THE APPOINTMENT

The APPOINTMENT

The Tale of Adaline Carson

A Novel by
John Keeble

LynxHousePress
Spokane, Washington

Copyright © 2019 by John Keeble.
All Rights Reserved.

FIRST EDITION

Cover Photograph: Christine Holbert
Author Photo: Debra Gwartney
Book and Cover Design: Christine Holbert

LYNX HOUSE PRESS books are distributed by the University of Washington Press, 4333 Brooklyn Avenue NE, Seattle, WA 98195-9570

LIBRARY OF CONGRESS CATALOGING-IN-PUBLICATION DATA
is available from the Library of Congress.
ISBN 978-0-89924-163-0

DISCLAIMER

The characters herein are based upon actual historical figures, but their motives and actions are the product of fiction.

Nez wanted to break in.
He had confessed,
I could have killed,
Maybe I did.
W., the Sioux,
Blunted his fingers
        on the wall.
Kit Carson Chapel at Ft. Lyons.
You know, we stood shivering
To some kind of error
That afternoon.

We could have become
Warriors again, rounded
Up the maniacs, made them hush.

High up, the stained glass
Blazed, fireless.

W. didn't know it
When he spoke soft fire,
But love, that's reasonable,
We're people, not like them.

—*Simon Ortiz,* from *Sand Creek,* 1981

Part 1

Chapter 1

April, 1851

ADALINE LAY AWAKE in the wrap of her buffalo robe beneath the Turners' wagon. Close by, her cousin Susan had a canvas dew break and a buffalo robe, and in addition a down-filled quilt her mother had sent off with her as part of her dowry. Susan was still asleep, snuggled deep in the robe and quilt. The sun was rising beyond the edge of the plain, the day beginning to seep in, and in the faint light Adaline glimpsed the ivory dome of her cousin's brow and a hank of blonde hair, so unlike her own. Just beyond, she saw a glimmering on the front axle and beyond it, the wagon tongue touched the ground. Directly above was the sling of hide lashed to the wagon's undercarriage, what was called a possum after the animal's way of carrying its young in a pouch.

The pouch held firewood. Adaline reached up to touch it, reassuring herself by its bulge that it was full. One of her duties was to keep the possum replenished, what seemed to have become a lifelong duty. She had fetched wood for her Aunt Mary Ann at the farm outside Fayette, Missouri, and at the convent school in Saint Louis to which she'd been sent for two years, then back in Fayette at the boarding school. Here the chore was more nagging, since in the six days of travel she'd seen that Mr. Turner built his fires too large and kept hectoring her for wood, while trees near to the trail grew scarce.

Adaline slipped her arm back under the robe and lay still, wondering what went on in her cousin's dreams that allowed for such untroubled sleep. She must have friendly beings in her night world, working to keep her at ease.

"Sweet dreams," Susan had said last night after the two of them settled in.

"And your dreams?" Adaline had asked. "Are they so?"

Susan laughed softly. "Oh, Ada, can't I say the simplest thing to you?" She paused a moment. "I hardly ever remember them. But you do, don't you?"

"More than I wish."

"I've heard you moaning in your sleep." Susan touched Adaline's hand. "But maybe soon the worst will pass away. Maybe only the best will prove true."

"Maybe."

Adaline's dreams came filled with circling birds and labyrinthine geometries as lunatic as the constellations overhead. She was haunted by shapes like larvae that grew huge and then spun away. They were like the whirlwind woman, Neyoooxetusei, whom she remembered her mother telling her about. Neyoooxetusei would put down for a moment, never resting, never waiting for the man who came after her, but twirling off again before he reached her, her fluttering skirts darkening the sun. Another man with no face walked across the plain.

Last night she had had no such dreams.

She rolled to her belly and gazed between the wheel spokes. It seemed as though she were sighting through the strike lines of a compass set on its deranged edge, the shapes on the far side of the oval like ghost wagons in the near darkness. Up along the oval to her right several oxen reclined. Cool air held their scents in check. One fire was lit and an early riser could be seen bent over it, blowing on the coals. Otherwise, the train remained still. The oxen did not stir, nor did the chickens nestled in coops hung from the sides of the wagons, including above her the Turners' prairie schooner.

•

At fifteen, Adaline was less than a year younger than her cousin. Susan was sixteen and just two weeks ago she'd been married, though to Adaline she seemed unchanged, still filled with trusting innocence. In ways, Adaline felt she was the elder. The painful hazards in life that had befallen her passed by Susan, she who had never even traveled from her parents' home outside Fayette to Saint Louis, but now journeyed westward across Kansas on the Santa Fé Trail into the Territories.

Susan's new husband, Jesse Nelson, was eight years her elder and not yet with the train but expected to catch up along with supply wagons from Kansas City. Other men were coming, too, Adaline's father for one. Adaline had taken measure of the men during the marriage festivities, including Jesús Silva, Jesús' brother-in-law, Tótilo, who had two young sons with him, and Louis Simmons, whose two small fingers on his left hand were cut off at the second knuckle. He wore a turquoise ring on one stub and his eyes had dwelled on her as she helped to serve the wedding dinner. It did not displease Adaline to be noticed by a man, yet given a choice she'd have preferred Jesús for his quick laugh and keen face, and she was disappointed to learn that he had a wife. Still, what she most looked forward to was the moment when her father would ride up with the other men to join the train, then take her westward as he had promised so long ago.

As to her birth date, she did not know it by the day but rather by the season, the end of winter and the demarcation of the heavens two moons past solstice. Her father had told her it was at a place called Fort Hall. Three winters later her mother, Waa-nibe, an Arapaho, had died of fever after giving birth to Adaline's sister at a fur camp on the Snake River. She remembered the cold of her mother's cheek, her white doeskin dress, and smoke from cedar curling upward.

And two years after that, her sister, whom her father had told her to watch over, perished in Taos. This memory produced a feeling of hopelessness. Always, she pushed it away to the place of the not-remembered.

3

•

Adaline lay still, stretching her toes under the robe, watching as the solitary fire flared up, and thinking about where they were.

She possessed a compass that she stored in a steamer trunk along with her "possibles" and other measuring instruments, as well, which she'd learned to use: a pocket chronometer, thermometer, siphon, barometer, and the sextant she had "lifted" from the apothecary in Fayette. By making her calculations and from the names she'd heard spoken on the train, Adaline knew that now on the sixth day out they were encamped on the Neosho River south of the Kaw, some thirty miles west of the Missouri. The air was soft. The Neosho ran a hundred paces behind in its bogan darkness, masked by ground fog, while scraggly hawthorns, birches, willows, and newly sprouted cottonwoods chased its course, these trees so far spared the ax. The bulk of the horses, mules, and oxen were set to their hobbles and pickets along the river's edge. To the south lay flatlands. Were there light enough and were she to walk clear of the train, the land would seem to stretch forever.

She might have camped at this very spot once before, but only bits of memory floated up to cling to her—this river, maybe, derived from a spring, and the trees along the banks, the recollected image of them full grown as they'd been in yesteryears. It made a symmetry she couldn't quite apprehend, this going back now on the same trail she'd covered ten years before, actually moving forward on the trail and at last in her life, yet also reversed on the path she had traveled before as a young child. Now, the trail had been widened by the tramping of thousands of gold seekers and the rolling of their wagons. Everything had changed.

She remembered her father from that earlier time, his face and his hat high in the sky. His hands, calloused by the reins, lifted her up to sit before him on the saddle. Later, he would dismount and put her down again in the travois and ride on. She remembered the skimming sound of the poles that cradled her as they slid over the ground.

And she remembered his departure, slouched upon his horse, cutting down the swale into the hollow, not looking back, and moving toward the woods while she stood on the verandah next to her aunt, a sob in her throat, tears in her eyes, and the terror of what would possibly happen here as she realized she was being left behind. She beheld his shadowy form and the pale of the horse flickering and vanishing into the dark woods, and the feel of boards under her bare feet, the wind gusting up from the hollow, and standing at her side her father's sister, Aunt Mary Ann, under whose supervision Adaline was placed. Mary Ann's skirt whipped at Adaline's legs, and her hand dropped to grasp the nape of Adaline's neck just as it would countless times thereafter, though at that moment it had been meant to steady her. Later, after she went to Saint Louis, then was sent back, it was to chase out the Devil and make her obey, one hand gripping her neck and the other pulling her by the ear.

•

Light silvered the sky. Over to Adaline's right, an ox rose in the ponderous way of its kind, hoisting first to its front knees and then pushing up from behind. Not far from it, Ferine, the mustered-out cavalry sergeant who provided security for the train, kicked loose and began rousting his dragoons. Her eyes were drawn to his hound, part mastiff, or wolfhound, or wolf, which began its ritual circuit within the circle, skirting the ox and moving clockwise, scouting for scraps or whatever might attract its demon nose.

Directly across from Adaline, Gish appeared and sparked his flint to start a fire for Mrs. MacReeve, a woman of means, who journeyed with her two children from Virginia to meet her husband in San Francisco, so went the gossip of the train. The MacReeves traveled in the column next to the Turners with their two wagons, one a scaled down Murphy filled with goods and the other an ambulance, a light carriage mounted on leaf springs, customized for the comfort of the children and Mrs. MacReeve. A tall, pale woman, she rarely appeared. Adaline could see the Murphy and the ambulance through the spokes of the wheel, the green box of the ambulance beginning to acquire its color in the dawn. Mrs. MacReeve had brought along four Negroes, an older man and woman, Josh and Linda, together with a younger man and woman, Gish and Yolanda. The Negroes cleaned, watched the children, prepared food, and managed the wagons.

Adaline puzzled over them: Could they still be slaves now that they'd crossed over the Missouri line? Had they been freed, or would they be considered so? Or if they went off on their own, would they be taken by the "slave catchers?" Were they kept back against their chocks, merely servants now, so habituated by their former lives? She was fascinated by Yolanda, who appeared from behind a canvas stretched from the side of the Murphy and came to stand beside Gish. She wore a pale dress and dark headscarf, and had long limbs, delicacy in her hands, and strength displayed when she lifted things. Adaline had yet to speak to her, but she recognized the cover drawn over Yolanda's eyes and their furtive way of darting to the side and looking down. Adaline knew well enough about that.

Susan stirred in her sleep. Several more pinpricks of fire dotted the oval. But by Adaline's divination the simple breathing of air still reigned within the hush of lungs of some eighty souls and the beasts, over two hundred oxen, a hundred and fifty mules, horses in and among the trees along the river banks behind. Two hooting owls measured the distance between the trees and the misty air along the Neosho, and then came the hound. It ducked beneath a wagon, then re-emerged. Adaline slid deeper into her robe and waited for it to pass, picturing the black on its back and flanks and the color of fire on its curly underbelly and snout. During the day, it trailed Ferine's horse, loping in the midst of the four dragoons on their military blacks, who followed Ferine on scouting forays ahead of the train. No matter what the pace, the hound stayed to its relentless stride always in the draft of Ferine's gelding, which was the color of a dead tooth and which Ferine had decorated with a beaded scabbard that held his percussion Hawken, also feathers, bits of metal, and a fluttering line of scalps.

If anyone dared approach the hound in camp, as Adaline, who fancied animals, had the second night out, the beast snarled and poised back on its hind legs ready to lunge. Ferine said the hound had a predilection for human flesh and most of all savored greasers and savages for their taste of sugar. He had boasted of this to a group gathered at his fire. The hound crouched at his side and Ferine dandled its ears with his fingers. Adaline and Susan hung several paces back. "Breeds, too. He favors 'em," Ferine said, his brass-colored eyes shifting toward Adaline. As soon as his gaze released her, she spun on her heel and left.

Susan came up behind her. "What is it?"

"Did you see the way that man looked at me?"

They reached the Turners' wagon, and Susan said, "It means nothing."

"No? Did you hear what he said?"

Susan inclined toward the light. "Once our men come, he'll be set in his place. You watch. He's a toplofty bully."

Adaline turned toward Susan. "Toplofty! Yes, and that was more than nothing!"

Now, as the hound came ever nearer, she peered at the bewhiskered snout nuzzling through the spokes. She could feel its breath in her hair. It took no interest in Susan, who slept on, but swung up its head to the Turners' chicken coop, startling the chickens. Adaline glimpsed their shapes between the floor slats as they squirmed to get under each other and otherwise, she imagined, ducked their heads beneath their wings and quieted down in a huddle in a corner, driven deep into their timidity. The hound passed, disappearing around the oxen and behind the ambulance, then materializing outside the circle. From beneath a wagon its legs were silhouetted against the light filtering from silver to faint yellow. The dog's legs moved to a pair of high boots—Ferine.

Within the circle, the hooves of oxen could be heard, and more people appeared. Gish was still there, crouching in front of Mrs. Mac-Reeve's ambulance and holding himself with one arm as he leaned forward to blow on the fire. Flames flashed, he added a chunk of wood, and stood up beside Yolanda. Adaline heard the Turners stirring in the wagon overhead. Mrs. Turner asked the question she asked every morning to which Adaline had yet to discern the words, only the voice curling out in the exact same, doleful note. Mr. Turner's voice always replied in an acid grumble.

The bed of the wagon creaked. Quickly, Adaline rolled out, dragging her dew break and buffalo robe behind. She held the oilcloth in which she had folded her skirt, smock, and cloak. She pulled on the clothing, set the bedding on the oilcloth, slipped on her moccasins, took up her gelding's halter, and picked her way through the scrub toward the river. Horses and mules stood half-hidden, their shapes obscure against the ground fog that hung near to the water. She turned back to face the wagons. Seeing no one, she ducked behind a tree, pulled up her skirts, and crouched, but then a voice broke out to her right: "I've been watching you, child."

Adaline clutched her knees, unsure whether to sink or stand. A figure emerged from the bush, tugging on a pair of buckskin trousers. The voice twanged: "Somebody better, I reckon."

Adaline rose, letting her skirt settle at her ankles. She did not look at the person, but stared straight ahead where some thirty paces distant she spied Mr. Turner stepping out to the doubletree, and hiking up the straps of his overalls. Susan slid out on her robe and pulled a skirt over her long johns. More men made their way toward the woods, while the rail-thin figure in buckskins approached, whom Adaline recognized as a mule-skinner whose wagon traveled near the head of the train. She'd marked him because he seemed small, too small for a mule-skinner. He, or so she at first presumed, sidled closer, swishing through the stubble, and reached out a hand as leathery as a lizard. "Mountain Frank. Frankie to you."

Now taken aback and looking closely, Adaline said, "You're a woman."

"The Lord did serve me up as such. They ain't many of us here, and only us two among the bunch lacking constraints, so far as I know, including your companion. But remember, you got a short allotment of mistakes out here if you're a woman. Some you ain't allowed at all."

Frankie looked down at her belt, cinched it tighter around the stick of her waist, and turned toward the wagons. A crashing exploded in the trees near the river, and one of Ferine's dragoons, dressed in military trousers and a long john shirt, led out a cluster of blacks and Ferine's off-white gelding toward the circle. Mr. Carlisle, the Master or "le maître de wagon" as he was known to the French drovers—Maître, they called him—strode out from the lead wagon and called, his voice brassy as a trumpet, "Turn out! Turn out!"

Emigrants began emerging from within and under wagons and from their tents. Their murmuring transformed into a commotion as they set about starting fires and striking the tents. Soon they would herd the oxen and come out to bring in the rest of the stock. There would be haranguing as mules were put to harness and braying and yips from the Mexican vaqueros capturing what broke loose, hooves beating crazily, young children crying, cacophonous chickens, bleating sheep, the squeal of hogs, and the creak and clatter of wagons.

"There, now," Frankie said. "Now, here we are. The mad bear garden." She gestured toward the train. "Next we got to get all them pilgrims forded over the river, which don't give a piss for their wishes. Did you see the discards?"

Adaline guessed she meant the portions of loads discarded. She'd seen several trunks, their contents littered, and a lonesome wreck of a sideboard poised on the bank of a stream.

"That's your first report from the trail," Frankie said. "Later, it'll be more than a few things tossed off to lighten loads, and like as not pilgrims themselves lightened for eternity. Sometimes it's news you should heed. Slaughter, mayhem, bones, and sorrow. A fair share of comedy, too." She nudged Adaline and cackled, showing the gap in her teeth. "Say now. I learnt who you be. A Carson."

Adaline looked away. Back in Fayette and among the people of that region—Boonesboro, Booneville, Boone's Lick where her father had been raised on the last of old Daniel Boone's settlements, and

Franklin, a point of embarkation upon the Missouri—there were many who considered themselves her father's familiars. She endured the long looks, the chatter, and sometimes loaded questions from strangers:

His whelp, are you?

He spreads his baggage around, don't he?

"You must be proud," Frankie said, thrusting her hands into the pockets of her coat and rocking back and forth on the balls of her feet.

In truth, Adaline was more than proud.

People gravitated toward the trees and river, while others moved amongst the wagons from which rose the din of animal noise, shouts of men herding their stock, and the rattle of iron. Thin columns of smoke rose into the sky and there was the scent of rashers. The sun had come up, quickly burning off the mist. The older Negro woman, Linda, who traveled with Mrs. MacReeve, emerged from the circle. Imposing in a purple dress, she carried a large chamber pot on behalf of her mistress, who Adaline envisioned laid out on a pallet inside the ambulance, as flat as a plank. The woman passed by Adaline and Frankie toward the river. She was a procession all in herself, striding and holding the vessel with both hands outstretched as if it were an offering. She looked at them solemnly and nodded.

"I see you ain't much of a talker," Frankie said.

Adaline felt cowed by this woman. "My father will be joining the train, soon."

"So I heared."

"I'm traveling to his home."

"Touse," Frankie said.

"Yes. Taos. Or first the Rayado. You must have heard from Mr. Turner."

Frankie squinted at Adaline, then nodded toward the Turners' wagon. "That's him?"

On the first day out, Adaline had heard Mr. Turner announce to another man that he had charge of her. There'd been a glitter in his eyes, something acquisitive that set her on edge. "I asked him not to speak of me."

"Well," Frankie said. "It don't appear he knows which way the stick floats."

Adaline wanted to explain further that she had no connection with the Turners, but that her aunt had arranged for her to travel with them at the outset of her journey, at any rate. They were abolitionist Methodists, as was her aunt, and since the Turners were believers, her aunt had concluded Adaline would be safe in their care and have the advantage of a woman's oversight. In exchange, Adaline was to help the Turners with their two little girls and the chores, yet in a lapse uncharacteristic of her Aunt Mary Ann, no consideration seemed to have been given to Mr. Turner's qualifications. He, too, was headed for the gold fields, and before that he'd been a shopkeeper. It soon became clear he knew nothing of journeying in this fashion.

She considered Mr. Turner standing at the front of his wagon, talking to Susan, jerking his head. Mrs. Turner arrived at his side, bearing her youngest daughter, leading the other by the hand, and the family vanished into the throng within the circle. They would find the other Methodists traveling with the train, and in the midst of the confusion they would gather together for a hymn and prayer. Susan bent to sort through her belongings.

"Look at the hips on that filly," Frankie said.

Startled, Adaline said, "That's my cousin."

Frankie chuckled. "I hear she's hooked up with Jesse Nelson. I reckon she'll learn to forebear. You never know what a man will get into his head, especially a jake like Jesse."

Amongst others sifting between the train and the trees, Susan now came near. "Mr. Turner's wanting his team put in the yoke, since, he says, you . . . he said you, not me . . ." Here, Susan raised her eyebrows in mock surprise. "Since, he says, you're not bothering with the morning prayers."

Adaline rolled her eyes. It wasn't the religion she objected to. She could take the religion. It was Mr. Turner's endless obdurateness that drove her to distraction.

Susan walked on. Forbearance she certainly had, and it was true enough that she had a gravity of body to go with her strong face, and since she had those physical gifts, and the gift of a mother's kindliness, though her father was said to be given to drink, she responded to the world with her own generosity, taking most everything at its face value. Adaline accepted nothing at face value.

Susan was rarely judgmental, while Adaline felt compelled to attach a verdict to everything that passed her way. Susan was guileless. What Adaline didn't understand, except half-disbelievingly, was how much Susan prized her, her dark, snapping eyes, the shine in her black hair, the sinew of her body, her touch with animals, the way she rode a horse, slouched and light upon it, her doubting ways, and for a girl, or young woman her age, her curiosity, her love for reading books, and the uncompromising razor of her thought.

"Well, now," Frankie said, again rocking back and forth. "Reckon I'll fetch my mules."

She moved off. Adaline checked around and decided it was safe to finish what she'd come for. She stepped deeper into the brush and made her way upstream until she found her horse, Hawk. She slipped the halter over Hawk's head, bent to remove the hobble, and led the horse to the train. A few of the emigrants had begun to move their wagons, heightening the confusion by opening alleys, while others still had their breakfast cooking. All along the verges, men on horseback chased mules and oxen inside. Skittish, Hawk danced behind Adaline and Adaline stopped and put her hand up on Hawk's neck and spoke softly: "Now, now, now. Easy."

The strains of "Rock of Ages" faded at the far end of the circle while the cacophony of animal cries kept rising, and there was the high-spirited cursing of French drovers, of vaqueros singing out. All manner of four-footed beasts shoved against the wagon sides, provoking more outbursts. Mothers called to their children. Wagons clattered and men bellowed at each other to clear the way. But for the last several mornings, Adaline had never witnessed anything like this, or maybe just once in an abridged form: the "disciples" she'd encountered in Saint Louis in the street before their church, who sang and bore witness in glossolalia, beat their chests, pulled at their hair, and kept dancing round and round. "Devils!" said Sister Simone, to whose charge Adaline and several other children had been consigned.

The master now sat astride his horse on top of a knoll, surveying it all and smiling a little, maybe wondering how many more mornings it would take for the train to settle into a regimen. Frankie came up from the river astride one of the eight mules in her team which she had already in harness. She went unperturbed into the tumult. Adaline scooped up her buffalo robe and canvas and moved around Hawk to the back of the wagon where Mr. Turner had permitted her the space to store her steamer trunk. A few yards away, one of the vaqueros struggled with a recalcitrant mule which he had roped around the fetlocks. He looped his reata around the mule's muzzle and pulled its head down, shouting, "Ay! Ay!" He lunged, jamming his shoulder into the animal's ribs and toppling it to the ground. The mule screamed and kicked. The vaquero danced away, clinging to the end of the reata.

Mr. Turner entered the throng with his four oxen, which miraculously he had herded up. He glowered in Adaline's direction. She took a hunk of pemmican from her trunk, put it in her pocket for later, closed the lid, and laid her robe and oilcloth over the top, tied them down, and then stepped out. Mr. Turner had begun to switch at the ox nearest him, but all four animals stood stolid.

"It's this one," Adaline said, touching the ox on the outside of the group.

Mr. Turner sucked air through his teeth. "It's what, you say?"

Adaline tapped the ox's flank with her hand. "He's used to being in the lead," she said, telling him once again what she'd already explained the previous morning. "When he moves, the others will follow. It's easier that way. He likes to be in position on the left of the yoke."

The ox moved. The others followed willingly to the wagon where Adaline helped Mr. Turner secure them in their yokes and bows two abreast, the wheelers and then the leaders. She clasped the chains and looked up ahead. A few of the wagons had rolled out, heading toward the ford in the river. She swung up on Hawk. Susan had located her bay mare in the trees and drew up alongside. The vaqueros drove the loose stock toward the river whereupon the animals fanned across the plain. The dragoons looped back along the trail, turned around and paraded beside the wagons, the four men on their blacks with mules on leads. Ferine rode his gelding with pennants of feathers and scalps a-fly. He whipped his horse and let out a shout. "Huzzah!" The dragoons leaned into their mounts and the hound loped apace of the horses and mules. All careened into the water, beating it into froth, and clambered up the far side, then tightened into a knot as they charged off into the distance.

Chapter 2

AFTER TEN DAYS on the trail the train stopped at Council Grove for a respite. Repairs were made to the wagons, the waterproof caulking was renewed, and the people reconnoitered for the trek ahead into "unsettled" country. Jesse Nelson appeared with eight Conestoga trade wagons, mostly driven by Mexican drovers and pulled by mule teams, but three were pulled by oversized animals known as "Conestoga horses." The wagons were painted blue with red running gear and had white canvas coverings drawn taut over hoops. They carried goods under consignment to the Army in the Territory, and ranch supplies for Adaline's father and his partner, Lucien Maxwell, who was at the Rayado, awaiting their arrival.

Adaline was disappointed to learn that her father, along with Jesús Silva and Louis Simmons, had sidetracked up the Missouri to Saint Joe to purchase mules for the army. Jesse said they'd learned that excellent animals were there, bred from draft mares and Mexican jacks. There would be profit in it. It would be several days before they caught up.

During the nights that followed, Susan went to the tent Jesse raised, leaving Adaline to sleep alone, but some days during afternoons Adaline escaped the Turners and rode Hawk up to Jesse's wagons, which were positioned at the front of the train. She would ease Hawk in next to Susan and her mare. As often as not Jesse was there, usually walking, but at times riding one of the wheel horses. He was a lean man who wore suspenders, canvas trousers, and a black flat-brimmed hat that made the remainder of his oval face look like a teacup with a nose and a pair of mischievous lips painted on it. He delighted in regaling the girls with stories, sometimes occasioned by what they had passed and other times as grim auguries of what might come.

He reported that up ahead a Pawnee raid once had left three men dead, and beyond that was a place where the Kaw set a fire at night, causing a train's oxen, mules, and horses to stampede. The drovers lit backfires to protect their wagons, but when they went looking for the stock they found them all perished in a hole. The drovers were thus stranded with a fortune in New Mexican goods.

"And that ain't the worst of the happenings," Jesse said. "Yet farther along is a place the Comanches favor for their killing raids."

Alarm sounded in Susan's voice. "We're not going into their country, are we?"

"Betimes, anywhere is Comanche country. They go where fancy strikes them."

Adaline held her peace, unsure whether to believe Jesse's stories or not.

On other days she rode to the head of the rightmost column and sought out Frankie. She tied Hawk to Frankie's wagon and accompanied Frankie on foot alongside her team. One day, the train was toiling up a grade made more difficult by a recent rain. Amongst the wagons one stood motionless, having tried a roundabout to purchase an easier climb and had sloughed into mud. An extra team of oxen was brought and hooked up to pull it out. Mud oozed from beneath the oxen's hooves while their necks grew chafed bloody by the yokes. A pair of drovers shouted and cracked their whips until the straining beasts pulled the wagon loose and labored up the hill.

Frankie looked back. "Them oxen is slow, but they'll pull for hours. They're strong all right. I fancy mules, though. Don't take as much feed, they're quicker, and get better footing than oxen."

Adaline took an interest in the margins between sustaining animals and the cost of their travail, for the freight animals what feed might be carried to improve the margins without overburdening the loads, and what in the way of forage might be expected from grass. There was something in the season—mid-spring—which emphasized the question of margins. New grass sprouted out of eaten-down root balls close to the trail and off in the distance the grass growing luxurious bent under the breeze. She'd heard that the country ahead would be dry. Also that swine and chickens would likely be slaughtered as food supplies dwindled. Milk cows would dry up from the lean pickings and be butchered. Already, they'd passed by several dead horses, abandoned and stinking. She told Frankie she was intrigued by the idea of lightening their load as the journey went on, stripping down to essentials.

"Intrigued!" Frankie said. "What's that? A fine word for what you don't want much of, lest you end up with skeletons pulling ghost wagons."

From the talk back in Fayette, Adaline had learned that traders used elaborate systems to take the measure of transport. When she asked Frankie how she made such calculations, Frankie laughed. The edge in her voice pierced the rumble of the wagons, the din of wheels and trembling loads, and the gee-hawing from behind. "Truth is, you never know what the devil will conspire to steal from you. Too, you got to allow for hazards waiting to stove you in. But I reckon after a time you get a notion of what's needed."

"Balance," Adaline said.

"Balance?"

"Balance what you have against what you might not need."

Frankie considered this for a moment, then said, "You cut your deck pretty deep, don't you child?"

They toiled up a particularly steep section, where surfaced a heap of trunks, crates, and broken up sideboards, stuffed chairs, cabinets and cases, which previous travelers had found to be too much for the grade. This was more than Adaline had seen in one place. Nor had she seen the furniture so hacked up, as if a gang of reapers had visited, chewing up the goods and strewing them around, leaving scraps of fabric to flutter from the stubble.

"That's the nomads ransacking 'em. The wastage," Frankie said.

"Nomads?"

"Injun nomads. Taking what they want and wrecking the rest. But there you have it. The emigrants'd be better off loading their wagons with feed as you say. Once it was eaten they'd arrive at the state of lightness with animals that had some life left in 'em." She retrieved her whip from the wagon and nicked the flank of her lead mule with it. The mule jerked and the team picked up the pace. "For years, it was traders on this road. But since the gold strikes, you get all manner of gawks. It's a different kind of greed with these pilgrims of Mammon. They want it easy."

The train passed a band of Indians, but they were far off. Frankie identified them as Pawnee. When Adaline told her about Jesse's tale of the Pawnee raid and the chance of encountering Comanches ahead, Frankie snorted. "Maybe once or twice in Jesse's time the Pawnees raided, but Jesse does like to coyote round the rim of truth. The Pawnee are now well settled in. We'll need to watch for Comanche, though more'n likely we'll see Cheyenne. Them Cheyenne ain't happy. What we got here I reckon is Cheyenne ransacking and taking, the gleaning. It's a uncodified trade. Trade in hatred and trade of the heart. Vanquished. Seems like the Injuns worship the vanquisher. They use his methods. But every little piece they gain, they give up more the big piece of what they're losing."

Adaline fell silent and looked down at her feet, her high moccasins tracing the gouges and ruts in the trail, and chewing on this thing, "uncodified trade."

She asked, "You mean it's for free?"

"Free? Could be costly. It ain't ordinary is all. And there's no record of it kept."

Adaline recalled an old chief back in Fayette, a displaced Unami Delaware who, according to the talk, had been taken West as a scout and mercenary by Frémont himself. The old man had been wounded during the return from Frémont's last expedition, then he landed in Fayette where he worked as a roustabout until he grew too infirm. She had eyed him as he sat on a bench in the square near her school, dressed in deerskin trousers, a military tunic and battered beaver hat. The sash he had draped across his chest was festooned with the feathers of birds, ribbons, military insignia, and Christian medallions. People called him Henry. One day, Adaline had stopped and asked him, "Is it true you were in John Frémont's service?"

She knew about Frémont, first from talk in Fayette, next from frequenting the tiny boarding school library. She had reason to seek out Frémont's journals there, *The Exploring Expedition to the Rocky Mountains in the Year 1842 and to Oregon and Northern California in the Years 1843-44*, and the maps that the journals contained, for her father, too, had traveled with Frémont. Just before setting out on her journey, she received a copy of the book. It came to her Aunt Mary Ann and her uncle's farm wrapped and secured in the bottom of a steamer trunk. Also, there was the buffalo robe. The trunk was addressed to her, but no name of the sender was included, nor was there a return address, only the name of a Saint Louis shipping company. The three things, book, robe, and trunk, were gifts sent to her by whom she still did not know.

The maps were dreamscapes with mountains drawn in, and in tiny print the names of forts, for waterways—Missouri, Kansas, Grand Saline, Neosho, Kaw, Arkansas, Platte—and for the tribes occupying the far-flung territories—Iowa, Pawnee, Sioux, Moache Utah, Pah-Utah, Snake, Jicarilla, Cheyenne. The trails followed by Frémont were marked. Timelines charted the progress. Distances were noted. Yet wondrous as the words and drawings were, the white expanses on the pages seemed even more so, the blanks conjuring a sense of mystery.

Henry didn't answer her at first. There seemed a riffle in his face like a current bending around a rock. She grew anxious, knowing how a dread value could be placed on words held back when a person did not acknowledge another's address. Finally he spoke, moving only his lips: "Frémont! Great chief! Great killer! Many Yanas for the chief!"

He looked away, along the road that ran down the hill, and said no more.

From then on, he merely followed her with his eyes from the bench as she passed. He kept his head imperiously erect, and if she tried to catch his attention, he would look away. She wasn't sure what he'd meant by "for the chief." That the killing was an honor paid to Frémont? And who or what were the Yanas?

Trudging up the hill beside Frankie, she wondered if Henry's apparel, his bowler hat, military tunic, and the decorative emblems on his sash, were meant to consecrate his vanquishers. Was this what was meant by "uncodified trade?"

Henry's people, she knew, had once lived far to the east in the original states, and had often served as scouts for the army. They were known to be ruthless. Frémont had written that the Delawares believed his expeditions were war parties, that they were always ready for a scalping. She'd also heard talk of a reserve, a farm community of Delawares near Saint Louis. There were other such places, which the train passed by. One for the Wyandot, one for the Potawatomi.

The Delawares called themselves "those who were left behind," Unalachtigo. They had ceremonies that caused some to accuse them of sorcery, yet they had fallen under the influence of Methodist missionaries. She wondered if those had once been Henry's people, and if so why he didn't return to them. She wondered how he sustained himself. One day, he was found dead outside town, stabbed in the throat, but why, or by whom—some killer filled with loathing, or one of the Osage still hiding out in the woods—no one seemed to know. These were more mysteries. How Henry lived, why he died, and what tales might have come into the world if he'd broken his silence.

•

The head of the train crested the grade and began a gentle diagonal across hard ground on the slope toward the Cottonwood River. Stretching out before them was the Valley of the Arkansas. "This be easier going on the animals," Frankie said, pulling herself up on the wagon and scooting over on the "lazy board," which was positioned next to the brake. "Skinny as the two of us be, there be room for you here. Let's set a spell."

To make sure she wasn't needed by the Turners, Adaline walked back to the crest of the hill and looked down, and there caught sight of the middle of the train and the cabalgata. She had an outlook on the variety of conveyances: Conestogas, prairie schooners, military wagons, diverse farm wagons, most with white canvas covers. There was even a Dearborn carriage or two. Some tried to manage the grade by tacking back and forth nearly to the mud. A couple of wagons had come nearly to a full stop. Well down the slope, she picked out Mrs. MacReeve's green ambulance and Murphy, and the Turners' Prairie schooner, Mr. and Mrs. Turner walking alongside, and the face of the older daughter catching the sun from inside. Of the Turner family, that child, Carrie, was the only one Adaline could say she liked.

She turned and caught up to Frankie's wagon and swung up onto the lazy board. They rolled near a solitary chair, its red upholstery cut to shreds. She said, "I think some of our own are thinking to lighten their loads."

"So I'd guess. There'll be more." Frankie pulled a tobacco plug from her pocket, bit off a hunk, and held out the remainder to Adaline.

"No, thank you." She'd tried chaw once and it made her throw up.

Frankie nodded at the chair. "There's fury in that demolition. Must've been dragged there. That chair's been there a while, but further on it might be news about some new anger. You got to look close for who was there and what they done, and keep your curious cocked. It's wise not to ever stop eyeing the meaning of what's before you."

In the last several days, Adaline had observed more corpses of pulling animals, most of which were oxen in various stages of corruption. Once, she'd spotted wolves retreating from an ox as the train approached, then a dozen crows rose up raucously from a nearby snag and dropped like tatters to rip at the entrails. Dung-eating blackbirds stalked the train, and it seemed there was always one or another killdeer darting alongside. Huge flocks of passenger pigeons darkened the sky overhead. On the ground lay buffalo bones and evidence by their droppings that vast herds had been here. Bois de vache, the Frenchmen called the chips. And now, stone cairns and a stand of makeshift crosses had shown up to the south.

Frankie followed Adaline's gaze. "Them souls didn't make it, did they? Likely just snatched off without warning. Us who's left behind alive has to pray for continued submission." Frankie leaned to her left in front of Adaline and spat out a stream of tobacco juice. She pulled back and said, "Cholera did wastage to the Injuns, Cheyenne especially. Some say old William Bent tried to scorch his fort and sanctify the ground afore moving downstream to Big Timbers."

"Bent's Fort." Again, Adaline thought of the maps in Frémont's journals. "Where the trail turns up ahead."

"Right. The old trading post," Frankie said. "But more'n likely he just don't want the army taking it over without payment."

Adaline knew Bent's Fort as a marker on a map. From it spurs cut north to Fort Laramie, south to Taos, Santa Fé, further to Fort Union, or all the way east to Saint Louis. And then a figment strove to decoct itself into memory, something from between her mother's death and her time in Taos with her father and sister, something about a fort as big as a castle, a village of tipis, beaver pelts, the smell of green hide, a woman who treated her cruelly, and the man who ran the fort, William Bent, and his wife, a Cheyenne woman who treated her kindly. William Bent was the brother to a man she'd heard talk of a few years back in Fayette—Charles Bent. She'd heard Charles had been killed in an uprising in Taos.

Frankie pulled back on the reins to slow the mules. "Them Cheyenne wouldn't go near Bent's Fort after the contagion. Same with the Arapaho."

Still entangled in her memory, Adaline said, "Arapaho?"

Frankie reached for her whip and flicked it at her mules, who by slowing too much had induced the wagon to roll into the ruts. The mules jerked, causing the whiskey casks Frankie carried to creak against their ropes. Frankie had been entrusted with the casks, she'd told Adaline, because the master knew she wouldn't gimlet them. "I swore off drink years ago," she'd said. One cask contained brandy to be delivered to Santa Fé. She also carried galena bars for molding to ammunition, and several bushels of corn.

"My mother was Arapaho."

"That a fact? You look it."

Adaline wondered what Frankie saw in her that she took for Arapaho. She had studied herself in her Aunt Mary Ann's hand mirror: wide-set, gray eyes she believed came from her father, while her dark hair and tawny skin must have come from her mother.

She stared at a long snake of a cut, what would be the Cottonwood, and beyond was the plain, the grass emerging out of dark earth. A flock of ducks glided above the cut. Adaline rocked with the motion of the wagon, her shoulder bumping against Frankie. The other day Frankie had said that she was from New Orleans, that she'd come out into the territories with her husband. He had been killed and she'd stayed on. "I loved my man," she said. "I still carry him with me. Don't have the need for any other. Ain't never been back to New Orleans, neither. What's the use returning to where your busted flush was begun in pleasure unless it's more sorrow you want?"

Adaline had looked at Frankie, at the cross-hatched wrinkles in her neck. "You don't mind being alone then?"

"Like I said, I never am. I got him with me." Frankie grinned. "Can't say much for the conversation he makes, though."

Struck by Frankie's words, Adaline stayed silent, wondering if she herself were ever filled with a beloved presence might she, too, stay full even if the beloved were lost from the earth.

On the far side of the Cottonwood a line of pack dogs and people mounted on horses came up out of a draw, heading southward.

"More Pawnees. Off to spring buffler camp." Frankie nodded at a trail that broke into the plain from the north. "Lucky it didn't rain more'n it did. These crossings can be nasty in high water." Bending forward, she peered at the river. "Reckon I ought to get down."

Adaline swung from the lazy board to the ground and Frankie came behind her, moving up beside the lead mule and gesturing with her head again, this time toward a rise to the south. "If you ride to that hummock, you'll see the blacksmith's shack across the river and his privies, and then the change in the country beyond. It'll soon commence being what it best is, jumping up into mountains. By God, I love them mountains!"

Beyond the hummock and back a ways from the Pawnees, three horsemen appeared against the sky, advancing on the trail and hauling two heavily laden carts. "It's hunters off the Republican herd more'n likely," Frankie said. "Likely meaning to confab. Go out and look if you like."

The dragoons pounded up from behind the train. They went by and soon surpassed the horsemen and carts and coursed along the high ground just this side of the Cottonwood River, a gnarl on their horses with mules on leads, the whole of them led by Ferine on his gelding and the hound running amongst the hooves. The men had not quite given the horses their heads and the animals verged on the edge of full gallop. The mules, their panniers draped with meat, extended their snouts and flattened their ears as if in furious humiliation. They ran in the level way of their kind, backs parallel to the ground, hooves dancing. The cluster flashed through a tributary creek, scared up a flock of geese, and bent southward in an arc for no reason but to provoke the Pawnees, and though not coming right upon the file they squeezed the invisible boundary laid out between peoples.

Adaline fetched Hawk's reins and mounted him. She rode to the hummock for a view of the three approaching riders with the carts and of the Pawnee passing away. Some Pawnee horses were dragging loaded travois. Other horses were amassed and the pack dogs trotted alongside. A phalanx of horsemen parted from the line to form a buffer against the dragoons. Geese winged westward toward the sun, drafting each other in a ragged -V-. The dragoons broke away, cutting a line straight back north to the Cottonwood, splashing across it and pulling up before a shack. Behind the shack and packed in a river bend, a stand of trees—cottonwood, box elder, willow—sheathed amongst them a village of tipis. Figures emerged like whispers from the shadows to the edge of the light.

Just below Adaline, the head of the train forded the river by making use of corduroy landings, the inclining rip-raps formed from logs. The remainder of the train had crested the hill where confusion once again exploded as the wagons descended. A few chose separate paths while the cabalgata, smelling water, scattered for the river. Vaqueros cracked their whips and wheeled on their mounts to keep the stock in hand, calling out: "Yip! Yip! Vaya!" The French drovers laughed and cursed. At a cry from the master, the head of the train commenced its circle on the flat. More wagons trundled up, some awaiting their turn at the corduroy ramp, while a few fought the banks. Another group stalled utterly, their teams declining to go on without a drink, and one of these, Adaline saw, was the Turners' prairie schooner.

Suddenly, as if to celebrate the tumult, the French drovers broke into song. Hawk's head swung up and he reset his feet beneath Adaline. The sky was bright, no clouds anywhere. A chill breeze blew up from the bottom and lifted her hair from her neck, while her legs luxuriated in the warmth of Hawk's ribs. The lilt of the drovers' song looped upwards. Far to the west, the land stretched out and arose ever so subtly to rack itself into benches. The Pawnee soon diminished to a distant stitching.

•

The next morning, at Jesse's behest, she and Susan took his stock out to forage. They brought along the Turners' oxen, and a bundle of the Turners' laundry and a washboard. Jesse had given them instructions to look for a place where the sun came through to call up the grass. "We need the animals flush for what's to follow," he'd said. "Haze 'em out ahead of the others and work 'em back come evening." His eyebrows went up nearly to his hat brim. "But don't go so far as to invite neighborly savages to hoodoo off our critters."

The two found good grass in a clearing bordered by a slow-moving creek and let their horses mix in with the other animals. Adaline knelt in a low place in the bank and scrubbed the Turners' clothing together with some of Susan's and her own. She and Susan draped the wash over willows to dry. They sat in the sun on a slab of rock above the creek where they purchased an outlook on their animals. A couple hundred yards beyond the Cottonwood two mule-drawn carts and horsemen, having crossed back again, made their departure from camp. They'd been the ones who had advanced on the train yesterday, five Wyandot braves in the company of a preacher and their buffalo meat packed in the carts.

Last night, some travelers had gathered to hear the preacher and Adaline and Susan had stopped to listen. He wore a belly gun tucked under his belt. He'd spoken of his mission in Indian Country, the pacification of Indians into Christians and farmers, including the Wyandots. By the grace of God, he'd said, he and his Wyandots had found buffalo down south ahead of a party of Cheyenne. His voice was dark with passion. Looking toward Mrs. MacReeve's ambulance his eyes burned as he condemned slavery as a poison upon the republic.

Now, Adaline said, "That man had frightening eyes."

Susan watched the entourage labor up the hill. "Jesse says his name's Chivington. Says that right or wrong he foments trouble wherever he goes. She unfolded a cloth in which she'd brought biscuits and passed one to Adaline, along with salt pork.

Men appeared thirty yards downstream with whipsaws and axes, since the blacksmith had granted permission to fell a bur oak. They cut the tree, which snapped as it fractured away, the wind rushed against its limbs, and it gave out a thud when it hit the ground. A cloud of blackbirds burst out of the bushes, sucking away above the trees, and a green-winged teal whipped by the girls. The preacher and his braves grew smaller as they receded eastward.

Susan said, "Jesse's a good man. I believe I'm lucky."

Adaline, who was constantly hungry due to the stinting ways of the Turners, devoured the food, relishing even the sharp salt and nearly rancid meat.

"He puts himself into me, as Mama said he would."

Adaline looked at her cousin, perplexed.

"At first, I didn't like it much, knowing him that way."

But Adaline understood what was meant, the pain and pleasure in it, and once more she was struck by Susan's guilelessness. "Then you came to him honestly," she said, startling herself with what she had almost revealed.

Susan brushed a fly off her arm. Downstream, the men axed limbs from the oak. Susan didn't seem to have caught Adaline's intimation. "Of course. And so will you when your time comes."

Adaline's knowledge came from her experience with the apothecary, Mr. Spender, in Fayette. She'd been sent to him with a toothache by her boarding house mother and the apothecary's applications of tinctures were followed by applications of himself. Soon, Mr. Spender arranged for Adaline to come clean his shop, seeking permission from her Aunt Mary Ann, the house mother, and the headmaster of the school. In return he defrayed a portion of her expenses, much to Mary Ann's satisfaction, and also gave Adaline a small wage. He was an amateur astronomer. In the room where he took her were stored treatises alongside his pharmaceuticals and divining equipment—sextants, barometers, thermometers, a telescope, and on a high bench an orrery. At first, Adaline felt trapped by the crushing sense of being surrounded by grownups who were indifferent to her treatment, but in time she tricked her way into a realization, which was that by gratifying Mr. Spender she gained sway.

She was fascinated by the orrery, a device made from polished wood, iron, and brass. It was a model of the solar system, and it seemed strange to her that what was considered to be in the beyond could be rendered as a mechanical contrivance with a crank to revolve it. Mr. Spender, a man with shaggy white hair and bristles bursting from his ears, induced her to recline in the examination chair, and then unclasped his belt and buttons to come on her, his breath quickening. She would gaze over his shoulder at the orrery on the bench and imagine the orbits of its planets. Afterwards, because of his sense of her dependence on him, or what more accurately came to be her desperately apportioned sham of willingness, he would let her dip her fingers into the spermaceti can, oil the orrery's gears, and turn its crank. As she did so, running it smoothly on its axles and gears and listening to its soft hissing sound, she grew entranced with the slowly spinning planets—Saturn, Venus, Mars, the very Earth. They turned around a sun that was made of brass and had a smiling face. The moon was a smaller brass piece circling the earth. Mr. Spender let her examine his sextant, too, and once showed her how it worked. It determined where they were on this earth. Other times, she peered through the telescope that was trained on the street running past the boarding house where the girls came and went.

Upon her departure, she lifted Mr. Spender's sextant, thermometer, barometer, and a bit of quicksilver. She'd have liked to take his telescope and most of all his orrery, but she didn't dare.

Here at the stream with Susan, she said, "Then before too long you'll be in travail."

"I will be proud."

Adaline thought: That, too, will come to her.

"Jesse says Louis Simmons might have an interest in you."

Adaline felt a blush at her neck. It was unnerving to hear named what she'd suspected but had kept back in a fog. She looked up the hill to where the preacher and his Wyandots had vanished and to the flatland where hundreds of prairie dogs appeared. A hawk skimmed close to the earth, its shadow prompting the prairie dogs to whistle alarm and dive back into their tunnels. Almost instantaneously, they reappeared, leaping into the air and barking.

Then a turtle surfaced from the stream below.

It made her think of the little beaded turtle, a gift from her mother, kept safe in a beaded bag in her trunk. The mud, the clay between the turtle's toes, her mother's soft voice, also came to her. The making of people here on the spinning earth, the Whirlwind Woman who flies away, forever disappointing the man who follows her.

Susan said, "He says Mr. Simmons may have already spoken to your father."

Adaline glanced at her cousin, then pictured Louis Simmons, his dark eyes, and the stub of a finger on which he wore his ring. She considered her life, how it might unfold with a match to him, but could not visualize it. She said, "Perhaps it's too soon yet."

By evening, she and Susan urged the stock back toward the train. Having found a clearing with sufficient grass, they drove pickets into the ground, and left the animals there. Nearer yet to the train, where the log rounds were being yarded, the air rang with mauls and wedges, more sawing, and a thud of axes again. Intermittent explosions reverberated as a powder-driven wedge was set off to split the rounds into lengths that would be carved into axles. Susan moved off to find Jesse while Adaline delivered the bundle of clothing to the Turners' wagon.

Mr. Turner appeared from around the side and reached up to feel the bundle. "Wet."

Adaline thought: Damp. It's still a little damp. Not wet.

She said, "The sun's going down. The dew will come up."

"Should've washed earlier. First thing."

Adaline let it pass and looked to the ground beneath the possum. She saw sticks and tinder he'd left there. "You'll have a fire, then?"

But Mr. Turner moved to the back of the wagon. The racket of axes and mauls had died away, and small fires flickered around the oval. At the head of the train Ferine's men had built a larger fire with the chunks of bur oak, giving rise to a festive spirit. She glimpsed people collecting in groups, where one of the Frenchmen was singing. His tenor voice pulled taut in the twilight. Carrie clambered down from the front of the wagon with the Lucifers, the phosphorous-tipped wooden matches that burst into flame when they were scratched. They came in blocks and Carrie busied herself with breaking one loose while Adaline gathered up kindling.

Mr. Turner returned and snatched the block from the child. "We need to save these." He looked at Adaline. "Use your flint." He disappeared back behind the wagon.

Anger flashed in Adaline, but she used her flint, employing Carrie to help shield the first flames. She lifted the child back into the wagon and moved toward the head of the train, leaving the fire to Mr. Turner. The Frenchman accompanied himself by playing a small bagpipe, squeezing it under his elbow to produce a drone. A countryman began playing a counter on a fiddle. The singer went higher, the tones hanging, his voice soaring while the fiddle wove around the drone of the bagpipe. At the musicians' backs, firelight danced on the white canvas of wagons. Beyond them rose the hills.

Adaline stopped between Susan and Frankie. Jesse was there and more people happened by to listen. Even Mrs. MacReeve materialized from her ambulance, her cloak hanging gracefully from her tall figure as she led her two children by their hands. Gish and Yolanda cautiously watched from the shadows. Other emigrants, their faces weary from the several days of hard traveling, softened with pleasure. At the edges of the fire the dragoons roasted slabs of buffalo meat and a savory smell suffused the air. The Frenchman's voice rose even higher, like a gleaming sinew that looped around and around. Upon the final turn of the cadence, his voice racked into a prolonged sob.

People were silent, held rapt by the feeling of melancholy the song had left them with. The musicians made off into the darkness and, in time, Mrs. MacReeve and others departed. Those who remained edged closer to the fire. Coyotes began to yip in the distance, and Adaline also heard the steady risible of the river, and in the shadows caught sight of drovers slipping off in ones and twos toward the tipi village behind the blacksmith's shack. She asked Frankie where they were going.

"Open air brothel I reckon is what it is, child."

Adaline looked again into the village and felt her eyes narrowing.

Frankie said, "The squaws get beads or some such. The blacksmith gets a silver piece."

Jesse leaned toward the fire, impaled two hunks of buffalo hump with a stick, and passed one each to Susan and Adaline. The pungent flavor of hump and of singed fat crackling against Adaline's gums made her feel almost delirious. Ferine had thrown his hound a joint, and when he shifted his feet the hound snarled, provoking Ferine to strike it on the head with his fist, silencing it. "I was under the command of Captain Grier in Santa Fé," he said, fixing his gaze on Adaline. "Whilst there, I rode with Kit Carson more than once."

Adaline froze, feeling the others respond to the name by looking at her. She knew Mr. Turner had been talking.

"And once," Ferine said, "was when the Jicarillas kidnapped Mrs. James White not far from the Point of Rocks. We had Bill Fisher and Joaquin Leroux with us, Leroux being the ranahan scout, every bit so as Kit Carson, but the major determined to have Carson, as well."

At her side she saw Jesse's head lift. Among the emigrants there fell a quiet, while across the fire Yolanda's eyes came to rest on Adaline. Ferine scratched his hound's ears. The hound, engrossed with the bone, emitted a muttering growl.

Ferine said, "Jim White had been trading along the Santa Fé for years. The country beyond Point of Rocks was believed to be pacified, and White was journeying with his wife and child, a young girl, bringing them out to his Santa Fé diggings. White determined that the pace of the train he was traveling with was slower than he wanted, so he went ahead with his family in a chaise in the company of his nigger and four men on horseback.

"When the train came a few days later they found the bodies of White, the nigger, and the four men in the river, scalped, the chaise overturned, and everything left behind in a ruin. The animals and Mrs. White and her daughter was gone, but there was a greaser boy there, hiding in the rocks, who said the Jicarillas had done the killing. Word reached the army and we formed a command, taking Leroux with us, and Fisher, and at the Rayado we picked up Carson. Him and Leroux found the Jicarilla trail. We followed it for two weeks southwest toward the Canadian River. Since the Jicarilla knew we were there, they made the trail hard to follow by breaking into twos and threes each daybreak. At times we came upon signalizing stones left alongside, and every time we came upon their camp we found a bit of Mrs. White's clothing left behind. A buckle, or strips torn from her skirt. We took that as signalizing. When finally we came in sight of the Jicarillas, your man, Carson, ordered a charge. Insubordinate is what it was, and he found himself ramping in on them alone because Grier, on the advice of Leroux, ordered a halt."

Now, Jesse spoke: "It's was Grier's choice, not Leroux's. Leroux agreed with Kit."

"You wasn't there," Ferine snarled.

"I know Kit. I know this tale. It was Grier. And Grier himself said he was mistaken."

"There's bad blood between Leroux and your Kit."

"Ain't so," Jesse said. "Kit begrudges no man his savvy, which in Leroux's case Kit would be the first to grant."

Ferine smiled coolly. "Well, Leroux begrudges Carson his, as I hear."

"Tell it right," Jesse said.

The others at the fire had taken on an air of even higher watchfulness during this exchange. A breeze bent the flames and scattered coals around Ferine's boots and against the flank of the hound, which was splintering the hunk of bone.

"As soon as the halt was called," Ferine continued, "the savages commenced packing up their things. One shot the major from some distance with a musket ball, so Grier was wounded, but it happened he had his gauntlet folded under his coat and that stopped the ball. He had a bruise, all right, and the wind taken from him. The Jicarillas went off. Then the captain ordered a charge. We found one Jicarilla left behind, trying to swim the river. He was shot and we pursued the others and soon found the body of Mrs. White, bloodied from cruel treatment, an arrow through her heart. Pinned to the ground that way, she was still warm. She'd tried an escape in the commotion, it was thought. If we'd parleyed we might have saved her."

"No Jicarilla will parley in the midst of it," Jesse said. "Once engaged, it's all fight to the death. And that's the truth of it."

Ferine's gaze came back to Adaline. "She had one of them Buntline books in her hand. It had Carson on the cover astride a white horse." Ferine chuckled. "I never seen him on such a horse or wearing such clothes as they had him in. Buckskins white as snow. *Prince of the Gold Hunters* it was called." One of his dragoons was bent over the fire, turning the meat, and he snorted, which caused Ferine to chuckle again.

"You're a damn fool," Jesse said.

Ferine's face twitched. "Well, Kit Carson never hunted gold, I'll give him that. There was hardly any word of gold anyways just then. Carson believed the woman hoped he would rescue her. We gave chase, killed another Jicarilla, and took prisoners. Some got away. What happened to the daughter, we never knew. Lost, I reckon, one way or another. Tortured, maybe, and killed. Or maybe raised up into a savage to make more of the same." He paused, then looked at Adaline, and said, "They like the breeds."

Adaline felt Frankie's hand slip inside her elbow, the touch meant to steady her against what she hadn't yet fully understood she needed to be steadied, a falsehood built upon another falsehood, and the marking of her by this man who wished to belittle her for no reason she could fathom.

Chapter 3

ON THE TWENTY-FIRST DAY out the noon stop was observed at Pawnee Rock, otherwise known, Adaline learned, as the Prairie Citadel, a towering sandstone extrusion beside the Great Bend in the Arkansas. From here the train would cross the Pawnee River and travel the open country along the north side of the Arkansas. During the respite, a small crowd gathered around the boulder, an anomaly upon the plain. Its wedge shape sloped to the west, and it prompted questions about the order of things: By what means had it been placed here? If indeed by God's design, for what reason?

It was said to mark the half-way point between Saint Louis and Santa Fé and was decorated with scrapes and petroglyphs. Adaline and little Carrie had joined the group to scrutinize the pictures, the meaning of which Adaline could only guess at:

The Cheyenne have entered into the country, so many days that way.

Or the Comanche have come from the south.

Or the Kiowa from the north.

Or there are many bluecoats and horses coming from the east.

Or we Shoshone have ridden away on this phase of the moon.

Some emigrants chiseled names in the rock, including Mr. Turner. With a mallet he thumped at an iron punch, laboring on his mark: N. Turner, 1851.

The sun had broken through the clouds. Carrie pointed up to where the rock formed a crevice from which more figures seemed to emerge, painted the color of blood. Carrie asked, "What's there?"

Adaline looked. "Buffalo, I think."

"Buffalo?"

"Maybe it's a message." Knowing the pictures were ancient, Adaline kept looking and in her mind's eye saw buffalo coming out of the rock one after another, making a herd. "Maybe it tells where to find the buffalo. Maybe they're coming from out there now."

Carrie turned to search across the vast prairie. "They're not coming yet," she said.

Adaline looked, taking up Carrie's hand. "No. Not yet."

•

That afternoon, the train moved on to the confluence of the Pawnee River with the Arkansas. The Pawnee was nearly at a flood stage, riding high on its banks and roiling into the cuts. The ford used most frequently lay some distance upstream, marked by the furrows of passing trains and by logs laid out to make another corduroy landing. She rode Hawk just behind the Turners' wagon, and caught sight of the master leading the train that way, but one lone wagon was poised above a less used crossing nearer to the low valley that defined the path of the Arkansas. Mr. Turner turned his team that direction, and what Adaline saw as she drew closer raised her foreboding. It was a slow, soft boil in the Pawnee above a scour hole. Rocks knocked against each other. She rode Hawk up beside Mr. Turner and said, "I wouldn't go there."

"Hush. Get the child." Mr. Turner jerked his head toward Carrie, who sat in the wagon, peering out.

"There will be trouble."

"Hush, I say." He drove the team into the water, following the other wagon.

Mrs. Turner was astride a horse, cradling her younger daughter. Quickly, Adaline snatched Carrie from the wagon and set her on the saddle before her. Mr. Turner moved into the water to the side of his team, and the lead ox sank to its shoulders. The wagon tilted precariously, and then no matter how much the oxen strained or how frantically Mr. Turner whipped them, they could not haul the wagon free. Following his lead, two more wagons entered the water. Attempting to pass by, they also foundered in the hole. Mr. Turner struggled to pull himself to the back of his wagon, clutching at the top of the wheel, his face fixed with fury. He shouted at Adaline and his wife to dismount and help. "We'll lose the wagon!"

Mrs. Turner, who'd started after her husband into the water, sat frozen, holding her baby. Adaline kicked Hawk over next to her and was about to hand her reins to her and drop into the water to help, but as Mr. Turner kept shouting at her, at Mrs. Turner, and at the next wagon close behind, she saw that he'd managed to clamber up the rear of his wagon and had her trunk levered out. Aghast, Adaline watched as he dumped it in the river. It caught in the current of the hole, turned end-over-end, reared up and sank again. Mr. Turner grappled in the wagon for a crate. Now snapping into action, and realizing that Mrs. Turner would soon be helpless with her child, Adaline shouted at her, "Go back! Go back to the bank!"

Mrs. Turner turned to Adaline, her face flat and eyes wide and blank as nickel slugs. Adaline tugged on her arm, as if to awaken her. "Go back! Cross with the others!"

Mrs. Turner reined her horse around. Adaline wheeled Hawk after her trunk which had plunged down again into the hole. Remaining in the shallows at first and moving toward a bend in the river just when her trunk broke free of the hole's hold, she came out ahead of it in an eddy, all the while clutching Carrie. She slid down into the water, the chill of which took her breath away. The trunk bobbed toward her. She'd left Carrie in the saddle, but she shouted, "Grab onto his mane!" Carrie lay forward and clutched at Hawk's mane. "Hang on tight!"

With Hawk and child, she slipped deeper into the river, and while gripping Hawk's reins with one hand, with the other she grabbed at one of the trunk's handles as it bounced by. The crate came next, skidding in a chute of water and breaking apart as soon as it cleared the bend. She let the crate go, hung on to the trunk, and with Hawk proceeded to cross the river. She plummeted into the water nearly to her chin, Hawk sank to his ribs, and Carrie was submerged up to her knees. The current pulled at Adaline's legs, and the trunk, broadsided by what was turning into a rapid, all but ripped away. It seemed hopeless, too hard to go forward, too late to turn back, but then somehow Hawk miraculously found purchase on the bottom. Adaline let the reins go, grabbed his tail, and the horse made off with Carrie, Adaline, trunk and all. Adaline's feet found the bottom and she scrambled with her legs. She let go of the horse, turned, and with both hands pulled her trunk to the bank.

She brought her face close Hawk's muzzle and murmured, "Good, Hawk. Hey." She lifted the child down and looked to the river where four wagons now foundered. Men flailed in the water, fighting to push the wagons clear. Articles drifted and bobbed away. More crates, furniture, loose things spinning through the vortex of the scour hole and hurtling toward the Arkansas. Some of the vaqueros had ridden back, one of them shouting, "¡Uno por uno! ¡Uno por uno!" Having finally understood his meaning, the men moved to push out one wagon at a time while the vaqueros tugged on the teams from horseback. The Turners' wagon came out, streaming water from its sides. The chicken cage had broken open and chickens floated downriver, flapping and squawking desperately. The next foundered wagon rolled out of the drink. Mr. Turner, his face dark with anger, fixed his eyes on Adaline and marched in her direction.

He stalked up the bank and coming upon her, leaned toward her: "Worthless!" She stumbled back. Mr. Turner pressed forward, swaying and bending down and spattering her with spittle: "You're worthless, I say!"

Adaline took another step back and felt a small hand in hers, Carrie reaching up for her. Mr. Turner stood quivering, his hands clenched shut. Adaline believed Mr. Turner had taken to striking Mrs. Turner in the night when she heard his voice going on. She recalled thuds, sometimes Mrs. Turner moaning, followed by quiet. This came to her now, and she feared for Carrie, too. Mrs. Turner's habit of turning away with her silvering eyes raced through Adaline's mind, and in a flash she decoded what thrived in Mr. Turner's face, what she herself knew by having received it before: More than one beating by the headmaster, and switchings by the nuns, and being boxed on the ear by Aunt Mary Ann, what she came to realize she somehow called out of people to make them put the blame on her.

She thought: No! Not now, not now, not from you.

Carrie tightened her hold on her hand.

Mr. Turner pointed at the trunk and snarled, "Not in my wagon! Not never again!"

Adaline felt her spine straightening and she stared directly into Mr. Turner's face. To her surprise, he rocked back. In an instant, Mr. Turner's expression altered into one of wretchedness, and she became aware that behind her the wagons that had made the crossing issued a familiar clatter as they formed their oval. People called out to each other. She looked away toward the eastern horizon. There, a line appeared as if drawn, black as ink in the fading sunlight.

She thought: Somebody's coming.

She looked upstream where Mrs. Turner, having crossed over at the proper ford and still clutching her infant, headed down this side of the river. The third foundered wagon hauled out of the water. Mr. Turner's team trundled off on its own toward the valley of the Arkansas.

Back at the horizon, the black line was thickening.

It's mules.

Looking back at Mr. Turner again, she thought: I've lived up to the bargain, cleaning after these people, washing their clothes, watching the children, starting fires for them, yoking up the team and taking my turn driving it. And I was right about the crossing.

She gestured to the side with her head and said, "Your team is wandering off."

Mr. Turner opened his mouth as if to speak, but nothing came out. He jerked away to chase his wagon. As the fourth wagon was hauled out, Frankie appeared from the high ground behind, coming down to Adaline's side. She bent to grab one of the trunk's handles. "Let's heft this thing up to my wagon." She picked up her end. "By God, it's heavy."

Adaline took up the other end, struggling to hold it. She released Carrie, grabbed Hawk's reins with her free hand, and followed Frankie's lead. Carrie fell in step with her, only hesitating when Mrs. Turner's voice suddenly cut through the noise: "Carrie! She's taking Carrie!" Adaline could imagine the woman's face, drained of color even as she shrieked. It was impossible to sympathize with her, chafed as everything was by her piteousness.

She bent toward Carrie. "Don't worry. Let's first get you warm."

When they reached the wagon, Adaline tied off Hawk and with Frankie lifted the trunk.

"Thank you," she said.

Frankie snorted. Her eyes flicked past Adaline. Adaline turned and saw Mr. Turner struggling to control his team, his legs rigid. Looking back half way between the Pawnee and the horizon, the dark mass had spread across the plain. They were mules, all right. There was a rider to one side who was unmistakably her father, and two more on point whom she recognized as Louis Simmons and Jesús Silva. Frankie pulled out a blanket and Adaline took it and wrapped Carrie in it, then fell into a tangle bright with contradictions: fury for Mr. Turner, a biting doubt emanating from her history, replete with the endless reprimanding yet elation that her father was finally here, and the telling conflict, a deepening unease now that he was here that the first report he might hear was that she'd done a wrong.

But I wasn't wrong. I was right.

On the opposite bank, the excited mules, all ears and tossing heads, first were worried into a bunch, then they spread out along the water's edge to drink. Louis Simmons and Jesús Silva swung downstream while her father rode upstream on the bank to just above the crossing. There was a stirring and she felt her scalp prickle when she heard a voice above her say, "It's him. Kit Carson."

Kit leaned into his pommel and peered across the river. Seeing her, he nodded, then turned toward the water and held position while the mules moved toward him with Louis and Jesús nudging them from behind. He sat upon his buckskin, almost shimmering as if the world on the other side of him might glide right through.

•

A fort was here, fashioned from poles and positioned in view of both rivers. Upstream along the Pawnee lay another Cheyenne village on the far reaches of which stood the trees and stumpage where the mules were to be picketed. On the high ground before the fort, the train had formed its oval. Mr. Turner had brought his wagon and it stood cockeyed, water still oozing out its floorboards. Mrs. Turner was there, too, having come to fetch Carrie and taken her off wrapped Frankie's blanket without so much as a word or glance for Adaline.

Under cover of the wagon, Adaline had put on the dry clothing Frankie found for her, then she busied herself spreading her "possibles" over the kegs. The buffalo robe, which had been tied outside her trunk, was drenched, as was the oil cloth. Her own changes of clothing and her stash of pemmican, which had been stored in the top of the trunk, were also wet. And then there were the Navy pistol she'd found at Boone's Lick and brought along, the apothecary's instrument cases, the corn frond doll that Josefa, her father's wife, had given her years ago, and the things she had from her mother, a beaded bag and within it the tiny turtle made of buffalo hide and beads. Last of all was the book, which was still wrapped in its own length of oilcloth. It was merely damp. She had the things all spread about, open to the air, and then heard her father's voice.

Astride his buckskin, he peered into the back of the wagon, and greeted her, using his childhood name for her. "Hola, Twister." He nodded toward Frankie, who was with her mules. "I see you're keeping good company."

She slipped down from the wagon and looked up at him, grinning broadly. "Pa."

He said, "Them mules is exacting, fighting against the commotion. We might've picked a better place to catch up, I reckon. There's a wild white one amongst them. A gambler's ghost Louay's taken a fancy to."

"Fancy!" Frankie was fingering a torn tie strap on her harness. "Maybe lynx-eyed suspicion is the most you'd best allow them hard tails."

"Suspicion, then. He's taken a fine suspicion to the white one. Say, ain't that Jim Ferine I seen with the dragoons?"

Frankie looked over. "He claims he rode with you once."

Adaline attended closely to this, but her father averred with a murmur and instead gazed toward the trees behind the fort where Jesús and Louis had driven the mulada. "We need to keep them mules back so they don't get snarled up with t'others." It was true that from the moment the strange-smelling, cavvy-broke mules had first stormed the Pawnee, there'd been a churning among the train's animals.

"I could help," Adaline said, and then remembering, incensed as she was, added, "Once I help the Turners with their chores."

"You might at that. You got a baptizing, I see."

"That I did," Adaline said.

"So did your trunk, it looks like. Glad to see you're making good use of it, though."

At first, Adaline didn't understand. Then suddenly she thought she did. "What do you mean? You sent me the trunk?"

"I asked Mrs Frémont to send it for me. I seen her afore setting out with Louay and Jesús after the mules."

"And the robe and the book?"

"Yes, the robe. But what book?" He smiled. "Not likely I'd think to send you a book."

"Frémont's journals?"

Kit squinted, saying, "Mrs. Frémont mebbe. Mebbe she put it in. I'd told her you was getting your schooling, that you liked to read."

Several mules from the mulada broke loose entirely, causing a tremor among the train's animals. There followed a raucous braying. Kit dug his heels into his buckskin, turned it, and hastened off. She saw him herding the mules back through a place where the trees parted, and they disappeared into darkness.

It fell quiet but for the murmuring of the people who were setting their tents or starting fires for cooking. Frankie worked on her tie-strap. Adaline walked to the Turners' wagon with fleeting thoughts about Mrs. Frémont, thinking that her pa must be right, and wondering what Mrs. Frémont, wife of the Pathfinder and daughter of the famous senator, was like. She lit a fire for the Turners, scratching out the spark with her flint. She found salt pork and beans in the stores, soaked as they were, and put them in a pot. Mrs. Turner stayed in the sleeping niche in the wagon, fussing with the children. Mr. Turner appeared with a stick and tub of grease with which he was coating the wagon's axles. He leaned up against a wheel in order to surveil Adaline. This incensed her, and unable to contain her anger any longer, she stood up to him once again. "There it is. Your food. We've got our agreement for me to help you and I'll live up to it. I'll honor your request, too, by not traveling with you at night, neither me nor my trunk."

Mr. Turner glared, his lantern-shaped face rigid.

She marched back to Frankie's wagon, whereupon she found that Frankie had gone to picket her team for the night. Adaline led Hawk behind the fort. She intended to see if she could help with the mules, but what she saw first behind the pole barricade were the remains of played out animals from previous trains, the bones and heaps of foul-smelling offal beset with crows that winged up as she approached, and then returned to light on the rotting flesh once she passed. Buffalo hides were stretched on racks, set out to the elements with bloody sides up. A mist rose from the rivers and the setting sun colored the sky crimson.

She went toward the village and smelled the smoke that wafted from the tipis, of bois de vache, alder and aspen, the latter unmistakable for its sultry, moldy odor. Other scents arose as she continued, one the smell of burning tar from the torches, the fuel crafted from woven grass wrapped onto sticks, which had been dipped into oil seeps. These flickering fires magnified the village's sepulchral look, and as she moved yet farther it began to reek of effluvium and corruption. She circled alongside the margin of the village where silhouettes moved to and fro. Between the fringe of woods and the Arkansas, she marked the outlines of livestock and shadowy horsemen still coaxing the mules into their picket. Indignant snorting infused the air and hoof beats twisted about. She paused. She would have to go through or around the village.

Three dogs came out, snaky as coyotes, snarling and flickering their snouts and weaving around each other in the opening to the village. She drew Hawk's lead in tight and spoke sternly to the dogs. When she advanced, they curled out again and sniffed at Hawk, and she felt him shift his weight. The dogs shied. A woman appeared from the shadows, opening the flap of a nearby tipi and leaning into it. A man emerged and scolded the dogs, who skulked back. The woman moved toward Adaline, muttering indecipherable words. Although she was old, she had an erect carriage, while the man who followed her was younger. He had a limp, a wrap around one leg, and to her surprise addressed her in English. He indicated that the woman wanted to know where she came from and if she had tobacco or sugar to trade.

"The train. From Missouri. Someone among them might trade." She added, "Before that I came first from the rivers to the north."

The man spoke to the old woman, and the two of them turned back to examine her. Others had emerged from the torch-lit backdrop, most of whom were bent and emaciated. A woman of middle years revealed a face drawn tight, as if she were in the early stages of starvation, yet in the cut of her, cheekbone to chin, and in her hard eyes lay defiance. Her head jerked and her lips twisted as she spewed out what Adaline sensed was a curse.

The young man asked again if there were tobacco or sugar for trade. "Or black powder?"

"I see you are hurt," she said.

"Musket ball," the man said.

"There is a doctor with the train."

"Your doctor."

"Perhaps I could speak for you." She felt foolish as soon as she said that.

"You should go now, but ask about powder. Also tobacco and sugar. And whiskey. And long guns. We have skins to trade."

She didn't move. A disturbance caught her eye. It was the white mule her father had spoken of, the gambler's ghost, stopping at the margin of the woods and village. A rawboned colt, like a phantom it hung poised for an instant at the far edge of the village and then suddenly spooked, broke and plowed over one of the tipis, and disappeared, heading toward the valley of the Arkansas. Louis Simmons intersected its path. His horse cantered, jumping over the flattened tipi. People turned to stare and then turned back to Adaline, faces stolid but for the woman who tossed her head and with one hand made a hacking gesture. Some distance away an outraged bray resounded. Hoof beats swirled in a loop back around the far side of the village, and as Adaline traced the sound a shadowy form seized her eye up high in the bare limbs of a cottonwood. Wings lifted against the fading light. Peering hard, Adaline could now make out dark shapes, big blots against the twilight, everywhere in the trees.

"What are they?" she asked the man.

"Our people are dying. You should go."

Then she understood: The dead, the source of the smell that cut through the smoke and burned the nose. The dead were secured in trees. Vultures bent to tear at the flesh, and she shuddered as she encountered a revenant flash of another village deep in the past, something she had once seen.

The young man and the old woman stayed still. "When we see an enemy we never retreat," the man said, his eyes growing luminous in the near dark. "But this new thing, the people just fall and die. Go now."

She retreated, leading Hawk around the village to the tall grass. Settled into their pickets and grazing, the mules, including the ghost mule, raised their heads. She hobbled Hawk near them. The breeze from the river blew across the village, carrying the death scent.

She tried to sort through the ghastly village and the memory. Why did some memories travel with her and others did not? She had long remembered her sick mother in the hut, and the hole her father dug, and the white doeskin dress, and she knew her sister had perished in Taos, yet until this moment she hadn't remembered the other village at all, the flames licking upward from the trees in which the dead were positioned, and the people there also had spikes coming out the top of their village like a crown of fire.

She made her way to Frankie's wagon, then to the master's where she'd spied figures assembled around the fire. Frankie was there, as was her father, and Louis, Jesús, Jesse, and Susan, next to whom Adaline moved. Several Mexican teamsters were also there, and Carlisle. Talk was about the weather, the rivers, how far it was to the cutoff Kit's company would take to travel its own way. Her father looked at her. Louis looked, too, then cast his eyes down to where he toed the embers.

Frankie asked where she'd been.

When she told her, Frankie said, "There's cholera there. Best stay clear. Do not drink the water from where the Little Pawnee goes round afore it enters the Arkansas."

Frogs started in with their croaking calls. Adaline looked into the fire, then across at her father, who drew a pipe and tobacco pouch from his pocket. She told him that the Cheyenne wanted to trade for sugar, tobacco, and also black powder, long guns, whiskey.

"Sugar and tobacco, mebbe." Her father loaded his pipe, picked up a brand from the fire, and puffed at the pipe. "I heard you had more'n a dousing at the crossing."

She felt the others waiting for what she would say, something restive in their waiting.

"That I did. But I will keep my part of Aunt Mary Ann's bargain with Mr. Turner."

She expected that word—bargain—to strike a resonance. Kit's expression quickened. He looked down the train at the Turners' prairie schooner where Mr. Turner could be seen struggling with a crate, then turned back to her. She wanted him to talk. She wanted to hear more about her mother. She wanted to hear in detail about the fort as big as a castle. She wanted to hear the story of the village with the crown of fire, the true story of Mrs. White. She wished to fill all the vacancies in her memory. She wished for him to tell stories, yet this was not the time to be inquiring closely into the like.

She tried something not so weighty, asking if it was true about him shooting his own mule at Pawnee Rock.

He looked at her quizzically.

"When you were seventeen."

Now, the others looked expectantly at him.

Susan stood next to her and took her hand, sliding her smooth, cool fingers into it.

"How would you hear about that?"

"I read it in a book."

"A book again?" Kit sucked on his pipe and said, "The trail was different then. When you're young, Twister, oft as not what you see ain't there."

Chapter 4

THREE YEARS AGO, as he returned from Washington, D.C. in 1848, where he'd delivered government dispatches from California and the first news of the gold strikes, Kit stopped over in Missouri. In his course eastward he'd passed through Taos and learned he'd received a letter from Mary Ann, which Josefa, his wife in the Territory, read to him. In it Mary Ann said that Adaline disobeyed the rules, that she was good at numbers and reading, and was a smart girl, yet impossibly willful. Adaline learned of this on Kit's first morning at the Missouri farm, when she came upon him and her aunt at a stall where her aunt was milking. Hearing her name, Adaline ducked behind a manure dray.

"Half the time, it's impossible to make out what she's thinking. She has a streak of the devil in her," Mary Ann said. Adaline heard her aunt's stool grating across the floor, and she strained to hear what came next. "Sometimes, I think she's touched."

The sound of the milking deepened as the cow's udder was stripped clean. Adaline couldn't make out her father's response, but in a moment her aunt went back to the house. Adaline peered around the edge of the dray and beheld her father in the doorway, lighting his pipe, the sun breaking through the slats in the wall behind him. She kept still as the first scent of tobacco drifted her way, and then she heard, "Twister. Come out, now." Filled with misgiving, she stepped out and slowly walked up next to him. "You heard your aunt?"

She gazed past the house toward the hollow where smoke from a campfire curled amongst the trees. "I did." She wanted to say: But I'm not. Not touched. Sometimes there's no doing right, nothing to be done that will make people happy with me.

And even as she thought this, she pictured Mary Ann in the house, skimming the cream off the milk, pouring it into the churn to make butter, and working the plunger up and down. There would be the eggs to candle and breakfast dishes to clean. Suddenly, Adaline had an urge to go in to help, to do everything Mary Ann wanted. Yet so tangled up in herself was she that all she longed for was to be at the campfire in the hollow where her father's men were making preparations to ride away with him. All she wished to say to him was: Please take me with you. You'll see. There's no devil in me.

Yet out of the provident sense, even at age twelve, that to deny what Aunt Mary Ann had said might merely affirm it, she said nothing at first. In her perceptions she was mature beyond her years, yet still a child, just as now at age fifteen, at this very moment in the midst of her journey west, walking with the creak and concussion of wagons all around her, she was nearly a woman, fetching toward culmination the recurrent nightmares and confused sensuality of childhood. In the barn three years ago, as if tottering at the edge of an abyss, she had puzzled: If the devil's in me, how do I get him out? What does he look like? How do I know him?

After a moment, she took a breath and spoke. "I couldn't help it, the eavesdropping. I came upon you. You were just there, and I heard my name. I'm sorry."

"Now, Twister," her father said. "The world ain't staying the same. You need your schooling." He then told her something that he told almost no one. Only his sisters and brothers knew, and they sketchily, and the children raised by him and his wife, they would know, and Josefa herself, of course, and certain of his friends and superiors. "I can't read a lick of the words on a page," he said. "I look at 'em and what I see ain't the same as what others see. I keep looking there and I can't see what it is. Them words dance around, the letters turning inside out and upside down. I can't for the life of me make 'em out."

She waited, feeling lightheaded.

He paused to draw on his pipe. "So you and me will make a bargain. We'll keep you in school here. Board you in Fayette, which'll put you in new company. Maybe that'll help."

She was crushed. "But I want to go with you. I'll do things right. I can go to school where you are. In Taos."

"Here it is," he said. "Three years here in school. Take your lessons to heart. Your aunt says you know your letters. Keep on learning, Twister. Learn your numbers. Then, God willing, I'll come and fetch you west."

Bargains. She kept hers as best she could through three years, on more than one occasion holding her fury in check against the belittlement, the Missouri people looking at her and thinking they knew her, their scurrilous chatter. Through it all, she cleaved always to the light of her father's favor, which she held up as a measure of her life.

Now, traveling with the train, her father finally had kept his.

And, with the value of bargains learned, Adaline also kept the one Mary Ann had struck with the Turners, what Mary Ann called the "benefits of their custodianship." Adaline understood that Aunt Mary Ann, knowing her father would have his own obligations, wished to have someone additional looking out for her. Mary Ann had grievously misjudged the "custodians," that was all, and although Adaline now spent her nights with Frankie, she still doggedly took her turn walking beside the Turners' oxen by day, unyoking them in the evenings, lighting the Turners' fires, gathering wood and bois de vache, and caring for the children. But she knew that soon the train would take the Cimarron Cut Off and her father's company would bypass it, continuing straight westward. Then she'd be done with the Turners.

Years ago, at the end of the conversation in the barn, her father knocked the embers from his pipe and looked down toward the campfire in the woods. She asked how she came by her names: Bee'eenii'eihii as she remembered her mother calling her in her own language, and her father calling her Red Bird, or just Bird when she was little, and lately more often Twister, and then Adaline, or Ada as her cousin Susan and Aunt Mary Ann's family called her. "Adaline is for your favorite cousin," she said. "But the others. Bird? How Bird? And how Twister?"

"You was blue when you first come out," he'd said.

"Blue? What?"

"You needed more air, as happens betimes. So you was blue. But then you turned red quick, after some hard gasping and twisting about. Your Ma believed the red bird inside you saved you from being killed by the blue one." He smiled at her. "Then you kept on like one of them twisters coming across the plains . . . look out!"

"Twister?"

"Like a dust devil. A whirlwind," he said. "Don't you remember your Ma's stories about the whirlwind woman named Neyoooxetusei?"

She had thought for a moment, back then in the barn. She did remember. "Wherever whirlwind woman puts down, she must always leave again. She gets no rest. And the man who comes to find her is always disappointed. Yet he chases after her just the same."

"Aye," he had said. "Your Ma chose them stories to tell and it makes me a little afeared for you. But Twister, you never know how things'll turn out."

•

1851.

On the thirty-fourth day of travel the prairie was radiant—endless vistas, spring grass bending under the breeze, birds in the sky, and frogs singing from the shallows of the river. But soon enough, buffalo carcasses began to appear, seemingly killed by ciboleros, the Mexican hunters who took their name from their prey. The remains were carved up, the hides, the best of the meat, the fat, and the tongues taken off for trade, and what remained left to rot. The more the train went forward the stronger became the malodor, since the buffalo must have come toward the trail before encountering the ciboleros. Ferine and his dragoons set out on a ride-about along the river in hopes of locating the herd, joined by several immigrants, including Mr. Turner.

After two hours or so the scent of decay was conjoined by another faintly rancid sweetness on the draft. The cabalgata of horses and sundry animals in the center of the train began to show hesitation, a restiveness and a willingness to turn. Susan walked beside Adaline, each leading her horse. Through an opening Adaline saw Mrs. MacReeve's green ambulance, for the master had reduced the train to two columns here due to the narrowness of passage between the Arkansas River and the hills to the north. The ambulance and Murphy had ended up ahead of the Turners' wagon, while the mulada and several trade Conestogas brought up the rear. She saw the ambulance go around a hummock, followed by other wagons, but then her view was blocked. She could only sense that something was changed by smelling it, and then by hearing beyond the creak of wagons a low rumbling. She gazed northerly to higher ground and there spied her father and the other two, Louis and Jesús, their silhouettes against the sky at the head of an arroyo.

"What is it?" Carrie asked from her perch next to her mother in the prairie schooner.

Adaline looked back and saw the girl trying to climb out. "Buffalo, maybe. Stay where you are."

"I need to see them." She had one leg over the ledge.

"You hear," Mrs. Turner snapped. "Stay put."

"Where are they now?" Carrie cried as she pulled back.

"Ahead, maybe," Adaline said, softening toward the child. "You'll see better from there."

Before long, there were reports of the dragoons' rifles from a couple miles ahead, and then the unmistakable boom of a Hawken. She studied her father, his silhouette turning to look westward, and her ears, her whole body, then, began to reverberate as the rumbling rose to something approaching thunder. Her father and his company cantered off the rise and vanished toward the rear of the train. The sound came nearer. Edging around the hummock, she saw the train at almost a full stop, and it dawned on her that the buffalo might have looped to come back. By instinct she got up on Hawk, feeling him twitching beneath her. Susan mounted and was forced to control her bay by turning it full around and then pulling close to Adaline. The oxen lurched against their yoke and the sound continued to rise as Adaline drew near the lead ox.

"Something ain't right," she called.

Susan tugged on her reins. "Jesse said buffalo don't like to be driven into water. Don't like to be near the trail, neither."

In the center of the train the cabalgata grew disarranged while from behind several mules brayed. The cabalgata turned back straight toward the disturbance ahead as if to ascertain that the noise was actually there, then suddenly it broke loose. The vaqueros could not hold it. Spare oxen, cows, mules, and the extra horses reversed direction and stampeded down the line, clamoring for an opening. They flooded out sieving through the mulada and breaking back down the trail, then the startled mulada whirled away, too. Adaline glimpsed all this happening behind her, and before her she saw animals in harness jerking frantically this way and that. For an interminable moment the stunned people ignored them, as if trapped within their confusion, but next, as if touching bottom and being shunted back out of themselves by the desperation of their animals, people began moving, pulling children close, shouting, and crazily leaping up into their wagons.

Adaline felt it now, and edging forward she could see it, the black horde swelling to darken the slopes a hundred yards away. It found a narrow chute along the left side of the train, and charged, not yet breaching the trail, but dilating close upon it. She rose up and tried to hold Hawk near to her lead ox, seeking protection there and also intending to keep the oxen from bolting. On her other side, Susan hugged her horse against Hawk. The air here was permeated with bellowing animals and up ahead with the pulsing throb and scent of buffalo. Pocks of rifle fire in the distance and the boom of the Hawken again punctured the din, and closer in, more gunfire within the bounds of the train, since some of the men had taken up the wild notion, utterly without hope of effect, to protect themselves with their guns. The buffalo kept coming, hundreds of them, maybe thousands, moving as though possessed of one mind. They crossed the trail and broke uphill into the arroyo to the north, some of them in their fervor of running being squeezed off their feet. The first fell, others cascaded over them, which in turn were overwhelmed by those behind, the rush combusting into a deadly implosion, a roiling, raucous, lethal piling up of massive bodies.

Adaline had Hawk at a diagonal to her team of oxen, nearly pushing against it, and in the corner of her eye she glimpsed Mrs. Turner and the two girls, clenching the rail at the front of the prairie schooner. The stampeding buffalo swelled again and completely overcame its own leading edge. Adaline and Susan were locked in place, desperately trying to hold their own against the flood of buffalo, just staring as the herd burst into a grunting deluge, trampling over the top of itself and goring itself and chasing the trace of itself up the arroyo to open ground until finally it began to dwindle. The roar diminished. Some of the injured struggled to their feet and pulled free, then trotted off after the herd. Others crawled forward out of the pile, dragging themselves with a shattered leg, broken hip, or bulging internal injury. The Turners' oxen lurched toward the river, still seeking escape. Adaline found herself swept along and soon she could see the water, rushing by the willows on her side. Susan's horse danced into the shallows, but she worked it back, turning it full around again, while Adaline pleaded with herself, Hawk, and her oxen, "Easy. Easy. Easy, now."

Hawk grew calmer. The oxen rolled their eyes. Susan came alongside, her face drawn. Adaline's attention focused on the dip ahead where the train appeared to be much as it had been all along, although just beyond the ambulance she perceived a wagon toppled. Men fired into the heap of buffalo, finishing off the injured. To the right, up the arroyo, the herd had disappeared on high ground, leaving in its path a litter of bodies. She turned and searched behind. Her father, Louis, and Jésus had reappeared, chasing after the vanished cabalgata and mulada. Looking forward again as she edged the Turners' team and prairie schooner back into the ruts of the trail, she tried to sort out what had happened, then as she advanced, she began to feel an intimation of horror—the Murphy, packed with Mrs. MacReeve's furniture, her ambulance pulled to the side behind, her two young children, Mrs. MacReeve herself, the old man, Josh, Linda, and Yolanda—but it was not Yolanda, nor Linda, nor any of the others, and not the ambulance, but the Murphy and lying prone amidst his mules a figure who looked to be Gish himself.

Several men had cleared a passageway around the Murphy. The train crept along, accompanied by the more benign sounds of creaking harnesses and turning wheels, the gee-hawing up ahead and behind, but softer now in the ordinariness of it all, and Carrie up in the wagon with her mother and little sister, asking "Can I get down? Let me see! Can I now?"

The sudden motion Adaline caught was Mrs. Turner jerking Carrie back again. Adaline slid off Hawk and tied him to the schooner and proceeded beside the oxen, her hand on the yoke. Susan came alongside her, leading her horse. When they came upon the point where the buffalo had crossed, they took in the full view of Gish with one of his legs broken and wrenched away from his hip at an impossible angle, his face a mass of blood and dirt, his chest stove in. Legs, torso, arms, and head no longer fit together, but seemed to make a crazy misappropriated version of himself. Two men picked him up and carried him to a cart, and Susan exclaimed, "Oh, Ada! Oh, my God!" Adaline watched Yolanda follow the men and Mrs. MacReeve and her two children taking care not to step on bloodied mules, picking their way through the confusion of the wreckage. Linda first tried to catch hold of Yolanda from behind and next came around and held her by the shoulders, then hugged her. Yolanda wanted to trail after the men with the cart and Gish's wrecked body, but Linda held her back. Josh, who had driven the ambulance to one side and set the brake, sat slouched on the jockey box, staring at his hands.

•

By mid-afternoon, the train succeeded in moving several miles past the far edge of the arroyo into which the buffalo had disappeared. Kit, William, and Jesús, joined by Jesse and several vaqueros, came up from behind driving more than half the runaway stock. Hardly pausing, they rode out, seeking the remainder of the mulada where they said it had been spotted off to the side of the trail, grazing. Josh and the two men, who by then had harnessed a mule to the cart, dug a grave. They buried Gish in the sand high on the bank of the river. Josh said words for him, and Frankie borrowed a team of oxen and walked them back and forth over the grave to pack the earth. Adaline, Susan, and a few of the women, including Mrs. MacReeve, sought out white stones to make a cairn. Then they left Yolanda and Linda at the site.

"He had too much mustard in him," Frankie said as she, Adaline, and Susan walked out to picket their animals. "He saved Yolanda, and Mrs. MacReeve, her ambulance, her two children, and God knows how many else coming up. He give the buffler space to come through ahead of him and told Yolanda to get in the ambulance right behind. That young man found his deadline wrote in the dirt and he stepped into it and went under, by God!"

Adaline and Susan looked over at Frankie, who had seen far more than they had.

She went on: "I reckon Ferine miscalculated and turned the buffalo too near the train. Maybe a band of Injuns helped'em along. The Cheyenne. Maybe they ran into the Mescaleros. Or maybe the Arapaho party we saw. Ferine ain't appeared yet to explain what he done. Could be him and his men will just run for the north till they gaunt up to rattling bones."

After setting the pickets they moved back. To the east, crows appeared, riding high on the drafts and calling out signals. Vultures circled in the sky and sailed down upon the carcasses. Sporadically, the operatic yowl of emboldened wolves sounded, also the high-pitched yelp of coyotes, and the distant bawling of wounded buffalo, residual to the raucousness of chaos. "I reckon the carrion grubbers'll get their fill, now," Frankie said grimly. "Us among them."

Susan went to her tent, and Adaline headed for the Turners' prairie schooner where Mr. Turner commenced to order her about. The fire needed to be started, the water barrel replenished, more firewood gathered. Mrs. Turner made her habitual escape into the wagon and

Adaline lit the fire. Mr. Turner retired to the wagon and Adaline heard him sliding things about to make room for sleeping. The younger child whimpered and Mrs. Turner's voice started in, a monotonous cast, as flat as the dish of her face and as lacking in nuance as her silvered eyes: "She'll die. She won't eat. We'll lose her." Adaline heard Mr. Turner's reply come not in words, but in the form of one thing slammed against another. She feared that Mrs. Turner might be right, that the toddler was in jeopardy. "It's a sin, what we're doing," Mrs. Turner complained. "There'll be payment for it if she passes on. And where are we, Ned? Why are we here in this God forsaken place? My God, what are we doing?"

Mr. Turner didn't respond, but Adaline could hear him stepping down. She sensed him, sidling behind where she was bent, coaxing the fire along, and then she felt his body inclining menacingly toward her: "We're better off without that wagon, loaded up for the rich. And by God, we're better off with one less nigger."

Adaline's whole being wrenched with a fury. Without speaking, she wheeled off toward the river, wondering how the insistent, bitter commonplace, the ordinary hatred, kept rising up into the extraordinary: the hordes of buffalo, the violence and wanton fury, the implosion, Gish passing over, followed by the deathly stillness which was an outcome to violence, broken now by Mr. Turner's denouncing voice. Nestled within it, as a Methodist abolitionist, was the astonishing hypocrisy of his belief.

She made her way to the river bank and cairn, stopping next to Yolanda. Yolanda stood gazing at the stones. The large hunks of quartzite were heaped up in a pattern, the meaning of which was mysterious, a language of the incomprehensible, *an imago ignota*. "I'm sorry," she said to Yolanda. "I'm so sorry about Gish."

Yolanda clutched at Adaline's hand and looked over the cairn with her tearless eyes. "Do you think this will keep him safe?"

After a pause, Adaline said, "Oh Yolanda, yes, I do." If other cairns along the way kept the wolves at bay, then this one surely would, she thought, but she knew Yolanda didn't mean that alone. She thought of Frankie and her love for her lost man, the way she held him close in her memory. "And so will you. You'll keep him safe."

Yolanda looked at Adaline. She seemed filled with a grief as implacable as had been her acceptance of ruin that Adaline had marked in her eyes days ago.

•

By twilight, an air of resolution and quiet settled over the encampment, the purposeful calm that follows calamity, the relief that it is over, and then the planning for the next day when the wagons that were damaged would need to be repaired. As light faded, more fires had sparked up. Adaline delivered a water bucket to the Turners' wagon and stole away again. From the far side of the train, the French fiddler had struck up a tune, but the melody found early completion passing through its cadences. She discovered Frankie, stirring a pot over her fire.

Mules' hoofbeats resounded as they trotted across the high ground just to the north of the train, and the shadowy figures of Louis, Jesús, Jesse, and three vaqueros were spotted, driving the mules toward home. The men pressed them in tight, the white one among them, its phantom-like shape near the lead. Voices rose on the other side of the master's wagon, and she spied her father there, together with three of the dragoons, and the master, who directed his comments at the dragoons. Her father's voice interposed, his voice soft, and the master's stentorian one came again, and suddenly the dragoons spun off, the drumbeats of hooves exploding into the black night. Her father went back the opposite way toward his men.

"They got the mules," she said to Frankie.

"The critters must've hung together. It's lucky," Frankie ladled out the stew she'd concocted. Hardtack was had for sopping.

The two sat on rocks, sucking at the food. Adaline closed her eyes for a moment and discovered the buffalo in her mind's eye, crashing through the train one after another, a slaughter. Next, she thought about the two colliding flocks of passenger pigeons they'd witnessed a week ago, thousands, hundreds of thousands. Injured and dead birds dropped like stones from the sky and the women walked over to gather them up. She remembered Missouri where these pigeons were yet more common, how sometimes the trees literally broke apart under their weight when they landed. They favored seed and nuts, but also ate berries and bugs, and they were passengers in the sense of those who passed by, always, always in the act of passing, darkening the sky just as the buffalo darkened the earth, passing by, for the historic diminution of them almost to zero had begun, and that of the Indians, too, Ute, Pawnee, Comanche, Cheyenne, and Arapaho, among others, for whom such wastage was anathema to their being.

The Indians were passing by.

The further the train had traveled, the more the side trails were frequented by Indians, including "removed" tribes from far away places to the north and east: Huron, Wyandot, Ottawa, Potawatomi, Osage, Cherokee, Creek, Chickasaw, Choctaw, and Kickapoo. The government prepared to excise the region the train traversed from what was still Indian Country and turn it into the Kansas Territory. This would occasion the further removal of "recalcitrants" into a newly conscribed Indian Country, where they conjoined with "free slaves." In the years that followed, that country would be squeezed again and again, divided first into Oklahoma Territory and finally into a diminished Indian Territory.

Gish had passed by.

At the top of the oval the master threw more wood on the fire. The three dragoons returned, their bodies lit up by the flames, and Ferine came in a farm wagon, his dead-tooth colored horse tied onto it and the hound following. Together with one of his dragoons, Ferine eased a man out of the back of the wagon and laid him down near the fire. Her father reappeared with Louis and Jesús.

After Frankie wiped the bowls clean, she and Adaline walked across to the master's fire. More people had congregated, including Susan and Jesse, and a collection of emigrants. Ferine's hound lay down a few feet away from the gathering, coveting a hunk of meat between its front paws, and Adaline noted that the man laid by the fire, the fourth dragoon, had taken an arrow in the leg. A doctor on the train, Doctor Steele, had been summoned and he crouched over the man, slitting his trouser leg up the seam and parting it around the arrow. Ferine began telling how he and his man had found themselves cornered by Arapaho, and with only one horse between them since the other had been driven off.

"What Arapaho?" Louis said. "Pretty far off, they was."

Ferine ignored this, telling how he'd taken cover in a copse of trees, that he'd held his own with his injured man until his dragoons came and lit into the Arapaho that remained. He said a band of ciboleros backed off from the fight. All this was told with a hint of injury, insinuating that others had abandoned him after the buffalo run. "I heard that nigger was killed. Could've been more'n him, if it hadn't been for us."

Adaline looked at her father, leaning against a wagon wheel. His face grew watchful.

"More light," Doctor Steele demanded.

Jesús dropped a few sticks on the fire and went to fetch a lamp. Upon his return, he knelt beside the doctor, holding the lamp over the dragoon's injured leg. The doctor took up his knife and held it to the coals of the fire. The dragoon's face was sallow, pockmarked, his yellow hair greasy, and his eyes narrowed to slits as he set himself for pain. Then with his knife the doctor made a cut on the uninjured side of the dragoon's thigh, at the same time working the buried point of the arrow toward the cut, levering and shoving the shaft. The dragoon sucked air through his teeth as his skin bulged and the point of the arrow cut through. The doctor sawed off the point, laid it aside, and eased the rest of the arrow back out the way it had come. Jesús lowered the lamp and placed his hand on the man's knee to keep him still.

"That should be the worst of it," the doctor said. "It's a good thing it missed the bone."

Suddenly a woman among the immigrants loosed a half-shriek and stumbled backwards. Adaline's gaze fell to one side of the hound, upon what it chewed, now revealed fully by the angle of light from the lamp. Between its paws lay not meat, not animal, but a child, a dark, bloodied baby, which the hound lifted by the back of the neck and shook.

The woman spun away, moaning, "Oh, my God! Oh, my God!"

Carlisle stepped out from his wagon wheel and barked, "Call that beast off."

Meantime, the wounded dragoon stopped moaning and his eyes widened.

"Beast, you say?" Ferine said.

"Call it off!"

The hound dropped the baby to the ground and picked it up again and shook it.

Ferine leered at Carlisle and circled around the fire toward his hound and commanded, "Off it!" When the dog didn't respond, he stepped to his horse, pulled out his Hawken, came back, and drove the butt of it into the hound's head. The hound dropped the baby and stood, stunned. Ferine drove the rifle butt into its head again, and the hound staggered. It rocked sideways and looked crazily about at the people.

Susan had wheeled around, turning away, and Jesse moved to her. More people at the fire were backing off. Adaline had edged back, as had Frankie at her side, and Louis positioned himself between them and the fire, on the other side of which were the wounded man and swaying hound. Slowly, the doctor stood up and inched away from his patient who lay motionless, his eyes wide and fixed upon the hound. At that instant, Adaline saw her father slide behind Ferine and reach for his Hawken, propped against the back of the master's wagon. Now, Jesús held the lamp up high and Louis leaned toward Kit, and Adaline saw the metal in her father's eyes. The hound lifted its head and emitted a low snarl. Kit nodded to Louis and Louis reached under his coat and withdrew the handgun from the holster he kept near the small of his back. He took one step over the prone man and around the edge of the fire, then lowered the handgun until its barrel nearly touched the hound's snout. The report thundered, slamming and reverberating through the train and into the night. The hound dropped.

"There'll be hell to pay for that," Ferine said.

"No," Carlisle said. "No such thing. I'll have you off this train."

Louis moved away, stepping once more over the prone man, who still lay motionless. Only the man's eyes moved, passing between Carlisle and Ferine, up to William, who stopped at Adaline's side, and across the fire to the prostrate hound, and now back up to Jesús, who held up the lamp and said, "Es un demonio. It's no business having the ogro like that in camp."

"It's dead," Ferine snapped, nudging the torn body of the baby with his boot toe.

"So now is the ogro," Jesús said.

Louis returned the gun to the holster, then Adaline felt his hand, holding her elbow.

Ferine shifted his gaze over to Kit, who stood with his rifle in the crook of his arm. "The dog found it. It was a dead savage, killed, or more likely left to die by its savage mother."

"Don't matter, even if it was true," Carlisle said.

Kit stepped out and picked up the end of the arrow shaft with the feathers on it, which he held out to the light. He looked at Ferine. "This fletching ain't Arapaho."

"Now, that don't matter," Ferine said. "They was hostile and they lay for us."

"They was Cheyenne. They caused the buffler to come into the train, provoked as they was." Kit looked over at the cart and back again, which in the firelight could be seen to have in it a stack of hides. "Reckon you was too busy to stop'em, what with thieving Cheyenne buffler robes for yourself. You ain't learned nothing about Injuns, neither. And you lied. Them ciboleros was long gone."

Chapter 5

To Adaline and Susan's left was the column, headed up by Jesús and her father while Louis and Jesse rode drag, moving the twenty or so mules and six spare horses behind the freight wagons. She and Susan rode not far off the main trail on a path that wound through sagebrush and juniper, and Susan kept remarking upon the plants. "Now, look at that strange thing," she would say, observing a pincushion, prickly pear, or disorderly cholla as tall as a tree and loaded with magenta buds soon to break open. For her part, Adaline was amazed how this place seemed so familiar. She rocked on Hawk, pleasuring in the full sunlight of June, her legs again warm against the horse's ribs. With half her mind, she kept alert for snake and cactus or watched the killdeer speeding alongside, while her other half fell into ruminations over where she was headed now, and where not, certainly not back to Missouri, not ever, and not down Cimarron Cut-off to Santa Fé, on what the pilgrims from the train would travel, and thence westward along the Puerco watershed to the Colorado Crossing and across the desert to gold country.

Three days ago, they had parted ways. Kit's company recomposed so that it included himself, Jesse, Louis, Jesús, Adaline and Susan, and the eight Mexican drovers with their freight wagons, including Jesús's brother-in-law, Tótilo, and his two young sons, Eliseo and Carlos. Adaline had taken a reading with the sextant and approximated their location at a latitude of 37° 40' and a longitude of 104° 40'.

Their travel would take them westward along the Arkansas beyond Bent's new trading post and the abandoned Old Fort, and then they would turn southward where the Rio Del Norte ran. Near to it lay Taos, and east of Taos stretched the spine of mountains where lay Rayado Creek, which by consulting the Fremont maps Adaline had calculated was not a hundred and fifty miles away. She was filled with anticipation for her destination, and for meeting Josefa again. Josefa was a luminous presence in Adaline's memory, tall and beautiful, and when she had known her not even as old as Adaline was now.

After they parted from the train, Adaline had looked back from her point of remove and seen the wagons curling away, the wheels and oxen legs beneath the dust, the green ambulance next to the Turners' prairie schooner, Frankie near the front, and Ferine and his dragoons trotting ahead. As it turned out, the master had not put Ferine off, having second thoughts about the need for protection. Adaline had thought how people, hoping for mending when disaster struck, so quickly rejoined the world of safety left to them. She'd said her goodbyes, reserving time for Carrie and Yolanda, with whom she'd become close, and for Frankie, who had transformed over time into something like an older alter ego.

"I'll keep an eye peeled for you. Big as this country is, our number be yet small in it," Frankie had said. "There's a chance we'll pass each other." They were carrying Adaline's trunk to secure it in one of the trade wagons of her father's company when Frankie paused, her eyes glistening, which had startled Adaline, and then her own eyes had welled. Frankie added, "So long as I don't get turtled up first."

•

Kit and Jesús pulled off the trail, and Kit gestured to Louis to take the lead ahead of the wagons, and back to Adaline and Susan to get on the main trail, and move next to Jesse to help watch over the mulada. She and Susan settled in while Kit and Jesús rode into a wash, their two tipped-down hats tracing a line against a limestone formation.

"Kit wants to see William Bent," Jesse said. "His new trading post is down that way."

Now and again, groups of buffalo had come into view, and once they passed through a narrow valley where bones and skulls pointed every direction. At other times carcasses were left with only the hide taken, and once in a while parts of a carcass strewn about. Jesse had already explained that this most likely came because the ciboleros sometimes abandoned the kill with the gut intact, which built up gas until it burst. "Neither of you girls would as soon be near one when it happens," he'd said. "Lest you get decorated with buffler belly."

The current of the Arkansas had quickened. To the northwest the Rocky Mountains ghosted upward, and south and west and much nearer rose the Sangre de Cristos, their slopes dark blue as though recently disgorged from the earth. Clouds trailed around the peaks, white and phantasmagoric as satin. It was marvelous how distances registered here, men, animal, and cactus so distinct as if cut into the backdrop. Sounds, too, reverberated on the hard dry air, a rock kicked by a hoof, the creak of Conestogas.

Kit and Jesús returned and confirmed that they'd found William Bent, also four Comanches trading hides. Kit said he knew the Comanches, led by a chief with whom he was friendly—Nokoni, who took his name from his band, The Wanderers. He thought there was no need to worry, as the Comanche's design was mainly upon buffalo, but still they should watch the company's stock at night, for the Comanche liked to raid horses. These Comanche had several good ones with them, including a familiar-looking military black.

Louis had drifted back and he said, "The dragoon's horse? Ferine said he met up with ciboleros and Cheyenne."

"Just so, then you got the proof of the lie along with the stolen horse," Jesse said.

Jesús, who was riding beside Kit, muttered, "¡Mentiras! ¿Y qué más?"

Kit ducked his head and chuckled. "Un sabueso muerto."

Jesse cut his eyes to Susan and Adaline. "A dead hound is what Ferine has along with his lies about causing the stampede. Ice in his belly, too. He lied, I'd wager, in hopes of not appearing to be the thief he was, stealing from the Cheyenne, and not looking exactly like the fool filled with bluster as he turned out to be, mistaking Comanche for Cibolero."

Kit and Jesús resumed the lead ahead of the wagons. Adaline and Susan fell in behind Louis and Jesse. In time, they came upon a desolate-looking village set a little back from the trail that Adaline judged to be Cheyenne by the way the tipis were thrown up in a line against the cottonwoods. Kit slowed to cast an examining eye upon the encampment. Adaline regarded the trees, seeking out the dead, but saw nothing. The village had meat, set aside to dry. The women and children were at work on the few hides they had stretched out. Some of the men looked up to coldly assess the passing company. Others made an open show of turning their backs on it.

Another three or four hours went by before the company drew up to make camp. It was agreed they would reach the Rayado the next day or the day after. The hills crept northerly and broke into low plateaus. Next to the camp stood a headland of rock with a hollow blackened by fires from previous travelers. The men built a fire, starting with a spark from Louis's flint and the kindling Kit split with his hatchet. They grilled meat and Tótilo produced maize meal and a flatiron for heating tortillas. The sky was lucid with afternoon spring light, and as evening came on the drovers were dispatched in shifts to watch over the stock.

Susan and Adaline sat next to each other in the hollow while the men left behind gathered around the fire. Talk at first was of Nokoni, the Comanche, then turned to the Comancheros. Texas, a part of the Union for six years, was deemed the fount of much trouble, and war was waged against all Indian peoples. The state hadn't set aside reserves for them, but instead forced the Indians and Mexicans out and gave over the lands to incoming settlers. Kit explained to the girls that it was important to separate the Comanches from the Comancheros, the ones out of Chihuahua that conjoined with Mexican bandits, the Mestizo Comanchero raiders. Also to separate the Comancheros from ciboleros, who came out of the Territory. The Comancheros, he said, were never to be trusted and lived by no one's law, only by a compact with murder and doom. They lived by their raids on trains and settlements and traded booty, including slaves of all races—Ute, Arapaho, Cheyenne, Mexican, Negro, and White.

"You said there was a buck breed with them Comanches," Louis said. "How do you make that out? A Parker chit?"

Her father said, "No. Too old. The raid on Parker Fort was in thirty-six. Don't know where he come from. Mebbe the Nokoni took him in trade."

Such judgments by her father of time and fact, and of names of people and places were rarely questioned. More than once Adaline had heard Jesse or Louis recounting something and her father would correct them. She puzzled over this, trained as she'd been to memorize from the page. Of the men present, she knew Louis could read some. Jesse read well enough and even possessed several books. Sometimes he might be seen poring over the Bible, tracing the words with a fingertip. As to Jesús and the others, she had her doubts, certainly not in English.

Louis leaned and poked at the fire with a willow stick. His look turned up to Adaline, then averted to the fire, and noting his solicitude of her, she wondered if he'd yet asked her father the permission Susan had spoken of. She wondered what her father would say. Then she began again to wonder about what it would be like being with Louis for the years to come. Her shoulder touching her cousin's shoulder, she sat motionless on tenterhooks in the stillness, and she felt the stirring, the probing that caused a shuddering within. Louis rose, walked into the shadows, and returned with a broken axletree left by other journeyers. He placed an end on a stone, stomped on it, breaking it with a crack, placed the pieces in the fire, and sat down again. The fire snapped, spewing sparks into the evening light. Geese parlayed at the river, and a pair of hawks spiraled on the drafts, calling out their piercing cries.

The men turned their speculations upon the behavior of the Cheyenne. Jesse said there was a change come upon those people. "Used to be by us being friendly they kept their noses far enough above water to accept what they had. Now with the settlers clambering in after gold, and with trade still going south to Santa Fé, Bent's Old Fort abandoned and infested with disease, so it was believed, and by diminishment of the buffler, them Cheyenne have to feel put upon."

"I hope it ain't no put upon in particular with them," Kit said. "Them in that village was uncommon unfriendly for Cheyenne."

"It's a fast freight of halos, what we've brung them," Jesse said. "But still it ain't yet exactly like it was with the Karankawa. With them and others, exterminated one way or t'other, so the chute of their life was shut down and the chute to perdition left wide open for them to slide into. Down they slide and there's the end of it."

A rise of attention stirred up around the fire and looks flickered from one man to another as it was perceived that Jesse was gravitating toward an expostulation, which was allowed by the prevailing sense of ease among them, being now in their own company and so near to home.

Kit said, "They had fresh meat in their camp. A short stack of hides. Some number had just come in from the east. I seen the son of a chief among them—Ah-man-nah-ko. William Bent said close though they be, they still ain't coming in to trade."

"He didn't say why?" Louis asked.

"It ain't like 'em is what he said," Kit replied. "Betimes, I reckon those were their hides Ferine had. That would provoke 'em." He turned his gaze to Adaline. "William Bent spoke of his wife, Owl Woman, who has died. She was Cheyenne. She'd of remembered you from the days after your Ma passed on and I was at the Old Fort with you and your sister."

A galvanic chemistry sizzled in Adaline: The name Owl Woman tied her to Bent's old Fort, and in the same breath her father had mentioned her sister, which was one of the few times she remembered him ever speaking of her. And there was something known to her about the Cheyenne village back at the Pawnee, added to the one they'd just passed today. She had memory of one called Owl Woman, who was kind to her, and of a younger Cheyenne woman, who was cruel. She thought of the country with its sand hills breaking ever more into benches, and things growing for which she'd been affirming names she'd heard before—cholla, sage, juniper, the prickly pear and tamarisk, grease bush, yucca, piñons, and bush mint in the river shallows. The calls of the hawks, the confabulating geese in the river, the feel of the air on her face, and all manner of things rang with mysterious familiarity.

Jesse picked up Louis's willow stick and stirred the fire. "Wise, however, to put up a store. The advantage lies in having stores in hand, not in what's hoped for, what would only bring on the perdition faster." Everyone around the fire fell quiet. "The chutes is narrow and spread all across the country, so per usual only a few at a time fall into it, but steady enough so their numbers go down faster than they can replace themselves. It's shifty like that in its workings. These chutes is most common in the mountains. The very bottom of the Colorado Canyon, I hear tell, is filling up with lost souls already from the dying, so we got these other hollows opening up every time the earth booms a bit. I seen one once, stumbled upon it when I was on a hunt. Couldn't hardly believe it, but strange things happen on a hunt, so you ain't sure if it's the phantoms you're seeing out of hunger and sleeplessness, that half-starved, lonely delirium, or if you've passed on to another world.

"It started with my horse, then my mule. I had the mule packed with elk and a few beaver pelts I'd picked out of a river, just gunning 'em down where they was thick. The mule was on a lead, and I on my bay, coming down from the mountains. This bay I had was long favored." Jesse nodded across at Kit. "It's the one I lost, as you'll remember, from when I came back to Touse on a jackass."

Susan put her hand inside Adaline's arm. Adaline leaned back a little, pleased to rest her head against the rock as she listened. At that moment, a lark sparrow high above on the sandstone began to sing, its sliding trills laddering up and dropping to a flourish like bright water passing over stones, a fancy lacing on the twilight. "Aye, boys, there she be already," Jesse said, twisting to look up. "The lively dirge."

He went on: "The mule balked. I couldn't get it to pass around a corner to where I thought I'd catch the trail back to camp. No matter what I tried, dismount and lead, or pull, it just stood there shivering. Critters know things, and more long I heard thundering in the distance. At about that time, the mule jumped its lead entirely and run up the trail from whence we'd come, carrying off my meat and provisions with it. All the while the bay stands there white-eyed, and then it bolts. Near pitched me off the edge, so I had to let it pass. It follows the mule, clattering to the ridge.

"I figured to look around the corner myself, then weary on up the rocks to cut off my stock. Maybe find some other way down more agreeable. I'd be destitute, otherwise, and it was afternoon coming into night, like now. What I heard was the thunder, or like an avalanche, which is like thunder, or it could have been the sound of the rocks coming down where the mule and bay had gone up into the cloud at the top. But it sounded over and over again, like somebody was at it there, striking a great bell. You as much felt it running up your legs as heard it. There was a half-moment between each, which ain't what thunder does, nor avalanches, since their rhythm is God's rhythm, which I don't pretend to understand. So I considered maybe it was a Howitzer being fired off, and expeditiously reloaded, and fired again, the which, unlikely as it seemed, give me some hope. When in such a state, you believe most anything.

"I eased on around the corner of the rock, and there was a mist there, too, the cloud just dangling down along a cut in the mountain, and what I saw was two white wolves with red shirts on and war bonnets standing up on their hind legs on either side of one of them chutes I've been telling you about. Behind them and going up the cut was a long file of savages, men, women, and children, more than I could tell on account of the mist. When them in front of the line seen me, they begun to beckon in a most friendly fashion, and I felt a strong urge to join them. I have observed friendly among their kind, but never the likes of that. The young women near to overpowered me, they made me feel so lonesome. They was smiling and dancing around happy as otters and waving at me to come along. Meantimes, the two wolves latched onto whichever savage come next to the front of the line. One by the shoulders. One by the ankles. They would swing the poor soul and heave 'em over the brink, each one scaring up more rock in the chute and causing a commotion of ringing rock as it plunged out of sight."

Jesse paused to poke at the fire. Sparks twirled into the air. All around, the faces of men were rapt in the firelight. Tótilo's two sons, having just enough of English, had been drawn to the tale, and they stood near their father behind the circle. Adaline and Susan reclined against the stone where by the fairness of the evening and radiance of the fire it had become warm enough for them to open their coats. The noise of the geese at the river had faded, yet somewhere above the lark sparrow began its warble all over again. Midway through, another sparrow chanted a counterpoint, a contralto to the liquid trills of the first, the two tunes weaving around each other and sketching out their jewels in the near darkness. The birds fell silent. The men at the fire awaited Jesse.

Jesús glanced over at his two nephews, and then grinned across at Jesse in a way that made his teeth flash. "¿Y entonces?"

But a low warning whistle issued from one of the drovers who stood guard. Heads turned, yet before the men could move Indians drifted into the camp in twos and threes, materializing from several directions—out of the willows near the river and from the gully that ran around to the west. They were Cheyenne. Fifteen or more converged, some with painted faces, some bare-chested, others draping blankets over their shoulders. Some bore rifles, others carried bows with arrows hanging from straps. The men at the fire rose as one to their feet while in the shadows the drovers shuffled. At the top of the hill to the west more Cheyenne appeared as dusky forms in silhouette on horseback. Those in the camp approached the fire, forming a barrier between the men there and the drovers. Susan's hand gripped Adaline's wrist, and Jesse looked up at the two girls, signaling them to keep quiet.

Kit spoke to one of the Cheyenne in English, addressing him by name, Ah-man-nah-ko, whom he'd seen in the village. He asked after his father, a chief called Old Bark. He praised the chief to the young man, who muttered, "Not here." Kit invited the Cheyenne to sit down and smoke, to which five of them, including Ah-man-nah-ko, assented, placing their weapons on the ground behind them. The others stood back between the circle and the drovers. Adaline and Susan stayed in place, still as the stone they leaned against. Ah-man-nah-ko sat beside Kit, and next to Ah-man-nah-ko sat a thickly built Cheyenne with a white scar snaking out of his hair to his jaw. Now he studied Adaline and Susan, marking them. Adaline felt Susan gripping her wrist more tightly, and saw Louis, seated across the fire, squinting at the man.

Kit took his pipe from his pouch, packed it with tobacco, lit it with a brand from the fire, and passed it to Ah-man-nah-ko. They talked in English and by signing. Adaline believed her father spoke some Cheyenne, but she did not hear him do that as the pipe went from Ah-man-nah-ko to the one with the scar, and further around, each man in turn drawing on the tobacco and blowing smoke toward the fire. Kit remarked upon the meat they had in their village. "A good hunt," the one with the scar said. One of the other three, a lean man with a red neck scarf knotted over a buffalo vest and slashes of white paint on his face, spoke in Cheyenne. The one with the scar answered, and in the moment of their exchange Adaline saw her father looking toward the hill where the Cheyenne on horseback had now transmuted into shadows. The pipe had come around to Jesse, who bent to re-ignite it with another brand. As he did so, he ventured to glance up where Kit was looking, then, puffing on the pipe, he turned his gaze to Louis, who held himself steady, not looking up, his face watchful and grim.

The one with the scar spoke again: "Yet there are too many hunters. Arapaho, Pawnee, Comanche. Gesturing toward the company's Conestogas, he said, "Too many wagons. Too many white men. Too many ciboleros. Too many blue coats. The blue coats have no honor.

Too much shooting buffalo for the pleasure." He lifted his fist, smote his chest with it, and sneered: "Big man! Kill buffalo!"

Adaline freed her wrist from where Susan gripped it, drew her hand up and grasped Susan's hand tightly. She could feel Susan's leg trembling. Her eyes tracked the scene—the men seated around the fire, the five Cheyenne, two of whom had remained silent, her father and Jesse next to each other, and Louis and Jesús across from them. The drovers seemed to have slipped away except for Tótilo and his two sons who stood near a wagon where several rifles leaned behind a wheel. The remaining Cheyenne in the camp stayed as they'd been in a line between the hill and the circle at the fire. She brought her gaze back, noting that only Jesse's rifle was visible, though Louis likely had his handgun under his coat. Jesús might have one hidden, too. Her father's long handled hatchet lay at his knee on the ground.

Kit asked the Cheyenne if they planned to take their hides to William Bent.

The one with the scar announced that the fort was no more.

"He's started again at Big Timbers," Kit said.

"The sickness came from the old fort," the man said. "It will come from the new one, too, once it's built. The sickness is in the trading."

Ah-man-nah-ko cradled the pipe again. "Yes, it will be the same."

He puffed on the pipe and passed it to the man with the scar, who took his time with it and spoke in Cheyenne to the one with the red scarf and face paint. The two Cheyenne next to him looked up. The man spoke again, causing the three to laugh. Susan's hand tightened the more in response to the ominous tone, and in her father's face Adaline saw the same countenance it had taken on before Louis shot Ferine's hound. He sat motionless. His eyes seemed to have metal in them. It was as if the world came to be atomized before him. When the Cheyenne with the scar spoke low again to his compatriots, Kit shouted out and leaped to his feet, bringing up the hatchet. Everybody snatched their weapons and sprang up.

The man with the scar held a dagger several inches from Kit's throat while Kit poised his hatchet ready to bury it in the man's skull.

Jesse's rifle clicked as it cocked and he leveled it on the man in the buffalo vest. Another of the Cheyenne had produced a military saber from under his blanket. Yet another had an arrow notched and lifted point blank on Jesse. Louis and Jesús produced handguns that they turned on Ah-man-nah-ko across the fire, who stood still, hanging back from raising his rifle, and in that instant of positioning in close quarters, Tótilo had edged to where the rifles leaned against the wagon behind the wheel and drew one out. The Cheyenne in the background stirred, approaching ever nearer, but stopped when Tótilo spoke to them, signaling that he knew they were there, and training his rifle on the nearest one. Next to the wagon, the two boys looked out, wide-eyed.

Without lowering his hatchet, Kit spoke to Ah-man-nah-ko in Cheyenne. Moving his head back and forth, now he leveled his words at both Ah-man-nah-ko and the man with the white scar, words completely enigmatic to Adaline except by their tone, clipped and ruthless, possessing a force she had never before heard from her father.

Ah-man-nah-ko responded to Kit and then turned to the man with the scar, who drew his knife away.

Kit persisted, his words unyielding.

Slowly, everyone lowered the weapons. The one with the scar spoke again, and in the same fashion by which they had first appeared in the camp, all the Cheyenne melted away. In a few moments, the only sound was the soft ringing of the talus on the hill, then faint hoof falls, then nothing.

Marking their passing, Kit said, "Catch the teams."

The call went out to the drovers, "Catch up! Catch up!"

As the drovers reappeared, Jesús cried, "¡Ensíllenlas! ¡Monten!"

The teams were harnessed and hitched, and the wagons rolled forward into the dark in close formation with the mulada tight in between. Along with the two boys, Eliseo and Carlos, Adaline and Susan were consigned to Tótilo's Conestoga while Kit and Jesse rode point and Jesús and Louis guarded the rear. The drovers had been warned, and each now had a rifle at the ready and whips to ensure that their teams move apace. For a time, the two boys kept sentry out the back of the wagon and then bedded down amongst the sacks of sugar, flour, and casks of molasses, bundled up in their serapes. Susan and Adaline knelt in the front, gazing ahead, looking around Tótilo and over his mules to the wagon ahead of them and at the obscure trail and hills against a slate-colored sky in which a quarter-moon emerged.

Susan said, "The night won't get any darker than it is now."

"No," Adaline said.

"Still not much moon, though."

"They will hear these wagons, light or no light."

Susan was silent for a moment. "I was thinking of Mrs. White."

"Best not to."

"You didn't seem afraid."

"But I was." Saying that, Adaline realized she had been near paralyzed with fear.

"I was thinking that what happened to Mrs. White might happen to us, or worse."

"How could it be worse?"

"If they kept us forever?"

"I didn't think it would happen. Besides, there is no forever on this earth."

"Oh, Ada," Susan said. "It would be good if what there is before the end of forever were a little easier than this."

Adaline chuckled.

"Your Pa knew what they were saying."

"Yes. But he didn't speak their language until the end. And the one, the son of a chief, he gave in."

"I wonder what he said."

"Pa? I guess he told them they would die."

Adaline hooked her arm into Susan's and held her close as she looked out at the penumbral shapes of hills on either side of the train. Ranks of junipers lined the washes and sometimes humped up along higher ground. She knew the Cheyenne band was out there, lurking to one side or another. She said, "I don't think we're done with it yet."

Before long, the company came to a range corral, which the men had judged they would reach before the Cheyenne band re-grouped. Also, they doubted that the Cheyenne would attack in the dark. They turned the mules and horses into the corral and wheeled the wagons around in a circle immediately next to it, leaving the pulling animals in harness, which they fed maize and afterward built a small fire near to one wagon for warmth. Adaline and Susan stood not far from the fire but not too close either, since Kit had told them they should not allow themselves to be outlined by the light. Next, he fell into conversation with Jesús, Tótilo, and the elder of the two boys, Eliseo. He bent to inspect Eliseo's feet and spoke to Tótilo, who in turn spoke to his son. Kit straightened up and gestured to the south, whereupon Eliseo set out at a run. His sand-colored serape flapped like an owl's wings in the sepulchral light as he vanished over a bench, racing toward the river. He was to alert the troops if they were bivouacked at the Rayado, or any others he might encounter, and to bid them to come.

What Adaline and Susan wouldn't know until later was that unless Eliseo encountered troops on the trail, it was thought to be unlikely that help would arrive by morning. The company waited through the remainder of the night, seizing snatches of sleep, and at the first light of dawn the same group of Cheyenne rode into the camp. They were backed by yet more horsemen who loomed on the hills across the flat beyond the corral.

Kit told them that troops were on the way.

The Cheyenne made no effort toward aggression at this moment, since every man in the company had arms at the ready, Louis, Jesús, Tótilo, Jesse, and Kit, and the drovers, who used their wagons as cover. Adaline, Susan, and Carlos hid behind the backboard of Tótilo's wagon.

The Cheyenne with the scar snaking out of his hair said, "The bluecoats are cowards."

A messenger had been sent, Kit said. Troops were near. He asked what it was, truly, that angered the Cheyenne, since his company had done nothing to trouble them.

The man looked away, declining to answer. It was a rebuff to the question, but Ah-man-nah-ko interceded, saying they would seek proof of sign.

Kit said they should do that. He nodded toward the mountains beyond the river where Eliseo had gone. "Look for moccasin tracks pointing out." He spoke in Cheyenne, and then English, "Those tracks were made in the night. I see how many you have with you, enough to kill us all, but some of you will die, too. Finally, the army will come and you will be no match for it. We will all die."

Chapter 6

ADALINE AWOKE, stretched out her legs, rubbed her toes against the woolen blanket, and looked up at the beams that bound the room together. Truly, she was at the Rayado and had been sleeping in the enfermería of the old Fort Union. She had measured the coordinates yesterday: Latitude 36° 29' North. Longitude 105° 17' East. It was also high, having an altitude of approximately 8,500 feet, and so still chill in the mornings.

She lay on her buffalo robe, snuggled into the blanket Josefa had given her. Nuthatches chipped and cowbirds called from the corral out back. As soon as the sun broke above the horizon, light would pass through the cracks in the shutter closed over the gun slot above her, casting the shape of a stick man on the opposite wall. The doorway to the former physician's quarters was there, and Susan slept in that room, where for two nights Jesse had also slept. Now, he'd gone off with Jesús, Louis, most of the drovers, and several troopers to deliver goods and mules to the army at the new Fort Union forty miles to the south. Kit's old friend, Lucien Maxwell, had also gone, having come up from Taos, leaving his wife, Luz, there, but bringing Josefa and the three children she cared for with him, so anxious was Josefa to be with Kit.

Manure eaters, the cowbirds.

They ate the seed in the shit.

But their call sounded crystalline, like silver coins cascading into a pool.

Adaline's mind came awake with the cowbird's call and with the myriad of things that had happened in the last four days—escaping the Cheyenne, arriving at the Rayado in the company of soldiers, learning what had caused the Cheyenne's anger, then being here in the enfermería surrounded by the sounds of a language she barely knew, and seeing Josefa for the first time in years. Josefa's face was more beautiful even than she remembered, yet there was a haunting in it, for her little boy had died while Kit had been away traveling with the train out of Missouri. The boy, Charles, Josefa's first born, Adaline hadn't even known about, so taciturn was her father, and Adaline couldn't get the image of Josefa's sadness out of her mind, how she had looked going to her husband when the Conestogas first pulled in, her knees bending beneath her skirt, her eyes in the shadow of grief. While Adaline, astride Hawk, looked on, Josefa waited for Kit to come to her, then buried her face in his shoulder.

As if that were not enough for Adaline to take in, just before leaving with the others Louis had proposed marriage to her.

•

The children, Teresina, Nicanor, and Juan, slept on robes along the wall where Adaline lay, these children formerly merely phantoms that Adaline knew only by their mention back in Fayette. Now they leapt into life as incarnations of the real. And at the far end of the wall, running to her left well past the children, were the kitchen and Josefa and Kit's bedroom, the two rooms separated by drapery. On the nearest side of the kitchen stood an archway that led to a back door. Faint light from a lamp now seeped from the kitchen, also the snapping noise of sticks being broken to make kindling, and the sound of bellows being pumped. Josefa, Adaline imagined, knelt before the fireplace. Beside it stood a earthen bottle filled with water.

Kit was up now, too. The sound of his footfalls headed to the back door and there was the thump of the latch string being pulled. She guessed he was seeing to the livestock out in the field. Faintly, she heard his voice and the voice of another, the herdsman Miguel perhaps. Or perhaps it was Tótilo, who had stayed behind with his wife and sons instead of traveling on with the others. Following separating out the wagons and mules that were to stay, the company had left on the third day, having agreed then that they had enough men to brave the trail to Fort Union. Maxwell had heard that the Jicarilla Apache had recently raided a pack train. He wanted them to think twice about raiding again once the wagons and mules were out in the open.

From the front of the enfermería, Adaline had watched as they departed. Seeing the soldiers who brought up the rear go down the trail, she spoke to her father who'd also been watching. She said how sorry she was about Charles.

Kit had said, "But Chipita . . ." That was the affectionate name he used for Josefa. "Chipita says he took to fevers and coughing. He weren't strong. Don't make it easier, but you got to consider maybe it was for the best, instead of watching him suffer."

Adaline thought of the woman on the train who lost her baby, and of Yolanda and the white stones, and of Frankie sealing the earth over Gish's grave with a team of oxen. "Yet it's hard on Josefa."

"Aye. It is." Kit filled his pipe. "Don't never lose that, Twister. Your being alive to what things mean, especially when they turn on others."

They stood in front of the house. Adaline looked across the clearing to the line of trees. It was true that she was alive to the meaning of things, including words she had learned.

Muerte.

Death.

Niño.

Little boy.

And as she'd seen in the camp on the Arkansas, knowing or not knowing the words of another language could be like standing before two doors: One could be an opening to life, the other opened to death. She had spoken of this, as well.

He replied, "Sometimes you don't want the other to ken what you hold, neither words nor equipage. Best to keep 'em close, though

I weren't certain about Ah-man-nah-ko. He was young when first I seen him in his father's company."

"We were lucky, then?"

"And lucky that it didn't go further."

The Cheyenne's reason for threatening Kit's company in the first place had become known. A chief had lifted a woman's ring. The ring was recovered and the chief was publicly flogged by one of Colonel Sumner's officers, who was the woman's husband. Adaline had heard her father say how foolish that was since the officer had the ring, the Cheyenne had offered no further provocation, and there was no greater shame for a chief than to be beaten without opportunity for a fight. Further, this chief had lost one son to the depredations of the army, and then there was the matter of Ferine and his dragoons and the stealing of the hides. Her father was furious with Colonel Sumner for countenancing the flogging. The officer, he'd said, must have had "courage oozing out his fingertips" once he had the blacksnake in hand and the chief in bonds. Also, the boy Eliseo who'd been sent out at night from the camp at the corral had come upon Sumner and his escort in the dawn, but Sumner, beset with arrogance, had declined to aid Kit's company. On the next day, Eliseo discovered Major Grier.

Grier, Adaline had thought. Was he the officer in Ferine's tale of Mrs. White?

Heeding Eliseo's urgent express, Grier had dispatched his lieutenant with a detachment. On the way, the detachment encountered Sumner, who to save face sent thirty men under the command of Major James Carleton. Had the Cheyenne attacked Kit's company that morning, the soldiers would have been too late.

•

Beyond the wall at the end of the long room she heard Josefa, still pumping the bellows to brighten the fire. The sweet scent of pine smoke crept down the length of the room while the first sunlight filtered through the shutters, beginning to light up the stick man. To her left, the three small figures lay in the near darkness, breathing softly. Teresina was the eldest, nine years old and the daughter of

Josefa's elder sister, Ignacia, the widow of the former governor of the territory, Charles Bent, who had been killed in the Taos Rebellion. Charles, the namesake of Josefa and Kit's little boy, was the brother of William Bent, as well as George Bent, who died soon after his older brother, Robert Bent, had been killed by Comanches in 1841. William Bent was the father of the second George, named for his uncle, and George's mother was Owl Woman, the one Adaline remembered from Bent's Fort. The brothers, Charles and William, were partners in the trading company with Ceran Saint Vrain, for whom Frankie had freighted the brandy cask.

Four years ago, during the Taos Rebellion of 1847, Charles Bent had let the insurrectionists in his house, believing he could reason with them. This was another doorway, not one to choose whether or not to step through, but rather one to not open, or to open, and yet in opening it Bent discovered he had miscalculated. Ignacia and the children were in the house, as were Romulda Boggs and Josefa, who'd been staying with her sister since at the time Kit was delivering dispatches from California to Washington. It was the same journey as brought him to visit Missouri on his way home.

As Bent attempted to convince the intruders that the rebellion was a mistake, he was shot with arrows, while in the next room the women desperately dug a hole with a spoon in a common adobe wall with another house. With the help of a woman wielding a poker on the other side, they cut through, widened the opening, then crawled through. Bent came last, his face streaming with blood, but the insurrectionists circled, knocked down the door to the second house, and summarily finished Bent off and scalped him. In the melee, the women and children escaped, and the next day Bent's scalp was pinned to a board and paraded through town. The revolt was put down by troops come up from Santa Fé, led by Saint Vrain, though not before Josefa's brother and an uncle were also killed. Josefa, Rumolda, Ignacia, and the children would have been taken, too, had they not disguised themselves as peasants and made away.

Teresina came to be raised by Josefa. Teresina's mother, Ignacia, still lived in Taos, albeit without her daughter. Here, Teresina and Nicanor, the son of Josefa's brother, the one who had been killed, and being truly an orphan since his mother had died in childbirth, and Juan, a Navajo boy whose freedom Kit had purchased from Ute slave traders at Josefa's urging, comprised the fetch of children to which Adaline was enjoined. This was the necessary and benevolent practice of the place and time, the taking in of children, yet Adaline couldn't help but wonder why Teresina, Nicanor, and Juan were here when ten years ago she'd been sent away. It was true that she had her Aunt Mary Ann in Missouri, guardian to her as Josefa was now to the three, and at that time Josefa had been very young. There had been the calamity of her, Adaline's, lost sister. Perhaps that was all there was to be found by way of explanation, but Adaline sensed the full answer had been driven deep down into the darkness where it was lost amongst her imponderables.

•

She heard the back door open and shut, and the sound of wood being stacked in the kitchen and the low voices of her father and Josefa, then the door again. From the outside, she heard her father's footsteps going to the front of the enfermería.

She rolled off her buffalo robe, pulled a dress over her shift, put on her cloak, and stole out to the porch that opened to a large meadow. Her father was there. Straight across the meadow stretched a margin of piñons and junipers, and rightward the sun rose above the horizon, glancing against the stacks of adobe bricks and hewn posts, and the stakes and batter boards by which the house he intended to build was marked out. He looked the other way, to the west toward the mountains. "Appears it'll be a good day for a spell."

She followed his gaze. To the far left stood the clump of water birch, fully leafed out, and beyond the peaks of the Sangre de Cristos blazed in the first light. Every time those mountains came to mind, she thought about those words.

Sangre de Cristos.

Blood of Christ.

The mystery stirred in her. How came they to be so called after a scripture?

What did that mean?

Drink ye all of it, for this is my blood.

Kit took out his pipe and filled it. "Storm tonight, mebbe, which we may need."

"Need, why?"

He didn't answer that at first, but said, "It's the wisp across the face of the peak. Something boiling over on the far side. It'll drop up on us."

Yesterday, he had pointed out an elk herd strolling into the meadow from the east. He studied the birds, crows and ravens, in particular, which, as he told Adaline, had the practice of signaling in the air, alerting the wolves, mountain panthers, coyotes, and bears where there might be food to kill and by-and-by carrion for themselves. He also reviewed what could be done with the day, what he called the "day's possibles," as with what one carried on the trail, but unlike the necessary items packed away, these possibles were kept in mind. He'd said, "Here you can tell the tale of the day afore it commences and it might turn out to be half a match for what you foresaw. On the trail, you can name ten things to be done, and it's luck if you get one, so unlike to scheming are the happenings."

This morning, he said, "Like them three horsemen. That's why a storm to keep 'em at bay would be welcome."

Adaline could not pick out anything until her father instructed her to look for the streak of blue upon the flank of one horse. That she saw first, emerging faintly from behind a juniper, then the horsemen came to light as they approached the edge of the meadow and rode along its hem before cutting back into the trees.

"Cheyenne again," Kit said. "I been watching 'em. This ain't their customary range and yet they keep coming. I don't like the war paint on the pony, but for now we be here, they see. And we see them, as expected." Formerly, he had thought the Cheyenne were unlikely to follow them into the mountains, leaving them only the Jicarillas, which were not likely to attack the old fort.

Now, knowing the Cheyenne were back at it, and the Utes, too, he said, "We better get the loose stock safe in the corral. And you and Susan be sure to take Miguel with you when you fetch water."

"All right," she said, seeing her "possibles" lining up.

She and Susan would hitch a burro to a cart, load the earthen jugs, and in Miguel's company make their way past the water birch to the place where an acequia had been dug to lead to the granite basin. Hemp hand loops wound around the earthen jugs to facilitate dipping them into the water. Afterwards, they would collect firewood, lugging the rounds to the stack in back of the enfermería. They would help Josefa in the kitchen, and once the stock was herded into the corral Adaline would address the feed and water, as she had taken it upon herself to do.

Kit gazed intently to the west. "Look there."

Black specks soared above the trees in the distance. "Crows?"

"Scared up," he said.

"More Cheyenne?"

"Reckon we'll know soon enough. It appears they ain't following them Conestogas to Fort Union." Then, as if by a sleight of hand, he added, "I hear Louay has spoken to you."

Her eyes went to her father. "He has."

"What say you?"

She took a breath, looked down at her feet, composing herself. "I told Mr. Simmons I would need to speak to you."

"He does not displease you?"

"Displease?" It hadn't occurred to her to think of it in that way. She only felt an inertia, a pleasuring in things just as they were, though she knew things would have to change. It was the "possibles" again, but of a life, not a day. "Perhaps you might think I'm a little young yet."

He scrutinized her. "Don't sound like you're certain."

She didn't know how certainty felt in such a matter.

"My Chipita was younger yet than you."

•

Louis had broached the subject two mornings ago while Adaline was pitching hay from a stack to the corral. There were Hawk, Susan's gelding, her father's buckskin, other riding horses, and the few mules, including the white one that Louis had kept in lieu of payment. The remainder, in preparation for their being herded to the army at Fort Union, had been separated and picketed the night before. Louis came up beside her and gazed into the corral.

She put her foot to the pitchfork, pushing it into the earth. Its prongs were four narrow branches joined to a thicker branch. She considered it a marvel, how the prongs had been sharpened and the handle cut to length. "I'm partial to your white mule," she said.

"He'll be big before he's done."

Strong boned and muscular, the yearling had already grown tall. She reached out to stroke its nose and the mule tossed its head and lifted one ear. It could move its ears independently, setting them like a semaphore. "He might make a fine riding animal."

"He'll pull, too," Louis said, turning to her.

"Yes, he would," Adaline said, though in her imagination she'd only envisioned the fine, smooth-gaited mule with her astride him.

Louis spoke again: "I mean to ask if you've considered marriage."

She shot a glance at him. She was surprised by the color that had risen to his cheeks, and the way he averted his eyes. She looked down, too, at her foot that had just pushed the pitchfork in the ground. Surely, she'd expected that some version of the question was to come, and now that it had she found herself almost breathless. She grasped the handle of the pitchfork as if it were a holdfast, and responded, "Perhaps I'd need to consult my father."

Louis's face grew stolid. "I spoke to him on the trail before the trouble with the Cheyenne."

So uttered this became another step taken, and she wondered if he meant that he thought it settled. It was one thing to be noticed and to feel the pleasure in that. It was another thing, altogether, to have the notice decocted into a proposition.

"He says I might speak to you. He would intend to, himself."

"Oh," she said, feeling a wave of relief. She saw that there was a conversation yet to be had, and that it needed to be laced into all the other conversations about the changes going on—her father's attending to Josefa in the wake of little Charles's death, the new home for the family in the Rayado, and the Rayado trading post established with Lucien Maxwell. There was talk of a trapping and hunting trip, come the following spring, a last farewell to the old life.

Hawk pushed against the rail and nosed the white yearling away. Adaline took up a swatch of fresh grass, fed it to Hawk, and looked toward the rest of the stock, their heads down at the troughs, and beyond the corral at the woods, the silvering crests of junipers where the sun struck them, and at the low hills over which the waiting mass of cavvy-broke mules and wagons were about to pass on their way to Santa Fé. Just then, a covey of quail hammered out of the bush and into the open. "I will speak to him," she said, "while remembering he is tending to his señora and otherwise to things here."

Louis pulled himself straight and stepped nearer to her. "I'll be gone for a time to Fort Union, and then it's back to the Rayado and another trading journey, I think. It'd be some time hence," he said. "Your Pa says Josefa will want things done proper. Likely there'll be ceremonies in Taos." His eyes went away for a moment and a shadow passed across his face, then returning his eyes to rest on her, he touched her shoulder. "A priest would officiate."

"I see." A part of her swelled with pleasure, yet she sensed a glimmering of how inertia might be instructive, warning her there might be a reason for not going too fast down that path. In some ways she was mature beyond her years; in others she did not yet know herself.

•

From within the enfermería footsteps could be heard, the sound of shutters being thrown open, and Josefa's voice and Susan's and chattering children. Josefa appeared, carrying a tray with three cups of chocolate, one of which she passed to Adaline. "Buenas, chica."

She passed another to Kit, who took it and addressed Adaline. "Betimes age is felt more'n measured. Louis is a good man. Say then, we'll know one year hence."

Adaline murmured and glanced at Josefa, who set the tray down on a stump. She smiled at Adaline and then hooked Kit's elbow with her free hand and walked with him to the site where their future house was marked out with batter boards and string lines. There were also several stacks of adobe bricks at the ready, and the house that would be there ghosted up through its outline, making Adaline feel strangely jittery. There was something oddly troubling about the phantom house. She sipped her chocolate, watched Kit and Josefa go, and allowed her mind to hover around the question of matrimony. She considered how her father and Josefa seemed to fit together. He was playful with the children. Josefa was composed with them, strict, and kept dominion over the household, though Kit's preeminence was not questioned. Her passion and natural charm were displayed on the surface, even when she was grief stricken. When he was away from his familiars, he could be fierce in his taciturnity. Josefa stood nearly an inch taller than he, and she was graceful, while he appeared awkward on foot. His grace manifested itself when he was astride a horse.

The pair stopped just as more Cheyenne rode from the woods, ten or so of them, coming out to ride in a promenade along the fringe of the meadow. The braves were attired in feathers, and ponies were decorated with paint. Kit and Josefa immediately started back, Kit attending closely to the distant high ground to the west. Adaline turned and saw four tight clouds floating northward, a signalizing by smoke. Her father called out, "Twister, you and Susan fetch water now. Take Miguel, you hear?"

And Josefa, too, called, "Cuidado, chica."

She found Susan inside and Miguel out back. The three took the burro and carreta along the path that led from the enfermería to the granite cisterns. When they came in view of the meadow, they searched every which way for trouble, though by then the Cheyenne had vanished. Miguel had brought along his rifle, and he spoke volubly and alarmingly in Spanish about the Indios, forgetting that Adaline and Susan hardly understood him. The botijas were dipped into the cistern, filled, placed back in the cart, then the three rushed back to the enfermería, arriving when Kit and Tótilo had just set out to bring in the remainder of the stock to the corral. Miguel joined them. Adaline and Susan placed the botijas at the back door, and Susan, who had grown increasingly rattled, worried that there were only women and children at the enfermería, including Tótilo's wife and his boys, who had come over from their little house.

"But Pa and Tótilo are right there," Adaline said. "Miguel, too. See? And Eliseo is not a child anymore."

Susan sighed.

"Be glad that we're not caught unawares like we were on the river," Adaline said.

Susan carried the botijas inside to the kitchen. Adaline employed the burro and carreta to transfer firewood from the stacks near the corral to the enfermería, then detached the burro from the cart and led it up to the corral. She filled the troughs so that the hay would be there for the stock when they came, and otherwise sized up the lay of things: here, the corral, below the enfermería and in between the wood pile, over there, the batter boards and string lines of the projected house, and on the other side, to the west, the Maxwell house and beyond it an old military bunkhouse, and beyond that a set of small buildings which included Tótilo's casa. The creek ran behind. Clear space had been cut around the buildings, and before it all spread the wide meadow, but under the cover of the woods there might be untold numbers of Indians. She again considered the smoke that drifted in puffs down the mountainside and also the clouds that had begun to spill over the peaks as her father had predicted.

Out of the enfermería came Teresina, fetching more wood. A moment later, smoke from the chimney turned dark as the fire was stoked. Aside from the muted voices in the kitchen, stillness had befallen the outdoors. Not even the birds called, as if a larger intellect were alerted to a fulmination gathering in the distance. Finally, she heard hoof beats. Her father, Tótilo, and Miguel were herding the stock toward the corral. Quickly, she opened the gate for them and the animals flooded in, churning up the dirt and swelling against the confines. She shut the gate and followed the men into the enfermería, marking the guns Josefa and Tótilo's wife had laid out on the table. Three percussion Hawkens and a double-barreled Hellinghaus smooth bore, a revolver, two Mills breech loaders, and a Colt rifle with a revolving chamber.

"Bueno," Kit said.

Teresina crouched before the fire, poking at it.

Tótilo's wife, Clara, mixed meal into a mush to feed the children, her wooden spoon clicking against the ceramic bowl.

Susan looked at Adaline. "We're to be attacked."

"No, no, chica," Josefa said. "We do not know that."

Kit spoke to Josefa. Adaline heard the words—"Dos ciento." He ended by issuing commands, which caused Teresina to add more wood to the fire and Clara to hang a small cauldron from a hook above the flames. Josefa stepped to a closet and from it brought out molds for balls and conical slugs, arranging them on the table, also a loading block. Clara placed a lead bar in the cauldron while Josefa snatched small crates containing paper wads and powder from the closet, all together comprising the differing forms of stored and yet-to-be-made ammunition for the several guns. Tótilo picked up the rifles one at a time, the revolver, and shotgun, loading them, then passed the shotgun to his son, Eliseo, gave a breech loader to Miguel, and laid hold of a Hawkens for himself. The three gathered up ammunition and moved outside. Adaline saw Miguel and Eliseo hurry behind a barricade at the wood stack from which they could watch the back of the enfermería, and Tótilo behind another barricade at the corral, which commanded a view of the grounds and the Maxwell house beyond. Tótilo's younger son stayed inside.

"You can shoot, right?" Kit asked Adaline. "I mean the breech loader."

"Yes." Her uncle in Missouri had taught her. "You let the sight fill up plumb."

"Can you be at the ready?" Kit said to Susan, who stood next to Adaline, and when she nodded, he said, "See what Twister'll need, and then you can look out with her and be ready to reload." To Adaline, he added, "You still got that Walker Colt?"

"But I don't have much ammunition for it."

"All right." Kit looked at Josefa who picked up one mold from the assortment. He nodded and then turned to Adaline and Susan. "It's the Cheyenne. But judging from the smoke it may be the Utes and Jicarillas, too. We might be all right, since we can't be sure what they intend. If them Cheyenne still have enough of the rage left in 'em, they'll turn on us. Then there'd likely be no talking them down. The Utes might be, even the Jicarillas if I can get to 'em."

"Two hundred you said?" Adaline asked.

A faint smile passed across his lips. "Mebbe."

"It's the same Cheyenne?"

"Same Cheyenne. The Utes are out in the woods. It's the Jicarilla signaling with smoke. The Jicarilla know the army's moved down to Fort Union, where Lucien and the others have gone. It's on the trail to Santa Fé, so the raiding there is hard for the Jicarilla. They don't want the Cheyenne up here." He paused and touched one Hawken that still lay on the table. "Take this. Bring out your revolver." He gestured with his head toward the physician's quarters. "Go to the far wall in there, but listen for what I say. If you see Injuns through the slot, if you see the fingers on their hands, say so. That'll be your range. That's when you let the sight fill up. They'll be close enough and we'll fire on 'em. But only if I say so. One at a time. Hear? Use your revolver only if you have to."

He went around, opening shutters and speaking in Spanish to Josefa, who herded the three young boys—Eliseo's brother Carlos, Nicanor, and Juan—onto Susan's pallet against a wall in the physician's quarters. They each had a bowl of mush and sat quietly, barely eating. Adaline hurried to fetch her Colt from her trunk and returned. Subdued voices and the soft clatter of preparations could be heard from the kitchen, and the scent of molten lead drifted through the house. Susan was there with Josefa, and then Clara went out to Tótilo near the corral, and Kit posted himself in the long room, near the entrada. Outside, it remained silent and still for a long time, but finally through her slot Adaline spotted a column of Indians spiriting from the cottonwoods at the creek, curling around the small dwellings, and halting in front of the Maxwell's adobe house. They formed three uneven rows. She called out to her father.

"Ay, Twister," he said from the other room. "How close would you say?"

"Right at Mr. Maxwell's house." She looked hard, thinking she picked out Ah-man-nah-ko and maybe the one with the scar. She could not see their fingers, though, only the shape of their hands holding reins and rifles. "It's the Cheyenne."

"Not close enough. How many do you count?"

"Maybe forty."

She heard his moccasins snicking in the long room, and then the latch pulled, the barricade lifted, and the creak of the door at the entrada. She saw some of the Cheyenne turn their heads toward the house, turn back, and turn to look again. They were conferring, Adaline thought, like crows on a fence line, not moving but attending to a new movement and noting it to each other. She thought: He's shown himself to them again, that's what. It was a form of acknowledgment, a salute to the Cheyenne presence and also meant to let it be clear that he showed himself openly, that if they wished to parley some two or three of them could come, and if they did not they would still know he was here and not afraid. The enfermería fell into a yet deeper silence. The Cheyenne stayed where they were. Adaline heard her father re-enter, and the latch and the barricade falling into its braces.

The clouds boiled over the mountains in earnest, and the sky to the west darkened, effecting the afternoon to seem more advanced than it actually was. Susan walked in, bearing more balls, wads, and powder for the Hawken and conical slugs for the revolver. Adaline loaded the revolver and left the Hawken where it was, already loaded and positioned against the wall. She pulled a stool close and set the Walker Colt on it. To Adaline's left a second slot had been cut. Susan peered through it. Behind them, the children began to murmur among themselves, but stopped when Susan said, "Ada! Do you see?"

What Adaline saw was the line of Cheyenne staying put, except for the occasional turning of a horse and vague stirrings in the back ranks. She could not judge whether the numbers had increased or diminished. "See what?"

"Come look," Susan said.

Adaline went. Through a better angle from Susan's slot located toward the front of the enfermería, she beheld another line of Indians advancing along the meadow. She could not pick out their numbers, but by their apparel—military tunics, hats, and bandoliers—she judged they were Jicarilla. She called out to her father, "Do you see in the meadow?"

"Ay, Twister," came the reply.

She carried her Hawken and revolver and dragged the stool to Susan's slot and sent Susan down to hers. They watched. Adaline presumed the fort's grounds had been thoroughly infiltrated and the enfermería surrounded. She wished her father would report his expectations, which he did not. There was merely the threat, like a wreath of thorns drawn about them, and she felt a a cool, deep, impatient panic.

She heard her father walking again. He stopped at the apex of the kitchen and physician's quarters where he could be heard in both rooms. Her father spoke in English so that, as Adaline later explained it to herself, Josefa could understand him, and Teresina might, and herself and Susan, while the boys likely would not, nor would Clara who was still at the wood pile with Eliseo: "If they breach inside on us, I will shoot you women and children afore I allow any one of you to be taken captive."

That was all. He walked back to his post. Adaline stared through her slot, thunderstruck, and filled suddenly with a coldness. The Cheyenne didn't move. The Jicarilla had passed from sight. She tried to understand. It was as if her father had been brought to imagine a feasible result which she could not allow herself to imagine. She looked back. Teresina now stood in the doorway beside the boys, wide eyed, beseeching Adaline while she held a basket with more balls. Grimly, Adaline shook her head and looked over at Susan, from whose face the color had drained. Susan looked back and ran her fingers through her hair, tugging on it. In their flash of looking, everything preliminary to this crisis that they'd shared passed: Gish and the buffalo, Gish and Yolanda, Louis and Ferine's hound, the hound and the baby, and the Cheyenne on the Arkansas. The gaze elongated into an eternity.

"But it ain't going to happen that way," she said.

Susan let out a long sigh.

"It ain't. It can't be." Glancing back at Teresina, she said, "Isn't it so?"

Teresina smiled wanly and pulled herself erect. She came forward and placed the basket on the stool and headed back for the kitchen.

Adaline believed it was her father's nature to match an extreme situation with extreme action. If he had learned anything living in the wilderness, he must have learned that. Those who were his enemies expected it of him because it was his way to pick up on what they had known since time immemorial.

She thought: He's trying to reassure us that he'll take care of us to the end and to make us stand together.

It seemed a mad balancing act in which the dross weight of loyalty and trust were in impossible disarray, everything thrown askew.

She thought: He might kill his own Josefa, and Clara, Susan, and even Teresina and the boys, I will not allow him to kill me. He will be surprised to learn that if I have to die I choose to die with him, in my way.

And then she thought: There.

Before nightfall, the Cheyenne withdrew, pulling back to invisibility, having not even bothered with Maxwell's house, which stood waiting to be raided. She watched through her gun slot and heeded the hoots of owls and a coyote bark. She wondered whether the sounds belonged to the actual owl and coyote, or if it was more signalizing. She did not see horsemen departing, but in time she perceived that either the shadows had deepened sufficiently to conceal them, or their numbers had truly diminished. After an interminable passage of time, she decided they were gone. Susan stood at her side. "They've left," Adaline said.

Susan looked.

"See?"

"But for where?"

Adaline called out, "Pa, they're gone."

She heard Tótilo's voice calling him from outside.

Kit crossed to the back door and called out to Tótilo, then back to Adaline. "You girls stay watching for a while."

•

After a time, they received permission to lay down, Adaline and Susan joining the children.

Early in the morning, Adaline rose from Susan's pallet. The children, all four of them now, and Susan, were in a jumble about and over each other. Adaline draped a blanket over her shoulders, noting the eerie whiteness coming through the slots. In the long room, too, the slots had been left open and the whiteness came in, the stick man was fully formed of light above the doorway, and below her father slumped in the soft chair. His revolving rifle lay across his knees and the Hawken leaned against the wall behind him. She looked out through the slot near the entrada. The moonlit night glowed over a hoary ground. "Snow," she murmured.

"Hail," a voice said behind her.

She turned. "I thought you were asleep."

"Couldn't hardly be called such."

"They're gone?"

"Mebbe."

Adaline said, "The storm? It wasn't much, was it?"

"Hail didn't hurt, unlikely as it is. They didn't want a fight bad enough to fight the weather, the night, and us, too, I reckon."

"And they feared you?"

"Likely the Cheyenne went off north. The Jicarillas, I don't know, but the Utes went north for sure. They got their own issues." Kit gave Adaline a hard look then. "I reckon they left all them doors shut for now, though they come close enough, Tótilo said, to take a bead on 'em."

Josefa appeared in the opening to the kitchen. Her dress was the color of the light that came into the room and above it her face shone the same hue.

"Did you mean what you said?" Adaline asked.

"The tribes are hard at each other, fighting for what's left to 'em."

"No. I mean about shooting us."

"I know what you mean. The army is a hard mark for 'em. But with what they had turning to scraps, they fight each other over it. It ain't good. It makes 'em crazy. So, yes, if it'd come to it, I'd of saved you and Josefa, and your cousin, and Teresina, and the niños from what you'd have to say would have been worse than death." He paused, glancing down the room toward Josefa, then back at Adaline. "I seen the like more'n once."

Part 2

Chapter 7

KIT HAD DETERMINED to move the women and children down from the Rayado to Taos where it would be safer. Within two days, he accomplished that mission, bringing along extra horses and mules, Louis's white mule among them. It was full dark when they arrived in Taos, and they found Jesse Nelson and Lucien Maxwell awaiting them, whereas Jesús, several drovers, and Louis had headed straight back from Fort Union to the Rayado. As Adaline helped put the stock in the corral above the house in Taos, she overheard her father telling Maxwell that the Jicarilla's alliance with the Cheyenne had to be passing. If there had been a fight, maybe neither they nor the Utes would have joined in earnest. And despite his misgivings about Colonel Sumner, he planned to proceed to Santa Fé in the morning to see about enlisting the aid of the army.

The women and children divided themselves between three places, Susan uniting with Jesse while Lucien Maxwell took Clara with him to where his wife, Luz, was staying with her family, the Beaubiens. Adaline arranged her pallet in a corner of her father and Josefa's house, spreading out her buffalo robe beneath a wall to which a plaster of tierra blanca had been applied. Its clean smell and its whiteness in the lamplight were familiar to her, but then she knew she had slept in this house as a child ten years before. When she'd picked her way down from the corral she found herself choosing to come along the paseo that ran alongside the house, feeling a foreboding of the shapes in the patio she might stumble over in the darkness, a fire pit, she believed, an horno.

In the morning she arose at the first sound of stirrings. She stepped out to the front where more memories were conjured—the scent of mesquite smoke from the morning's fires, the first light striking the adobes, and from afar the bell at the church, San Francisco de Asis, tolling for matins. She made her way toward the corral, passing not by the paseo but on the other side of the house, around it and across the patio with its horno, the open mouth of the fire pit, the stones ringing it like teeth, and a metate. The earth bore a patina from people treading upon it. She slowed to a stop, looked upon the stones that girded the fire pit, and heard a child's voice:

One.

Uno.

Two.

Dos.

Adaline turned round to the doorway, searching for the source of the voice. The kitchen window was there and vigas coming through adobe walls. She heard hissing and jerked back to face the fire pit. There was a cry, yet when Adaline turned again all she saw was a big crow with its head tipped sideways, scolding her from its perch near the top of a cerro hawthorne that had grown up next to the door. She escaped to the paseo and hurried down to the front of the house where her father stood, smoking his morning pipe. She took a deep breath and let the air shudder out. She said, "I can feed the stock. And take in some wood."

"Aye, Twister." He looked searchingly at her. "Bueno."

She heard the clop of hooves. A horseman passed by, heading northward. He touched the brim of his hat. Roosters crowed, and the bleating of goats and sheep echoed against their paddocks. Down south toward the church, westward to the flat above the river, and up north to the Indian pueblo, the entire town came to be measured by animal sounds. Far to the east the coyotes' wails rippled down the slopes to the domestic dogs that answered them. The air all around was strung together by an unruly anthem. This, too, was familiar.

Her father said, "A fine time for them wild dogs to celebrate a kill." He looked to the mountains, the sun rising behind them. "Six o'clock. Do you see?" He meant to show her how season and time in Taos could be measured by the sun's position amongst the crags of the Sangre de Cristo. "Just now, between them two promontories?"

She studied the mountains, fixing the position of the sun in her mind.

After a spell, he knocked the ash out of his pipe and said, "I'd best be heading out for Santa Fé. Else Colonel Sumner'll turn the whole of this country over to the Injuns." He smiled. "I reckon that's how he determines not to be inconvenienced by 'em."

He went inside. She stood at the root of her long, early morning shadow, still trying to settle herself, and imagined the tilt of the earth and the oval compass of it swinging around the sun, as with Mr. Spender's orrery. The time piece of mountain crags was a part of the great movement. Two women strolled by, talking and gesticulating, and after them a young man led a burro loaded with poles. In a few moments, she heard the creak of the back door followed by the sounds of a horse being readied. She walked around the side of the house by the paseo just as her father swung up onto his buckskin. He nudged it forward and the two boys, Juan and Nicanor, darted after him, calling out, "¡Adiós! ¡Adiós!"

Kit flicked a grin at the boys as he rode into the full slant of light.

Josefa and Teresina were there and Adaline stood beside them. Kit's figure shrank as he rode down the paseo. At her back, she again heard the counting in English and Spanish, and the shuffling of feet.

Three.

Trés.

Four.

Quatro.

"¡Adiós, Papá Kit!" the boys cried, still running after him.

Teresina remained quiet next to Adaline, who turned her head toward the stones of the fire pit that were black on the inside and white on the outside. Nothing. No one there, not a soul. When Josefa lightly touched her arm. Adaline jumped.

"You remember your sister here. ¿Verdad?"

•

The little girl writhed on the ground. She had boils on her legs and arms.

A man bent over her, wiping her face with a handkerchief. He pulled back just when the luster passed from her eyes.

An old woman behind moaned in pain, and another younger woman lurched into view. A young man restrained the young woman. To one side, a cauldron was filled with bubbling liquid, and on the other side stood a room being built next to the paseo.

•

"I can tell by your face," Josefa said. "Sometimes a child does not remember such things. We hoped it would be so, but now I see we were wrong. The patio is just as it was, except that the room by the paseo is finished, and the tree. Of course, the tree has grown up."

Adaline gazed at the hawthorne. All over it grew little fruits.

"We prepare the manzanillas," Josefa said.

"They are sour at first," Teresina said. "Then sweet."

"Lupe," Adaline said, remembering the name of the old woman who long ago had made jelly from those fruits, and terrified her with her scolding voice, and Felicia, the other, younger woman who had let her taste the jelly and the candies drawn from cactus, and who could be heard at times singing sweetly through the kitchen window.

"Sí, Lupe. She is here," Josefa said. "She lives with my mother. She knew some day you were to come back, and now you are here. She said she forgives you."

"Forgives me? She?"

"Sí."

Profoundly disconcerted, Adaline did not go on to ask: Forgives me for what?

•

It wasn't that she didn't know her sister had died here. That not quite repressed glimmering she kept in her stores of memory, but brought face-to-face with the place, the glimmering came vividly back to her. It was like a building arising from an idea, laid out in abbreviated form with batter boards, posts, and stringlines, and kept that way as a phantom of itself. It was like the room here had been, like the house at the Rayado would be. Her father, having secured permission from Don Jaramillo and Doña Apolonia to marry their daughter, Josefa, had bought this house, arranged to have a room added, brought his two daughters here to be cared for by Doña Apolonia's servant, Lupe, while he went away to work as a hunter for Bent's Fort. A man named Mateo had charge of the construction, helped by his son, Pepe, and sometimes accompanied by another son, Pablo, who was three or four years older than Adaline. Perhaps he was eight or nine. Adaline remembered him, his air of inquisitive calm, and how he frowned when Lupe went off on one of her tirades, which Adaline understood by their inflection: "¡Silencio! ¡No vengan aquí! ¡Vayanse!"

She saw the hump of Lupe's spine moving up and down like a fornicating dog as she ground maize in the metate. She saw her feet, gnarled and bulging from her sandals. She remembered the two women, Lupe and Felicia, appearing from the front of the house, groaning under the weight of a great basin filled with ash. They bent to place the basin on stones positioned in the fire pit. Felicia stirred the coals while Lupe placed a flat stone next to the basin. The stone had a groove worn into it that led to a curved tile, which in turn led to a pot placed in a depression outside the pit.

Lupe poured water over the ash, and all afternoon and into the evening, while Mateo and Pepe worked on the new room, Felicia added water to the cauldron. Eventually, thick liquid flowed through a perforation in the basin and onto the stone. Adaline imagined how the groove in the stone was like a channel that elongated to the tile and finally to the pot. Josefa came to visit sometimes. She festooned the wall by the door with ropes of freshly picked peppers, and before she went away she drew Adaline and her sister aside and made gifts of Lupe's sweets that she carried wrapped in her shawl. She also gave Adaline the corn frond doll with the blue dress and the painted gourd for a head. Josefa was then a slip of a young woman, and beautiful, though hardly as beautiful as she would become. She smelled crisp like the water in the creek. Mateo and Pepe had finished the walls of the new room and climbed the ladders to mount poles for the roof. Adaline gave her sister the doll to hold and climbed up to see the nearly complete room for herself. She called out, "Nihanca! Nihanca!"

Pepe said, "¡Chica! ¡Chica!" And he laughed.

Adaline spoke into the room, having discovered the echo that spoke back. She was learning the numbers and how to say hello. "¡Hola!"

Pepe called out to her, "Uno."

Tottering on the ladder, she cried, "¡Uno!"

"Uno," the echo said.

Lupe came out and shrieked at Adaline, causing her to stumble down the ladder. She took her doll and escaped to the edge of the paseo with her sister.

There broke out music from the plaza below. Three old men marched along, one playing a violin, another a guitar, and the last beating a tombé. As they passed, she saw that the man with the guitar had only one eye and was clad in rags. The one with the violin had his trousers open from the hips down, exposing voluminous drawers. The third one had curls of hair brimming out of his ears and he struck the tombé against the violin's repeated arpeggiation. The men were announcing a fandango to be held in a hall that night. Later, in the darkness, Adaline lay cuddled next to her sister on her pallet within the casa, and she strained to hear the music—the guitar, tambourine, tombé, the violin descending, the low voice of a woman singing, the shouts, and what seemed a wild percussion of feet striking the floor.

Come morning, Adaline saw a cart arriving in the patio filled with hunks of animal parts. Felicia went to work cutting the bones and meat from the fat, and the fat and quantities of water were poured into the cauldron that had replaced the basin over the fire. It hissed and a cloud of steam arose. Village dogs crept in and made off with the bones, disappearing down the side of the house toward the brush at the creek where they snarled and gnashed at each other. The fat boiled. Lupe and Felicia carefully moved the cauldron to one side until it cooled enough for Lupe to pick out all the remaining bits of bone and meat. They replaced the cauldron where again the fat came to a boil. Overnight, the fire dwindled. In the morning the women could be heard working again.

With her sister, Adaline ventured out and circled to the passageway. She saw that Lupe had skimmed the fat away with a large wooden ladle and dropped it into bowls. Felicia rinsed the cauldron and poured the fat back into it along with more water. Lupe added the liquid from the ash. It had transformed into lye. They were making soap. After the women put more wood into the fire and the contents of the cauldron frothed near to a boil, they walked off into the house. Pablo had come that day. He sat up on the top of a wall between two roof poles, swinging his feet. A wind came up and blew his hat loose. Pepe, who had entered the patio with a cart filled with roofing tiles, snatched it with a sweep just before it blew into the cauldron. "¡Ay, qué castigo!" he cried.

The wind turned into a dust devil in the passageway, enveloping the girls. Her sister's eyes grew wide with surprise and Adaline felt her skin prickle. She had brought her doll with her and held it tightly, also her sister's hand. Pepe carefully placed the hat within Pablo's grasp before carrying a pallet of tiles up the ladder to Mateo. The wind darted away. Over time, the great boils in the cauldron would stretch and grow shiny before bursting, and instantly they were replaced by another boil. The sun began to descend, the air turned a peach color, while shadows grew longer. Crows cried, winging over the town, and an owl hooted, signaling that before long it would be dark.

Adaline and her sister edged toward the cauldron. Her sister climbed onto the black stones that encircled the fire pit. Adaline looked for Lupe, but the old woman was nowhere to be seen. Just as Felicia would begin singing again, or come outside and make her skirt snap in defiance if Lupe wasn't nearby, or pull her blouse lower, baring her shoulders for Pepe, and just as Pepe would become playful, so, too, Adaline let her sister be. She taught her numbers in her father's language and in what she knew of the language spoken here. Her sister counted her steps as she moved from stone to stone. Adaline spoke the numbers to her sister and soon grew lost in the counting. Her sister spread her arms and chortled after each tottering step.

"One. Uno."

"Two. Dos."

"Three. Trés."

The door of the house creaked open and footsteps approached. Adaline lurched back and shot a look up into the sky where the bottoms of the clouds glowed. From the kitchen Felicia's voice could yet be heard singing.

"Four," her sister said, making another delighted sound. "Quatro."

Adaline glanced back at her sister and in that next moment, what made a crazy sparking across a dark place, what as the years passed loomed larger even as it was driven down and grew to be more and more concealed because of her deep mortification, a permanent, uncognizant way of consigning herself to the nagual of the shadowland. At first the sparking became a scream, transmogrifying into Lupe's repeated shrieking. Her little sister twisted to look toward Lupe, then swayed wildly and tumbled into the boiling cauldron. There was a hissing sound. Again, Lupe shrieked. Felicia's singing stopped. Adaline stood petrified and seconds distended into one long horror. Her sister lay face down in the cauldron, her short legs kicking. Lupe rushed to the cauldron and leaned over it, struggling to gain purchase.

One of Lupe's legs kicked straight out as she pulled, and then at last she dragged Adaline's sister over the cauldron's lip, bouncing her over the stones to the ground. She turned her over. Adaline still couldn't move. Her sister was covered with the steaming, viscid liquid and, in a spasm, she swiped at her eyes with one hand, then her hand dropped to the ground. She was quivering, bleeding from the forehead where she'd hit a rock. Beside her, Lupe bent double, clutching at her own hand and lifting her face, which was twisted with pain. She fixed on Adaline and loosed a guttural, subhuman noise, "¡Diabla!"

Not understanding, Adaline foundered in the terror. It was like plummeting through space. The air passed through her. She heard it hissing as she whirled. It was as if Neyoooxetusei had come to take her away. Felicia lurched into view, tracing Lupe's footsteps, and now hung beside the child and groaning woman. Mateo vaulted from the roof and ran to the fire pit. Pepe came behind, and Pablo clambered down. Mateo crouched over Adaline's sister and took out a yellow handkerchief to wipe the froth from her face, then from her arms and legs. Still locked in place, unable to move, Adaline stared at the little girl, who writhed slowly on the ground and upon whom blisters like small versions of the boils in the cauldron were now erupting.

As Lupe's voice descended into a hollowed-out moan of pain, Felicia's sobbing rose. Pepe drew Felicia away. "Ay. Ay. Felicia, ay."

Only then did Mateo pull back with a sorrowful resignation on his face. "Por Dios," he whispered. Adaline clutched her doll. Pablo came up to her, put his hand on her shoulder, shook her lightly as if to awaken her from a dream.

•

Josefa was holding both Adaline's arms now and she drew her close, then held her at arms' length and said. "But you were so young. And it is true that we all are born to suffering in this world. See Teresina here, whose father was killed, and Nicanor also. Who knows what Juan suffered? It is so that Lupe forgives you."

But Adaline found a troubling idea taking shape. Josefa must mean that she had committed a sin for which Lupe somehow had the power of forgiveness. Adaline remembered her own agony, conjoined with the far greater agony of her sister, and still she was fixed on the questions: Forgiveness for what? Who forgives? Yet she did not ask, fearful of seeming disrespectful to Josefa, whom for all the world she did not wish to displease.

Instead, she led Teresina and Josefa inside to her pallet and opened up her trunk to where she kept her prized possessions—the book, the turtle, the doll. She took out the doll, given her ten years ago by Josefa, and showed it to Teresina and Josefa. Josefa ran her hand over the water-damaged remains of the corn frond body and blue dress and the face that was still barely visible on the gourd.

"Sí," Josefa said, smiling wanly. "I remember. You kept it all this time?"

"Yes. It got dumped in a river."

Josefa said, "Some things survive, no?"

In the days that followed, Adaline managed her foreboding of the patio by simply not looking at it at all. At times the sound of a crow startled her, and every time she saw an old woman, she wondered if this might be Lupe. She kept uneasy counsel with herself as she fed and watered the stock and found welcome distraction in her new project to accustom the white mule to the hackamore. She gave the mule a name—Ghost. She made herself useful in the kitchen, watched over the children, or tended to Josefa's garden. Time came to harvest the chiles and Teresina showed her how to braid them into ropes that were hung on posts next to the doorway to dry. It was as Josefa had done long ago.

Kit returned from Santa Fé and in a week rode up to the Rayado to oversee the building of the house. It was believed that the Indians were subdued now. Jesse and Susan had made their way up, and Clara, Jesús's wife, and children, and Lucien and Luz Maxwell. Louis and Jesús, it was said, had gone back to Missouri for more mules. Meanwhile, Colonel Sumner had given his word that the army would watch over the new settlement. Soon, the Jicarilla would be removed to the west side of the Río Bravo del Norte. By early winter, Kit expected to come down for Josefa and the niños. Until that time Adaline would stay with them in Taos.

One morning as she stood at the front portico, surveying the town in the first light, an old woman came laboring up the hill and off the paseo toward her. Her feet were misshapen, swollen with gout, and Adaline imagined a chimera of entangled roots under her black shawl. She was tiny, ancient, betraying years beyond measure. Her nose was a beak and implanted in dark pits her eyes glittered. The handle of a basket hung from the crook of one elbow as she reached for the latch.

Adaline glimpsed the other hand clutching at her shawl, a twisted, featherless wing, skin like dirty vellum. Adaline felt something knock in her, then remembering her manners she reached for the latch and said, "Buenas, señora."

The old woman muttered under her breath and pushed past Adaline. The door clicked shut, but out of the figment of her person something wafted in the air. The memory of the smell of moss and rancid earth elicited sounds and visions: ¡Diabla! ¡El Demonio! There was a crashing. The woman fell to her knees while the little girl writhed on the ground. Lupe wailed and sank to the earth, clutching her hand to her belly.

Adaline escaped down to where the Rio Fernando de Taos flowed into an acequia, henceforward into the garden. She began pulling the desiccate maize, its dry fronds rattling in the breeze. The clods of dirt that clung to the balled up roots displayed wizened faces. The few remaining negro de valle chiles lay frost bitten, bearing the color of a sickly shroud drawn over bone. At the bottom of the acequia long weeds waved to and fro, like the hair of corpses. Hearing voices, Adaline looked up and saw that Josefa had stepped outside the house, wearing a white shift and blue shawl. A dark clump came beside her, Lupe, who then crept toward the paseo and passed from sight. Josefa walked to the garden, whereupon she unfolded the end of the shawl, revealing a small loaf with white decoration in the shape of a cross. "Lupe brought this for you."

Adaline was startled. "For me?"

"Sí, chica. Tomorrow is Día de los Muertos. El primero de Noviembre. The day we remember the young who have died. The next day is for the older ones. Taste it."

Adaline broke off a piece and put it to her mouth. It was sweet.

"Está bien. No? She brought one for little Charles, too. Also, we have sweets for your sister, as well as for the other Charles, Teresina's father, for Nicanor's mother, for my brother, and for her daughter, Felicia."

"Her daughter?"

"Lupe's. You do not remember Felicia?"

Adaline remembered, but this other news, that Felicia was Lupe's daughter and that now she was dead raised more questions. What about Mateo, Pepe, and Pablo? Why had Lupe disappeared, leaving Felicia to watch over Adaline? Why had her father taken her away?

Josefa was preoccupied with the gifts: "And my uncle, Cornelio, Narcisse Beaubien, brother-in-law of Lucien Maxwell, six of your father's friends all of whom were killed in the rebellion. And my own father now has passed on. There are so many. Your father has sent word that he will soon be coming down to Taos but not in time to visit the cemeteries. The kitchen is filled with sweetbreads."

The next day, Adaline went on a processional with Josefa and the children to visit the graves, including little Charles's and one where Adaline's sister lay, marked only by a wooden cross. Josefa had given her a tiny wooden carving of a heart, and the children carried little figures and images, what Josefa called milagritos, with which they sought the intercession of a saint. Adaline put her heart by the feet of the statue of the Virgin de Guadalupe, then all at once remembering Yolanda and her grief, she found a white stone and placed it at the head of her sister's grave. On the second day, she returned, carrying the doll from her trunk, which she placed next to the stone.

Watching her, Josefa said, "You still feel your sister cannot rest?"

Adaline thought a moment. "Perhaps it's my sister not resting. Perhaps it's the blame Lupe places upon me, too. It makes it hard for me to rest."

"Chica, you were little. She forgives you for your sister and for her hand. And for Felicia, her daughter, who died giving birth. She believed you should not have been left here, that your being here made things happen as they did. She does her own penance every Easter by approaching the Virgin de Guadalupe on her knees."

Josefa straightened. Her black hair shone and she smiled, and Adaline could not possibly tell her how Lupe had kept her in a state of terror, and how she'd shrieked when her sister walked on the stones around the cauldron. She felt something grievously incomplete, the counting her sister never finished, the circle not completed, like a cutworm, like the whorl of hair on top of a head. She was compelled to carry within her two warring metaphysics: the one, correct and drastic, as she studied how to take her share of the blame while leaving the other part of it affixed elsewhere where it belonged, on the old woman; and the other the old woman's delusion that she might sanctify herself by forgiving others for sins they had not committed.

Chapter 8

JOSEFA AND ADALINE WORKED in the garden down by the acequia. It was well into November and they stripped out the plants in earnest. They had finished the beans and chiles and pulled up the squash, abandoning the fruit blackened by frost. They yanked up what was left of the dry maize stalks and, intending to feed them to the animals, dragged them up past the fire pit, around which Adaline routinely made small detours. At the corral, the white mule pushed forward and tore at the stalks, stripping off the leaves and favoring the partially formed cobs and the residue of huitlacoche, the fungus, which Adaline had seen Josefa stirring into soups. Also, she had begun the process of breaking the mule to a hackamore and noseband. She reported, "He's still a little wild. But I believe it will work."

Kit had come down from the Rayado. He walked down the hill into town, arranging for the purchase of supplies. Josefa had announced to Adaline that he meant to leave again for the Rayado in a couple of days and then return to Taos. He had wondered if Adaline might wish to go with him. Josefa added, "Luz would be glad for your help for a few days. Your cousin is there with Jesse. You would be glad to see her, no?" They set about closing off the acequia so that the plot wouldn't wash out in the spring. Adaline slid boards between the staves of the acequia gate and secured them. A trickle of water began building behind it, slowly inundating the weeds in the bottom. "As well, Louis is there," Josefa said.

Adaline gazed out toward the paseo, then at the sky above the casas. She suspected the journey would occasion a return to the question of marriage, recalling how her father back at the Rayado had put forward "one year hence." The year was yet to pass, but she accepted the arrangements, determined as she believed they were. She wondered, though, how it happened that for all the time she had spent in Taos she had rarely thought of Louis.

In the morning several days later, she pulled on her canvas trousers, a fine beaded doeskin shirt purchased with her coins, and her cloak, since the Rayado was expected to be cold. The buffalo robe she lashed behind Hawk's saddle. She and her father rode up the trail, two pack horses trailing Kit and one trailing her. She waited for him to broach the subject, but it was not to be. Of course, she remembered that her father's taciturnity could be extreme, that just the right moment for speaking needed to arise, as if by accident. So she bided her time, settling for the satisfaction of listening to her father's observations on what they passed.

On the first evening after they'd journeyed above the juniper and piñon stands, he gestured off the trail to the right. "See there, Twister, that spruce island chasing out of the draw to lean upland and branch to the lee and the air in their uppermost. Ain't never tried that spot, but it reckons to offer runoff and grass below." They cut off the trail and made a night's camp where lay carpets of mountain fescue and couch grass for their animals, a narrow stream just as he'd promised, and protected nooks for bedding. She was amazed by how he could conjecture in such detail—the spruce and the course of air—and know how a place lying completely hidden would turn out. It was as if he willed things to be as they became.

As the moon rose, she heard the stock stirring in their pickets beneath them and a clicking sound. She jerked up to a sitting position, finding her father already upright and gazing to where a herd of elk weaved like specters amongst the trees above them. Their ankle cartilage made the clicking, an ominous noise as their silvery forms passed in the dark. Her father leaned toward her, his face masked with shadows. "Headed for the valleys and found us in their path. They got tolerable winter coats on. Hard winter coming."

The next morning they set forth on a trail she'd ridden before. At the time there'd been too much worry over the Indians to pay attention to the sights, but now the ruggedness of the mountain pass leading to the Rayado made her blood pulse—the escarpments, sudden drops into watersheds, dwarf trees, and other-worldly, chalk-white palisades set like mineralized waterfalls against a barren of granite. They arrived at the Rayado in the afternoon, the horses leaving hoofprints in the shallow snow as they proceeded toward the enfermería. The Maxwell house and the several little casas near the trees where last June the Cheyenne had hovered were visible to the right, and a couple hundred yards above and to the left the creek and corral could be discerned, and men there, working. Lower down stood the partially built Carson house. She'd learned from her father that after the Cheyenne had been routed, the Moache Ute had migrated northeasterly back into their home country. Numbers of Jicarilla had journeyed across the Río Bravo del Norte to join others of their band and the Membreño Apache near a place called Abiquiú.

At the front of the enfermería, Kit tied off her packhorse, together with his own two and his buckskin. Since the enfermería had been completely taken over by men, he carried his things inside while she rode across to the Maxwell house where she was to stay. She dismounted, unfastened her buffalo robe, and entered the plaza. She passed a carreta that had empty botijónes in it and another loaded with freshly butchered deer. Through a open doorway she saw Luz, along with Clara, another woman, and Susan. To one side a fire blazed in the hearth. When Susan spied her standing in the light she cried out, "Ada! Oh, I so hoped you would come!" She rushed outside and held Adaline at arm's length. "My, how you've changed. Just look at you."

Adaline glanced down at the beaded bodice of her doeskin shirt beneath her open cloak, at her canvas trousers, and soiled moccasins, and smiled. "For the better I hope," then, looking back at her cousin and marking the fullness of her face, she added, "You are changed, too. Settling down must agree with you."

"I suppose it does." Susan hooked her arm in Adaline's arm and led her inside to the kitchen where the women were cutting venison into strips.

Luz and Clara greeted her and she was introduced to DeLaguna, Jesús's wife. Luz showed her a place that would be set aside for her, and when Adaline put down her robe a detonation shook the floor. She glanced up. Luz, brushing a strand of hair away from her eyes, announced, "That's your Louis."

"Louis?"

Susan hooked her arm once again. "Come see."

Out back they saw Louis's form moving toward a flat above the corral, and through a cloud of snow and dirt Tótilo and Jesse pulling up with a mule team. In the corral below, the stock were just turning from a corner to which they had bolted. She and Susan picked up Hawk, also skittish, and took him to the corral where he was unsaddled and brushed down, then they proceeded up higher toward the flat, where Louis called out to them and lifted an arm in salute. At his back lay a big fir tree, its roots still clutching loose rock and red clay, and a gash yawed deep in the ground. Several other trees—aspen, pine, and more fir—had been decked out thirty yards to the side. Tótilo had tied the mule team's harness to the fir. Jesse shook the reins and shouted, "Hiya!" The mules strained to pull it out, Jesse shouted again, giving them slack to start with. The mules moved the tree perhaps several inches.

Louis drew near to where Adaline and Susan stood. "Could use a couple of them big Missouri mules now, the likes of which we delivered to the Army." He glanced over toward the corrals. "Or my white mule, which somehow ended up down in Taos when everybody turned tail." He shot Adaline an amused look.

"That tree," Adaline said. "You blew it up."

"Tried to blow it out of the ground." he said. "Just like in the mines, as I used to do back home. We'll make a water tank." He nodded at the creek, which flowed above the tree and hole. "An acequia to here. Enlarge the corral for sorting animals. Put a sawmill on the creek." He gestured toward the corral and enfermería, and Adaline glimpsed his ring on the stub of his finger. "Then run water to the Carson house down there. We got a lot to do."

Adaline hadn't known he'd worked in mines, nor did she know where "back home" was. She watched as he stepped into the hole, ax in hand, which he used to sever a half-buried root from its holdfast, then he vaulted out. Jesse shouted at the mules one more time to get them to pull, whereupon the tree rode right up out of the cut. As Adaline traced its trajectory toward the other trees, she caught sight of adobe bricks on a hod hanging in mid air, held by a gin pole to a wall of the house under construction. Her father was down there, inspecting the progress with Jesús, Miguel, and Maxwell. Louis walked over to where Tótilo and Jesse were and started in limbing the trees, deftly swinging the ax as he moved up one tree, then another. Tótilo produced a two-man saw and he and Jesse came behind Louis and began sawing the logs into lengths.

"They won't stop until dark," Susan said. "I'm going to fetch water for Luz."

Adaline turned away with Susan. "I saw the botijónes awaiting. I'll help. It'll be just like the old days, except no Cheyenne, I hope."

•

In the morning, Adaline went out to find her father and Maxwell, along with several Mexican men, loading more bricks on the gin pole. Jesús and Miguel had begun to mark out the acequia from the creek. Louis was positioning iron wedges in the short rounds left by Tótilo and Jesse and striking them with a maul. The rounds exploded into halves and quarters.

She had marked Louis's manner toward her, which by his way of holding her with his eyes and sitting across from her at the table the night before, seemed proprietary. She didn't think she minded. And on that second night when she lay deep in her buffalo robe, listening to the songs of coyotes and the mournful hooting of owls, she recollected Frankie, how she'd chosen the man's life of journeying after losing her husband. Adaline wondered how that would be. She pictured herself having already been a married woman and going on alone in life, and then suddenly she felt a chill, a goose walking across her mother's grave. Death, Frankie had told her once, was a foremost ordinary of the earth, along with the things that caused it, love and birth. "'Cept I reckon none of 'em ain't never ordinary headed your way. More like bepuzzling is the best you can make of it." Frankie had put her hand on Adaline's arm. "As to the end of it, why the reaper takes his satisfaction, and when, and with who, he gives no answer. He just traipses along on his own time."

This conversation had taken place not long before Kit's company and the train parted trails. Frankie sat up on her lazy board and Adaline was squeezed in beside her. Frankie had said, "In between the beginning of your engendering and the end when you've engendered all you can, or want to, you still got your needs. The need of it you got to piece together with all these other ordinaries. The lead and hide, the casks, vittles, hardware, and all the goods, and the cost attached, going back and forth like they got minds of their own. The men, strong as they be, requires caring for more'n you'd expect. That's what you do. That's living. But get what you can to keep your needs down because soon you may be on your own if it's not you the reaper has yet taken. Love is always a hard one to master."

Adaline's mind wandered again as she thought of Howard County where men spent their days in the fields or sometimes pilgrimed to Saint Louis. Missouri was nothing like this place where the men regularly went off for months, or a year, traversing several hundred or thousands of miles, as she gathered her father meant to do on a spring beaver hunt, accompanied by Lucien Maxwell, Louis, and Jesús. She'd heard the confabulations before the fire in the parlor while Luz, Clara, and DeLaguna again were working in the kitchen. Adaline and Susan stood in the archway between the kitchen and parlor, near enough to hear the talk and see in the firelight the interest sharpening the younger men's faces. For some of them, the hunt posed a chance to taste a way of life they'd never known. Maxwell, being nearly ten years younger than Kit, had been mentored by him, and Kit in turn had picked up the way of life from the old mountain men—Ewing Young, Jim Bridger, Thomas Fitzpatrick.

The younger men had prodded Maxwell and Kit for stories of their beaver days, the troubles with the Blackfeet who slipped in on snowshoes during the winter to steal horses, and the skirmish in which they killed five of the trappers, and the time Kit had to climb a tree to escape two grizzly bears. They asked about the time Maxwell had lost eighty horses and mules and six hundred tanned buckskins to the Jicarillas, but Maxwell preferred not to talk about that. Jesse Nelson, ever ready for a good story, asked Kit about the Frenchman, Chouinard. Adaline's interest quickened because once she'd read an account of her father and Chouinard dueling at close range on horseback. Kit put a ball through the Frenchman's arm and the Frenchman's ball creased Kit's scalp. The version she'd read said that the fight was over an Arapaho woman who Adaline presumed was her mother. But instead of answering Jesse's question, Kit bent and tapped his pipe against the hearth. Straightening, he glanced toward the kitchen, where Luz looked up at Adaline from the slicing. Hers was a searching look and came with a mysterious smile.

Adaline thought she understood it: *It's us, the women. Your pa won't speak of this when women are within earshot.*

The men returned to their plans about the hunt. The market in pelts had been in collapse for twenty years, but Maxwell calculated that if they found good supplies of beaver this time out, they might expect to catch a rebound of past demand. Maxwell's upright carriage and demeanor were very different from her father's, and his face more open. He drew on his cigar. "We might niche into what wanting for beaver resurges to come out a little ahead." He paused, then said, "Maybe buy those sheep."

To the competencies commonly possessed by this group, Maxwell added knowledge of commerce. Because of her interest in the value of goods, and in numbers, and because of something she did not completely understand yet in herself, but subliminally rising, the inchoate and somehow prophetic sense that she might want to master these matters in order to satisfy what Frankie called "your need," Adaline paid close attention when Maxwell spoke, as did the others while the fire blazed behind them. Jesús sat, lithe and alert, and Tótilo, Jesse, and Louis, who tipped his head toward Maxwell, and all the while Kit puffed on his pipe. Maxwell's ancestry traced back to merchants from Illinois and Saint Louis, so his commercial propensity was "in the boot," as was said. Moreover, Maxwell expected before long to come into ownership of vast tracts of land on the Rayado and further to the northeast by virtue of the grant held by his father-in-law, Judge Carlos Beaubien of Taos. Adaline considered that her father, who was anxious to settle in and find steady income, might be a little awed by Maxwell's business acumen.

After a week at the Rayado, Kit returned with her to Taos. As he'd predicted, it turned out to be a hard winter. The snow hung on in the Sangre de Cristos unseasonably, well past the beginning of March. Nevertheless, he prepared to set out with his company. Although the purpose of the hunt was to raise money for his and Maxwell's outpost, and ostensibly to buy sheep for a drive to California, the purpose of which was also to raise money, she knew by the misty look in his eye that it was as much as anything the recapturing of bygone days that drew him away.

Chapter 9

1852

Soon April would come, and Santa Semana and Easter.

Kit was away with the other men on the hunt.

Josefa and the children stayed in Taos and as March advanced the town began to bustle. Orbits of order were created in the chaos left by winter. Women could be seen wielding brooms all up and down the paseo. Lupe appeared, sent up by Josefa's mother, Doña Apolonia. The walls of the house were dusted and one was newly whitened. Bedclothes were washed. Lupe swept the floors and the cobblestone in front of the house clear out to the paseo. Adaline fetched water from the creek, heated it in a pot at the kitchen fire, and carried it outside for the old woman, who scoured the cooking vessels that Josefa brought. Adaline had a good look at her hand, two of its fingers fused together and the skin stretched and scarred to above the wrist. The old woman clutched the vessels with this hand, while with her other hand she wielded a pumice stone, grunting softly as she labored.

Josefa sent Adaline with Lupe to the mercado, the various shops located a quarter mile down from the house near the town plaza. Adaline was to help carry the purchases that Lupe thrust at her—shoes for Teresina, one shirt each for Juan and Nicanor, two ceramic bowls, candle holders and candles. Adaline was struck by how the old woman, invoking the saints and her mistress, Doña Apolonia, could drive a price down almost to nothing.

The candlemaker ducked his head and grinned and said to Adaline, "Qué es esto? No caballo, no mula?"

Adaline had taken to exploring the pueblo while training Ghost. She rode Hawk at first and lately had advanced Ghost to a lead tied to his hackamore in order to accustom him to the distractions of the street. Their circuit went down past the plaza, markets, and fandango halls where soldiers, drovers, or bands of Indians lounged. She wended her way amongst these men and also sheep, goats, burros, and dogs. The candlemaker recognized her from those forays.

Further down was the church, where the circuit took her westward toward the Hacienda Martínez. Sometimes she would explore side trails. On occasion she rode past the hacienda as far as the bluffs that overlooked the Río del Norte, though she preferred to make the hacienda her destination since it seemed an appropriate distance. There was an impressive system of acequias here, fed by the Río Pueblo, out of which Hawk and Ghost could drink, and small fields cultivated for spring planting, and a stone mill to which the people brought their seeds to have them ground. A group of men were building an expansion to the dwelling space, already a fortress with high adobe walls and tall gates not unlike Lucien Maxwell's house at the Rayado. She admired an apparatus where a mule was harnessed to a line that ran through pulleys attached to a gin pole by which adobe bricks could be lifted to the wall under construction, this, the same method as what she'd seen at the Rayado. After several visits, a young man walked up to her. His white trousers were stained with red clay. He came to where she stood next to the stream where her animals drank. She'd dropped Hawk's reins but kept hold of the mule's lead. As he moved closer, Ghost twitched and dipped his ears, but Adaline held the animal still. He said, "You have your father's way, picking out everything."

She was startled not only by his directness but by his English. He was a sparely built young man of perhaps twenty, a Pueblan, she thought. He had shining, cropped hair and a striking face as if it had been crafted to be just so. Two white scars ran parallel on one cheek, which were like a decoration that heightened his handsome aspect. She glanced down at her hands, holding the mule's lead, and back at him.

"You have been coming here often."

"It's a good distance for a ride. To train the mule."

"And you are curious."

What he said was true, of course. She had grown curious about the proprietor, Padre Martínez, whom she knew her father distrusted. Adaline had seen the padre several times at services and once during Día de los Muertos and heard his resonant voice rising as if out of a deep hollow, filling the sanctuary, at times becoming almost like an animal cry that she could feel in her belly. Here at the hacienda, she'd seen him only once from afar as he rode off in a black cassock and striped trousers. It was said that he spent much of his time in Santa Fé, serving as president of the newly formed Territorial Assembly. She said, "You know me?"

"Everyone knows Señorita Carson. Don't you know me?"

She looked at him closely, thinking that maybe she knew him, but how she had no idea.

"I am Pablo," he said, gesturing back to where the wall was being built. He smiled. "Now I lay the adobe. Do you remember?"

She glanced up to the gin pole which at that moment was lifting a pallet of bricks, and then back at the young man. Could it be? The knitted brow set against the impish smile in its grown-up version of the same watching little boy? "Pablo? Mateo's son?"

"The same," he said. "It is I."

She peered more closely, and now the first glimmering transformed in a rush of recognition. Further, he had an air as if he were haloed by something yet more recognizable to her than his actual features, his way of looking closely at one thing and seeming to see another, or as if the other were contained in his eyes as he looked. "I do remember," she said, and foolishly added, "But you're so tall, not little like you were."

This made him laugh. He nodded to her. "And you?" Looking at the mule, he said, "If you say tall, which I am not, there's that mule as tall already as your tall horse." He reached to touch Ghost's neck, and the mule flattened its ears. "That is a proud mule."

"So it is," she said.

"I remember your sister," he said. "I am sorry."

Adaline looked away across the fields to an open patch, where a tree cholla with magenta blossoms grew amongst the sagebrush. On the side of it, willows with their pale blue stems like smoke followed the irregular course of the stream as it fed itself from the hacienda's acequia.

•

After five days, Lupe was satisfied with her work at the Carson house—all the pots scoured, the walls freshly brightened, candles mounted, everything swept clean. She returned to Josefa's mother just before the beginning of Holy Week, or Santa Semana. Josefa accompanied her, taking the children and asking Adaline to come, too, which Adaline did with some reluctance, for the few times she had been in the Doña's company she'd sensed disapproval.

They strolled through the mercado, past tabernas and fandango halls, picking their way amongst the sheep, goats, burros, chickens, and prowling dogs. From the change in season, the number of trade trains passing through the pueblo had increased, and on this day a dozen wagons stood waiting. They began to pull forward, the metal in the outfits gnashing, loads thudding, axles screeching, and men barking out commands. The women and children progressed downhill a mile, passed by the church, and came to the home of Josefa's family. Josefa's mother scrutinized Adaline from the straight-backed chair that stood at the head of the room. Adaline looked away. To one side hung a silver crucifix and beneath it a shrine rested on a table. Adaline sat on a bench against the wall and examined the shrine, finding respite in her fascination with candles and small carved figures, tiny swathes of lace, a bowl of cactus blossoms, bits of bone, curls of smoke from sage leaves smoldering in a dish, and in the background a plate standing on edge with a scene painted of Jesus walking on water. It was a tiny world, like the village of Taos itself with its low adobe huts running back from the paseo, the makeshift fences, carretas in the alleys, plucked chickens and gourds hanging from the porticos, guns leaning against walls, and women appearing in the doorways. Several times Doña Apolonia turned to gaze straight at Adaline, never speaking to her directly. It seemed as if the old woman had commenced raveling upon her skein a tangle of unspoken remonstrance.

Lupe doted on the doña, going off to bring a shawl for her, and then joining forces with another servant to gather pastries. Doña Apolonia was a descendant of a prominent family named Vigil, and without doubt she had been beautiful, perhaps as beautiful as Josefa. Her face now betrayed a pallor, offset by coal black eyebrows and silvered hair. Adaline sat motionless on the bench while Josefa and her mother spoke earnestly in Spanish. Several times she heard the name Lamy, the Vicar Apostolic who'd been sent here by the pope, but now was away during the Easter season. She noted the affection with which Apolonia treated the other children—Teresina, Nicanor, even Juan. Lupe presented the pastries and retreated to fetch a plate filled with pale fruit.

Adaline accepted one pastry, which she slipped into her pocket, and one of the fruits. Josefa leaned toward her and informed her it was called opuncia, a fruit of the cactus, which had appeared early this year because of the precipitous snow melt. Adaline discovered that it possessed two tastes, the sweetness surrounding her tongue and the bitterness making her cheeks pucker. Doña Apolonia sat in repose, hands resting on the arms of the chair, her stilled face like stone.

•

Adaline kept riding to the hacienda, bringing the mule along. By degrees she had put a blanket, a pack, and a saddle on it, and then finally riding Ghost herself and drawing Hawk on a lead. She believed her project of discipline would be seen by Josefa's household, and even by herself, as a service performed for Louis. Usually, she found

Pablo at the hacienda. He would take leave of his labor and they would sit next to each other on the apron of a broken down carreta near a peach tree and just above the acequia that watered a newly planted field. She told him how the old woman, Lupe, sought to forgive her for sins she had not committed.

"I saw it all," he said.

"From the wall," she said.

"Sí. You have nothing to fear from her. She is foolish, but she does not choose to be so. She and her acts of penance have made her famous in Taos."

Again Adaline envisioned her sister. "It was a cruel way for her to die."

"Your sister, sí." Lightly, he touched her hand. "For Lupe, it is a way of explaining it to herself, that is all."

She stared out at the field, finding that his touch made her body ache.

Sometimes, his fingers were darkly stained, which he said came from rolling ink onto the padre's printing press. "By day it's the bricks. By night it's words. Words have their own mortar which they supply to other words, making a bed for them. Bricks are good labor. I have the clay on my trousers, but the ink is on my hands. I now know several languages," he added. "Español, English, the language of my pueblo, and even a little Latin from studying in the padre's seminary."

Adaline listened carefully, thinking that she, too, had almost enough Spanish now to say she had two languages. He related to her how he'd been taken captive by the Utes one day when he was out hunting with his brother, from whom he became separated. "That is how I got these," he said, touching the scars on his cheek.

"You were with Pepe?"

A shadow passed across Pablo's face. "Yes, my brother, Pepe. We fear he is dead." Pablo said he himself had been sold by the Utes to a man who ran a trading post because he spoke Spanish and a little English. He'd made his escape to his pueblo not long after the revolt and found his mother and one sister, but his father, another sister, and an uncle had been killed. Pepe had disappeared. Another uncle had been hanged in his people's pueblo outside the mission church, Saint Jerome, which was left in ruins when Colonel Price followed Ceran Saint Vrain up from Santa Fé with his troops. "This was five years ago," Pablo said. "If I'd been here, I'd have fought with the others. I would have been old enough. I would likely be dead. Your father's friend, Governor Bent, had come up from Santa Fé, and he was killed, too. And the troops killed over a hundred of my people who had taken refuge in Saint Jerome by shooting their cannons into it. One governor and a few men in exchange for hundreds. Who places the value?"

She knew this story, but she had never heard it told by one who had lost family inside Saint Jerome.

"So much killing," Pablo said. "Your father was away then, too. It is said he blames the padre and other priests for his friend's death. Some say if he had been here he would be dead, too, but I am not sure. It seems he does not die."

She thought for a moment. "There were other friends, too. Stephen Lee was one, and his señora's brother. And her uncle. I have not heard my father say that he blames the padre, but I believe he doesn't trust him for giving refuge to some from the uprising. I am sure the Señora Carson would not want to blame him, though she still remembers what she endured. And to this day she cares for Teresina, the governor's and her sister Ignacia's daughter, and for her brother's son, Nicanor. As to my father's not dying, how can that be true?"

He did not answer. Instead, he said, "Pablo is what I am called here. It is not my name."

She waited for him to tell her his true name, but he did not.

Whenever he spoke, she felt she was brimming with things to say in response, but she remained cautious. This made her think about the book of Shakespeare and the other book, *Tales From Shakespeare*, that she slipped into the Fayette library to read, and of the story of Romeo and Juliet, who came from warring families but loved each other nevertheless. She remembered Josefa calling out to her, "¡Ten cuidado, chica!" Her mind spun awhirl and her breath was taken away.

Pablo said, "They say it started when three of my people were put in jail for stealing. It was winter and they were hungry. Then the Mejicanos started in. For them it was about the Americans taking possession here. Before that the Mejicanos took possession of the pueblos and called it Méjico Nuevo. It was about the war that is always here and will be forever."

Pablo said the man at the trading post had never treated him cruelly. "He gave me my freedom to go about so long as I did my work. I learned better English from him. I taught myself to read both English and Spanish, and that is how I have become useful to the padre here as a helper with his printing. These days, it seems he is always running it." He looked at his stained fingers. "I heard about the revolt in Taos. I was still up north beyond the Arkansas at the trading post and my heart ached for my people. I walked away to return home. Why I did not do that before, I don't know. Maybe because the agent was not a bad man, or maybe it was meant that I should stay there for just so long and that I knew when to leave."

This rang in Adaline, how she'd longed to leave Missouri to be with her father and his family and dreamed of setting out on her own, but she waited in accordance with her bargain. She told this to Pablo.

"We all have our journeys and our bargains," he said.

"When I was there, I thought about being here every day."

"I believe I am meant for something," Pablo said. "I am to do something. I am attending the padre's seminary, too, along with this work, and the padre says he may wish to send me to Méjico as an emissary. I don't think I am to be a priest, though. I am seeking what it is. Perhaps it is so with you, too."

This sent a pulse through Adaline. The feeling of the need to play her own part in the world, as Pablo wished to do, and the question of what that might be, was as strong in her and as soaring as the emotion she felt in Pablo's presence.

They fell quiet. They looked out over the field where crows had swooped down to thieve the planted seed. She said, "Governor Bent was in Taos to be with his family, too. As you wished to be, and I."

"Ay! There is no end to it."

•

It was now Good, or Spy, Wednesday, and several days ago Padre Antonio had returned from his duties with the Assembly in Santa Fé, and Adaline sometimes caught sight of him. She also observed young women emerging from their adobes to work in the plantings or washing clothes in the stream and carrying them in baskets to be hung on a rope line. Occasionally, one or two of them would follow the padre when he stopped to inspect the construction. Even when the padre was visible, Pablo felt free to sit with Adaline. He explained that the young women were the padre's mujeres. "He is known for his appetite. But he is also famous for inspiring penance in others." Pablo smiled at Adaline. "He loves his people. He is a great man, since he understands fear and the power of poverty. He understands pleasure. His memory is perfect. After he reads a book, he can close it and turn the pages in his mind and speak the words just as they are. He says it is a gift God gave him to further his work."

This brought Adaline to consider her father again, who could not read but who saw in his mind wherever he'd been in the land and never forgot it.

"At first, the padre made books for his seminarians with his printing press," Pablo said. "Now, he wages battle with the new vicar by what he writes. The vicar is away, consulting with American bishops in hopes the pope will grant him authority over Santa Fé in place of Bishop Zubiria of Mexico. Soon, Padre Antonio will go to Abiquiú, his true home, to remind himself of his people's poverty, their fear of penalty, and of the means to redemption. Perhaps we should also go to see."

Adaline felt a rush of curiosity about the place called Abiquiú. "How far would it be?"

"A day's journey," Pablo said, his head gesturing to the west. "Over Cerro Coronado and toward Cerro Perdernal to the Rio Chamas."

At first, she felt crushed by the distance, which seemed impossible, but then her overpowering curiosity and desire came to supplant any misgivings with thoughts of how she might arrange to go. Josefa had spoken of staying with her mother for several nights during Santa Semana. She had assured Adaline that she could join them, but Adaline preferred not to, which she trusted Josefa would understand. She felt the ache, an unfathomable longing as if Pablo had touched her again. "A day's journey there?" she finally asked.

"Yes. And a day back, or all night."

"I would have to see."

Pablo murmured softly.

In the field before them, the seeds had sprouted, making green lines against the dark earth. The padre appeared on horseback, evidently having just ridden from town. He drew up to them, wheeled his horse around, and dismounted, displaying his striped trousers and boots fitted with spurs under his cassock. The rowels rang when his heels struck the ground. He wore a rakish black hat with a crimson chin strap and about his neck a silver cross. Pablo had informed her that the padre was nearly sixty years old, yet up close he seemed like a young bull, filled with vigor. His jaw and massive forehead seemed too large for his body, like a heavy flower out of proportion to its stalk. He surveyed Ghost, which she'd tethered to the peach tree.

Then he surveyed her. She had on the canvas trousers and doeskin shirt, but she felt embarrassed to be seen by the padre in such garb. Next, she came to realize that she'd just been appraised by him like the mule before her, or as if she were a lump of metal. A jolt of offense shot through her and yet also wonderment as to what thaumaturge a woman might be sucked into if she fell under the padre's sway. He spoke to Pablo in Spanish, his deep voice waxing passionate, intimating the same animal resonance as that which surged when he stood behind the pulpit in church. It seemed he had a pressing matter to tell Pablo, something about the vicar, Lamy. When finally he paused, she heard Pablo say her name, and the padre's eyes turned back to her in a different way now. Something brooding surfaced in his measurement.

He removed his hat, revealing a bald pate and a fringe of hair drenched with sweat. He pressed the hat against his chest and bowed deeply to her. "Buenas, Señorita Carson." He reset his hat, swung onto his horse, and rode off toward the hacienda.

"Do not worry. He will not wish to provoke Kit Carson," Pablo said, seeming to have read her mind. "It's the vicar, Jean Baptiste Lamy, who has sought to remove two priests from their parishes. These are men Padre Antonio trained in his seminary and proposed for ordination. Soon we will be printing another letter of protest."

Chapter 10

THE FRIDAY FOLLOWING—Good Friday—they stole away down the paseo, the animals' clopping hooves softly breaking the quiet. They turned westward at the church, passed the Hacienda Martínez, and proceeded to the brink of the canyon from where they could hear the day's first rooster crows behind them. They descended into the canyon on a trail that traced its edge, coming out to the Río del Norte which had engorged its banks because of the mountain thaw. Pablo knew of a wide place not far upstream, whereupon they discovered the banks littered with boulders, driven down by high water. Pablo tied his mule to a willow, motioned to Adaline to do the same with Hawk, removed his poncho, and said, "First, we have to cross halfway on foot, seeking the river's permission."

Adaline removed the poncho Pablo had brought for her, her moccasins, and the belt to which she'd attached her holster to keep her Navy Colt snug against the small of her back. When Pablo caught sight of the pistol, he smiled. In a scabbard, he had an old Hawken he said had belonged to his father. She rolled up her trousers and followed his steps into the river. They picked their way along the rock shelves, the brutally cold current tugging at Adaline's legs. She could hear the rocks bouncing along the bottom and several times they knocked against her ankles. As they neared the center, the river deepened to her thighs but after a few steps grew shallower. Pablo stopped and turned back. "Bien. The animals will make it."

They returned and rode across without incident. They ascended a precipitous, jackknifing trail that scaled a basalt bluff. Finally, they attained a mesa from which they caught sight of far-off mountains to the southwest and in between more mesas and pyramid-shaped formations. They continued westward, going side by side. Her legs, chilled by the river, now felt warm from pressing against Hawk, and the sun rose above the Sangre de Cristos from behind to warm her back through the poncho. Pablo's straight-spined mule maintained a level parallel to whatever incline the earth took, and Pablo easily kept his balance, his poncho draped over his knees. To one side swayed the scabbard. Adaline was struck by how much in command Pablo was now that they were removed from the hacienda, and older, too, and how handsome.

He'd confirmed that Padre Antonio had traveled to Abiquiú in order to give the people confidence. "The conflict between padre and the vicar grows worse," he said. "When Lamy first came he could not speak the language. He sent one of his French priests to deliver mass in the pueblos. The priest also spoke no Spanish and delivered his homily in French. Some people believed he was Satan disguised in priest's clothing."

"Why would a French priest be sent here?" Adaline asked.

"The better to reform us, no doubt. He's a Jesuit. It's a power that comes from far away, as do the soldiers and traders. In the case of Lamy, it's the power of the Holy Father." Pablo squeezed his knees into his mule and lifted himself clear of the saddle, stretching his legs. The mule carried on with its smooth gait, uninterrupted. Settling back down, Pablo said, "There are two great seas, one to the east and one to the west. I would like to see them some day."

"The Atlantic to the east. Europe. To the west, the Pacific. I would choose the Pacific."

"Where the gold is."

"Yes, if I had to choose one, but not for the gold."

"For what then?"

"To see it. I have heard there is no blue like it in the world."

"But the miners are there. They are a plague, also come from afar."

"If you have something to sell to them, you can make your way is what I hear," Adaline said. "My father intends to drive sheep there along with his friend, Lucien Maxwell."

"Sheep? So far? There are more mountains to cross before reaching that place, mountains far more difficult than what we have here, I have heard. Why sheep?"

"For meat. Easier to drive than cattle. They forage for anything."

"Ah," he said. "But then most anything will eat them, too."

"It is true. I would prefer cattle for the interest in them."

Pablo looked over at her. "Sheep are not interesting enough?"

"My aunt and uncle in Missouri kept cows. It seems a cow has more of a mind of its own," she said, "within the one mind it shares with the herd. Sheep only have one mind. Each one does whatever the others do. It's not always so with cows. Some mothers will protect their calves to the death. Sheep run and hide their heads."

"Do you know sheep?"

She smiled. "No. But cows are surely more interesting."

Pablo leaned forward and chuckled softly. After a moment, he said, "The miners and these traders who come in here and the ranchers also have only one mind, which is to take everything. And they offer their excuses for it. They say we Pueblans are weak, or the Mejicanos are dirty and lazy, or that they, the Americans, are superior and only do what God wants them to do, and that whoever obstructs their path should be killed off like the wolves. It is true that they are superior but only in their numbers and in the weapons they have fashioned for killing. They are not superior in the way they think. In time, they will be shown to be a passing thing."

In silence, they dipped down into an arroyo and toiled up the opposite bank along a transverse in order to avoid a heap of rocks. Adaline wondered what Pablo had in mind to cause this superiority to pass away and how much time it might take, but before she could ask he leaned to one side to study the rocks and said, "It is too cold yet for the snakes."

"Good."

"The snakes seem to live alone, except to mate. There are other animals like that, such as the mountain panther. This mule would kill a snake by leaping on it, given the chance."

"Horses are more interesting yet than cows."

"Mules even more so. Sometimes more interesting than you wish. Pablo leaned forward and patted his mule. "They are confused about who they are. Two sexes in one."

Adaline let that pass, and said, "I thought about riding Ghost today. But I was afraid he might make trouble on a ride of this length."

"You were wise."

Adaline wished she hadn't mentioned the sheep because it called forth her concern about Louis Simmons's plan to go on the drive and probably stay in California and that very soon she was to give her answer to him, which she knew was not an answer at all, not one of choosing between this thing and that, but simply to assent. Since meeting Pablo, she'd all but shut the sheep out from her mind, like a bag of lizards she kept hidden deep in the shadows. Yet she'd found her hopes rising when she and Pablo spoke of California as if it were a place to which they might journey together. She wondered what words could be used to form such an idea, but it seemed risky because the thought was well ahead of what she felt certain of between Pablo and herself. She did not dislike Louis. It was only that he was not Pablo. She felt a terrible discord, a fragility. Now, the lizards gathered around her and grew still and poised, awaiting the signal to scatter. She must not think about this. She sighed and thought: *My God!*

They began a descent into a broad valley. The trail wound around juniper stands, and they crossed more dry washes strewn with rocks and heaps of branches discarded by recent floods. To the south, Cerro Perdernal, high and black in the distance, slipped in and out of sight. They were coming upon a village, what Pablo told her was El Rito. A waterway passed by from which acequias had been dug to irrigate the fields. The two stopped to let their animals drink and forage, and they sat on a bank to eat some of the tortillas Pablo had brought, preserved in a basket and bundled in white cloth. Maize husks were wrapped around the tortillas, and within the tortillas were goat meat, beans, and a mole Pablo's mother had prepared. He also provided two gourds filled with a tea.

Pablo said, "Perhaps the goat is more interesting yet."

"They are independent, though they travel in a herd. The mothers protect their young as well. They are surely preferable to sheep."

"But have you looked into their eyes?" Pablo was toying with her. "With little rectangles for pupils? Some say there are devils behind those boxes. And of course a goat can never be as powerful as a mule."

Adaline did not mention Pablo's own eyes and his perpetual way of having something else he had seen set against what he saw at the moment. She still puzzled over that. "I have heard that the goat and sheep, the horse, too, and the cow all came from far away like so many things that are living here."

"But we have had them for a long time. They are definitely ours, especially the sheep and the horse. Truly, the burro is ours, the coyotes and wolves, and the buffalo that lives in numbers to the east." He turned his eyes back toward the river and Adaline imagined he envisioned buffalo in the tens of thousands, hunted down as they now were by the Americans, ciboleros, and by Indians in their desperation. She knew well how the buffalo's singularity of mind grew formidable when they were panicked, all moving as one like a ferocious wind.

After finishing her tortilla, she drank some tea. "We had a buffalo stampede against our train. When I came West." She envisioned the buffalo perishing, piling on top of each other, and Gish's act to protect those behind him, only to perish himself. "A young man was killed." She felt the palpable grief of Yolanda, and remembered Yolanda's confusion over the white stones.

Pablo murmured. "When the buffalo run they drive all the earth into tremors." He took a drink, put the gourd down, clapped the stopper in its top, and pondered an old man in a cream-colored poncho, moving slowly along a row of small maize plants in a field next to them. "And the maize. It seems it was always ours, too."

Every few steps the man halted and bent to the ground. He looked back at them, pulling his hat brim to shade his eyes. Pablo raised a hand to greet him. The man waved back and resumed moving along the row. Pablo said he thought the man was checking the maize, perhaps pulling the weak plants and leaving room for the strong. He said this was done every spring, and at the end of the season the very strongest would be kept for next year's seeds. "We have done the same with the horses, sheep, and goats. For a long time we have saved the best."

A flat-roofed church stood in the center of the town. Pablo put away the gourds and carefully wrapped into the cloth the remaining food. They tied off their animals to a rail and entered the church through a side door. It was cool and so silent that all Adaline could hear was the sound still inside her head of Hawk's hooves grinding in the sand and the creak of leather. Pablo explained that the walls were built thick—five feet, he said—in order to hold up the massive beams and for protection against attack, since the Apaches were in this region. All around the sanctuary, up the two side walls in the positions of the Stations of the Cross, hung carvings of the saints illuminated by candles in holders crafted out of tin and bone. Adaline moved in a circuit, examining each. She had observed similar carvings in the church in Taos, but nothing so twisted as these, so grotesquely misshapen. She circled back to the front where Christ hung above an altar. His figure was life size, painted a ghostly white. Crimson splotches erupted from his hands and streamed down his left side. A blue cloth was draped over his hips and his legs contorted downward toward his mutilated feet. His eyes were cast down, his cheeks were hollow, and more blood trickled into his beard from a crown of thorns.

Light flashed from behind her as Pablo opened the door to make his exit. She followed him out. He said, "The new vicar and his friend, Machebeuf, have not been here yet to replace the Santos with porcelain."

"Why would they do that?"

"They say the Santos are vile appearing and that those chosen to carve them, the santeros, court certain doom."

She did not understand the import of it. "What do you mean?"

"There is the power of doom to frighten people. If one persists in sacrilege, or in any sin, excommunication is the result. The vicar sees such Santos as a sign of the corruption that comes when people are left without guidance. Thus, the santeros and the people, too, are doomed not to receive the Lord's blessing and they will rot in Hell."

They mounted and turned southward. "The vicar is wrong about that. Guidance! What is meant by that?" She urged Hawk up beside Pablo's mule. "Because the Santos are powerful. Is it not good to discover the source of power, for good or for ill and thus to know it? How can the struggle of the santeros to discover this be sacrilege?"

"Do you mean the discovery of the power lies in the santeros skill at depicting such things," Pablo said. "Or is it in the power of the Santos as they are revealed?"

Without hesitation, she said, "It's the second. The power the Santos are revealed to have as they are caught up by the santeros, whose skill in carving is simply their way of discovering what is in the wood. The power of the Santos, truly, rests in the wood that makes them."

"Ah!" Pablo said. "And it is a different order of power from that which Lamy sees. He prefers the French porcelain, which has no shape of its own. It merely takes the shape of the molds from which many may be made exactly the same. Porcelain is nothing."

She stared at her hands, holding the leather thong of the reins looped between her thumbs. They rested against the saddle horn, and her fingers folded into each other made partial circles like the cocoons of caterpillars. She looked up. The path they had chosen showed more signs of travel, hoofprints, footprints, and the furrows of carretas. The trail, which marked the course of the river that passed through El Rito, was bounded on either side by large sandstone outcrops. Some had flat mesas on top, some were jagged, some were eroded as if carved into all manner of strange forms, and some had alcoves that appeared to lead to rooms within. As the sun began to sink, the pair came upon the Rio Chama. They forded it easily, passing over a place where flat stones had been laid in the water. Within a hundred yards, a hacienda cropped up and beyond it atop a mesa buildings materialized—Abiquiú. Pablo chose a side trail to an adjacent mesa to show her the remains of a settlement he said was older than anyone knew.

"This is called Poshuouinge. My mother's people in the Pueblo de Taos came from here."

They picked their way through the ruins, leading their animals. Under their feet ceramic shards and bits of stone rattled. A road runner bolted from its hiding place in a clump of cholla and disappeared over the edge of the flat. The sight made Pablo smile. "A good sign. It will clear the way for us." In most places the old adobes had all but dissolved away, leaving lines of clay to seep slowly back into the ground. Here and there, a wall remnant stood a foot or two high, on one of which a decaying ladder lay propped.

Pablo led her to the back of the mesa and to a rock face near a route that soared yet higher to yet another mesa. This one displayed incisions in the rock—snakes, a man plunging downwards headfirst, whom Pablo said was a shaman going to his death. There was a bounding deer pierced with an arrow, blood spurting from its mouth, and a writhing serpent with a plume on its head to which had been scraped a topknot in the shape of a cross.

"You see," Pablo continued, "Hidden there is everything known to us, the snake, Avanyu, with the plume on its head. Sometimes the plume is of feathers. This one is a cactus bloom. It is the old way, old as the snake itself and the cactus that always grows there and sends out its flower after the spring rains. The cruz was added much later," he said, running his finger down the shape of the cross to the bloom on the snake head. "Perhaps by one of the traveling priests, whether in kindness or unkindness, who can say? If what is given by the strangers, the Castillas, carries a power that speaks to the people, then it is permitted to speak."

Pablo fell silent for a few moments, and then unexpectedly he turned to the subject of Lupe. "You were a child. And much less, as well, an Indio, but in the next breath an Indio that grew up with more power than Lupe ever imagined was possible because of who your father was. I believe Lupe is afraid of you. You surprised her by increasing to who you are. He shrugged. "She's alone with her penance. Accept her forgiveness."

They stood. The horse and mule stopped straining to reach for tufts of grass that protruded through the fissures in the packed earth. Pablo's face had grown calm as he looked up at the sky, which was emptied of clouds. Adaline heard him breathing as though he'd fallen into a trance. In a piñon at the base of the rock wall a nuthatch jumped from branch to branch and abruptly halted upside-down on the trunk. Adaline attempted to sort all this out and considered the two concepts jittering back-and-forth, as if Lupe carried on a dialogue without words—one side misrepresenting the truth, the other in secret knowing not to misrepresent? Truly, it was all Lupe could do. In the darkening skies, birds flared up like scattered buckshot.

"We should go," he said.

They mounted and rode down to the Chama, picking up the trail that led to the mesa. Near the river lay fields, configured by an acequia that flowed from the river. Pablo gestured toward a long, isolated building, indicating it was a morada. "See. One door on the end. One window on this side. One cross above." He gestured up to the mesa. "There is another morada up there, which is where we will go, now. On the other side of the mesa is a valley fed by the Chama and the Rio Abiquiú, and a hacienda where Padre comes from. There are two pueblos here, populated by what we call the Genizaro—a people begotten by ancient ancestors of different nations. I am one of them because of my mother."

This was another new idea to Adaline—not that there wouldn't be such people, but a name for them. "As I must be, too."

"But you are a new Genizaro. We are old. True, they include the Castillas and the mixed blood Méjicanos, like my father. The true ancestors are Pueblan, perhaps Apache or Diné, and some older than we can say. Some day they will return, moving up from the south. Some call them the enemy Diné, others the Anasazi. Their homeland has become Aztlán."

They pushed forward up the trail from the river and passed a church half-encircled on the south side by dwellings. People began to appear. Further along a pathway lined with narrow crosses was another building. "The Via Cruces." Pablo gestured upwards. "The morada."

They rode to one side where they hobbled Hawk and the mule in the stand of piñons at the edge of a small field. There was an abundance of grass there and an acequia near enough for Hawk and the mule to drink. Pablo left his Hawken in the scabbard, and Adaline did not disturb her Walker Colt beneath the poncho. She followed Pablo back uphill to the side of the Via Cruces where people made room for them. Since the cold was imminent, men wore ponchos and the women shawls, and they had gathered in clusters, as had the group on the other side of the via. Over there, several also had yellow bandanas wrapped around their heads.

"Those are pretending to be the Jews," Pablo said. "That is why they are marked with yellow. Yesterday, the Cristo was betrayed and taken captive. He has seen his mother, the Holy Virgin, and Santa Veronica has wiped his forehead with her cloth. Now, the cloth has his image upon it. He will be coming soon." A faint smile glimmered across his face.

An old woman stepped up. As Pablo had spoken, her bright black eyes darted back and forth between him and Adaline, then she addressed Pablo in Spanish. He replied and Adaline heard her name uttered. The old woman took Adaline's hand in her hands, which were knobby at the knuckles and hard as leather. She spoke as though delivering a pronouncement. Pablo chuckled. "She says you are welcome here. She wants to know when we will be married."

Adaline stared at the ground, a flush rising to her neck. This was far more direct than anything that had passed between them and not knowing his precise meaning made her feel tremulous, which startled her as much as what had just been said. These responses of her body jolted her. The old woman took a gourd from under her shawl and turned it in her hands, rattling the seeds within. She pressed it into Adaline's hands. It felt light and dry.

"She says you should have that for the Tineablas," Pablo said. "You will see."

Just then, two columns of men marched up the hill from the church, dressed in white trousers. The ones on the left wore white shirts, too, while the ones on the right were shrouded in dark hoods. They bore small, carved statues. "Las Muertes," Pablo whispered. "The santos of protection. These men near us are the Hermanos de Luz. On the other side are the Hermanos de Tinieblas. Brothers of Light. Brothers of Darkness."

Behind the columns of men rolled a cart, pulled with great effort by three more men because three young men stood inside it. The cart's wooden wheels wobbled. Pablo touched his shoulder to Adaline's and whispered that the young men were initiates, newly admitted hermanos. From all around arose a murmuring and bodies pressed closer. The old woman leaned in again, her elbow against Adaline's ribs. Another old woman came from behind, laying a hand on Adaline's shoulder. The murmuring found its way into a chant, then a hymn with the refrain:

"Arrastrada y escupido,
Con tormento feroz."

Pablo whispered, "They are singing of Cristo's coming suffering—ferocious torment."

A second cart came, also drawn by three men. In it loomed a carved life-sized figure, a hag enveloped in a pitch-black veil, which was topped by a black crown that had sprouted scraggly wisps of dark yellow hair fashioned from maize silk. Through the rails of the cart, Adaline saw oversized feet, the figure's gargantuan toes, and bony knees rupturing a slit in the veil. In her hands, thick fingers clutched a bow and arrow. Her mouth hung agape and the teeth were colossal, matching her fingers and toes. Her obsidian eyes glittered in the last incandescence of the sun. Pablo whispered, "La Muerte. She is the death that passes before the Cristo."

Behind the cart shuffled three men bearing unwieldy crosses—the two thieves, and then the Cristo. They wore white trousers. The backs of the thieves dripped with blood from self-flagellation, and the Cristo staggered beneath a crown of cactus thorns, blood streaming down his face and down his back. They struggled up the last rise to the bench of rock upon which towered the morada. The volume of the singing rose. All took part except the Jews, who leered across the via and produced flutes and single-stringed instruments akin to violins. Some of these were fabricated from skulls, the string a sinew drawn taut between a cranial cavity and jaw. Then the flutes screeched raucously, slicing through the strains of the hymn, accompanied by the stringed instruments that droned under stickbows. In the midst of this racket, and in the path of the crossbearers, filed six more hermanos, again attired in white trousers and hoods, and whipping behind their shoulders with scourges.

Adaline looked toward the morada and saw the Cristo struggle, then fall from view behind the procession. She felt Pablo tugging on her elbow. He nodded toward the last of the hermanos who now passed directly in front of them. Behind them walked an older man dressed in a hooded cloak. He carried but did not use a scourge, his pace was measured, and unlike the others, he had a thick body and massive head, which when he lifted it, letting the hood fall partly away, revealed himself. There he was. Padre Antonio.

People from both sides of the via crowded behind him and followed in his steps. The music faded, and the hushed air filled with a sibilance of feet sliding over rock. Adaline fell in with them, clutching Pablo's arm. A cross swung up, pulled by two guy lines, and to which the Cristo was bound. He had donned a hood and white cape. The doorway to the morada was thrown open and before it several hermanos prostrated themselves. People kept moving, some walking on top of the hermanos, but Adaline sought out footholds in between. Still clutching Pablo's arm, she was swept inside. On the altar at one end of the room blazed a candelabra. Running the length of two walls, dozens of candles burned beneath carvings and paintings. Bodies pressed close together. There was only the sound of their breathing, and then the voice that could only have been the padre's spun out:

"Adiós por última vez."

The words were sung over and over, increasing in magnitude. Adaline barely caught sight of his figure ghosting down along a wall, extinguishing one candle at a time. His voice reverberated. He glided along another wall toward the altar, extinguishing candles one by one, and upon approaching the altar he snuffed out the candelabra in one dramatic sweep. Absolute darkness overwhelmed the morada. His voice soared to a long, pure, high lament and then plummeted, breaking with inconsolable grief:

"No me vayan a olvidar,
No me vayan a olvidar.
Fin. Fin. Fin. Amen."

The final echoes trailed away and for what seemed an eternity everyone stood in deep silence, and then suddenly, as from the pit of darkness, a shattering shout rose up, chased by a clamor of flutes, chains, pitas, cajas, and matracas, and a thunderous stomping. Adaline's scalp prickled with the vibration penetrating to her feet through the earth. She recalled the old woman's gourd, what had been tucked away underneath her poncho, and she drew it out to join the throng—the Tenebrae. A curtain was pulled clear of the window, revealing a square of crimson, and people spilled outside into luminous twilight, whereupon the Cristo was lowered from his cross. Everyone spread out, reassembling in smaller groups. Padre Antonio, now lingering outside the morada and just before La Muerte in her cart, was illuminated by a torch. When he threw his head back to speak, she saw his jawline bulge as if he were biting through bone.

•

Adaline and Pablo rode off into the night, now and then passing up others along the way. The others traveled on foot or were riding burros. At each encounter they greeted Pablo and Adaline, wishing them

God's blessing, which Pablo reciprocated. Sometimes, the two rode in silence, drowsing in their saddles. At other times, reenergized, they talked in what much later in Adaline's reminiscences would signify the closing stages of a long, weighty, and intense conversation. She could not cast off the spell of La Muerte, nor of the entire ceremony, nor of Padre Antonio. She said the vicar's wish to abolish the rituals made her exceedingly uneasy.

"That is not all he wishes to change," Pablo said. "Years ago, Padre, with the permission of his bishop, Zubiria, suspended the tithes for sacraments because the poor could not pay. The vicar, Lamy, is collecting them again to build his church, which will be filled with porcelain statues. He cannot understand how formidable is the knife in the hands of a santero. You were right. The power is inside. How the santos look arises from what the knife discovers."

"Yes," she said. "If the santero comes upon a boll in the wood that resists him, he must imagine what shape it wants. When he finds it, the santo comes out with a shape all its own."

A waxing half-moon gave off just enough light for them to discern the trail. The darkness beyond was laced with the cries of coyotes. Pablo said, "Perros de cantos. They are constantly reminding each other that they are not alone."

"Signalizing," Adaline said.

"You want to be sure it is not the Jicarilla, but there are too many moving from place to place to be them, I think."

Their animals' hooves hissed through the sand. The spectral mesas and stone formations took shape in the blue moonlight, and it seemed that they passed through an ending of the world, barren, desolate, yet ineffably beautiful. Pablo said that like the Santos the same was true of the procession and scourging, which had been practiced by the first priests here, the Franciscans. "But then there was a time when the people had no priests for years, especially during the wars, or else the priests were of their own people, and so the ceremony became their own. If they cannot pay the tithes it doesn't mean they are not devoted." He paused for a few minutes and then added, "Now it is political, as all things must come to be."

"You mean they are resisting?" Adaline asked.

"But who would call it that? It is who they are and what they have. It is so with the procession and the santos, who come from their feeling. It comes from what is known and felt. Sometimes what is felt is too strong. Then the people learn what it is to be political."

The two fell quiet. They plodded northward toward El Rito where they would stop to recruit their mounts on the spring grass close to the river. Hawk was so steady that Adaline could loop the reins once around the horn, only touching them with her fingertips, and let her chin drop to her chest and nod off. In her dreaming she lost track of time. She would hear Pablo talking in her dream and thus even in her dreaming she thought he didn't know she'd fallen asleep and she'd make herself wake up.

At other times, she awoke to discover he had picked up the conversation where it left off, as when he said, "To know what is necessary and truly felt is still possible for these people because they are not quite slaves. The peones and Indios among them were sent here to work. Sometimes their families were broken, but mostly they are not bought, sold, or traded, unlike the Africanos in Los Estados. They were sent to labor for the hacendados, such as Padre's ancestors and the ancestors of your father's señora. The hacendados were given the land, yet still the poor have something of their own life, their own little plots." Then Adaline heard him smile in the sound of his voice: "They are free to celebrate as they wish and to be lazy, which is another kind of resistance. This is why Padre came to Abiquiú. The vicar, Lamy, will blame him if he finds out, but Padre only does it to reassure the people that they should take heart. He wants them to know he understands their suffering. He is too old for the trial of the scourge, as you saw, but just walking in the procession is also political, coming out of his love."

When they drew closer to El Rito, they came abreast of a man and woman standing alone near the trail. Behind them was a small house with a light in a window. The man invited Pablo and Adaline to spend the night. He had a stable, he said, where they could sleep and keep their animals. Pablo responded that they were grateful, but they should go on because they were expected at dawn. When they parted ways, Pablo told Adaline, "We should stop where we did before to let our animals rest. I thought it would take too long back there at that house." Just beyond the town, they stopped, taking care to hobble their animals. Pablo slipped his Hawken free of its scabbard. "We have come so far without trouble."

They ate more tortillas with meat, beans, and mole and drank the tea. Pablo had taken down the extra horse blanket and spread it on the ground. They lay close, Pablo on his back and she, once she had taken her Colt and placed it on the ground above her head, lay on her side, facing him, and they covered themselves with the two ponchos. She watched him searching the stars. "We have an hour," he said.

She decided he had made that determination by how the moon was positioned relative to the constellations. She put her hand under his shirt and ran it up to the smoothness of his ribs.

"¡Ten cuidado!"

"Te amo," she said.

"Sí, lo sé," he said.

They were still for a few minutes, and then he turned and embraced her, pressing his lips to her. She felt the scars on his cheek and also felt his fiery hardness beneath his trousers. She would gladly have opened herself for him, but he pulled back, still holding her arm with one hand. "We should not do this thing. Your father would not forgive me."

She asked a question she knew was wrong. "How would he know?"

After another moment, he said, "Do you want to lie to him?"

"You are right," she said. She felt deeply uneasy, yet her desire for Pablo had increased. "I might lie to almost anyone but not to him. And not to you, either."

"Bueno."

"When will we be together?"

"Some day, perhaps."

She fell asleep. Her dreams shimmered with all they had shared.

When she awoke she found him crouched beside her and holding the reins of their mounts. It seemed no time had passed.

"Now we should go," he said.

They rode eastward out of El Rito, toward the river. They would descend into the gorge and cross where they had come before. Pablo again insisted that first they proceed halfway in order to secure permission for the crossing from the river. Once they had done that they rode up the other side and paused, whereupon he reached out and took her hand, passing something into it. She felt his fingers curl against hers. She opened her hand and saw a small carved wooden crucifix with the twisted form of the Cristo impaled upon it. She gazed at Pablo, then secured the crucifix in her pocket. They kept on, making their way past the Hacienda Martínez and to the paseo just as the sun began to radiate from behind the Sangre de Cristos.

No me vayan a olvidar.

Chapter 11

As she rode up the paseo with Pablo at first light and approached the house, she saw Nicanor, returning from the privy. Her heart sank. She knew that if Nicanor were here, so too were the others. She watched as Nicanor passed inside, going by the back door, but not before he looked at her and raised his hand. From the chimney a narrow trail of smoke emerged. Pablo looked across at her, the exchange by their eyes struck with portent. He nudged his mule near, reached out, and touched her hand. Then he nodded and rode away. Adaline pulled Hawk up and watched his form diminish until it disappeared over the crest of the paseo, going toward the Taos Pueblo.

She led Hawk into the corral, first removing the saddle and bridle. She fetched him a swatch of grass and brushed him down, going slowly through these motions as if they were ceremonial. Stepping out to the paseo again, she looked northward. A cart pulled by a burro appeared and advanced toward the house, but there was no sign of Pablo. She walked to the house and went inside, passing Teresina and Juan, who were still wrapped in their night covers. She found Josefa breaking sticks into a fire and beside her Nicanor, who gave Adaline a long look.

Had he spoken to Josefa? Had he told her? Or had he said nothing? And did it matter?

"Buenos, chica," Josefa said.

By the firmness of Josefa's tone, Adaline realized she could no more lie to her than to her father. She said, "I've been to Abiquiú." Josefa glanced at her with a look that showed as much curiosity as judgment. "Sola? Alone? So far?"

Adaline was aware that Josefa knew about her journeys to the Hacienda Martinéz. She probably knew about Pablo, as well. Josefa had a way of knowing things. Adaline said simply, "Nothing happened. To me, I mean. Nothing at all."

"Bien." That was all. Josefa said they would have to wait until her father returned to speak further on the subject, but perhaps she should keep her riding near this part of the pueblo.

•

A week later, a traveler called out to the house from the road. When Josefa emerged, he dismounted, removed his hat, and held it before him. His boots and leggings were caked with mud, as was his horse, muddy from hock to shoulder. His face was grizzled with beard, and under his coat he wore a bandolier with silver studs that sparked in the sunlight. Adaline had followed Josefa out and observed the deference the man displayed in Josefa's presence. He introduced himself as Henry Mercure. He said he'd encountered Kit and his party at Fort Saint Vrain on Crow Creek. Kit had asked him to tell the señora they were having a good hunt and that soon they would head south to home.

"He might be on his way right now," the man said.

Josefa offered him food, but Mercure nodded toward the paseo where another rider and two mule-drawn wagons awaited him and thanked Josefa, saying they had people expecting their arrival down at the Río Baja. He said he hoped to join Kit and Lucien Maxwell on a sheep drive. Perhaps he could stop over then.

Josefa thanked him for his trouble. Beneath her composure, Adaline saw a flickering of emotion. She had learned to read the gradients of Josefa's feelings, revealed by slight movement at the edge of her lips and subtle shading of eye and brow. Only her smile, when she was pleased or amused, could completely alter her reserved expression.

Now surely she must have felt relief, after what had been stoic acceptance when Kit left, and concern during the interim, which had come to be shared by others once they learned she was pregnant again.

Mercure replaced his hat. His spurs rang as he remounted and he nodded at Adaline, causing her to stare at the ground. He set off toward the paseo.

And now the smile. Josefa suddenly smiled openly. "Bueno. It is good."

"He'll be home by May, then. And the others? Most will go to the Rayado?"

"Sí."

"Louis, too?"

"Sí. Perhaps."

"Then they'll go on the sheep drive?"

Josefa shrugged, "Sí, to California. Por dinero. I wish they would not, but the dinero will supply the rancho."

And when her father did come, Adaline found herself suddenly filled with trepidation. His first morning home she went out early to the front of the house. She found him there and stopped beside him, standing while he lit his pipe.

Finally, she asked, "Did you have a good hunt?"

"A fine hunt, Twister."

"We missed you." Saying that, her mind flew off into a wild dissonance. Surely, he'd been missed, and if he'd been here, she thought perhaps she would never have gone off as she had. But as soon as her thoughts ran that direction, she saw that it was a falsehood at its root, a cover up. She felt evermore warring emotions: her passion for Pablo, the deep, gnawing sadness, and yet her fear of displeasing her father.

"Chipita was worried for you," he said. "She says you took to riding about. On Easter you were gone for so long, way into the night. This is a hard country for a young woman."

She said, "Yes, I should have told Josefa where I was going."

He scrutinized her and what he saw, as she imagined it, were all manner of signs, bits of things, small broken things like the shards in the ruin, Poshuouinge, shallow depressions and incisions, and nearly invisible imprints only he could see. She saw the sharpness of curiosity in his face. "And going to Abiquiú. Why Abiquiú?"

He was interested in these things. Behaviors. Customs. The strangeness of the night came vividly back to her, the resplendence of the journey, crossing the river, Cerro Perdernal in the distance, what Pablo said about the Genizaro, the procession, the figure of La Muerte, the man lashed to the cross, Padre Antonio's thunderous voice, and the din of the Tenebrae. What new detail her father might have added hung in the air between them.

"I heard Padre Antonio was there."

Remembering how Pablo had explained it, she said, "He cares for his people."

Kit drew on his pipe and looked closely at her. "Could be, Twister. You were in the company of Pablo Morales, Chipita says."

The two carts could be heard rumbling nearer, and he looked past her toward the paseo. The carts rolled by, their wooden wheels creaking against the cobblestone. As they were loaded with goods, they incited in Adaline a flashing thought of the carts pulled by men in Abiquiú. These two were pulled by burros, driven by two women in long skirts and black shawls, one of whom tapped her burro with a stick.

Finally, she said, "That is true." She yearned to explain again that nothing untoward had happened, no transgression, no violation in fact. Her father should understand that and believe her, just as he would know the fascinations of a place like Abiquiú, but she could not bring herself to say it to him. She was silenced by the taboo against speaking of such a thing to her father. She felt encircled and felt next a velvet hammer descending, deposited in the hand of another.

"Chipita will speak of this to you," he said.

●

Three days later, her father came up to the corral to fetch his horse and a pack mule. He loaded the mule with the last of the beaver pelts, which he meant to sell in Santa Fé. He paused to watch while she rode Ghost in a clearing above the corral. She had a halter and a blanket on the mule, and kept it in tight figure eights. When she returned, he said, "That mule takes well to gentling."

She said, "Yes."

He mounted his horse and went on his way, not mentioning her journey to Abiquiú, nor Louis who had gone first over to the Rayado and had yet to come down, nor of what otherwise awaited her. She ached for Pablo. She had seen him once. The model of composure, he told her that Padre Antonio was sending him to Durango to complete his novitiate under Bishop Zubiria.

The next evening, she was tending to the animals when Josefa called her from the back of the house, bidding her to come inside when she was finished. She found Josefa in the room where she and Kit slept and was startled to see Lupe, too, come up once again from Doña Apolonia's house and crouched before the hearth. Lupe had an uncommon aspect to her face—her hawk nose and eyes like pokers surrounded by an other-worldly glow. Her face twisted into a smile as she glanced up. Confused, Adaline hovered at the lintel of the bedroom. Josefa turned lightly on her toes. She paused, a white dress with blue satin trim draped over one arm, and beckoned for Adaline to come in.

Adaline stepped inside and Josefa unfurled the dress and held it up against her. "Hold it there," Josefa said, touching Adaline's shoulders. Adaline did so. Josefa smoothed the dress around Adaline's ribs and ran her hands down Adaline's arms. "Here it would fit," she said. She stepped back to appraise Adaline, frowning. "It is as I thought. We are much the same." She looked down where several inches of the dress's hemline lay crumpled around Adaline's moccasins. "Except there." She laughed, then put her hands on her expanded belly. "And here just now." She took the dress away and called to Lupe, who entered the room. In a state of consternation, Adaline had not moved. "We will try it," Josefa said. "Your dress. Take it off."

Adaline pulled her pinafore over her head. Beneath the pinafore were her canvas trousers and a blouse that had a patch on the side which she'd sewn on. She was embarrassed by the patch, by her soiled moccasins, which she also removed at Josefa's bidding, and then by her calloused feet. All business, now, but leaving the trousers alone, Josefa lifted the dress over Adaline's head. Adaline wriggled into it and looked down at the expanse of white linen. The blue borders felt smooth against her arms. It was a wondrous thing.

Josefa stood back to survey her, frowning and smiling faintly at the same time. "Bueno," she said. She stepped forward, tested the fit of the shoulders, then walked behind Adaline. Adaline felt Josefa's fingers manipulating the fastens up her spine until the dress wrapped snug around her neck, and then Josefa drew a stool out from under the small table and spoke to Lupe. Lupe produced a sewing box. Josefa told Adaline to stand on the stool, and when she complied Josefa arranged the hem of the dress, draping it over the stool, then straightened and gazed into Adaline's eyes, again smiling faintly, which unnerved Adaline. "So different, you are," Josefa said. "So changed from when you first came to the Rayado."

Lupe produced a pin cushion and chalk and knelt on the floor. Adaline could smell the odor of earth on her. Josefa knelt beside her. The two women murmured as they worked, and Adaline marveled at their hands guiding the hem of the dress in concert, Josefa's two delicate ones, and Lupe's distressed ones, the one of Lupe's like a wing with its skin-covered bone above the wrist, the fingers fused together, yet still deft in its unlikely contortions as it secured the hem. Adaline felt hopelessly out of place atop the stool, like a dark animal.

The two women moved around her, marking with the chalk and inserting pins in place for shortening the dress. Adaline inhaled deeply and looked around the room, luminous in the evening light that flooded through a west window. The walls were like the walls of the kitchen and sitting room where Adaline slept, finished with the tierra blanca, the fine plaster of diatomaceous earth that elicited an enchanting white the hue of pearls. The four poster bed stood before her, the polished table with two straight-backed chairs, a dresser with a mirror against a far wall, and next to it on the floor a rolled-up buffalo robe and her father's weathered bag and a small heap of disparate articles—deeply soiled shin-high moccasins, a braided rawhide quirt, and a revolver. His Hawken with its scarred-up stock leaned against the wall in a corner. His things, the evidence of his person in this room, seemed like a seasoning of wildness.

Josefa stood up and stepped back. Lupe followed. Josefa came forward and pulled the dress at Adaline's shoulders, testing the fit. She exchanged words in Spanish with Lupe. Lupe murmured and gestured with her bony wing, and Adaline caught a waft of her again, the rankness of fetid earth warring with the sweetness of Josefa. Lupe's black eyes were furtive, and her gnarled form hunched up and tiny. Adaline glimpsed her good hand, marred with cuts, and it occurred to her that Lupe must have performed her penance, crawling to the chapel devoted to Guadalupe. She remembered what Pablo had said, that Lupe was afraid of her. She thought Lupe looked akin to La Muerte, protuberant toes, sharp nose, fused bones for a hand, her hair frazzled like corn silk, a living relic.

Again Josefa spoke to Lupe, and suddenly Lupe left the room. Josefa turned to Adaline: "We will change this for you," she said. "It is my wedding dress."

"Oh," Adaline said, startled. She looked down, again marveling at the fine linen and the satin that ran along the seams. "You are kind to me," she said.

"My mother had it made for me. It is only for you to wear for the ceremony."

Adaline felt a flush race to her neck, which came from embarrassment that what she'd said might have suggested she thought the dress was being given to her. She didn't think that, had not. Josefa was behind her, now, undoing the fastens. Adaline pulled the dress off over her head and carefully laid it out on the bed. She put on her patched blouse and threadbare pinafore over the canvas trousers and found Josefa seated in one of the chairs at the table.

"Sit with me."

Adaline sat.

On the table between them were three votive candles, unlit, and a set of silver earrings and a cross on a chain. Next to the jewelry rested a small wooden case. "Señor Simmons is a good man," Josefa said. "He will care for you. It is decided. Your father and I had wished to give you time to find yourself here."

Adaline sat poised with her hands in her lap, but now that the inevitable had been spoken, and so directly, she felt an inward quaking. Her eyes went again to the heap of her father's things in the corner and found herself wishing desperately for their solace—the quirt, bag, the guns, the buffalo robe. She brought her eyes back to Josefa. It occurred to her that just now Josefa seemed not unlike her mother, Doña Apolonia. Josefa said, "Love can be studied and learned like so much else in the world we are given to."

Adaline said, "But what if I have learned to love another." She said this not to challenge Josefa, but in hopes she would understand the matter.

A smile played at the lips of Josefa. "It is not for the best."

Josefa's face softened and Adaline wondered whether or not she had needed to learn to love her husband. It seemed so unlikely that one would not love Kit Carson. How could one not love him? As she thought that, the fatefulness, the dust devil skittering across the desert, her bag of lizards yawning open and the creatures scattering willy-nilly, her regard for Louis transformed not into the promise of something magical but into into a dread of the future.

"It will not do," Josefa said. "The future for you is in an Americano, not a poor Indio. Not in your friend, Pablo Morales."

Adaline's eyes darted away and back. "Genizaro," she said.

Josefa smiled. "Sí, bueno. He is unusual, I hear." Her voice became firm. "But he will become one of Padre Antonio's seminarians. He will not do for you."

Tears came to Adaline's eyes. She looked down at her hands. "I am sorry."

"I, too, am sorry for you. But we speak of this now. Afterward we will not again. Only your papá and I know how long you were gone into the night."

The mortification nearly overwhelmed her. "Nothing happened," she said again, fervently wanting Josefa to believe her. "Nothing. Nothing at all."

"Bueno . . . that is good. Señor Simmons is coming down. He will join us on Sunday after mass. Your . . . how do you say it? ¿Esponsales? Your betrothal will be announced."

Adaline put her hands on the table and stared at them. Josefa placed her hands over Adaline's hands. Josefa's hands were cool. Then Josefa gathered up the chain with the cross and the earrings, which she passed to Adaline. "Those were my great-grandmother's, my grandmother's, then my mother's, and finally given to me. They are from the days the Vigils first came to this country. You have no mother and do not know of your grandmother. You have no one among your ancestors, so these are for you to keep." She slid the wooden case into the center of the table and opened it. An herbal aroma rose to Adaline's nose. "And these, as well."

The case had compartments in which were positioned several small packets and two glass vials. Each had a label with a name written out in Spanish:

Cardo, Aquilea, Liquen, Salvia . . .

Josefa touched each in turn, first the packets, saying the names and what they would remedy. She removed the two glass vials and set them on the table. She touched one and said, "Lechecho. It is what the Americanos call milkweed. It has a juice in its stem that looks like milk. You will know it, no?" When Adaline nodded, Josefa went on: "Por intervenciónes." She paused, looking straight at Adaline. "And this . . ." She touched the second vial. "Pasquaflora. Anticonceptivo. Aborto. Do you understand?"

Adaline nodded, listening intently now.

Josefa touched the vial that contained pasquaflora. "But if you do this, do not tell him. Never. And if you do use it, be sure you have a woman nearby whom you trust. And it is the same if you become pregnant. Be careful." She told Adaline about the moon and the cycles and how the times when her desire was the greatest, as it had been, Adaline knew, when she lay down with Pablo, were the times to avoid until she was ready, how she was most vulnerable when she was most willing. "With that, and with these," she said, touching the two vials again, "you are entrusting your life. Only a rare man would be of help. Understand?"

"Yes." Adaline was certain Josefa had lost at least one other child in addition to the one-year-old Charles. Now, she was pregnant again. Adaline felt a rush of gratitude for Josefa's telling her what she'd only known before in the most approximate way, taking instruction from her own body and her fear, since her Aunt Mary Ann had never troubled to tell her. She also had a sudden impulse to wish Josefa well and to tell her she would pray for her and her infant. She leaned forward and did that.

"Gracias, chica." Josefa gestured with her hand, opening it and passing it between them. "Here you would have me. Or even Lupe. At the Rayado you might have Señor Maxwell's Luz or Jesus's DeLaguna. Of course, it will not happen so soon. But listen now, wherever you are, you must find someone."

Adaline was listening. She nodded.

"Your father will take sheep to California in winter. Señor Simmons will go, and he intends to stay in California, I believe. We will miss you."

•

Several months later it came to be what Adaline would see as one of the several retrogrades in her life, everything going contrary to where she wanted it and she left to reckon with the consequences. The emanation of Louis as he would become later on that year, his form in the window, darker than dark itself, crazed with drink, blocking out the gaslights in Sacramento, and before that his looming in the tent on the trail to Sacramento, before that the sweetness on his breath in the Taos rooming house after her wedding, the drink, her torn chemise, and before that on the trail from Missouri west, him watching her, and, first, the primogeniture at the outset, him standing next to her father in front of Susan's parents' house after Susan's marriage, his dark eyes slanting toward her, then turning to her father. She would have to go clear back to that time when it was not evident that Louis's pleasure was not for her but rather for pleasing her father. And her acquiescence, too, was for her father. Now, Josefa's intercession perpetuating this service was for her father, as well.

On her wedding day, she walked down the paseo to the church in the company of her father, Josefa, Lupe, and the children. When they entered the sanctuary and took their turn toward the aisle that would lead to the altar, her eyes moved instinctively to the figure in the back of the room. Her mind did not follow at first. Dazed as she was by what was happening, she did not think to do it. Her eyes simply went there and found Pablo, who had come up to Taos on a respite from Durango and the bishop there. Then her mind went, too. He gazed evenly at her, and she believed the light came into his eyes from the other thing that he saw, the whole puzzle of their fractured destiny. As she made her turn into the aisle, she found herself silently forming the words: "Amor mio." Suddenly, she was deeply embarrassed by the white and blue dress she wore, so great was its contrast to how she saw him in his white canvas pants, the coarsely woven poncho, the stains on his hands. The flush rose to her brow, what would be taken by others as a flush for her wedding. She looked fiercely down at her feet as they made their way past the pew where the Vigils and Jaramillos sat, including the Doña, who cast her eyes over Adaline and down the dress with, as Adaline framed it, disdain.

When Louis came to her side, he tipped his head back to look at her. He was freshly shaven. His hair had been cut close. She looked away and stared at her feet. It was either that, look down at her feet, or at the rail before her, or up at the padre who was not Padre Antonio but one of the vicar's padres sent up by Machebeuf to stand in for Padre Antonio, who in the meantime had traveled down to Santa Fé. As the ceremony went on, she came more and more to stare fixedly at this padre as he delivered the prayers, incantations, and scripture in French, and finally the homily in French, too, but with a few Spanish words thrown in. She grew increasingly transfixed by his language, which, delivered in a thin voice, became more and more laughable, a cacophonous, clown's façade. She listened and thought of Padre Antonio, the voice that contained all the beauty of the hard rock country, its rise to a sensual cry against the vastness and loneliness of this place, a howling wolf in it, and the pain it carried bespeaking the agony she felt for the figure in the back of the sanctuary.

Chapter 12

EARLY IN THE WINTER OF 1853, Kit secured Josefa and the children in Taos and rode to the Rio Abajo where he and Lucien Maxwell negotiated with Mexican hacendados for the purchase of ten thousand sheep. A third partner, John Hatcher, had already set out for the California gold fields, and Kit left the Rio Abajo a week ahead of Maxwell. Divided into its three components—Hatcher's, Kit's, and Maxwell's, with whom Kit's old friend, Tom Boggs, was traveling, and whose wife, Romulda, would help to watch over Josefa and her babe in arms, William, named for William Bent—the drive would be the second of its kind from the Territory. The first had been led the year before by Dick Wooten, thus demonstrating that such a journey was possible and notching up the American perception of how the continent might be crossed, with what, and from where. Now, meat on the hoof migrated out of the southern extreme of New Mexico Territory.

Wooten had gone by the desert and his account of the condition of his stock by the time he arrived led Kit to urge a more leisurely route north from the Rayado along the east slope of the Rockies to Fort Laramie at the confluence of the Laramie and Platte Rivers. With everything lensed in upon thaw, river flow, grass, and the conjectured levels of tribal animosity (wise to keep clear of the Blackfeet, Gros Ventre, Crow, and Cheyenne), spring forage would be sought in the watersheds on the western edge of the Great Plains. From Fort Laramie they'd stay with the forage as they came through South Pass, nearly to the Snake River, and down the California Trail to the high country crossing south of what was written on Frémont's maps as Mount Tsashtl, and along the valley to Sacramento where the sheep would be sold. Finally, they would stop over in San Francisco, what lingered in Kit and Lucien Maxwell's memory from their days with Frémont as a scattering of seashore shacks called Yerba Buena—good grass.

The whole of the journey to Sacramento would be two thousand miles. If the sheep were herded ten miles a day, laying up at times and at other times pressing hard, it would take better than two hundred days. Kit was accompanied by two sheep men who had settled in New Mexico, a Spaniard named Bernavette, and the French Canadian, Mercure, who months ago had ventured by the Taos house and reported to Josefa from Kit's hunting party. A few Mexican herders were also with them, and a couple of Basque herders traveled with Maxwell. In the company of Bernavette was another Spaniard, Don Ramón de Zumalacárregui, a man of learning who was inquiring into the American West, and who came to favor Adaline with his knowledge.

Kit's flock was divided into three bands with Kit leading the first and Bernavette and Mercure the second and third. When the first band reached the Rayado where Louis and Adaline were waiting, the sheep spread across the meadow before the settlement. Kit, his several Mexican herders, a cook and his supply wagon, and Louis and Adaline set out just as the second band of sheep caught up. Adaline rode Hawk and at times she rode Ghost, for she had succeeded in gentling the mule that Louis had relinquished to her. She seemed a woman, now, fully a woman despite her sixteen years, and she had the hardness of eye, the watchfulness, and the wary sense of self that came with full womanhood. She studied Josefa's advice and avoided heartache by thinking as little as possible of Pablo.

Within two weeks they arrived at the confluence of the Purgatoire and Arkansas Rivers where they successfully forded the sheep. They set up camp, well in sight of the singed walls of Bent's Old Fort, which stood crippled above the flats. A fire was started and the first shift of lookouts posted. Adaline pitched her and Louis's tent and retrieved her Frémont maps from her trunk, which was stored in the cook's wagon, and pored over them. Louis followed her, bending in and looking down at what she scrutinized—the mappings of Smith's Fork, Thomas's Fork, Tullich's Fork, Beer Spring, and the Port Neuf River that flowed south from Fort Hall where her father had told her she'd been born.

He said, "They ain't much lest you need them, which ain't likely with your pa in this company. Ain't it just dreaming you're doing, looking at them maps?"

She said simply, "I like the dreams."

Once he closed the flap of the tent and moved off, she looked down at the map again, running her eyes along the delicately etched ridge lines to Fort Hall. She thought about the people trekking westward, her father running sheep to stake his outpost, Louis with his store of black powder and his intentions of staying in California and using the powder to find gold. Wasn't all of that dreaming? Her own was a familiar deep dreaming that moved backwards. What she knew of the trail the sheep drive would follow seemed to track her life back to when memory was little more than a patchwork. In this dreaming she ever so slowly inhaled the enigma of who she'd been before she came to the earth.

Early the next day, the sheep Adaline was watching ventured into a marsh between the fort and river where all at once they ran the risk of foundering. She and the Mexican pastore her father had partnered her with, an older man named Juan, worked the sheep back toward the Old Fort. She pleasured in the dogs the pastores had brought along—Juan's sharp-nosed fyce that nipped at the sheep's heels and ranged suddenly back and forth like a lightening bolt and also the larger ones spread out over the three bands and used as guards. Juan's fyce worried the sheep alongside a wall of the fort, causing them to raise a half-smothered bleating, then abruptly a number of them burst through a breach in the wall.

Juan remained with the sheep on the outside of the wall and gestured to Adaline to chase the others, but once inside she stopped and looked about at the strewn scraps of iron, the charred timbers, barrel hoops, staves, scorched hemp sacks, and in the center of the courtyard the remains of a fur press, and spilled trade beads in swirls, bright as constellations against the dirt. She was seeing the place the Cheyenne blamed for their contagion and would not enter, yet some other tribe had come to ransack the detritus after the fort burned, thus engaging in what Frankie had called "uncodified trade," the act of giving value to what was considered valueless. Adaline slipped down from Hawk and moved behind the sheep, pushing them out through what had been a gateway, and there stopped and stood still for a second time, looking about. First, it had been the scent of clay that emanated from the rained-on adobe, the odor of the nearby marsh, and the things cast about that got her attention. Now, it was the sight of the mysterious circles of stone on the ground, one after another of them arranged in lines, and then she remembered that the stones had once held down the outer hems of tipis. There were also holes from pins. There'd been a village mounted just outside the fort. A scrap of memory stitched itself together as if a quill of scattered beads were gathered. She had indeed been here before. She turned and looked through the gateway. She'd been at this very spot with the sun to her left sliding upward behind the ground fog.

She remembered a Cheyenne woman. She remembered being scolded and remembered the tipi, the robe on the ground where she lay with her sister, and the flap closing to make darkness, or closing behind when she was sent out. She recalled the smoke swirling from the tipis, the Cheyenne people, the men in the fort, and a black woman named Charlotte Green in the kitchen lifting the iron pans atop a stove, wagons trundling in and out, horsemen arriving with pack animals, travois, provisions, the racket of it all, the hooves, the creaking, the shouts. She remembered wondering where her father was. She remembered struggling to carry her sister, and sometimes Charlotte coming out and lifting her sister high and her sister kicking with delight. Charlotte took the two of them into the kitchen, which smelled of sizzling meat and boiling beans. Charlotte would laugh and sit her and her sister down and give them food.

She stood, looking toward where the kitchen had been, and then she heard Juan's voice. "Hola! Adalina!"

He gestured to her to look to the side where her sheep were making for the marsh again. She swung up on Hawk and rode along the wall, turning the sheep back to the gateway. Her sheep merged with Juan's, veering away from the fort and river.

"Que pasa?" Juan asked when they came alongside each other.

"I've been here before."

Juan wore a broad hat, a red bandana, and his chin was grizzled to silver. "Es verdad?"

"When I was little," she said.

•

The company followed a trail beside a creek, the Fontaine-qui-bouille. The three bands moved at varying paces and at differing distances from each other according to the forage. From behind the clouds, the Rocky Mountains shouldered in and out of sight, these, the same mountains Adaline had seen from a distance when she'd journeyed along the Santa Fé Trail. In their nearer proximity, they were huge and jagged with snow-filled chutes. Frémont had written that he'd forayed up into the mountains in search of the source of the Fontaine-qui-bouille and had found an opening below a rock formation from which the torrent exploded. The water was charged with gaseous effervescence, and Frémont extolled its taste, comparing it to the Seltzer Springs of the Grand Duchy of Nassau, although just what that was evaded Adaline.

She looked at the rocks that glimmered through the crystalline waters of the creek—granite, tumbled-down limestone, quartz, agate. The Spaniard who accompanied Bernavette, Don Rámon, had taken to passing between Kit's and Bernavette's bands. He came up to her. A gangly man, everything about him was longer than it seemed it should have been, even his face. He wore a flat brimmed hat, a black frock coat, and rode an elaborately outfitted piebald horse, the riggings, rings, and buckles of its saddle ornamented with silver inlays. He led a mule, from the aparejo of which he extracted a mallet, then he found a rock and chipped at it, showing her bits that exhibited imprints etched upon them. "Fossils," he said.

Adaline remembered that Frémont had written of them.

"They are left on the sedimentary rocks," Don Rámon said. "Mollusks or univalves. Sea plants, too." He stood and spread his arms like a great heron about to take flight. "They were left here thousands of years ago beneath the sea that once filled the lowlands." He leaned toward her. "I've seen you reading. I don't suppose you know Jean-Baptiste Lamarck. The transmutation of species? Or Charles Darwin's writings on marine invertebrates?"

"No, I haven't." Adaline had no idea what he was referring to, but she countered the way he'd put his question with, "But I have my John Frémont."

"So you do. I have seen you with him." Don Rámon chuckled. "And a fine guide he is."

He let her use his mallet to break off pieces of fossil for herself, which she carted to her trunk in the cook's wagon. Just then, Louis came up from behind, saying, "It's rocks, now, is it? Ain't we got enough of them underfoot?"

She showed him the etchings of ancient stems and leaves, the shells. "From thousands of years ago," she said. "There was a sea here."

"A sea, you say?" He touched a fossil with his fingers, then looked toward Don Rámon, who was returning his mallet to his mule. "The Spaniard says that now, does he?"

•

The weather grew changeable as the season passed spring equinox. On occasion, the ground was dusted with snow and at other times turned to mud. The creeks ran high. Adaline customarily kept to the rear of the sheep with Juan, riding drag behind the trailing edge of the band that undulated through the swales. At intervals, she saw her father depart from point, ride straight into the foothills or the other way, eastward, toward the flats. He sought the fords and gauged the grass and what or who might lie ahead.

The last night that the company camped near the Fontaine-qui-bouille, the men gathered around the fire to feast on a doe one of the pastores had shot. Pinpricks of torches the watch had lit marked the flock's compass, and from it issued a soft rumbling sound like a wide river flowing over stones. Hundreds of sheep were edging forward and pulling the grass from the ground. The bark of a guard dog might be heard in the distance, as might the low wailing of wolves, and an obligato draped by the coyotes from the hills. Among them was the yowling of feral dogs, too, escaped Indian dogs, and dogs loosed from the immigrant trains.

Adaline heard her father announce that for the time being most of the tribes had moved to the east and south after buffalo. He said the feral dogs were what the sheepmen needed to watch for. They might lure away the pastores's dogs. They were bloodthirsty killers, unafraid of men. "Them dogs be the shadow of trouble among peoples, now, ganging up in farrago," he said, then he smiled a little. "Though they ain't bad eating if you're hungry enough."

"Not much is, if you're that hungry," Louis said.

Adaline had taken a hunk of meat from the fire. She had beans on her plate and biscuits prepared in an iron oven. She ripped away savory ribbons of meat with her teeth and wiped her fingers on her trousers. The moon rose from the east, silvery amongst lenticular clouds.

As often as not, either Bernavette or Mercure were here at the fire, and Don Rámon regularly joined them. On other nights, he'd asked about Kit's associations from his trapping days: Jim Bridger, Ewing Young, the Sublettes, William New, who'd been killed by the Apaches. Referring to the time Kit had been in the service of Frémont, Don Rámon had asked about the mutilations wrought by the Klamaths and in return the scores of Klamaths killed after Basil Lajeunesse was found with a Klamath hatchet buried in his skull. What about Kit's trek through the desert at night on his bare feet to San Diego, seeking reinforcements for Frémont's men who were surrounded by the Mexican army? These were among Don Rámon's many questions that Kit sometimes answered cautiously, seemingly wishing to deflect attention, at other times not answering at all. On this night, Don Rámon asked, "It was from about here, Señor Carson, that you awaited Señor Maxwell, was it not? But doubting his arrival, your captain sent you down to Bent's Fort for provisions?"

The other men present—Bernavette, Louis, and a pastore or two—looked over at Kit. Adaline edged nearer the fire alongside Louis. The incident, Adaline knew from her Frémont, came during the second expedition.

"In July of forty-three," Kit said. "But from further south on the crick."

"And from where we camped a few nights ago," Don Rámon said. "Your captain journeyed to explore the headwaters, seeking the springs? Was he searching out a suitable course for the railroad then, as he did later in these mountains?"

Don Rámon's beard heightened his appearance of mystic elongation. Adaline remembered her father saying they'd have "to fold the man up and peg him down if a need arose to take cover." Now, he said "I heard he done that up to the ridges. I myself had mules for him and didn't catch up until Saint Vrain's Fort. More'n once I herded mules toward Fort Laramie to sell to the emigrants, the last time in 1850. But the railway survey come afore that."

"Ah, I see, Señor Carson. Was Bill Williams with you then?"

Kit paused, then he said, "He come along in forty-five, joining up with us at Old Pueblo, since he knew them mountains."

"And your captain's winter survey of 1848? Bill Williams guided then, did he not?" Don Rámon said. "They were stranded in the snow. Men died. There were reports that a portion of the party that survived did so by cannibalizing the others."

The silence of the men deepened as they looked to Kit. Though not written, Adaline nevertheless knew this story, how the ill-advised search for a pass in the Rockies on which to build a railroad ended with the party trapped in the snow, and since others, including her father, had declined to guide the venture, Frémont had engaged Bill Williams. Word had it that over a hundred animals died, men starved, and a small fortune in bullion that Frémont was to deliver to California was lost. The party separated into two and Frémont's group escaped with the aid of Alexis Godey, who went up after them, and Frémont recovered in Kit and Josefa's Taos house, while the men left in the mountains, including Williams, cannibalized the dead to survive. The following spring Williams ventured back, looking for the lost treasure and was killed by the Utes.

Kit said, "In starving times no man walked a trail ahead of old Bill." He bent to tap out his pipe on a stone. "Best see to the mounts." Without another word, he walked toward where the horses and mules were picketed, skirting the edge of the sheep. Adaline looked after him, his shoulders catching the firelight as he went, then she looked back at Don Rámon, whose eyes looked harrowed. Louis had told her he'd been caught up in a war in his country, that he'd lost two sons to it. The Spanish queen had marked him by putting a death warrant on his head.

•

In the following days the company headed toward Vermillion Creek, the Crow, and further yet along the South Platte toward Fort Saint Vrain, the three bands moving at varying paces according to the forage. If Don Rámon encountered Adaline fetching firewood, he began offering to help carry her load. Adaline always declined. At other times he rode along beside her, expostulating about the North American journeys taken centuries before by his countrymen, Hernando de Soto, Hernán Cortés, Vasco Núñez de Balboa, or Cabeza de Vaca. Adaline knew nothing of these men. Don Rámon also told her about Rousseau, the philosopher, who believed in what he called the "natural man" and in the rightness of a return to nature.

"Take your father," he said. On this day, she was riding drag on her band and he had coaxed his piebald and mule beside her. "He has none of the slavish vices which are taught by civilization. Servility, envy, greed, contempt, and arrogance. Frémont, who himself was something of an outlander, saw this in him."

Adaline stared intently at her father who rode far ahead, slouched low on his horse and making his way toward the South Platte.

Don Rámon wished to visit the Yellow Stone country, and he clung to this hope, though others reminded him that they would not journey so far north. He told her he'd read that in the Yellow Stone wild game—buffalo, elk, deer, antelope—formed vast herds. He said it had "infernal regions" where there were tracts of pure white salt, molten earth so hot it boiled, sulphurous steam hissing from within, and springs emitting a black combustible oil which if lit would burn until doomsday. Don Rámon's eyes shone and he took on a jittery smile, revealing squared-off teeth behind his whiskers. "It is said that in places it's like Hell."

One evening several days later, Adaline watched as he disappeared into a canyon on his horse, leading his mule. Louis, who just then was riding beside her, chilled her by saying, "He's going to provoke something before he's done. Watch out."

They pushed on close to the Platte, whereupon a party of Utes showed up in their camp. With them was a chief named Ka-ni-ache whose face was broad and whose skin seemed as soft as dust. The Utes sat around a fire with Kit, Louis, Bernavette, and Mercure. Don Rámon was also there. Adaline was some distance away, standing with Juan and another of the pastores. A pipe was smoked while Kit and Ka-ni-ache conversed in pidgin English, Spanish and some Ute. Kit asked about the Cheyenne and Arapaho. Ka-ni-ache indicated that in the spring the buffalo began to move east to new grass. He believed the Cheyenne, or Tsetschestahase, had gone that way to hunt. Perhaps the Arapaho had gone there, too.

The Tsetschestahase were hungry, he said, and had the sickness, the pox, and the bad belly the white men called cholera. They were angry that the big treaty at Fort Laramie of two years before had not been honored. So, too, Ka-ni-ache said, were the Crow and Gros

Ventre, Sioux, Arikara, and Shoshone. The agreed-to hunting ground that they were to keep as their own was now overrun with Americans killing the buffalo, cutting the trees, and spoiling the water. His people were hungry. On the other side of the mountains, the Wasatch and the Mormons were at war with the Ute bands, as were the Jicarillas coming up from the south, and even the Comanches. "The river of wagons is ever widening," Ka-ni-ache added. "My people are dancing the Nanissáanah, the Sun Dance. Soon they will dance the Cry Down. There will be trouble."

They were quiet for a time, passing the pipe, then Ka-ni-ache said, "I see you have ovejas." He looked toward the valley where the sheep had been secured for the night, the herd stretching into the hills bounding the valley and making their rumbling sound as they ate. "I have never seen so many."

"And more behind," Kit said. "But we will pass."

"They eat the grass down to the earth," Ka-ni-ache said. "What do they not eat? What will replace the grass? It will give no seed. The buffalo and antelope and other creatures will travel away. Those other vacas your people bring eat the grass, too, but not down to the root. Soon there will be nothing."

"I cannot speak for the others," Kit said. "Only for this company. We will pass by and never come again in this way."

Ka-ni-ache said, "Your word has been good. But others come in all kinds. Many lie. You are here now and that means others will be here. We know the grass will not last forever. It can disappear, just as the cottonwoods along the rivers disappear, as the buffalo are disappearing. Your people are like the ants coming out of a great hill. They keep coming and coming."

"I cannot speak for them," Kit repeated. "We will pass. If we are hindered, we will fight."

Ka-ni-ache paused and looked over the top of the fire at the hills beyond. "We know that when you say you will fight, it is so. We will fight, too, if it comes to that. But our people are hungry. The people to the north, our enemies, the Blackfeet, also the Arapaho and Tsetschestahase, are hungry, and the Crow, too."

In the morning, Kit ordered some ewes with lambs to be cut out and given to Ka-ni-ache together with a pouch of tobacco. It came to be the practice as they traveled deeper into country frequented by the Indians. From then on, his forays in the company either of Louis or one of the pastores would often be followed by conferences at a far reach of the flock and the subsequent cutting out of animals as tribute for safe passage.

They forged up along the Platte, the sheep scouring eastward toward the plains under the falling rain. They took their time, but if the grass was sparse, they moved quickly, cognizant of Maxwell coming up behind. During breaks in the weather, Adaline studied the mountains to the west, angular, soaring, and glazed with ice. They traveled past ramshackle and ruined trading posts of the fur trade from bygone days. Fort Luxton, Fort Jackson, Fort Vasquez, were hardly forts, but merely trading establishments set upon the most used pathways. Within a week, just upland of the South Fork of the Platte, they came upon Fort Saint Vrain, also called Fort George and before that Fort Lookout, opened up years ago by Ceran Saint Vrain's brother, Marcellin, as an armature of Bent's Fort.

This day was warm, the sky cloudless and clear. To the west, Long's Peak towered. While Louis and the pastores drove the lead band of sheep into a shallow valley vivid with new grass, Kit cut to the side, going toward the fort. Juan was in his company and Adaline trailed behind. They found the fort in an abandoned condition, crumbling away and sinking into the ground but for stone foundations, a few upright posts, and one remnant of a stockade wall that had been put to use as a windbreak against which several rogue hovels had been fashioned out of hide and willow.

A fire was ablaze, snapping with brushwood. Two old men slouched at it, both with white hair that fell to their shoulders, and staring as Kit, Juan, and Adaline approached. Next to the hovels lay a buffalo hide staked to the ground, green side up, also a wreckage of wheels and bits of iron, old broken-up barrels, and the ubiquitous trade beads. Kit dismounted and engaged one of the men. They spoke on at length, gliding back and forth in a language Adaline marked as one her father knew well. She scrutinized the men as the conversation continued, also the several children and women clutching ragged blankets around their shoulders as they emerged from the hovels, and a feeling of sadness surged through her. She was near her home country. She believed these were her people. They were in bad shape, emaciated and pockmarked. Two of the children had the onset of starvation bellies.

The conversation over, Kit instructed Juan to tell the others to set camp upriver and to the north where the valley was bounded by rock shelves. Addressing Juan in Spanish, he cocked his head in the direction he meant. To Adaline, he said, "Tell Louay to keep them critters in the valley but let 'em trail eastward for a time." He gestured again. "Come morning, we'll backtrack a ways and ford where the river breaks below."

"Are these Arapaho?" Adaline said.

"Aye." Kit looked eastward along the rim of the depression upon which the fort on its high ground allowed a vantage. He remained still, scrutinizing hard and filling in the unseen. "I reckon more coming."

Adaline turned, seeing just beyond the not yet leafed out cottonwoods and above the horizon a thin veil of dust. "Arapaho?"

"Likely." Still looking, he added, "Geese. Scared up by someone off the bend in the crick." She saw specks rising into the air. "Send Louay up to me. Tell him to cut out a ewe that's lost its kid. Stay back with Juan and the sheep til we're certain it's safe."

"Wait," she said. "Pa, these are my people."

He looked at her. In the full sunlight more of the blue surfaced in his eyes. Behind the cool of his look she caught movement, like water flowing beneath a skiff of ice. "I hear you. Go on, now."

She rode off to tell Louis and waited amongst the trailing edge of the sheep. A short column of Indians took shape along the high edge of the valley, outlined against the pale gray limestone, a dozen or more in all closing in on the fort. Louis cut out a ewe, which bleated desperately when he shackled its legs and hoisted it up but fell silent when he draped it across his saddle. He advanced to Kit's position just when the party of Indians arrived. The party slid down from their mounts and formed an arc around where Kit and Louis stood.

In the valley, the sheep had become docile in the grass and a low risible reverberated with their grazing. Bernavette's band advanced, and two miles back the leading edge of Mercure's band appeared, fanning out over the bottom land to the south. Louis rode away from the fort and to the north along the bottom of the plateau. A half mile away lay the site where the company would set up camp, what Adaline now understood had been chosen for its prospect upon the valley and for the rock that rose above it, a natural fortification. Several pastores had already gone there and were picketing their mounts. Kit remained at the fort. He looked in her direction and gestured for her to come, and checking to see that the sheep were quiet under the watch of Juan, she headed toward her father. He conversed with two of the new arrivals, one of whom inclined his head toward her. He displayed scarifications on his arms and his nose was turned sideways as if it had been broken.

The new arrivals were in better health than the others. Behind the two white-haired men, their fire was now in full blaze. A few buffalo hides lay piled upon a travois, yet no meat was in evidence. One of the men had already crouched over the ewe where Louis had delivered it. He cut its throat and with a second incision opened up its belly. The man cracked open the skull and one of the women dipped her fingers into it and lifted out bits of brain to proffer to the destitute children. Another woman parted the hide from the flesh with a knife. Soon, the intestine would be cut out and the hide stretched between pegs.

Kit nodded at the man with the crooked nose. "This be your mother's brother, Half Crow."

A jolt ran through her and she searched Half Crow's face, imprinting it upon her mind. Besides the askew nose, his mouth was set in a line and his hair was down to his shoulders. He had stern eyes. She looked sidelong toward the now disemboweled sheep, then back up at her father. "Tell him I am honored to be in his company."

Kit spoke to the man, who struck his chest with his fist.

"We should go now," Kit said, mounting his horse.

Adaline's legs moved woodenly. After Hawk had taken a few steps, she turned to look back and found the man still looking at her.

"He heard I be here," Kit said, speaking back to her. "Word travels. That's why they come in from their buffler camp. Seeing you, he says your mother's blood was good."

Her disquiet now changed into a disequilibrium, something in herself she could not name. She urged Hawk forward. "Why do you not speak of my mother?"

"Speak?" He interrupted his trajectory by reining in, causing Hawk to skitter away from his horse. "She was a good woman, I say."

She drew back up beside him. "But why do you never speak of her?"

Kit looked out to the south side of the valley where its grade stretched to the flat. In the distance Mercure's band could be seen coming down into it, and nearer was Bernavette's band, and nearer yet Don Rámon rode in the margin between. Kit swung to her, almost sighing. "You know, it ain't a good thing to do in the presence of women." He lifted his gaze to the north where the cook's wagon had rolled into place. Two tents had already been mounted there. "Them Arapaho wanted to trade their few buffler robes. I told 'em we wasn't here for such, that they should go on to Fort Laramie. But I said we'd give 'em sheep in exchange for safe passage. There's nearly fifty of them Arapaho out there, he says. Together with Cheyenne." He looked down at his stirrup and turned his foot. His moccasin had a hole in it. "Ain't you a woman?"

"I am your daughter. And hers."

Now, he looked straight at her and a crinkling went up into the crow's feet around his eyes. "And not a child any longer. A full-grown woman. A smart young woman, too, as was the child. Waa-nibe was a good woman. She prepared the pelts and she could fight alongside the men. She would be a good woman among any class of women. I'm sorry she died as she did."

"Died how?" Adaline was struck that she didn't have words to describe it but only images she'd been carrying, her mother dead in the tipi, her father digging the grave.

"In birthing your sister. It was too much for her after the first loss of blood, though it took her some time to pass on."

"You are not ashamed?"

"What?"

"You do not speak of her," Adaline said, exasperated. "Are you ashamed of me?"

"Shame? I am not ashamed of her. And I reckon I'm proud of you."

He fell quiet and she looked into his eyes, blue again and seeming to move under a shroud of ice.

Chapter 13

THE DRIVE WAS far from inconspicuous and according to Kit they were constantly watched. Now and then, he took Adaline along with him on a scout and showed her what to look for—tracks in the earth, smudges left by fires, smoke from the hills, stones set in signalizing code. Several times he pointed out horsemen on a distant hill, or closer in, all but invisible figures peering from cover. One night, a sheep was lost to a mountain panther. It screamed like a woman and brought Adaline straight up from her buffalo robe, her skin prickling. There was a report from a rifle fired off by one of the pastores on watch, followed by silence. Next to her, Louis muttered, "Panther," and lay still with his eyes open. "Don't think they got it." The only sound was of sheep stirring from bed ground, hooves muttering against the earth. Come morning a party searched and found the remains of the kill, but not the panther. Kit seemed sanguine, saying, "'Cept for the consternation, or if it gets into the dogs and makes the sheep run, ain't much use in finding it. I reckon it takes its share."

The sheepmen stayed on the lookout for bears, too, but none approached. A few sheep left as stragglers in the brush or unhealthy ones lagging behind had been lost to the wolves. This was a greater concern because the sheep, accustomed to the herding dogs, might let the wolves come in close, but so far the flares the pastores lit at night and their mastiffs kept them at bay. Then came the coyotes and feral dogs, which would be heard again in a widening chorus that emblazed the night and caused speculations over whether or not they were the same ones, amassing and trailing along, or different packs the company passed.

The drive had journeyed generally northward, following the trace of Horse Creek and along the way fording several smaller creeks. The sheep were averse to walking in water, for once saturated their wool might pull them under. They required shallows for crossing. Within a few days' travel of Fort Laramie, the company made camp in a long valley, not far south of a place Kit called Goshen Hole, and where deep grass flourished. Spied a distance away through an opening in the "hole," white marl and limestone cliffs enclosed a mineralized bottom where sagebrush and greasewood grew. It was as if the earth were at war with itself, for fecundity thrived where they made camp while within the hole lay a barren. The cliffs had the appearance of an illusory city, revealing seams cut in the walls, and there were alcoves, balconies, parapets, and high up the still snow-covered domes, chimneys, and spindly minarets.

Don Rámon said the cliffs were formed from sea deposits many centuries ago, that all of this land once had been buried beneath a sea. The carving, he said, was the result of the softness of limestone and centuries of scouring winds and rains. This provoked wonder among the men who'd gathered at the evening fire. Adaline looked toward the formations, which were pale in the twilight. Louis, who stood at her side whittling a peg, said, "You must mean from the time of Noah."

Don Rámon replied, "If we could presume that Noah built his ark in a certain place and at a certain time, and that the diluvium epoch was general upon the earth, indeed, it might be so."

Louis stopped whittling. "Diluvium? And what might that mean?"

Don Rámon bowed toward Louis. "Just as you say, Señor Simmons. The time of the flood. Though one must think," he added, "that the fertile Land of Goshen to which the name of that place refers must be what one would behold coming out of that desolate hollow."

Louis took a step back, glowering. "Snakes in there, I reckon. Here, too, maybe."

The company planned to stay in this vicinity for three nights, recruiting the animals in preparation for the trek toward Fort Laramie and westward across the mountains. Bernavette's band settled a half-mile off, and behind it came Mercure's band so that the landscape was animated by sheep as far as the eye could see. On the second night, feral dogs ventured out nearby, their racket of yelps and barks echoing back and forth across the rock, discordant noise to the wailing antiphony of coyotes or wolves. Kit didn't like this. He said, "Come early morning we'd best move a ways up the valley. Them dogs think they know us."

They set out before dawn. Adaline rode drag again, with Ghost on a lead. Louis was nearby and the supply wagon rolled out front of the sheep, which just then passed by the "Hole." Juan joined another pastore in squeezing the sheep toward the river and away from the opening. The spectacle loomed sepulchral, the white sheep, the dark silhouettes of the wagon and horsemen, and then the first rays of sunlight glanced down. Sparrows chattered in the bush. A pair of hawks gyred, whistling at each other, and Adaline observed her father cutting a line oblique from the wagons, breaking back between the edge of the sheep and the opening, and pulling out his carbine. He surveyed the hawks gimleting upward far above the cliffs. The pastores's mastiffs stood with their ears perked. Adaline cast about, marking Louis's alertness and that of the pastores, and then there escalated a sound like a babble. Glancing back through the opening, she spied the dogs, at first a flickering along the base of the cliffs and then a dark mass pouring across the barren. The babble enlarged into a yowling throb, and Adaline sat frozen, watching while Hawk twitched beneath her, and at her side Ghosts's ears bolted upright.

Now the guard mastiffs began to bay. The herding dog whipped back and forth at the edge of the band. Kit rode that edge, gesturing at the pastores and turning to call out something to Louis that Adaline couldn't make out, and Louis, flinging his head her direction barked, "Hold them sheep together!" He spun off, circling around the back and cutting up just inside the edge of the flock, separating out a small wedge. She did as she'd been told, riding the back hem, which forged ahead again, the sheep breaking into a trot and joining the din, mothering ewes calling for their lambs, the lambs bleating back, and far to her right she saw the twisting shapes of dogs tearing into the wedge, and men shouting, and gun shots, and adding to the confusion the acrid haze of powder. She glimpsed Don Rámon, his angular figure on his piebald. She saw him raise a gun and fire. In a moment he fired again. Through the dust and bedlam she saw Louis returning at a canter, wheeling before Dan Rámon.

She urged Hawk behind the sheep, still bringing Ghost along. The main body of the band before her rushed toward the creek but tried to scatter before reaching water. She pressed after them, and as she passed nearer the carnage at the edge she had a better look at the dogs and was astonished by their many forms—thickly built and lean, wolf-like Indian dogs, white and black and brown, flat and sharp snouted, smooth haired and shaggy. They behaved as though they were impervious to the guns. The pandemonium of snarling and yowling persisted while more gunshots echoed against the rocks. She saw it all, now realizing that the quickly formed strategy had been to chance sacrificing a few sheep at the edge of the action and let the remainder move nearer the river. It worked, for quite suddenly as if by some deranged index the dogs curled off toward Bernavette's band while the men there, having had time to make ready, greeted them with a barrage of gunfire. The dogs retreated a second time, flooding back across the barren, snarling as they passed and diminished into the distance.

Juan drew up beside her. He surveyed the sheep skirting the river, some wading in it, and said, "Bueno, chica." Along the edge against which Adaline carved an arch to cut the band away lay the few bodies of the unfortunates that had been in the wedge, blood now saturating their matted wool. A few more were mortally injured, alongside which lay dead and half-dead dogs. Louis waded into the carnage with his long knife, finishing off the wounded animals, while another two pastores joined Juan and Adaline in working the band behind Kit's lead. Don Rámon sat astride his horse, riding slowly on the outskirts. The pastores called softly to the sheep to calm them. Their voices lilted like a lullaby in the aftermath, joining the soughing of the wind.

•

The talk at the fire that night dwelled upon the events of the day. The men knew about dog attacks but none had ever witnessed anything on this scale. Adaline's mind turned to the wolf-like dogs she'd seen in the Indian camps, the half-wild dogs that roamed Taos, and to Jesse Nelson's tale of the dressed up wolves at the head of the chute to perdition. Kit said, "It's the immigrant trains, not wanting to feed what they brought, and the Indians not able to feed in winter. The buffler killing, mebbe, going on everywhere, and leaving carrion for them to take. The wolves breed with 'em, the coyotes kill 'em. The dogs git a taste for even human flesh if they get advantage on it." He looked across at Louis. "Like that one of Ferine's."

Next to Adaline, Louis shifted his feet. "We bucked him out, all right."

Adaline envisioned Louis leaning forward and shooting the hound between the eyes. It spooked her.

"Dogs be most akin to us. Mebbe they's acting out what's coming," Kit said.

The men fell silent, staring into the flames. Mercure had joined them, while Bernavette remained with his band in the center. A few pastores were present.

Don Rámon, seated on a stone, spoke. "But did you see the mix? What has been here from time immemorial, the Indian dogs crossed with wolves, or like Asiatic dogs from the far north. I saw what looked to be a Hungarian Puli among those killed. And what De Soto and Cortez brought in, briards, wolfhounds, salukis, and the Great Pyrenees. De Soto's company told of greyhounds brought as animals of war, given royal names—Becerrillo, Leoncillo—and paid them in gold for the Indians they killed."

Kit looked over, squinting at Don Rámon.

Mercure toyed with the fire, making sparks fly.

The pastores kept their silence.

Louis said, "I reckon them greyhounds made good use of the gold."

Don Rámon lifted his face in the twilight. The reflection of flames glimmered in his eyes. Adaline sensed his gaze touching her and she felt an uneasiness for him. Louis was baiting him.

"De Soto had litters built for the greyhounds," Don Rámon said. "And they were carried by men. It saved the hounds' legs for the chase. There is so much talk of the horse, the gift of Cortez to Norte America, but it was dogs as much. There were herding animals from España, and the hounds, and from Britannia, the watchdogs. Everything here in the new world is finding its way to new form. Killing, wanton destruction, death in its heat is driven into the cauldron of the country where in time it will vulcanize into new forms never before imagined by man."

Adaline didn't know what to make of that, and still no one answered. Louis looked away and snorted, causing Adaline to fear for Don Rámon, but the talk moved on to the oncoming journey, to Fort Laramie. Later, as the fire dwindled, Louis and Adaline retired to their tent. She began unrolling her buffalo robe and Louis said, "Don Rámon is a damn fool."

"He has strange ideas, it seems."

As she came straight, he put his hand on her shoulder and twisted her around to face him. "He's crazy! If he ain't watched he's sure to get himself killed, or somebody else'll be killed trying to remedy him. What the hell does he mean, 'vulcanize?'"

Startled by the heat in his hostility, Adaline said, "What is it?"

He clenched her more tightly. "During that dog attack, he commenced to shooting ever which way. Same as his talk. Like a scatter gun! He's lucky he didn't shoot someone."

She pulled her shoulder away. "But you stopped him didn't you?"

"I can't abide the man."

"Clearly," she said with more irony than intended. In the moonlight that filtered through the open flap, she made out Louis's features, his brow descended toward his eyes, and she felt what up to then had been merely nascent between them now rising toward a full resistance. It came as her old feeling of refusal. She realized what Louis compelled her to beat down—her fascinations, her openness to new ideas, and the excitement of learning things. What she had feared became obvious as she thought the unthinkable: Louis envied Don Rámon's interest in her.

In his face she made out his scowl and saw one hand closing to a fist, then opening, the ring on the stub of his finger catching the light. She found her body bracing for a blow, something else she had learned years ago and something Louis had not done but which she felt just then coming near as it had once with Mr. Turner. It nearly brushed her as Louis came toward her, but he stopped then and turned away. She sat down, pulled her moccasins off, and folded her robe over her, glancing over at him. There was something disconsolate in the slope of his shoulders. She heard him slowly sucking in his breath and letting it out.

Deep in the night, she heard him stirring. He came upon her and under his touch she discovered that there was not an ounce of pleasure in the act. Previously, she'd held her true regard for Louis in abeyance, balanced between her wish to do right, to follow Josefa's precept by "learning to love him," and her deep disappointment, now transformed into enduring the dross of his weight while he took his satisfaction. Later, while he lay snoring, she slipped from the tent to the cook's wagon where her trunk was kept. Softly, she searched for the potion Josefa had given her, and finding it picked her way to the creek where she waded out on a sand bar into the frigid water and, holding up her skirts, washed herself. She stepped out and stood on the bank, not feeling her feet at all, nor her legs below the knees, so numb were they. She felt a panic, remembering Josefa's advice to keep a woman near her, but she was the only woman on this expedition. She lifted her gaze to the sheep reclined on the flat, the whiteness of them trailing into the night, and beyond the flickering torches of the watch, and to the side downstream the horses and mules on picket, the faintly discernible forms of men asleep on the ground, several tents, and the coals left smoldering. A breeze ran through the pines. The night sky was spiked with stars. The moon had just sunk behind the ridge line. An owl took wing, darted close to her head and she came alert with the rushing air from its wings, and then it dodged away among the trees.

•

As the company came near Fort Laramie, the three bands stayed near to each other. A contingent, consisting of a supply wagon, and Kit, Louis, the cook, and an ever-persistent Don Rámon set out for the fort. Bernavette, Mercure, and Juan stayed behind to keep command of the sheep, and Adaline was to help them, along with the pastores. Louis hoped to purchase additional black powder from the army's stores, and Kit planned to check in with the commander. The cook would secure additional supplies. That evening Adaline saw on the horizon a trail of dust raised by a long line of prairie schooners, making its way west. The men returned the next day with two additional kegs of powder and food supplies loaded into the wagon. At the campfire, Don Rámon talked about the agent at the fort who had further excited him with more tales of the famous Yellow Stone: the dazzling white castles composed of salt, mud flats that swallowed up whoever dared to walk there, creeks that leapt out of the ground at a full boil, and everywhere tiny-leafed plants that took steam, mineral, and tar oil as their sustenance. "Don't you see? Before long even plant forms will be changed." His voice had risen as he spoke and in response the silence of the company grew uneasy. It waited to go on to the next thing.

Over the next few days, the drive crossed the double divide where all waters flowed inward. They advanced to the Green River by a northward detour Kit had determined to offer fewer fords than this trail promised, but at a ferry crossing they would spend three days transporting the sheep in bunches across the river. The ferrymen did this work at reduced rates in exchange for the honor of calling the route Carson's Cut Off. With Louis and Juan, Adaline watched over the growing numbers of sheep on the far side of the ferry, and she detected Don Rámon veering off to the north, leading his burro. She couldn't shake the dark premonition that Don Rámon might actually be setting out for Yellow Stone, but said nothing.

When morning revealed that Don Rámon hadn't returned, her foreboding increased. He was gone another day, and another, and finally Kit sent Louis and Juan to backtrack and search for him. The next morning they reappeared, leading Don Ràmon's mule. The horse had been taken, they said. They'd found the Spaniard's body, snatched off the path where he'd been making his way, presumably toward Yellow Stone. The mule's aparejo had notebooks and artifacts in them, arrows, stones chipped into points. That night in their tent, Louis told Adaline that they'd buried him, but Don Rámon had been scalped and his ears cut off. His skull was cracked open. He'd been staked to the ground and his testicles and penis were crammed into his mouth. "I reckon he got the adventure he wanted," Louis said.

Adaline's imagining of the horror of Don Rámon's suffering, and her remorse for not doing something to stop him, left her feeling hollow. That night, she dreamt of a dust devil which appeared at the mouth of Goshen Hole and danced across the ground, taking up into the sky all manner of dogs and a disfigured Don Rámon. The man with no face walked beneath the whirlwind, which made a low roar like the endless muttering of sheep. When she awoke, she was groaning while Louis lay snoring at her side.

She crept to the flap of the tent, opened it, and looked to the sky. There was no wind, only brilliant constellations. Noticing a spark of fire before her, she went to it and found her father up already with Juan and the cook. Her father said, "Listen. Seems like Don Rámon wanted to die. We didn't understand him, none of us did, but I'm sorry he had to go that way."

•

By June the drive had dropped to follow the westerly line of what had been variously called Mary's River, or Ogden's River, but which Frémont had renamed in honor of Alexander von Humboldt, the German explorer and naturalist. Difficulty was expected in the coming dry country, and Adaline had seen her father probing the earth in order to check its moisture. When she asked, he'd said he believed the forage would be suitable for now, but that the wet didn't go far down. Speed was important, yet they had to keep the sheep in good shape for the desert ahead and then high country crossing. Also, they'd lost two horses and a mule. The mule had broken a leg on a talus crossing, and the horses had bolted away one night. There was no telling where the horses went. The company had seen a band of Shoshone, who might have scared them off, and another band of Bannocks, or "Diggers," as they were called.

They made camp in a valley timbered with aspen and cottonwoods, encircled by low hills and fed by streams. The Humboldt Range rose to the east and far to the west snow still glistened from the ridges of the Sierra and Cascade Mountains. A wide marsh lay between the stream and river where large numbers of red and yellow-winged blackbirds perched on the cattails and reeds. There were egrets, herons, cranes, and thousands upon thousands of ducks and geese and as a consequence a constant din. The pastores had built an evening fire against a high water cutbank above the river and unpacked chunks of mutton. The sheep in Kit's band branched out from the marsh and toward the hills, favoring the northern slopes where grass grew thick.

That night they were visited by five Comanche, led, Adaline would learn, by the same old chief, Nokoni, that her father had encountered nearly two years before. She'd observed how her father's face quickened when he turned toward the sheep, then she spied the group on horseback weaving down from the hills and driving a string of twenty or more horses. Louis, who kept sentry, drew his carbine from its scabbard, laid it across his pommel, and looped between the Indians and the flock. Her father said to the pastores, "We're all right, I reckon. I'm thinking they be still friendly, but keep your guns at hand." He swung up on his buckskin and rode along the edge of the sheep, then with Louis pulled up directly in front of the Comanches.

Adaline saw her father's arms gesturing broadly and snatches of barely audible but seemingly friendly conversation drifted in on the breeze. Kit turned his horse back with three of the Comanches trailing, leaving the others with the string of animals. Louis drew up the rear. As the group came near and dismounted, she saw the old chief among them, and that was when she heard her father address him as Nokoni. A flashing cross was tied with a thong to his saddle. Another man was dressed in a tunic and flat-brimmed hat, and the third was a tall one with gray eyes and tawny skin. Adaline remembered the men in Kit's company talking about such a man two years ago, a mezclado. He wore buckskin leggings, had a beaded comb with a feather in his hair, and he sat astride a grulla-colored horse.

Kit and Nokoni communicated in a mixture of English, Spanish, and signing. As best Adaline had learned, it was the customary decorous greeting that included accounts of where one had been, whether the rains were kind or not, and who had been seen. The Comanches were invited to take part in the meal, to which they assented. Two pastores began roasting mutton on skewers and the cook brought over bird eggs and added them to the beans he had boiling in a pot. All along, the cook had made full use of the provisions of what they had brought or what they killed—deer, antelope, turkey, sage grouse. The three Comanche carefully laid down their excellently preserved Mills and Hawken breechloaders. They sat. Kit sat, and Louis joined him. Juan kept his distance by the wagon and Adaline moved near him. Two pastores hunkered on the other side of the fire, turning the sizzling meat and occasionally stirring the beans.

Nokoni spoke in his language, and then the mezclado spoke up on his own for the first time—in good English: "He wonders where you are going with all these ovejas. So many of them. We know there are many more yet behind you."

Kit gestured westward with his head, saying, "They are for trade."

The mezclado said, "It is as we thought. We are told it is not an easy crossing, and yet you propose to go with the ovejas. The rock that the Americans value is out there, and now these floods of Americans go there and kill the game along the way. They dig in the ground and change the way of the rivers for this yellow rock."

Kit said, "The sheep are to be sold as meat to those people."

The mezclado translated this to Nokoni, then they went back and forth, speaking in their language, and Adaline studied her father, who had straightened his back, alert to the talk. Next to Kit, Louis poked at the coals with a stick. Kit said, "We would trade you six sheep for two good horses. We would pass over some tobacco, as well."

The mezclado told this to the old man, who nodded gravely at Kit and spoke in Comanche again. While this transpired, Kit nodded at one of the pastores. The pastore walked away to the wagon, returning with three additional plates and a tobacco pouch. He busied himself putting food on the plates for the Comanches.

The mezclado said, "The tobacco we will take. Maybe the ovejas, too."

Kit said, "Horses is what we would like. I see you have many good ones."

The Comanches proceeded to eat with their knives, including the beans, picking up a line with the knife edge and sliding the beans into their mouths. The pastores ate, as did Louis and Kit. Adaline followed Juan, circling behind the Comanches to fetch food for herself. She felt the mezclado's eyes on her as she walked back.

Kit said, "You are far from home. I have never heard of Comanche in these parts."

"Back where we come from," the mezclado said, "the hunting is not good. We have all these people coming in, now, the Americans, the Mejicanos, the ciboleros. Soon, the ground will be worn out from all the walking upon it. We wanted to see what was in this country. The hunting is not good here, either. These Indian people are able only to dig the earth for roots. They eat seeds and lizards." He smiled. "It is hard to believe, but some even eat flies."

"It is dry country we're coming into," Kit said.

"So it is." The mezclado spoke to Nokoni again and when the old man responded Adaline assumed he said what terms to ask about next.

The man in the tunic kept eating his beans with the knife and the meat with his fingers, wiping his chin on his buckskin sleeve and his fingers on the bottoms of his leggings. Once finished, he tipped up the plate and sucked down the juice that remained. He spoke to the mezclado and then directed his gaze over toward the marsh from where a great clamor of geese had just arisen. He took out a long pipe from inside his tunic and tapped the ground with it. One of the pastores stood and retrieved a stick to add to the fire, whipping up sparks into the darkening air.

Then the mezclado said, "We would take two ovejas for meat, but as we are traveling we would kill them. We have need of balls and powder."

"You are the travelers," Kit said. "Nokoni."

"We are wandering to see how the world is changing." The mezclado said.

Kit took up the tobacco pouch and passed it to Louis, who handed it around to the man with the pipe, who gently drew open the string on the pouch and lifted it to his nose. He took out a pinch of tobacco, packed the pipe, and lit it with a brand from the fire.

"We could trade some balls and powder for horses," Kit said.

The mezclado's eyes came up again. Adaline looked at him and felt the lure of an alien world. This man spoke as masterfully as he bore himself, tall and straight, and in a rushing instant she felt as though she were floating away, filled with attenuation and fear. At that moment, the mezclado turned to Kit and said, "You have a woman with you. Would you trade her?"

Without hesitation, as if he'd known what was coming, Kit said, "Ain't likely. No. She be married to Louay here." His hand went out to touch Louis's knee.

Juan shuffled his feet and looked down, then edged nearer to Adaline as if to protect her. The cook stepped close to the back of his wagon. The third Comanche and the old man gazed at her, and Louis squinted up at her, his lips drawn tight in a line. The mezclado said, "I see." He nodded solemnly at Louis and checked Adaline again as if to appraise once more what was unavailable, and now Adaline felt warring emotions—the alluring mystery of what being sent off with him might mean, and the sheer, cold, abject terror of the idea that she, a woman, could have been handed over in an exchange of animals, black powder, balls, and tobacco.

The parties agreed that the transaction would be finalized next morning—two horses for the meat from four sheep, a quantity of lead balls and black powder, and tobacco. The Comanches departed, picking up their guns and removing their horses to an encampment some distance away behind the hills. As they passed by, the noise from the marsh quieted. Within a few minutes it welled up again, the cacophony of birds enjoined by croaking frogs. Kit put up extra guards, told everyone to have their weapons ready at their sides, and sent two pastores off to warn Bernavette and Mercure. "Half them horses is army horses, do you see? No telling how they come by the weapons they need balls and powder for."

In the twilight, Adaline and Louis walked back to their tent. By the way his boot heels came down hard on the dirt, she knew he was angry. Once they reached the tent, he stopped and turned on her. "What do you mean leading on the breed?"

Adaline stepped back. She sensed fury in his body. A matching fury arose from her own. Her voice was tight: "Leading on? I lead no one on."

"I seen you inviting him with your eyes," Louis snarled. "And twitching your hips at him when you moved. What do you want? To be carried off by savages? That don't scare you? First, it's the Greaser in Taos, then the spider, Don Rámon, now a Comanche breed. Truth is you're worse than all them put together."

She took another step away, but Louis grabbed her arm and yanked her back, which made her lurch angrily. She had a flashing image in her mind of Pablo, the "Greaser," and about whom all this time she'd hoped against hope that Louis knew nothing. She'd kept Pablo to herself, buried him within her. She felt herself bristling. And who did Louis think he was to not object, either here or at the fire, to her being treated as an item of barter? "Scare me? Yes, I was afraid," she said. "And now I'm afraid of you, Louis. Let loose of me," she said, pulling against his grasp, but Louis held on to her and then jerked her yet closer.

Suddenly desperate, Adaline wrenched free and a guttural noise expelled from her chest: "No!" She was shuddering and she stared fiercely at him. She brought up her hands in front of her face and shook them at him. "No! Leave me be!"

Louis stood still. He glanced furtively back toward the fire, which told her that he'd gone beyond himself, and so had she, and that her shout had been loud enough for others to hear. She beheld Louis's face change before her, his eyes growing slatted as if he were peering out of a cage. She looked over to the fire. Only Juan was there and the cook. They were staring at the coals. Her father was walking away almost out of sight. She knew full well then that it was he whom Louis feared, that his dread of being shamed in her father's eyes was as strong as her own.

She bent through the open flap, pulled out her buffalo robe, and dragged it away nearer the cutbank, where she would be hidden by the tent. She slipped inside the robe and lay still, staring into the sky, listening to the bleating of ewes and the lambs calling back.

Chapter 14

IN AUGUST, the company continued to where the Cascades and the Sierras nearly met. It had to negotiate an arduous canyon, the way impeded by thick underbrush and fallen trees, and then in a few days it came out on a valley surrounded by what appeared to be low mountains, though they were not. It was the height of the land that made the mountains appear low. They encountered no Indians here, although Adaline had felt there must have been watchers amongst the tangled growth that lined the streams. On this evening, she stood near her father and inquired after them. He surveyed the sheep that blanketed the valley, and said, "I reckon they be too timidified to come down on us."

After a pause, Adaline said, "This is hard going."

"Aye, Twister," he said. "But it's nothing like when we first come over. February, it was then, and it took us days way down south where we was. Snow up to the treetops in some places and the Injuns walked right over the top of it in their snowshoes while our animals foundered to their bellies. We sent out parties with mauls to beat down the snow into a ice road."

The pastores had built a fire against a low hill. Louis was there, casting a long glance at her and her father. She was sleeping in the tent with Louis again, but now he was reluctant to touch her except when his need became too much for him to resist and then expressed with a kind of suppressed anger. Mostly, he barely acknowledged her, and she was grateful for this. Within this uneasy truce, she was engaged in an inward war, her consciousness telling her one thing—to keep up appearances, to keep trying—and her unconsciousness telling her another truth—that somehow and sometime she'd have to leave him. She'd taken to coming near her father when the opportunity afforded itself and otherwise staying close to Juan. She believed Juan was too old, too kindly, and too subservient to raise Louis's suspicions.

When they set out in the morning, she took the drag position behind Juan. What ensued was harder than they'd yet undergone, the way winding tortuously along a string of switchbacks. At one turnabout the wagon had to be maneuvered with levers by the pastores in order to pivot it around a boulder, but then after it ascended the trail flattened again. She gathered they'd crossed a summit. They made camp next to a lake. She detected a blazing whiteness to the north in the mist. She looked to the fire, and seeing Louis there with her father, slipped off to the cook's wagon to retrieve her Frémont, barometer, and sextant. She searched the journal by candlelight, determining that Frémont's company had twice passed near here, and that, indeed, the radiance in the gloaming must be Mount Tsashtel. The sheep and mounts were winded and she, too, felt short of breath. She calculated their elevation with the barometer, finding it to be four thousand feet, then took her sextant and measured their coordinates to be at a latitude of 41° 29" North and a longitude of 120° 32" West.

In the morning the company made an easier transit through another pass and began its descent in earnest for several days. At outlooks, perspectives opened upon towering rock walls, snowy peaks like dagger tips, and closer in, basins teeming with water. By afternoon, they passed into the dense foliage of cedars and firs. From one promontory a long valley below came into view veiled by a rose-colored haze. Far across the valley the outlines of more mountains stood against the sky. The further the company descended, the more the trail widened, and emboldened by the abundance of grass the sheep fanned out. Red pine manifested, mixing in with the fir, and next the trail was skirted by stumpage. From the woods one could hear a clamor of axes. Double-yoke ox teams and men now appeared, skidding out logs.

The trail grew wider yet. Bunchgrass and manzanita held sway amongst the great California oaks with their spreading limbs. Blue jays rode the drafts between trees, and dust kicked up by the animals filled the air. The slope modulated into foothills, and as the trail turned gently upon the crests and cut downward in a long diagonal, it opened more vistas of the valley below. A cluster of tents appeared alongside a stream that fed into the Sacramento River. The river was the color of pewter and ran the length of the valley. The mountains seemed to rise ever higher the more the company descended. Beyond them, she thought, lay the Pacific.

They worked their way toward a flat, the sheep spilling over the sides of the trail, but Juan's fyce harassed the sheep to keep them from straying. From up front came a whining sound, and she saw her father and Louis draw their mounts onto a ledge and gaze down. They moved off and once she reached the overlook Adaline had a clear view of the stream and emplacements along the bottom, including a platform that extended over a pool where logs floated. More logs were brought in by teams of oxen. On the platform a blade spun, and a log was hoisted by ropes and pulleys. Men were pulling the ropes. Two more hooked the log with pikes and dragged it onto log dogs that drew it into the blade, which then pierced the air with its whine. It was a sawmill, a larger version of what had been built at the Rayado.

Above the opposite bank stood all manner of tents, and logs stacked up in squares to make cabins with canvas roofs. Upstream of the mill, men dug and shoveled dirt into contraptions that were like giant sieves mounted at the bottoms of the banks. In addition to the teams of oxen hauling back and forth between the mill and the felled trees up the trail, a mule team pulled a wagon loaded with lumber toward a wooden flume, which Adaline could track from where it first lifted on its stilts. Between the river and the mouth of the flume, more men excavated a trench that would channel the river to the flume. Adaline pieced it together in her imagination: the machines, the trench, the long flume, the big sieves, all for extracting gold. A gang of men struggled to move a huge rock from the ditch, and she fetched from her memory Ka-ni-ache's words. The trails worn into the bush looked like ant paths. The boulder looked like a load transported by ants struggling beneath it. They carted it out of the way, returned, and resumed digging like ants.

At Juan's call, she wheeled Hawk, driving a half-dozen sheep back into the fold and resuming her position at drag. As the company moved away from the river, the din vanished. By evening they reached an open pasture in the hills where a spring discharged from a granite formation. They would stay here for three days, allowing the animals to recruit themselves before making the last drive to Sacramento. At night a breeze wafted up the slope, and Adaline lay in the tent on her robe with only a light blanket over her, luxuriating in the dry air. Louis, next to her, dark in his long johns, fell asleep instantly. She rolled to her side and studied his brow traveling down to his nose, his left hand, the truncated fingers, one of which was squeezed by his silver and turquoise ring. His breath caught in his throat.

•

When they weren't watching the sheep, the pastores busied themselves checking through their equipage, mending leather, sharpening knives, and cleaning their guns. Some wanted to try the gold pans on the stream that ran out of the pond, but Kit forbade it because everyone needed to be kept on the mark of delivering healthy sheep. Louis inventoried his drilling augers, fuses, and the kegs of black powder he'd stored in the supply wagon. Adaline tended to her trunk, sorted through her books and maps, her instruments, clothing, and recounted the cache of coins she'd been keeping in the bottom compartment.

One of the pastores had warned the company about thieves around here. There was a bandit called Joaquín, he said, with the powers of a phantom. He could be anywhere. Adaline asked Juan about him as they minded a chaparral of scrub oak into which the sheep had sifted. Hawk, Ghost, and Juan's mule stood behind them, picking at the grass. "Joaquín Murrieta," Juan said. "Murrieta and his men ride like the wind. His wife was taken by the Yanquis. He is from Sonora, a soldier. They say he comes here to fight for his people. It's true, he might even be invisible." Juan looked away and chuckled, yet when he looked back his eyes were filled with light. "Ay! El Mago! He'd have to be one to set things right!"

In the last evening there, the group engaged in a colloquy on what awaited them. Most of the pastores meant to stay on in California to join a mining team for a spell. Bernavette and Mercure had brought their bands close in and joined the group at the fire. Mercure took out a leather-bound ledger and Adaline was caught a glimpse of its carefully written columns, marked in a precise hand. Mercure had kept a count and now set it against costs and in anticipation of what they would draw upon sheep. Strangers began showing up, curious about reports that Kit Carson was encamped here. They hoped to lay eyes on the famous scout, but whenever they arrived, sometimes in the company of a newspaperman, Kit fell quiet. This evening, another knot of horsemen appeared, kicking the powdery dust up in the trace of the valley. Adaline watched her father scrutinizing their approach, then he caught her eye and gestured to her with his head. They walked to where the horses and mules were picketed. "Let's ride out a ways," he said.

She and her father took their halters from the supply wagon, disengaged his buckskin and Hawk from their pickets, and rode past the far edge of the sheep's bed ground, heading deeper into the hills. A jackass rabbit bounded before them and disappeared into the brush. They climbed to a flat atop a low hill, slid from their mounts, and dropped the reins. The sun slipped down toward the mountain range on the far side of the valley.

Kit said, "Once we sell these sheep and after Lucien and Tom Boggs catch up, we'll go down to Sonoma for a time to see my brother, Lindsey, and Tom's people."

Adaline stood still. She knew she had relations in this country: Moses, her father's older half-brother; Robert, another brother and Susan's father, who was said to have grown dissolute from drink; and

Lindsey, her father's younger brother. Tom Boggs also had a brother here and his father. Adaline had wondered if she might meet up with these Missouri people.

Kit broke out his pipe, filled the bowl, and sparked it with his flint. "After, Lucien and myself and likely Tom Boggs will head home by the Mojave Road. Louay says he's looking for a proper place to do his powdering. Once he finds it, you'll likely be off, too."

She saw that her father's drawing her away was ceremonial to their parting. He had brought her West, as promised, and now, come so near the closing of a chapter, she still found in this turn that there was nothing she feared more than failing him. On the other side of the hill to their left the sheep busied themselves pulling at the ground cover and at the leaves of the shrubs. A couple hundred yards beyond the men's voices could be heard. A condor traced a wide arc in the iridescence of the sky.

"You might keep the filly the Comanche traded us," he said. "I see you favor it."

The strawberry roan, dappled on the rump, was a sprightly creature, hardly broke for riding. The Comanches had thrown it in along with the other two horses they traded for sheep, powder, and balls. "I did not expect that." She gazed at the condor, whose loops seemed to shape the air up the valley. "I've thought I might raise a few cows, if Louis would allow it."

Kit said, "I hear tell there are herds of 'em coming in by the trail to Oregon. I reckon there used to be more, the slicks and mavericks from the hacendias." He pulled on his pipe and sent out a stream of smoke. "You asked about Injuns. Used to be more. When I was first here with Ewing Young, and with Frémont, as well, back then at the missions and haciendas they had the Injuns, and thousands of cows. They was other Injuns betimes coming in on raids."

"It seems meat would be in demand."

"Reckon we heard the like."

She grinned at her foolishness, then said, "I'm thinking for longer duration."

"Something there, maybe. Maybe still a person could start in with the slicks."

She was pleased by his affirmation, but close on its heels arose her unsolvable, inward war, her near-desperate unease over what she was to do. Tomorrow, they'd be delivering sheep. Lucien Maxwell and Tom Boggs would follow them in. Her father would ride away and she'd be left with Louis.

Kit went on. "If Louay goes southward, could be you might make agreement on pasturing with the Colonel. The Colonel might let you start up a little herd from his slicks. Mrs. Frémont'll be coming West, and I reckon she'll be disposed to you. Or further south on the flats of the San Joaquin, Alexis Godey's running beeves for the Colonel."

Her attention quickened at these possibilities. "Mrs. Frémont? And Godey from your exploration days?"

"Sooner or later Mrs. Frémont'll be out here. And aye, Godey, my old compadre, has hung on with the colonel. As I say, if you get down there, seek him out. You'd need to watch your figuring close, though, in whoever you sell to. You got to watch Godey, but then Louay be there with you." There was a light that seemed to shine through his face. "Watch your numbers, in critters and dollars. Like Mercure has. You need the numbers to keep your footing. And the words to keep others true."

He had just informed her what he thought the best use of her schooling was, digging at the crack he'd just opened, whereas for him always, if a document became an issue, a bit of information, or back in Taos one of Padre Martínez's pamphlets, he would step away just as he had when here the strangers turned up in the evenings.

Once, she'd asked Josefa about it and Josefa had said, "He doesn't see what we see. When he looks at a page of words they mix up together like a . . . how do you call it . . . bucket? Like a bucket full of differing seeds."

"Yet there is no one better for reading sign," Adaline had said to Josefa.

"Sí. Yo sé." Josefa's hands had rested lightly on the arms of a chair.

She smiled in a way that said this quality in her husband pleased her. "And minds, too. He can read them and know what people think before they do, sometimes. I have wondered about this thing."

"My aunt told me he had a little schooling," Adaline said.

"Sí. Más pequeño. He couldn't stay still within the room."

"I loved the books, but I couldn't stay still, either. Seems I was in trouble always. The books were the only way I could keep calm."

"¿Sí?" Josefa gazed at Adaline with amusement.

Now, standing beside him on the hillside while he puffed on his pipe, Adaline also remembered the cruel discipline, the mockery, the whippings. Her sense of aching loneliness washed anew over her, but she made herself say, "I think I'll ask Henry Mercure to show me exactly how he keeps the ledger."

Kit looked at her. "This country ain't unkind. You'll make it out. It's why the Injuns here be easy to bend, though they have their hardship, too. When I was first here furring with Ewing, they was villages filled with bones, the Injuns killed off by ague faster than they could dispose of the dead. Still, but for a few they weren't never like Blackfeet or Sioux, trued by the cold country, or dried hard like the Jicarilla or Chiricahua by the Sonora. Not like them warrior tribes. Here, things more or less fall into your hands."

"You don't favor slaving."

Again he paused and sucked on his pipe. "I do not," he finally said. "It makes some few people soft and mean and breaks the rest. It's spoilage. It ain't no way no good."

She guessed he was thinking of the farmers back in Howard County who kept Negroes. The slaves worked the fields and lived in shanties, and some lived in town as house servants. She'd seen them on the steamers, too, where they fed wood into the fire, served the meals, and rowed the lightering vessels. "I mean the Indians."

"I know what you mean. In the end, it comes out the same."

"What about the killing of them?"

"Time is ending for the killing. The Injuns has to give in."

The enslavement, killing, and decimation had an enormity to it, and as she looked across the valley, she felt a shuddering to go along with her ache. A slot in the mountains over yonder opened to San Francisco Bay, she'd heard, what Frémont had called the Golden Gate. Low as the sun sank at this instant, its light might have been ensconced and gleaming in that slot. The condor drifted back their way with another one behind it, the two spiraling around in ever lowering loops.

Kit watched them. "They got the scent from in the hills. There's plenty carrion for 'em with the draft animals left exhausted. Them birds will drop down soon up there. Least ways you hope so." He took his pipe out. "You hope it ain't us they's waiting on."

Adaline watched the birds. They had tightened their loops, then broke out to cruise near the land. They flapped their great wings to lift above an obstacle of tree or the brow of a hill, and the white ridges on the fronts of their wings flashed in the sunlight, which burnished to their undersides, and they coasted and vanished into the shadows like specters.

"They say you killed a thousand Indians up on the Sacramento River."

Her father's eyes nicked back at her. "They who say such?"

"Don Rámon."

Kit looked away and Adaline saw the muscle in his jaw working, but his response to the mention of Don Rámon was nothing like Louis's would have been. "I'll tell you, Twister. It's the talking. In its passing around the truth gets racked by folks that's got more lip than they know what to do with. They just talk on, pleasuring in the sound of it. Worst is in the end a body has to answer to all the lies told along with the truth."

He turned to see where the horses had gone, which was into a swale toward the first of the hills and behind which the condors had spirited. He gave a low whistle. The buckskin drifted back and Hawk followed, their movement rattling the bush, each holding its head sideways so as not to step on the reins. Kit tamped his pipe and relit it. Adaline felt the cool of the evening dew upon her ankles.

He said, "There was maybe a thousand in all, counting them what lay hidden in the hills. That's what I mean about them tales, rounding everything up to bugaboo. Yanas I believe they was in the main. They'd been threatening the settlers on the river. The colonel, or the captain, then, sent us after 'em. We took no casualties and they was taught a lesson."

What she asked next was not the question, or not the string of them she most wanted to ask: A lesson you say? How many lessons? No casualties to Frémont's men? And to the Indians, who were not ready to fight you? What? What happened? Why? Yanas? Remembering that Henry, the Delaware, had named the Yanas way back in Fayette, she wanted to ask who were they? A people, a tribe? Instead, feeling her sadness compounded by the fact that she knew her father would leave her before she had all the answers, answers to questions she didn't know how to ask, she said, "He himself didn't go along? Captain Frémont?"

"Not into that fight since he had his business to conduct. But not long before when a Klamath drew a bead on me, Frémont ran him down with his horse. It's one reason that I'm forever beholding to him. Reckon otherwise I'd not be here."

Don Rámon had told her that some considered Frémont a coward because he avoided bloodshed. Adaline harbored questions about this, though surely such expeditions into dangerous country as were Frémont's could hardly be considered the acts of a coward. He had enlisted men in his company experienced with killing. Don Rámon had turned his face skyward and spoke so softly that she had to step toward him to hear. "It's an ancient compact," he had said, "the killers who travel in the company of the lofty. Captain Frémont had the advantage of their sword edge, and they the honor of feasting on his scraps. But your father," he added, touching his hand to her arm, "has something noble in him. Something Rousseauian. Small as he is in stature, look at his cranium."

He had nodded toward Kit, who sat at the far side of the fire and who held his hat between his knees, slowly revolving it with his fingertips as he gazed into the flames.

"The fullness of the brow," Don Rámon had said. "The arch to the parietal eminence. His faculties of perception, the honed edge of his mind, and superior sentiments of belief and firmness, and the inquisitiveness and compassion that go together in the best. The depth of bone about the ears and above the neck, his balancing willingness to destroy. Given a better station in life, he could have been a statesman. You, too," Don Rámon said, touching Adaline's forehead and then the top of her head. "Not unlike him. The perceptive faculties, faculties of language and wonder, just so. But your force in the company of others, being a woman, will only cause you grief. His lack of it in the company of those considered his superiors is his affliction."

Adaline shifted her weight from one foot to another, listening to the horses behind them swishing in the grass. The sun dipped nearer yet to the ocean, while clouds changed to the color of steel. She still wasn't certain how to phrase her questions, how to make them come out clean.

"Them Indians," Kit said, "was rendezvousing on the river. They fought a little and ran, and flanked us and come back, and some of the men went crazy. It happens when you're askeered, always watching and losing out to the renegades. The trace of it makes some lose track of their minds. Ferine on the train. Them Cheyenne. But if I had to do it over with the Yanas I wouldn't. The Indians' time is over here. My time is near over. The gold frenzy, I reckon it'll be over soon, too."

He knocked his pipe bowl against the butt of his hand and discarded the flakes. "If you get the long look, maybe killing was like taking the whip to the hard-tail mule instead of forever fussing with the critter. But I'll grant that killing up on the Sacramento turned loco. One man catches the loco and others jump in as loco rips through 'em like wild fire. They didn't even trouble to reload once they started in. They just waded into the wretches with their cutlasses."

The buckskin and Hawk had moved closer, pulling at the grass. Kit reached back and took up the buckskin's reins. Adaline walked a few steps to Hawk and led him up. She and Kit stood, gazing across the valley with the horses waiting behind them. Sparrows scuttered in the manzanita at their side, and the nut birds chipped in the oaks.

"I wanted to ask you about Mrs. White."

Her father's eyes flickered back. "Don Rámon again?"

"No. I heard it from the dragoon, Ferine."

"That dog more dog himself than was his dog, speaking of dogs," Kit said. "Some of them coming out of the army is the worst. They was renegades afore they ever went in. And then they just git hardened in it. He said we found Mrs. White dead, Ferine did?"

Adaline nodded. "He said you wanted to go in after the Jicarillas, but the officer in command held back on the advice of Leroux. He said you didn't insist."

"Weren't nothing to do with Leroux. The captain, Grier, called me out from the Rayado to go along with Leroux in tracking them."

"It's the same Grier as with the Cheyenne, right?"

"Aye. Back then I did want to go in after the woman, Mrs. White. So did Leroux. There's no bargaining with Jicarillas in such a corner, but the captain wanted to parley and besides he'd taken a ball in the shoulder. I do not question him. We disagreed and he has since said he was in the wrong. Force was the right recourse in that case."

"Jesse was there when Ferine was telling this," Adaline said. "Jesse said it was as you say. The daughter was lost, too?" She was probing to get the facts of the tale straight, yet with each question she felt she was inching away from what she most wanted to know. When her thoughts turned dark, Mrs. White and her daughter became frightening images of her own abandonment. She believed her father saw this moment as the opportunity to engage with her, yet the true, if mysterious, substance of what remained unsaid was unbeknownst to her. Even as they talked, she had the crushing feeling that she was on her own.

"Aye, it's so," Kit said. "And the Negro woman traveling with them, killed, and her little girl and Mr. White aforehand. Two other little girls was taken, too. Could be the Jicarillas have them still, or they've been traded off as slaves."

"And she had the book about you, Mrs. White did?"

"It was the first I'd seen such. At the camp where we found Mrs. White with the book held close, which Grier told me was about me rescuing folks from the Injuns, I feared she believed I'd come to her rescue." As Kit went on, his voice grew husky with emotion, which was something Adaline could not remember having ever heard from him, not in this way. "The lady was left in an unspeakable condition," he said. "Cut up, abused, left to die. Still warm when we come upon her. It aggrieved me to think she held out the hope for me that I failed to requite. It give me a long pause thinking on it, Twister."

He drew his buckskin alongside and swung up on it. Adaline went up on Hawk. They sat still. After a moment, Adaline said, "I am sorry for her."

"Aye," Kit said, nudging his buckskin forward. She followed and they rode a loop above the sheep, which had settled into a broad hollow.

Adaline had long seen herself as Mrs. White, or her daughter, left alone and not rescued in time. That was the horror the story had conjured in her. What details her father had added, and what scrim of the background his emotion provided, and what beforehand she'd marked as a changing in him, only made clearer what her feeling was, what she could explain to no one but only keep close as a growing and inconsolable sadness.

"So," Kit said. They traced a path through the manzanita, aiming for the fire which had reduced to a glow of red coals. "It's likely soon to be adiós for a time."

Chapter 15

THE COMPANY MOVED its encampment north of Sacramento near the American River. When in early evening they first entered the bottomland, mallards, wood ducks, coots, and a flock of Canada geese exploded upward, circled, and descended raucously into the adjoining marshland. The numbers of sheep, horsemen, and dogs had spooked them, though these seemed merely to extend the ravages already wreaked upon the river: the mining debris, the wastage of animal bones and rotting innards, the garbage, the stinking makeshift latrines.

At dawn, Kit, Louis, Mercure, and Juan drove a portion of the lead band to the yards at the edge of Sacramento. Kit and Mercure negotiated the sale of the flock, while Juan stayed behind to watch over the sheep, and Louis rode ahead to arrange for lodging. The remaining sheep were rousted and the entire company moved to the pastures outside the yards. Adaline, riding flank along the edge of the flock, peered at the distant buildings to the west where ranks of two, three, and four-story brick structures soared against the sky. Once at the yards, she rode up beside Juan, while Kit, Bernavette, and Mercure passed into the yard master's shack to finalize the sale. Realizing that Louis was nowhere to be seen and knowing she was to go with him, she asked Juan about him. Juan shrugged and said that Louis must have been detained.

She tied off Hawk at a corral where the company's mules and horses had been tethered and walked past the yard master's shack along an alley to a shed where men, wielding prods, forced cattle down a chute. The cattle bawled and as the chute narrowed, more men hit them between the eyes with sledges. One had to be struck several times and then finally hooked in the hip and dragged along. The chute reverberated with its bellowing until it was raised by block and tackle to hang head down and have its jugular cut. It joined others in the line, twitching violently, and shuttled from one worker to the next where it was beheaded and eviscerated. Hooves were cut off, its hide shoved down over its body and thrown onto a growing pile.

More cattle entered the chute, and she heard their wailing, their fright at the scent of blood of their own kind as if they knew what was coming. She moved further along and came upon an alley next to the river into which several men shoveled stinking offal. A stack of hides towered over her head. Still further, she found another yard, a holding pen, this one filled with Indians, mostly men, but also women and children huddling in clusters or squatting with their backs against the fences. There were forty or so of them, half-naked with protruding ribs and, in the case of the children, starvation bellies. Near the alley stood two troughs, one with water covered with a skim of grime and another with a semblance of a mush, above which hovered a cloud of flies. A man bent over it, ladling with his hand to his mouth. He looked up at her with dull eyes and beckoned to her.

Just then Juan appeared. "You should not be here."

"What is it? Why are they here?"

"Son esclavos," Juan said.

"¿Esclavos?" At the far corner of the pen, a white man leaned with his elbows upon the top rail. He glanced over at Juan and Adaline. A whip hung from his belt.

Juan shrugged. "To rent."

"To rent?"

"Sí. Por las minas," Juan said. "Come away from here. Señor Louis is waiting for you."

She did not move. "You mean somebody owns them?"

Again, Juan shrugged.

Adaline remembered what her father had said, that most Indians here were easy to bend. She said, "It would be better if they would fight. Better to break out and die than this."

"Están quebrados. They had the Franciscans to shackle them first."

"You mean at the missions?" Then, her passion taking hold of her, she said, "This is not good. None of this is good."

"Come away now. Louis is waiting."

They moved back along the alley, past the slaughtered cattle. A little further on, she saw that the sheep were being funneled into vast holding pens. Her father stood watching. He had one foot up on a rail and beside him stood the yard master, Bernavette, and Mercure, marking columns in his ledger. Louis was up at the mouth of the alley with a buckboard and two mules harnessed to it.

Juan said, "We pastores are going off come morning." His beard was silver against his dark face and he smiled as he took her elbows in his hands. "Vaya con Dios, chica." He moved off. Adaline watched him go, his fyce at his heels, and the sadness took hold of her again as he passed beyond the sheep and toward the pastores who awaited him.

She drifted toward Louis, who already had loaded her trunk into the buckboard, together with his two bags. He said he'd left his kegs of black powder in another wagon, stored behind the corral. "I reckon it's safe. You'd best turn your horse in with the others." He added, "That dang trunk's a lot of trouble. Without it we likely wouldn't need the wagon."

Adaline had no intention of parting with her trunk, which she knew he was intimating. She turned Hawk into the corral, stored her tack in the wagon beside the kegs of black powder, returned to the buckboard and pulled herself up. Louis flicked the reins and they drove away from the yards, first passing tents, lean-tos, and makeshift houses with canvas roofs, and finally the brick buildings under construction, their walls festooned with precarious-appearing scaffolding. Hod carriers scrambled up and down. Gin poles lifted pallets loaded with bricks. As they passed deeper into it, the city grew unmasked in her mind's eye, a cacophonous, disordered place, unlike anything she'd ever seen. People were out in the streets. Many of the men were disheveled and clothed in rags, some staggered against walls, yet a few among them wore fine coats. Here and there were women. A barker on the boardwalk hawked shovels and gold pans. They passed a brightly painted cart with a cage on its bed and inside a grizzly bear that leveled its beady eyes upon passersby, a man with a monkey and a hurdy-gurdy, then a saloon from which the tinkling of a piano floated. Louis pulled sharply on the reins, maneuvering the wagon around a man who lay face down in the dirt street. He shouted at the mules, "Hiya!" Then, leaning close to Adaline, he laughed, "Dead or just dead drunk? Who knows!"

She pulled away from the sweetness on his breath.

Whiskey!

She was taken back to the tempestuous marriage night in Taos when he'd had too much to drink.

Be careful!

There stood a brick works, a packing house called Mohr and Yoerk, the Sitka Ice Company where great, blue blocks packed in sawdust were visible in a warehouse and a bank called Wells Fargo. They passed the Stanford Brothers Mercantile, which displayed a sign:

Importers and Wholesale Dealers of Provisions, Groceries, Wines, Liquor, Cigars, Oils and Camphors, Flour, Game and Produce, Mining Implements, Miners' Supplies, Etc.

In a line was an exhibition of vehicles of conveyance: several small steam engines, one on tracks, common wagons, fancy wagons. Men picked over tools. As Louis drove on to the river, the embarcadero emerged. Ships were tied to the wharves, gin poles mounted for offloading, and men loading cargo onto drays. In the background a stern-wheeler wended its way up the river.

They passed another saloon, a Chinese laundry, and came to a hotel, a three-story brick edifice. Louis stepped down, tied off the mules, and shouldered her trunk. In the opposite hand he carried one of his bags after handing her the other one. Dazed, Adaline followed inside, startled by the opulence of the room, which was replete with Oriental rugs, paneled walls, glass windows, and a painting hanging on one wall of a half-naked, buxom woman. Soft chairs encircled low tables on which were placed vases with yellow and red roses, and off to one side a dining area filled with men. On a table near her lay a newspaper with the headline, SHEEP DRIVE, and a subheading, *The Scout Kit Carson a Day Away*. Adaline snatched the paper up, tucking it under her arm, and moved to the counter where the clerk eyed her disdainfully.

"My wife," Louis said. "Kit Carson's daughter."

The disdain vanished from the face as if a shade had been snapped up, and an unctuous voice issued: "Would the lady like a bath drawn?"

Louis snorted. "I reckon she needs it."

She stepped back and glanced down at herself—the man's shirt, canvas trousers, high moccasins, the knife strapped to her leg. On her head rested the slouch hat she'd worn for months, and her face, she imagined, was as grimy as Louis's. He picked up the keys from the counter, shouldered her trunk again, grasped his bag, and labored up the stairway. She followed with the other bag. They came into a hallway and went through a doorway that opened to a room with a bed in its center, heaped up pillows, and alongside a table, chairs, gas lamps, a white curtain swelling with breeze in a window, and a tall mirror. She glimpsed herself in it—as filthy as she'd thought, a dark druid, behind her the equally filthy man, who grunted as he lowered the trunk. He handed her a key whereupon she found herself recoiling from the scent of his breath again. "I'll take the wagon back. Wait here when you're done."

The door closed. Adaline set his bag next to the other one, opened her trunk and crouched over it for a moment. She dug out clean underthings, a pair of moccasins, and the one dress she'd brought along.

She moved out into the hallway where she spotted another door that hung open. There, she came upon a Negro woman filling a zinc tub with steaming water taken from a wood-burning stove.

"I'm a sight, ain't I?" Adaline said.

The woman laughed. "Might have to peel that shirt off you and hope we leave some skin behind." A round mirror hung on the wall and Adaline peered into it, amazed that it was herself there. The woman poured salts into the tub, took down a towel and bar soap from a shelf, and touched the sliding latch as she made her exit. "Honey, there's a latch to lock."

Adaline set the latch, put her fresh clothes and the key on the commode, and slipped into the tub, amazed by the warmth of the water that slid over her skin. She scrubbed her back with a brush, washed her hair, and sank down into the tub, staring at her toes poking out of the water. Then she climbed out, dried, put on the clothes, and combed her hair straight, pulling the teeth of the comb gently through the tangles.

She went down the hallway back to the room, finding that Louis had not yet returned. She piled her dirty clothes and—going on to do her duty—opened Louis's bags and searched for what of his could be washed. She felt a heavy pouch. A formidable urge swept over her to look into it, but quickly she shoved it deep within and set Louis's clothes in a pile next to hers. She studied herself again in the wall mirror, finding her face clean and bright. Her ankles beneath the hem of the cream-colored dress and her arms were hard with sinew.

She knelt before her trunk, drew out the buffalo robe, and perused her books and the Frémont maps, the instruments, the box of potions Josefa had given her, the rocks with fossils she'd collected at Don Rámon's urging. The items recounted her tale since leaving Missouri, and again she succumbed to melancholy. She came upon the jewelry Josefa had proffered, and also the carved crucifix given by Pablo, and remembered precisely what Pablo's fingers had felt like on her hand, his fingers curling open, the gift tenderly slipping into her palm and his hand lingering there. She remembered the sin she had not committed that Lupe forgave her for, and Josefa, the milagritos, the baby that died on the trail, the inconsolable grief of its mother, wolves, buffalo, Gish, Yolanda's anguish over his loss, and the white stones, and Frankie. Oh, Frankie.

She looked up at the white curtain before the darkening window, then lit an oil lamp with one of the lucifers that had been left on the stand, and thought of Mr. Turner, his hoarding of them. She wondered if he had survived, accompanied by his worrying wife and his daughters, to arrive into the gold fields. Positioning herself in a chair beside the lamp, she took up the newspaper she'd absconded with and settled in to read.

The story, no doubt written by one of the newspapermen who visited the sheep camp, reported how long the journey had taken, how many sheep were driven, and by what course, which the story noted as a remarkable feat, coming out of the Lower Rio del Norte in late winter to Fort Cheyenne and thence westward and over the mountains. Yet if anyone were up to the task, the story said, it would be "the legendary guide and Indian fighter, the Nestor of the mountains, Kit Carson." Only one man had been lost, a touring Spaniard who wandered off into Blackfeet country where he had been cruelly tortured by the savages. Otherwise the ferocious tribes of the Northern Plains had left the company undisturbed, "no doubt daunted by the formidable presence of its leader." The writer added that Kit Carson was as modest and unassuming as he was reputed to be fearless, that he shrugged off approbation and avoided the admiring crowd.

Another sheep company was soon to arrive, the story continued, led by Lucien Maxwell, Kit's old comrade and fellow "Bear-Flagger" in the service of the former senator, Colonel John Frémont. Others in Kit's company were named: the New Mexico merchants, Bernavette and Mercure, and Carson's son-in-law, Louis Simmons, and then what caused Adaline's blood to jump as soon as her eyes fell upon it—a daughter! She was named and described as "a comely and sprightly young woman of proud Arapaho descent." At this, Adaline let the newspaper sink to her knees and stared at the wall opposite her as she was overtaken again by a rush of emotion. She felt the quebrado, the pain, of something come apart in her, and also requital at seeing her life entered into the record, and not just spoken of, but actually written down.

At her side, a waft of evening air drifted through the window. For the better part of an hour, she listened to wagons passing, stopping and starting out, men calling. She smoothed the newspaper and read again, studying every word until she heard the key releasing the lock in the door to the room. The door swung open and Louis appeared, regaled in new corduroy trousers and a red shirt, a pair of black boots, carrying yet another bag, which he flung in the direction of the bed. She watched him sway between the jambs. He stumbled to the bags she'd left open on the floor, poked one with his boot toe and snarled. "What's this?"

Startled, Adaline gestured at the heaps of clothing against the wall. "I meant to take your clothes out to laundry. There's one just up the street."

"That so?" he said.

Fearful, she backtracked. "With your permission, I mean."

He came near and leaned over her so that she could smell the drink yet stronger on his breath. His body lurched sideways and he caught himself by putting a hand on the wall. "You've been squirreling in my bags."

"Clothes is all," she said.

"The likes of you ain't safe down on the street, not dressed out like that."

But even as she warned herself—Watch out!—the anger rose in her and she blurted out: "What then? Back to my canvas trousers?"

His body jerked at her. He bent and lifted her by the shoulders. "None of your lip, I say." When she struggled to break loose, he swung around, and tangling a foot in his pile of clothing so that he almost pitched over, but hanging on to her, he pressed her against the wall.

She stood as straight as she could, reaching into herself for the strength to forbear. "No," she said.

"No what?"

"I won't go. I'll wait. All right."

"All right, you say? The hell! What's all right?"

"Easy, Louay." The familiar version of his name further infuriated him. Violence welled into his face and he jumped at her, clutching her bodice and shoving her yet harder against the wall. In desperation, she pushed him away, or tried to. His bulk was overpowering and her resistance enraged him even more. He bore down upon her, leaning close, reeking, and leaned back and lifted her, slid her up the wall and tore the top of her dress, lifting her with one hand, the hand that had the coldness of his ring on his stub, digging into her throat. With the other hand, he struck her on the side of the face, not once, but twice, twice at least. Everything inside her shattered and fell away, and the world went black.

•

She came to with a part of the bed beneath her, feeling the floor under her feet. She was nearly naked and cold. Her back and head were on the flat of the bottom of the bed. The ticking of the rumpled quilt pressed against her neck, and her head and face throbbed. She lay still, afraid at first to move. Finally, she rolled and slid to her knees on the floor and by sheer will found her equilibrium. She stood, used the chamber pot, her head reeling. She came back to the bedstead and picked out Louis in the near darkness, lying on his side with one arm dangling toward the floor. Her dress lay in a tangle at the bottom of the bed. She gathered it up, her head swimming again with the motion. She moved to her trunk and softly dragged her buffalo robe to the far corner of the room, sat against the wall, and pulled up her pantalets and drew the robe over her. She was shivering. She saw the newspaper on the floor next to the chair and above it the oil lamp sputtering. The white curtain hung straight down. The street noises and men talking outside seemed eerie. She fell asleep again.

At the break of dawn she awoke. She looked down at her dress, running her finger along the ripped seams, then crept across to retrieve the needle and thread she kept in her trunk. She crawled back to the corner. She pulled her robe around her shoulders and bent close to the fabric. Carefully, she stitched until she dozed off. She awoke again, the needle poised in her hand. Louis was on his back now, snoring. The oil lamp had burned out. She heard a wagon rumbling slowly down the street outside, and from directly beneath the window a delirious, mournful voice singing, "Asleep in Jesus, blessed sleep . . ."

Her thoughts were invaded by the bargain she'd struck with her father in her aunt's barn. If only he had brought her West with him then, things would have turned out so differently. She'd have finished growing up in Taos. Or if she'd stolen away with Pablo, as she desperately wished she had, everything would have been changed, and if there'd been any change in the course of events once she found her way West, everything that followed might have occurred in a different order. She thought about her father, remembering the stories of how, filled with wanderlust and bored by his apprenticeship to the saddler, he'd lit out on the Santa Fé Trail, but he was a young man, or a boy soon to be a man, whereas she was a woman.

She proceeded to mend around the bodice of the dress. The stitching was too wide at first but improved along the arm. She pushed the work away and leaned her head back against the wall, closing her eyes. Her head ached. She tongued her jaw and on the left side felt the one tooth knocked loose. The street sounds magnified, horses, men talking again, hoofbeats, more wagons trundling back and forth. She fell asleep, but when her eyes opened morning light flooded through the window and Louis was up, pissing into the chamber pot. He pulled on his corduroy trousers and red shirt.

He sat in a chair to put on his boots and spied her watching him, and frowned as if surprised that she was there. He walked to the door, opened it, stopped to look back at her, and frowned again. "Breakfast," he said. His eyes turned to her trunk, then to her, examining her dress, apparently not registering that she'd been sewing it. He fished in his pocket, took out a ten-dollar gold piece, which he plunked on the table. "For your work on the drive," he said. "If you need to buy something, do it soon. We'll be leaving." He went out, clicking the door shut.

He had given up keeping her off the street, or he didn't care. Or he didn't remember that he cared. Or there were two of him, one that cared and one that did not, one that was darkly sane, and one that became degraded and loco, as her father had said could happen to men. She flattened her work over her knee, knotted the thread, and bit it off. She eased her head back, inhaled, then exhaled slowly and eyed the soiled clothes he'd left against the wall. She believed the not remembering was caused by the drink and was in the mind, while at the same time everything was stored in his blood for remembering. It was his stance in relation to her, a deep remembering, invoking a commotion between his ferocity and his fear of her father. It struck her again that he had to be cautious so long as her father was near, but if he drank as he had, twice now, she imagined some incremental change occurred as if by detonations that gradually shook him loose from his moorings. Now that her father was going away, there'd be no ameliorating force left to care for her, and she was caught in her own war between wanting to be worthy of trust and a escalating, manic urge to exact a penalty for every instance of her suffering. So long as her father was here, she could moderate her tumult. Once he was gone, she would fill with disorder and panic.

She stood, put on the dress, then mechanically moved to her trunk and opened it, took her things out one by one until she could get at the secret compartment. She took out her money, adding the ten dollar gold piece and running the coinage through her fingers, feeling its weight. In addition to the occasional measurements as to location, elevation, and temperature that she wrote down, she'd begun a ledger in her notebook, too, inspired by Mercure. With a graphite pencil, she entered the number: 10.00. She wrote: Sheep drive. She added the 10.00 to the 37.00 she already had and wrote: 47.00. She returned the money and the ledger to the compartment, put everything else back, including the newspaper which she'd retrieved from the floor by the window, and closed the compartment. She took up her canvas trousers and put them on under the shirtwaist, shut and latched the trunk. She looked once again at the mirror, at the ludicrous figure she cut wearing her moccasins, canvas trousers, and crudely mended shirtwaist. She strapped the knife to her leg and arranged her hair so that it half-covered the bruise on her cheek, and donned the slouch hat and a coat. She went out into the hallway, descended the stairs, and moved across the lobby, slowing as she approached the dining hall, then seeing the men before her—her father, Bernavette, Mercure, and with his back to her, Louis—she stopped, loathe to go in. She stepped back. She would wait, stunned, deranged, barely understanding, yet filled with fury for Louis's violation.

Part 3

Chapter 16

1853

As he said he would, Adaline's father journeyed from Sacramento to Sonoma along with Lucien Maxwell, John Hatcher, and Tom Boggs. From Sonoma they were to head southward, then eastward via the Mojave to Taos and the Rayado. Adaline and Louis went as far as Sonoma and on the day of their parting from the others she was astride Hawk and had Ghost and the filly on leads. Her trunk had been loaded in the wagon where Louis sat, holding the reins. "Adiós, Louay," her father said, then he looked searchingly at her, marking once again, she believed, the bruise on her cheek. He would not want to intercede but instead exercised his care within his taciturnity. "Twister. Vaya con Dios." He swung up onto his buckskin, turned back, nodded at her, and started out with the others. Watching, Adaline's breath caught in her throat at the sight of the figures on horseback riding into the golden hills. It was a moment eerily like what she remembered watching him leave Fayette when she was a child, except that now she was a child no longer.

She then traveled inland with Louis and for a short time she lived in the town of Grass Valley where Louis plied his skills as a blaster in the mines. She worked as a housekeeper to help defray the expenses of lodging: dust mop and rag, the flatiron heavy in her hand, iron pans to be washed. In the meantime, she strove to encircle herself with calm, imagining this as a saucer of milk with her brain in its center, slowly revolving, taking in everything and awaiting an opportunity to escape. She formed the habit of sucking at the empty space left by the tooth in her mouth, which gave her a slightly different demeanor, a kind of sullen squint. Not long before November arrived, Louis went into the hills to blast out a mine with his black powder. He would be gone a week. This was her chance to slip away without confrontation.

She'd been eyeing a contraption at the mercantile, what the proprietor called a sulky, but it looked like a travois with a seat, two wooden wheels, iron strapping for tires, and an iron axle. She purchased it for eight dollars, fashioned a rope harness to attach its two poles to Ghost, and replaced the seat with boards. Very early the next morning, she dressed in her canvas trousers, doeskin shirt, a red poncho, knee high moccasins, and her slouch hat. She wore the Navy pistol in the small of her back. So outfitted, she fancied that from a distance at least she might be taken for a man. She lifted the small crucifix with the Cristo from her trunk, ran a thong through its eyelet, and put it around her neck and tucked it under her shirt, keeping the twisted figure close against her breast. Up to then she had been unwilling to wear it, not so much because she feared Louis would remark on it as because it was hers and hers alone. She left, heading southward, which seemed right for seeking out Alexis Godey, or even Colonel Frémont. Of course, she ached to return to Taos, but she was certain Pablo was gone and there would be the shame and difficulty of facing her father and Josefa.

She first followed the trace of the Yuba River astride Hawk, and taking with her the filly, which she'd named Manchada. She took Ghost and the travois with wheels which was loaded with an old Hawken breech loader she'd purchased, also her trunk which containing Josefa's jewelry and potions, Don Rámon's rocks, Frémont's journals and maps, her mother's beaded bag, the turtle, and the newspaper article from Sacramento. Strapped over the top of it all was her buffalo robe.

By a stroke of fortune, she fell in with two of Mercure's pastores. They had tried their hand at placer mining, but disliking the cold of the mountains they decided to journey to the lowlands of the San

Joaquin River from whence they'd received word of a compatriot who operated an arrastra. She asked about Juan. The pastores informed her that he'd gone straight back to the New Mexico Territory. They had two red cows in their possession, which they'd happened upon during their descent, and observing Adaline's interest in them, gave them to her. She continued with the pastores down the valley, but after two weeks of traveling and eating beans and pemmican, she fell into a pain like none she'd ever experienced. She'd missed her monthlies four months in succession. She remembered Josefa's advice to find the company of a woman were anything like this to happen, but there was no other woman here.

They neared the river and she made off on her own, finding a place to make camp on the other side of a hill from the men, and there aborted with only the company of her animals. She pried up a large stone with a stick, intending to bury the child in the cavity she hollowed out, first swaddling it in the cloth she used to clean up her blood. She did not know whether it was a boy or girl, but in the moonlight caught a fleeting glimpse of its fontanelle and a wisp of black hair curling over it and of its wrinkled face adhering together as if jammed out of gummi arabicum. It was a death expelled from her womb, following a furious conception. She felt empty, cold, and bereft. Laying the tiny body in the cavity, she put the rock back and said a prayer for what she'd given over and waited for the pain to subside. She thought of Josefa's first born, Charles, having survived barely a year, and of Josefa at the gravesite, of the Día de los Muertos, and of placing milagritos on all the graves, including her sister's. She found a white stone and put it at the head of the rock. In addition to the sound of her mule, horses, and cows pulling on the grass, she detected geese talking to each other. They made a muted sound like a hymn of tineablas, ghost words as the moon sank.

The night passed. She and the pastores parted company the next morning when the men gave her some rock salt for the cows and turned to trek up the San Joaquin to the hills. Alone again, she grew determined to find Alexis Godey and continued to the south in the valley, giving wide berth to the settlements, the ramshackle houses with canvas roofs, the little groups of round dwellings used by Indians. It began to rain. The next day, she came upon three vaqueros driving some twenty cows before them. One rider broke company and trotted toward her. She pulled her hat down and circled her animals in close. The man stopped and asked where her cows had come from. In a low voice, she said from up north. The man, a grizzled Mexican, gave her a hard look and looked at the cows.

He has marked me.

He knows I am a woman.

She asked if he knew how much farther it was to Alexis Godey's house. He said it was a half-day's ride down this trail. He gestured vaguely at the hills to the east. "I hear the colonel himself has just come over from San Francisco. We're cleaning up his slicks. I suppose you are all right with the red ones, verdad?" He cast his eyes to the cows again and then back at her.

Filled with misgiving, she fabricated. "I'm to deliver them to Godey."

"I see." He then studied her travois on wheels. "Half a wagon."

She nodded and glanced at her mud-streaked trunk and buffalo robe on the travois. She inquired as to how she would know Godey's place when she came upon it.

He described it as a big adobe with corrals de vacas and a number of Indian huts. "It's when the tule swamp starts up," he said. "Maybe he's not there. Maybe he's with the colonel."

Sensing a trap, she said, "I've been instructed to deliver these cows." She swung Hawk around in order to put the cows before her, leaving room for Manchada and Ghost, and set out. By late afternoon she came upon a swamp fringed with wintered tules and alive with thousands of pelicans, cormorants, bitterns, and huge flocks of geese and ducks. Sandhill cranes flew in a gray sky, and then she saw the house. As she approached, a woman with yellow hair appeared in the doorway and stood with one hand on her hip. "Godey's not here," she announced. Adaline removed her hat, showing her hair, and said she was the daughter of Kit Carson, an old fellow traveler of Alexis Godey. Now, she half-fabricated, saying that her father had sent her here.

The woman laughed, the sound burnishing like brass as it descended. Adaline's red cows skittered, and Adaline restrained them and tried to explain, but it only made the woman renew her laughter. "There's no telling when he'll be back." Had Adaline known then what the woman knew, and what the vaquero back on the trail had likely known as well, what her father must have known, that Godey was an infamous philanderer, that he'd already been married three times and had at least as many common-law wives, innumerable liaisons with Mexicans, white women, and Indians, uncountable children, she might have concluded that the woman considered her a lovesick rival.

She determined to backtrack. She rode past the tule swamp, scaring up the birds again, and then wearied along for a few more days up into the hills, searching for Colonel Frémont. She met several empty freight wagons making their way down and passed several others going up with four, six, even eight mules in harness. Though this way, what in later years would be called the "Old Highway," was an easy enough climb, the loaded wagons labored under the weight of heavy supplies, including parts she recognized as being for stamp mills and big cast iron things that looked like cannons, which in time she would learn were called monitors. A man affirmed that Colonel Frémont was up there at his rancho, though not in the town of Mariposa, as she had believed, but in what was called Biddle's Camp. It began to snow, and she followed the muddy trail that went around a mountain, then found the town with its row of houses and the Frémont rancho set back from the road. A slender man appeared on the portico and asked what her business was. His cheekbones seemed pinched out of clay and in the obscurity of falling snow he affixed her with his bright, black eyes as he inclined his head toward her. She told him who she was. He went inside, and in a moment the colonel himself appeared.

"Kit's daughter?" he said. "Then come down." She dismounted and stepped up onto the portico whereupon the colonel peered into her face. "By God, it must be."

The colonel's thick hair hung down to his collar. He glanced toward her desultory cavalcade of snow-bedecked animals, then back at her. Suddenly, Adaline was astonished by what she'd accomplished, that the colonel stood right before her, the commander of the expeditions and author of the journals. While her image of him had fashioned a younger, more rugged man, he was as tall and regal appearing as she had expected yet enveloped by something delicate, his sallow cheeks, his aquiline nose, and haunted eyes.

He told her that a daughter of Kit Carson was always welcome here. He invited her in, but when she hesitated, looking to her animals, he summoned the man with the sharp cheekbones to lead them to a corral. George, he called him. Frémont explained that two men had recently arrived to confer with him, but she would be given the room that would be Mrs. Frémont's. For now, Frémont led her into a parlor and explained he hoped that soon Mrs. Frémont would be here. He gestured at a sideboard supplied with teacups, then a small shelf in which were placed several books. She spied the colonel's own expedition journal there, also a book called *White-Jacket*, one called *The Scarlet Letter*, and small stacks of weekly newspapers, the *Alta California*, *Sacramento Union*, *Mariposa Gazette*. Two chairs were placed on a flowered rug. "What do you think?" he asked. "Will it be suitable?"

Adaline glanced about in confusion. "What? I? You mean the parlor? Suitable for Mrs. Frémont?"

He smiled. "Won't you sit?"

She didn't move but looked down at her soiled trousers.

"Sit," he said.

She positioned her pistol and sat as lightly as possible in one of the chairs. "It's perfect," she said, looking away in embarrassment, then blurted out that she hoped to graze her stock in order to secure a means for herself.

"But aren't you married?" he said, taking a seat himself.

Fearing his perception of her failure, she fell tongue-tied. There were waves, shimmering waves moving through the air from her absent father to the colonel; she felt relief, gratitude that she had found him, and still disbelief, and also a terror that at any moment she might be turned out, that she'd have to return to near starvation on the trail. She looked down at her feet, only to be appalled anew by her soiled moccasins resting on the fine rug.

"To Louis Simmons?" the colonel asked.

Adaline looked up. The colonel peered at her, leaning from his chair. She was overwhelmed. She took a shuddering breath and said, "I left him."

Colonel Frémont pulled back. "Isn't he a friend of your father's?"

This was the subject she feared. "He's gone home. I mean Pa has, after the sheep were delivered to Sacramento." She took another breath. It occurred to her that the colonel might not know about the sheep drive. "We brought sheep to California."

"Yes, I know. I'm sorry I missed seeing Kit and Maxwell," he said. "So, you're in the rift of it still."

She said, "Pa told me to find Mr. Godey if it came to that because . . . because I think he knew the marriage would be short-lived. I mean Pa. I went to Godey's ranch, but Godey wasn't there," she said. "A woman was there."

Colonel Frémont said simply, "At Godey's ranch?"

Something glimmered deep in the recesses of her consciousness. It was an inchoate response to the way he surveyed her. Later in the night when she lay in Mrs. Frémont's room it would take full form, but now all the further she went was to wonder what the colonel knew about the woman. It was merely a glimmering, a briefly flashing light, overwhelmed once again by the sense of whose company she was in and her anxiety over having put him in an difficult position. "I saw three men. One directed me to Godey's house. He'd heard you were here, too, and said he was gathering slicks for you."

"More likely they were thieving slicks. And you were lucky," he said. "But you're saying you came alone down the valley and then all the way up here with those cows?"

She considered the seeming foolishness of that, her struggling to bring the cows along, and she wondered why she had, and then she hit on it, the true reason: They were a counterweight to the vastness of her emptiness, they gave her a sense of her own obligation, and giving her that they made her feel less terrified of the pain of being irretrievably lost. "They and the horses, and the mule are all I have."

He looked away toward the dining room where windows revealed an evening sun beginning to break through the dizzying snowfall. His brow furrowed and he looked back at her. "Godey's off to the Sierras doing a survey for the railroad. At my behest. But this won't do, your coming here in these straits."

Suddenly, she found herself saying that she'd read his journals and reports, that she considered them fascinating, and that she admired his science and wondered how a man so sure of himself in a dangerous world could also have such facility with words. Even as she spoke, and as her eyes fell on the little bookshelf, which included his expedition journal, she felt the mortification creeping up on her again, now for her forwardness. Yet it seemed that he was pleased, though it was unfathomable that a compliment from the likes of her could find a way to the pinnacle of his greatness. One thing she had yet to learn was that the chief vulnerability of any egotist, which Colonel Frémont certainly was, was to flattery.

"My science?" he said. He struck a lucifer and turned to light an oil lamp, as the deepening twilight had made the room dim. "You are interested in the science? You say you've read my reports?"

How could she explain that for years she'd pored over the drawings of plants and the names given to them, and to previously unknown creatures, and the description of rivers, springs emanating from under rocks, fossils imprinted upon stones, and astronomical data, the numbers given to location in all the places the colonel and his troop of men had traveled? She wanted to tell him about how she could take measurements, too, determine location by sextant, how she'd traveled to places he'd been, such as Bent's Fort, and the Fontaine-qui-bouille, and the hole at the Land of Goshen, and about the dogs, about Don Rámon, who also had admired his science and who had encouraged her interest. She wanted to tell him that Don Rámon had been killed for his curiosity, and mocked by the same man, her husband, whom she'd left. But she considered that she'd gone far enough already. She said softly, "Yes." And added that her father, whilst arranging over two years ago in Missouri to have a trunk shipped to her by Mrs. Frémont, believed that she had slipped the expedition journal in anonymously.

The colonel's face lit up. "Well. I don't know about that, but it sounds like something Jessie would do." He turned again to adjust the lamp, then faced her. "I remember when I first met your father, he was delivering you to Missouri to be educated."

She stared at him for a moment, thunderstruck that so much of her life was circumscribed by him. She sighed deeply and said she did not want to impose on him, that all she had hoped for was to find a place where she might provide for herself. "I didn't know where else to turn. I am not even sure why I came here. If I have burdened you, then I am sorry."

"Nonsense. It's well you came."

There was a commotion outside, the whinny of a horse and men talking, the sound of boots on the portico floor. The colonel rose and walked out to the dining room where he peered through the windows. George came through a doorway from another part of the house, but the colonel stopped him, saying he would see to the visitors. To Adaline, he said, "It's my banker and an attorney. Will you forgive me?" He gave her a look, the expression in equal parts grave and bemused. "They're worried about my holdings."

He directed George to tell Johanna—a woman, as it turned out, who awaited them in the kitchen—to give Adaline food and to heat water for a bath. He started out to see to the arrivals and Adaline noticed how gingerly he turned. She recalled that back in Taos she'd heard her father and Josefa talking about how his feet had been frostbitten on the last, calamitous expedition into the Rockies. The care in his face was apparent, yet when he opened the door the wind ruffled his hair and he looked back at her with a shine in his eyes. "Don't worry."

George led her into the kitchen where he spoke to the woman in a language Adaline had never before heard. The woman's hair was cut straight across her forehead and lopped just short of her shoulders. She wore bone jewelry in her ears, a necklace of what Adaline learned was dentalium, a mollusk from the sea. On her face two tattoos traced diagonals from the sides of her lips up to her cheekbones. George said, "She is called Johanna, just as I am called George," which Adaline took to mean those were not their proper names. "She is my sister."

Johanna touched Adaline's shoulder, then placed a pot of water on a stove. She served up a gruel that Adaline guessed was made of acorns and venison. While Adaline ate, Johanna looked on, smiling in a way that made her appear she had little live things in her cheeks. George left and once Adaline had finished the gruel Johanna led her into yet another chamber where she poured the water into a copper tub, produced a nightgown, and took Adaline's clothes away. A half hour later, she returned to show Adaline into what would be Mrs. Frémont's room.

It had ceased snowing and the moonlight bore through the glass and fell upon the ticking of a quilt. The wind rustled in the pine trees. Instantly Adaline fell into a drowse, only faintly hearing the men in the parlor. One of them paced back and forth and his voice seemed vexed as he inquired into the colonel's Mariposa Grant. In time, Adaline would hear more about the land grant. It was enormous, better than seventy square miles, and as it happened the colonel was in the process of turning it, in fact increasing its size. He was literally revolving it ninety degrees on the maps so that its new boundaries would allow him to hold onto both the rich mines in the Sierras and the pastures that adjoined Mariposa Creek and descended clear down into the bottomland of the valley.

    The drowse overcame her. She entered sleep speculating about the colonel's interest in romancing other women in his wife's absence. The colonel's habits were, of course, not known to her, but she dreamed of him in the room, his face thin, regal, and silvery. Then she reawakened, her breath taken away by the fright of such a possibility.

Chapter 17

THE COLONEL SENT her in the company of George back into the San Joaquin Valley, heading southward near the Kern River. There she would find a dwelling among the casas left over from the Rancho San Emidio, also pastures and corrals. José Pérez, a vaquero who'd worked for the hacienda, and now worked for Frémont and Godey, was there, too. The colonel struck an agreement with Adaline to join José in searching for cattle running wild, or slicks, as the three Mexicans had been gathering, though without permission. The colonel said he'd driven a herd up north to sell a year ago, but that there should be more than a few left. Once Godey returned, the cattle would be delivered to the new Fort Tejón, built to protect the settlers against attacks by discontented Californios and Indians. She could keep one-tenth of the cattle for herself for her efforts. He had a similar arrangement with José Pérez. What remained of the other owners, the old hacendados, were so reduced in stature that they'd forfeited all claims. "You can help me," he said, giving her a paper that affirmed his intentions. "José will be glad for your help, too. And you'll be safe traveling with George. Don't worry."

They were down by the stable. George separated out her animals and looked at her with his shining eyes. For his part, the colonel seemed a tall, curiously delicate figure implanted in her imagination. Little did she know that before she saw him again late in 1856, and not long before she met his wife for the first time, he would be fabulously wealthy, the subject of controversy, lawsuits, vitriol and hatred, famous for his abolitionist views, and the first candidate of the Republican Party for President of the United States.

•

As they journeyed down, George told her that he and Johanna had the same mother but different fathers. Johanna had been raised among her people and he had been taken to the valley by his American father, a man named Stilts. Later, after George began working for Colonel Frémont, he arranged for Johanna to join him. During the nights, Adaline noticed that George always set his bedroll nearest the trail and placed her some distance away in cover, which she believed must follow the Colonel's instructions. George also played the banjo in the evenings, which he said his father had taught him to do. It was a way of calming the animals, he said. He had an unusual way of playing, rarely chording but plucking out the notes of a tune.

In due time, they found the casas and pastures, and George headed back, leaving her with people she would come to hold dear, José, Juana, their twin sons, and three little ones. She was younger than Juana, who was fifteen years younger than her husband, and before long she became like a sister to Juana and aunt to the children. She stayed the first year—1854—tending to her expanding herd and pleasuring in the things Juana harvested from her garden—maize, chiles, tomatoes, squash. Later in the spring, she joined José and the twins in running cows to the foothills of the Tehachapi, what conjoined the Sierras with the Coast Mountains.

By her second year there—1855—and through breeding and finding slicks, she had increased her herd to nearly twenty animals. Up in the hills, she cut out the colonel's slicks, folded them in with ones José intended for Frémont, and with the twins drove them down to the pasture before the casas. One twin rode off to tell Godey where they were while she and the other twin returned to the hills. When she reappeared at the settlement later that summer, Juana told her that Godey had twice come and gone and that he'd left a newspaper. In it was a notice that Louis Simmons had obtained a writ of divorce, claiming that Adaline did not behave properly, that she was wild and a thief. It asked for anyone who knew of her whereabouts to inform her of the notice, or if anyone had reason to not allow the divorce to proceed they should inform the newspaper by a certain date, which was long past. Adaline was glad that Juana did not read or speak English and glad to know that Louis considered their marriage dissolved, yet the thought that word of the false accusations might reach her father and Josefa in Taos, or already had, or Colonel Frémont here in California, filled her with the old anger.

Juana said that on his second trip Godey had gone dancing down south with some Indians. A woman traveled with him. He came back with two more women. "Y preguntare por tu."

"¿Por mí?" Adaline said, seeing in Juana's expression her distaste. Adaline was well content with her abstemiousness and extremely wary of Godey.

•

During her third spring in California—it was April of 1856—as she, José, and the now fifteen-year-old twins were driving the stock into the hills, they spied two slicks a couple hundred yards off the trail. José rode into the bush to retrieve them. It took some time to chase them down, and when he returned he reported that he'd come across a man dragging a bucket of water from a creek, that the man had asked for her by name.

"He knows me?" Adaline said.

José shrugged. The man's name, he said, was Turner. This gave Adaline pause, as she wondered if it could possibly be her old tormenting custodian.

"No one is with him?" she asked.

"No, está solo." José's way was to speak either Spanish or English to Adaline, according to his sounding of the occasion. He'd carried the man's water and helped him back into his choza. The man was very sick. "Y no tiene más que un pata," José said, striking the ground with a boot heel and causing the rowels of his spur to jangle.

"One foot?"

"Sí."

The next morning Adaline rode her horse where José had directed her. She rode Slate now, a gray gelding birthed by Manchada that Adaline had kept and recently broke. She had taken to riding either him or Ghost and customarily brought both along when she traveled into the hills. She crossed the Kern River, then after some time riding discovered the creek, a wrecked long Tom, and just across the creek the choza, a hut with a torn canvas roof and rotting posts for walls. A dozen or so pileated woodpeckers that had been working over the posts winged off, swirling in a flying sash of gray, white, and the red of their heads. A pine snag stood to one side and in it a turkey vulture watched as she lifted the latch to the door, which creaked as she pushed it open.

She was greeted by a sound of mice skittering off from underfoot and the stench of waste. Though there were no windows, light slanted through the doorway and a slash of it passed through a rip in the canvas to the floor. Then she heard breath like a rasp and made out a form lying on a pallet against the far wall. The smell of rot grew stronger as she approached. A bucket stood near the head of the pallet. Adaline studied the emaciated form, the footless left leg wrapped in a rag and drooping down toward the floor, a pair of white and bony hands resting on the blanket, a skull-like head propped up on a poke bag, and hair and a wisp of beard white as snow. A pair of fevered eyes looked back at her. She inquired: "Mr. Turner, is it?"

After a moment, the voice came. "They're gone, Louise and Carrie, and the little one gone for good." He whispered hoarsely, "Dead."

"Dead?" Now certain this was Ned Turner, Adaline had a rush of feeling for the little girl she'd known what seemed an eternity ago. "And Carrie? Dead too?"

"Back to Missouri with her mother," he said. "The little one not so lucky."

Adaline understood that it was the infant girl who had died, but still she wondered about Carrie living with her disturbed mother. She glanced at the stump of leg poised above the floor.

"It was too hard for my girls." Turner fell silent, then tried to raise himself from the pallet and whispered, "It's greed. The Devil's quicksand. Death."

"Easy," Adaline said, bending down and touching his shoulder.

Turner succeeded in positioning his elbows so as to prop himself up. Outside, the woodpeckers had returned to drum at the posts, and as if by resonance with the racket Mr. Turner's head and shoulders quivered. "They left me," he said. "The little one dead. Never laid eyes on California. She blamed me, Louise did, and took Carrie back to Missouri." He turned his head toward the far side of the hut. "Frostbite. I cut it myself." His head sank and he fell into a paroxysm of wheezing, his hands clutched together above his chest, falling to his sides while he caught his breath. "Such pain. It's the smoke of Hell. Pity them that feels the fire at the bottom of the pit. I heard you was in these parts and prayed you would come for me."

It seemed strange to have her presence wished for by this man, and suddenly she was appalled that she was here, being called to administer to the invalid, who, true to his foolishness, had come south into this region where the arrastras, chili mills, and stamp mills were already marginal undertakings.

"Wait here," she told him, as if he were capable of doing anything else. She walked outside to her horse, meaning to get food for him and causing the woodpeckers, who had circled back again, to explode into the air. The vulture, a purple-faced watchman motionless on its roost between the hut and rise to the creek, had been drawn to its vigil by the scent of death. Adaline's horse worried its tether while she rummaged through her poke for tortillas, a hunk of salt beef, a candle, all of which she carried back to the hut. Once lit, the candle gave her a better aspect on the evidence of squalor—shovels, picks, pans, a heap of soiled clothes, a second bucket that had been used as a chamber pot, and a boot. In the corner next to the door stood a table littered with paraphernalia. She stepped back quickly, catching sight of the bloody rags beneath a handsaw.

She spotted a stool and carried it next to Turner's pallet and set the food and a jar of water on it. "Here," she said. He lay still. She placed her hand on his forehead, which was dry and burning with fever, then knelt to look at his stump but was assaulted by a waft of urine from the pallet. She unwrapped the rag, holding it gingerly with her fingertips. The rank smell of rotting flesh overwhelmed all other scents. She held up her candle and regarded the rag soaked in ooze, and a second rag wrapped tight above where he'd cut, the lines of crimson, the poison that ran in the veins from the stump.

He hadn't cut high enough, and she thought again about his foolishness, his nerve to cut off his own foot yet not making the cut above the infection, just as he'd had the nerve to set out from Missouri for the gold fields when he was barely competent to survive the trail. More of the leg would have to come off, or surely he would die.

She looked around and thought—not here, though, not me, or not me alone, not without clean linen and enough laudanum or whiskey to put him out, for God's sake, not without help.

She glanced into his eyes, which were hooded like a reptile's. "The boot," he said.

What he meant, Adaline had no idea, some woeful fascination, maybe, with the boot that had covered the dismembered foot. She slid over on her knees, set the candle on the stool, and picked up the water jar. "Drink this." She held the jar to his lips and lifted his head. He swallowed a little while the remainder drooled down his chin. "Try this." She set the jar down, tore off a sliver of beef, and put it to his lips. "I have a wagon back in the hills. I'll fetch it." She ground down on herself, reconciling to the prospect that she was going to have to help this man.

Turner tongued the meat into his cheek. "Look to the boot."

She glanced back at the solitary boot on the floor. "I see it."

"Look. The left. The Devil!"

Not knowing what that meant either, be it admonition or curse, she walked to the boot, which was the right hand one.

His head lolled sideways. "No. The other. Under the table."

She moved to the corner and bent to look, perceiving what might have been the boot jammed beneath the table. She heard the voice again: "Look." She reached out and tugged on the heel. The boot yielded, but at the same instant a dark creature slithered out the top of it and scurried over Adaline's arm, its claws dry on her skin. Adaline jerked back and frantically crawled out and clambered to her feet, gasping. It was a rat, running in circles and squeaking. Abruptly it vanished through the far wall. Adaline sucked in air. "Damnation, by God!"

Turner had rolled to his side to face her. "Look in."

"The hell!"

"Look."

She retrieved her candle from where she'd left it on the stump, glaring at him. His eyes were fevered. He waved one hand weakly, pulled up his knees, and quivered as if trying to muster the strength to stand up on his one foot. "Stay where you are," she said. "I'll look." She walked back and bent, holding the candle to the boot. The nearer she drew the stronger became the stink. She saw a form squashed inside and realized it was Turner's foot, left to rot. She lurched back. "The hell, Mr. Turner!"

"Inside," he said.

She gingerly held the candle near as possible, keeping as much distance as she could from the mouth of the boot. Something else was pressed next to the glutinous, half-eaten foot.

"Take it out."

She slipped her fingers alongside the dank leather. She felt a piece of thong and tugged on it. A leather pouch came out with a sucking exhalation, covered in slime. She dangled it away from her body and looked over at Turner, who watched her intently. "I dredged and scraped the bottom like a Heathen Chinee. That's all I got, what I kept for Louise." He fell into another paroxysm of wheezing and rolled to his back again, gasping for air.

"All right," Adaline said. She still held the bag, which must have weighed two pounds.

Turner's words hissed, dark like air narrowed in a billows: "See that she gets it."

By its heft, she was sure it was his cache, everything he had for his dreams, his atonement in the form of lucre placed in her hands, which were shaking, and accompanied by a demand that was more like the old Mr. Turner than she preferred. "I'm going to fetch my wagon," she said. "We'll help you away from here and you can keep it for her."

Turner lay flat, seemingly ephemeral under the blanket. His face was white, his stump floated above the floor, and his voice was weak: "You have to do this for them. Louise and Carrie." And then the whisper: "Death is cruel in its making, and proud, but kind in the end. I'll be gone, cleansed by the blood of Jesus."

Pneumoniac, Mr. Turner had been granted the final gift of hallucination, which even in this extremity would be uncarnal and cold, washed hard like stones in an unforgiving torrent, rain, snow, and stone crumbling into the earth and the plants and animals that lived upon it, and the unyielding Santos glaring out from their niches.

Once outside, she opened the pouch. She was startled by the actual sight of it. She found herself straightening to look around to be sure no one was watching. No one was, not alongside the creek, not up over the bank, nor on the flat beyond, nor from the hills where the river was, and not back toward Mr. Turner's hut, either. Only the vulture lingered on its limb, still as the tree in the windless air. She slipped a finger inside the pouch to stir the dust and nuggets, what she thought must be close to seven hundred dollars worth. She cinched the draw string tight, walked to Slate and pressed the pouch into the bottom of her poke.

•

She returned that afternoon, she on her horse and José with the wagon, having left the herd under the care of his sons. Because of the wagon, they were compelled to circle to the east in order to cross the Kern. When they reached the hut six hours later, Mr. Turner was dead.

She and José appropriated Mr. Turner's spades to dig a grave near the creek. José kept a vigilance toward the vulture with its stare fixed on the hut but otherwise stayed on task. He peeled off leaves of earth from the sides, carving the walls straight, and shoveled out the earth in piles. Each time Adaline stopped to rest, José admonished, "El olor, señorita. Hondo." Soon, they had it deep enough to contain the smell, a rectangular opening five feet down that was cool and moist in its bottom. They walked to the hut, spread Mr. Turner's blanket on the floor, lifted him onto it, and half-lifted, half-dragged the body out, each grasping an end of the blanket. It seemed impossible how heavy Mr. Turner had become, like iron. The vulture flicked its head, its eyes little round pebbles. Adaline and José lowered everything into the hole, body, blanket, bloodstained rags, and the pair of boots, one with the glutinous remains of a foot in it, then Adaline's shovel hissed for every time José's shovel went hiss hiss.

Once, while José kept shoveling, she returned to the hut to retrieve the last of the personal articles—a hymnal, Bible, a pair of glasses, pocketknife, and a watch. Coming out, she caught sight of a horseman with a mule on a lead brushing through the willows just this side of the creek. He wore a duster and a Mexican poncho. His horse was the color of pearl and outfitted with a saddle in the Mexican style— wide fenders and a high horn, metal buckles and rings. The mule was black as obsidian with a rolled aparejo. The man dismounted and walked to the gravesite, dripping a trail of water from the hems of his duster. He had a limp. He peered into the grave where all that remained visible were the tops of two boots, the toes of Mr. Turner's intact foot, and the features of his face. "Ned Turner," the stranger said.

Adaline and José stood with their shovels, not speaking.

"I didn't expect him to be in this bad a way," the man said. "As bad as it could be."

He was not Mexican, despite his garb. His accent was not Mexican. His face was half-concealed under the hat brim. As if signaled by her examining him, he took the hat off, revealing his shining black hair and high brow. Handsome, he was. His hazel eyes were flecked with blue.

Adaline said, "You knew him."

The man glanced at the ramshackle hut. "Somewhat."

Uncertain as to the man's intentions, she said, "He was barely alive when I found him." She gestured with the hymnal, Bible, watch, pocket knife, and glasses, which she had stacked in her hands, then lied. "This is all he had left, or at least all I found. I'm meaning to bury them with him." When she'd first picked them up, the hymnal and Bible conjured visions of Mr. Turner from the Santa Fé Trail: his theological expostulations, the hullabaloo with his oxen in the mornings, his prairie schooner trapped in the river, the trunk she almost lost, and the ineffectuality of his anger. "I came West with him," she said.

The man did not respond but looked toward the hut again. She dropped the articles into the grave and fell to her task with José. She piled dirt over the remains of Mr. Turner in order to obliterate the evidence of his person, while José systematically worked from one end to the other. The stranger removed his duster, spread it over a bush, and reached out to take Adaline's shovel.

"I'm Adaline Carson," she said, again noting the slight gimp in his walk.

"I know. Your reputation precedes you," he said. "Gerard. Gerard Perlot."

She nodded toward José. "This is José Perez."

Perlot nodded at José. The two men topped off the grave and she fashioned a cross out of planks and pounded it into the ground with a stone. The vulture had vanished. As she and José fetched stones to make a midden, crows circled overhead and the woodpeckers returned to raid one wall of the hut.

The stranger's eyes followed them. "No metal in there?"

She shrugged, revealing nothing. "Not that I could see."

She thought something should be said for Mr. Turner, and as she searched for it she discovered tears welling in her eyes. The tears were not for Mr. Turner himself but for mortality in general, as death had come to haunt her, lying low wherever she went, and for something reciprocal lost in herself—the hopefulness of that time on the

Santa Fé Trail, the passionate desire for her future while heading toward the Rayado and Taos. She looked up toward the darkening mountains. "Take this soul. He loved his daughters. He had good in him, maybe enough to dog his way into heaven. He wanted to do right, though he didn't know what it was. He's taken the big jump, now. Be kind to him, like nobody much else was, since he was a damn fool."

These words caused José to flick his eyes at her and as he made the sign of the cross a grin began to evidence itself. The stranger looked up and scrutinized her directly, provoking a bodily response from Adaline, the lighting of a fusee smoldering toward its charge.

Chapter 18

Spring, 1856

ADALINE WAS NINETEEN, fully a young woman, and yet mainly distrustful of men except to work with them, as with José. She'd grown beautiful after a fashion, though from her habit of sucking on the empty space left by the missing molar, she had developed a faint crease in her cheek and the slight, winnowing droop in one eye. She gave the impression that one would do well not to cross her, and usually a look from her drove the men away. She ran her cow business. She sometimes delivered a calf in the breech, placing her small hands in the opening, finding the calf's legs, turning it, then setting her legs to pull it free.

Late that spring, she left the bulk of her herd in the hills under the charge of the twin brothers. José had ventured higher into the Tehachapi, seeking new pasture, and she'd come down, bringing thirty-four head of cattle to the corrals and pastures at the casas with the help of one of José's dogs, Naja. Of the cattle Adaline had brought, five were heifers still carrying their first calves and two were heifers that had recently calved. Adaline planned to stay until the last of the heifers gave birth, keeping them penned in the corral nearby and feeding them from the adjacent hay yard. The remaining twenty-seven cows constituted her and José's consignment to the colonel, for which Godey's men would travel down. They'd fold them into a bunch to be sold to the army at Fort Tejon.

One evening, Naja gave out a low bark at the front door of the casa. Adaline followed her and stepped outside. Down along the pathway to José and Juana's casa she glimpsed pale lamplight glowing through the kitchen window and lighting the side breezeway. Juana hovered there, the outline of her figure in a white chemise. No sound came from coyotes in the hills, nor from the chickens, which had gone to roost, nor from the pigs in the pen near to the house, nor from the three steers, one of which Adaline was to help Juana slaughter the next morning. Naja pressed against Adaline's knee and emitted another low bark. The dog Juana kept, Yeso, issued a string of them as he loped out from the breezeway. Now, from the shadows to the east came the rhythmic sound of hooves. Adaline thought it might be José or one of the twins returning home, but nevertheless went to fetch her double-barreled Damascus, a shotgun she'd added to her arms. She returned to the doorway as the rider emanated nearer her casa and dismounted, looping his horse's reins on a rail. She recognized the mule and pearl-colored horse and the man's gait as he approached. There was something in the motion of his knees and feet that made it seem he was angling off on an oblique to his actual target. She silenced Naja by touching her hand to her head and called out to Yeso, then, lowering the gun, said, "Gerard Perlot."

"I heard you lived here."

She looked out at the horse and mule and marked the shiny burnishings of the saddle with which the gelding was outfitted. Just beyond was the corral with her heifers, the hay yard, then the pasture which held Slate, Manchada, Hawk, and Ghost. The trail on which Perlot had appeared ran outside the pasture and turned northward as it followed the trace of the river. Then there were the hills to the south, catching light from the descending sun. Up there spread an incandescence while here grew a pool of darkness under a sky the color of blood.

"What I hoped," he said, removing his hat, "was that I might water my animals and with your permission lodge for the night."

Naja and Yeso trotted off to sniff at the strange horse and mule. Adaline called out to Juana, saying everything was all right. She nodded toward the stable at the head of the corral, and allowing herself to be courteous enough, but also guarding against his presumption, said, "There's clean stalls. You could bed down in one. There's a water tank on the far side of the stable." She gave Perlot another close look and found her fusée smoldering again. "I could offer you eggs and coffee come morning."

•

At sunup, after replenishing the fire in her stove, she went out to tend to her stock, finding her heifers as before. Dawn spread across the valley and the two calves chased each other, gamboling around their mothers. She pitched hay into the feeder and moved to the stable in the corner of the corral where Perlot had quartered his mounts. The horse and mule were motionless, and one stall further down the saddle and rolled up aparejo were perched on a rail, and outside in the morning sunlight stood Perlot himself.

She said, "You could let your animals out for a time."

"Obliged." He gestured toward her heifers. "Looks like you'll have your hands full."

She studied them. "With luck, there'll be no trouble."

She returned to her casa, leaving the front door open. When he appeared, she again was struck by his odd way of moving, seeming to throw his body off the course it actually followed. She broke eggs into a pan and set the pan on her stove. He sat down and said he was on his way to Stockton to get what he could for the played-out claims, including the one Ned Turner had worked. "He didn't say anything about a stake holder?"

"He was near dead when I found him."

"The pickings are lean here. Not enough gold for the placers. Not enough water for the long toms, and for what there is during the rainy season, not really enough drop to the valley to make much of a go of it in any way."

She poured coffee into two cups she had set on the table, and at the stove turned sweet peppers into the eggs. She'd cooked rashers, heated beans, and fashioned quesadillas from the tortillas that Juana had given her. She put everything on platters and sat opposite him.

"If the water is impounded and flumes built, maybe the hydraulics will come here," he said. "I am told they have full sway now in the North."

She now knew that hydraulics meant machines with huge nozzles for shooting water, the monitors. They were hooked up to hose connections that extended from the flumes and washed the gold-bearing earth and gravel off the hillsides, making a slurry. They were what she'd at first puzzled over two-and-a-half years ago on her ascent to Las Mariposas.

"It's another change in the measure of operation. Small measures are falling off. The mines are becoming company mines, like the Merced Company, which is trying to move in on Frémont," he said. "So, lacking a fortune to invest, it's best to devise something that the operators cannot do without. Everything is changing. You're wise to raise cattle since the miners will always want their measure of meat."

He'd caught her attention with his use of the word, "measure." She'd come to take her measure of things, whether it was counting the cost of the horse-drawn mower she had purchased, the hay it produced, her calves on a ledger, how many birthed, how many sold, how many to keep. She'd studied the costs of commodities, many of which were rushing pell-mell into California. When purchasing, she always drove a price down to the quick. When selling, she insisted upon payment in cash, either with a currency she knew was not counterfeit, or preferably in metal. She accepted promissory scrip only as a measure of what was owed her by Colonel Frémont, via Godey, or the men Godey sent down to gather up the beeves. She had learned to take the measure of these men. Were they or were they not trustworthy. Often, she thought of Henri Mercure's admonitions: "Be careful of your whims. Be careful of a gamble. Gauge your risk against result. Most of all be cautious with romance." She understood that by romance Mercure had meant not simply any fascination that might overwhelm reason, but in particular, and in his prescience, attachments to men.

To Perlot, she said, "Your business is buying and selling claims on Las Mariposas?"

"I stake claims. But I can't compete with the big banks. Easy pickings are playing out." He looked over her head at the shelves mounted on the wall for kitchen stores. "How well did you know Ned Turner?"

"As I said, I came West with him and was put under his and his wife's care so long as my father was absent. So I knew him. I despised him then."

Perlot smiled. "There was some heat in your benediction over his grave."

"And you?"

"He was to have paid me back out of his proceeds."

The kitchen door was open, and outside it was where she had buried Turner's gold in a strong box. She was half-heartedly seeking out a way of getting it to Carrie and her mother, whom she had yet to track down. Naja lay nearly on top of the spot, her ears pricked toward Juana's casa. The front door was open, too, and cool morning air wafted from one end of the house to the other. She heard the sound of Juana's rooster crowing, also the pigs worrying over the scraps Juana fed them in the mornings, and she smelled smoke from Juana's fire pit.

Perlot lifted his cup to his lips and clicked it back down. "That was the arrangement."

She retrieved the percolator from the stove. "Mr. Turner's measure of himself was what he never had track of. His wife and daughter are somewhere back in the states. Whatever profit is taken from his claim should be sent to them." She filled the cups, returned the percolator, and sat back down. "So, when you appeared, you weren't seeing to his health?"

"I guess not." Perlot fished in one trouser pocket. He took out a small thing, unwrapped it from a bit of canvas, and set it on the table. It was a nugget not unlike the ones Adaline had, and it glimmered.

"He had this."

Growing alert, Adaline reached out to touch it. "At his cabin?"

He nodded. "Under his cot. I figured there'd be more."

Adaline rolled the nugget over. "And who do you settle accounts with in your business of buying and selling claims, or of staking them, as you put it?"

"Frémont." He took a pipe and tobacco pouch from his coat pocket. She waited, watching his fingers pack tobacco in the pipe. He rose, went to the stove, took out a smoldering stick, cupped his hand with it close to his pipe, and sucked on the pipe, then walked back through the cloud of blue smoke to his chair. "But Frémont doesn't know me, nor I him. Never met the man. No doubt he regards me and others like me as cleaning things up for him. He gets a cut of what we take. It's not that different from your cleaning up cattle for him."

Her knowledge of the colonel's recent transactions had come to be a patchwork, gleaned mainly from issues of the Sacramento Union and from what she heard. She knew that Biddle's Camp was now known as Bear Valley. She knew, too, that the colonel was back East, in anticipation of receiving the Republican party's nomination for president of the country. It was said that the dominant issue was abolition, but already he was being demagogued by Democrats for the fact that his father was a French foreigner and Catholic to boot. His mother, some claimed, was a prostitute. Others averred that Frémont's own marriage to Jessie had been performed by a Catholic priest. His reputation was further besmirched by tales of corruption and philandering.

The legal wrangling over his Mariposa Grant, she'd come to understand, had only deepened. Originally, the purchase was arranged by Thomas Larkin, the American consul in Monterey. The land was legally passed to Frémont by Governor Juan Bautista Alvarado in 1847, who had taken receipt of it from his predecessor before the Mexican-American War. Las Mariposas had been obscurely described as the land lying between the Merced, Chowchilla, and San Joaquin Rivers and bounded to the east by the Yosemite Valley. When Frémont had marked it out and turned it on the maps it came out well in excess of the original seventy square miles. There had been lucrative gold strikes on it, one of which was known as the Mother Lode. Now, the Mariposa Grant was infested with road agents and countless unscrupulous miners, hence Frémont's increased reliance on what were called "vigilance committees."

She said, "You must be one of the enforcers I've heard about."

"Some call us that. The truth is that the real trouble comes from the big claim jumpers like the Merced Company, which now wants to control the outcome in the courts. It's a different order of threat." He paused to tamp his pipe. "Banks are involved. It's turned much too expensive for me. I'll get Turner's nugget assayed and sell his claim, along with other played out claims I've got. But what I'd really like is to be put in touch with your man. Water is in short supply at his diggings, hydraulics are feasible only up to a point, and he's hit a vein. I'd propose building a percussion rock drill for him and building it up there, near him. He's going to need that drill."

She'd suspected that he had plans to use her, but this was matched by her curiosity over what she had no image of, or had only what she could form from what he called it—percussion rock drill. She reached out to touch the nugget, turning it over again in the sunlight.

Perot said, "Seems I need someone to approach him on my behalf."

"I see." She stood and gathered the plates, carried them to the counter where she set them in the dry sink. She put a pot of water on the fire. She'd felt a bump in herself, the concupiscence again. She'd all but forgotten what it felt like, and she would have to admit she liked his insistency and refusal to be disarmed by her.

"They say you have a thousand head in the hills."

"They? Well, they exaggerate wildly, as they do with everything."

"They say you ride like the wind, like an Indian."

"I am an Indian. I ride like my father used to, who is not one, but who rides like one."

"They say you sell to the army for the highest price. They say your father arranged this."

"It's true I sell to the army, or Alexis Godey does, his cattle, some of mine and Jose's, and Frémont's, and it's true that through his old friendship with Godey my father might be said to facilitate that," she said. "But I'm on my own. I'd sell to the Indian commissioner or to the mine brokers, if I could get more."

She glanced out the back doorway. Juana's chickens had appeared, turned loose to grouse. Naja still lay with her head on her front paws, surveying the chickens as they passed. The rooster crowed. Hens scratched for insects and seeds. Adaline picked up her frying pan, stepped outside, and dumped the grease on the ground. Naja came to lick the dirt while the chickens clucked, hoping she would throw something out for them. Across the way, she saw Yeso sniffing the air and then Juana in a blue smock, leading the steer to be slaughtered. She guided it into a small containment pen in the breezeway at the back of the casa. Above it, hanging by hemp rope from a viga, was a hook and a double block and tackle.

Adaline often thought about how glad she was that the colonel had sent her here where there lived just a few families on the site of the old hacendado and far enough away from the river, thus from the miners and from the main trail north to Stockton and Sacramento. The place was desolate. She loved the sear and the dry, and even cherished what she felt but did not speak of the haunting of her father in it, the translucent specter of the old ways before the war. She also read about him sometimes in the newspapers and knew that he'd been appointed Indian Agent, stationed in Taos, that nowadays he negotiated settlements with the Utes, Cheyennes, and Arapahos, and joined military expeditions to skirmish with the Jicarillas and Navajos.

Perlot had come outside to stand beside her.

She took the pan to the kitchen and returned. "That's Juana. I'm to help her."

She set out across the flat and Perlot came along, followed by Naja. They stopped to watch when Juana produced a sledge and stood at the rails where the steer, nervous now, sensing something in the air, its eyes showing their whites, turned to pass by her. Juana grasped the hammer with two hands and surprised the steer by hitting it between the eyes. The steer went down. Juana opened the pen, positioned a bowl with her foot, produced a knife, and cut its jugular. She held the animal by an ear so that the blood flowed into the bowl.

"It'll be chorizo," Adaline said, starting off again. When they came close she introduced him to Juana, speaking in Spanish, explaining that he was on his way to Stockton.

So the day began. Perlot stepped in to help. He raised the steer on the block and tackle, setting his weight against it. He tied the rope off, then proceeded to skin the steer, pulling the hide over the sides and back, down the legs. The three children, Maria, Pedro, and Marta, watched from against a wall. Adaline and Juana staked the hide to the ground. Perlot cut the head loose, and Juana probed with a knife to cut out the tongue, cheeks, eyes, and to scrape at the brain.

"It's for tamales," Adaline said. "Juana will want the intestine, too. The small stomach. And tendons in the lower legs. The librilla meat for soup. Nothing is wasted."

Juana had stepped back. Her face was soft as dust, yet she had a way of standing as if roots thrust out from the bottoms of her feet into the ground. She smiled at the two of them. Adaline and Perlot dragged the canvas with the intestines and stomachs over to a basin and Juana began cutting them up.

Perlot stayed that day, and another, and yet another helping Adaline with the heifers. In the corral, a red heifer gave birth without incident, lying on the ground and easing the calf out, then standing up to lick it dry. Back in Juana's breezeway, the steer's intestines, stomach and tendons had been washed and on the third morning Juana began making a broth from them. They were heated in water while Juana's eldest daughter, Maria, skimmed off the foam to keep the broth clear. Juana enlisted Adaline and Perlot's help sawing the carcass into quarters and letting it down for roasting, salting, and drying. On that night, Perlot, or Gerard, as Adaline took to calling him, slept on Adaline's pallet. His way of appearing to be headed where he was not was the way of his lovemaking, too. Adaline was aware that his presence and his manner in the bed raised a yearning in her, and then suddenly he was there.

José returned, escorting another two dozen cows and leaving the remainder in the hills under the charge of the twins. Adaline and Gerard rode out to help him and José seemed unfazed by Gerard's appearance, and the sight of his little son, Pedro, gave him great pleasure. He scooped the boy up onto his sorrel and placed the little hands on the saddle horn and rode with him out back, there setting him down. The two girls and their brother ran wide concentric circles around the house, calling out to each other. José dismounted and walked to Juana and the two of them disappeared into their casa.

Afterwards, Adaline and Gerard sat on the bench under the eave of her casa. He gestured at the low, broken walls beyond the corrals. "Are those not breastworks?"

"It's the war," Adaline said. "José says the soldiers were stationed there for two nights, but then when the Americans came they left. There were many more casas here, but they were demolished. He says the Mexicans were cowards and the Americans showed no mercy." She gazed at the low, sandy walls, and wondered as she had before whether her father had been among those Americans. She remembered how José had bristled and then walked away from the ruins when she inquired after them. It was the only time she had seen such a reaction from him. "José will not talk about it. He says that the war ending as it did would have been all right if gold had not been discovered. He wants no part of it, the search for gold. There's a living for him, yes, with cattle. With what he's done all his life."

Gerard shifted his weight and murmured.

She looked across the flat beyond her pasture toward the mountains. It had been hot for the season and the landscape shimmered. "I've come to love my cows," she said, remembering how so often they had countered her emptiness, the vastness of her loneliness.

"Wait here," he said. He walked to the stable where his tack remained. He came back carrying a cylinder and sat down next to Adaline. "Look." He lifted one end of the cylinder in his mouth and blew on it. It had a fitting inside it, meant to open and shut, and it opened, projecting a couple of inches. Gerard set it down and looked at Adaline expectantly.

Adaline chuckled at his expression. "So?"

He lifted the cylinder back to his mouth and sucked on it. The fitting went back inside. He blew out and sucked it in, lowered the cylinder, and looked at her again. "Do you see?"

"No, I do not."

"It's the drill. I was sitting in a hotel in Stockton one night. There were some old steam cylinders like this one lying around and for no reason I put one in my mouth and blew the rod in and out, just like that. There were some loose tacks in the wall. To amuse myself, I used the steam cylinder to drive them in. Then suddenly, it came to me. A machine rock drill."

He picked up a stick and scratched a picture in the dirt of a long tube mounted like a cannon. "If you tunnel, as Frémont must, you have to break up the rock and bring it out. Hand drills, blasting, picks, sledges, carts, windlasses. It's very slow. What about a steam powered machine rock drill? Steam here," he said, drawing a large cylinder with his stick. "And here a piston and a drill rod." He touched the part of the drawing that looked like a cannon. "The piston throws the rod forward. It rebounds and is caught by grippers behind the piston, only to be thrown forward again. You'll need tracks to bring the steam machine to it, and water for the boiler. In concept it's simple."

Adaline studied the picture. Gerard had told her he'd been a shipwright once. He also had been a blacksmith, along with having spent some time digging for gold, and finally working as one of Frémont's "enforcers." His knowledge of ships included the ways of moving water by bilges and pumps. There were the blacksmithing tools she'd seen in the mule's rolled-up aparejo. And she liked his way of disappearing into an idea, and of staying there, rapt, then surfacing with a glow in his face.

"What is it that you want?" she asked.

"Your good offices to recommend me to Colonel Frémont."

She looked away. Out in the pasture a flock of redwing blackbirds flashed from one spot to another. Overhead, a nighthawk could be heard buzzing as it dove. A slate color crept slowly up the mountains. She loved the way at this time of day the valley fell into darkness while the emblazure on the mountains came slowly to be overwhelmed.

She looked back at him. "Maybe I could do that."

"Then to bring you in on it," he said.

"Hmm."

Gerard bent toward his picture again and touched it with his stick. "See here, a ratchet and pawl to drive the drill rod. Screw jacks to adjust its trajectory there." He scratched out more lines in the dirt. "What if you put it on a tripod so you could drill sideways or upwards. It'd be like a deck gun on a ship, a turret with a swivel. If only I could figure a way to use compressed air instead of steam . . . like the wind." He stopped and gazed at her. "No one has thought of that yet, I believe, let alone tried it." He went on. "I have a place in mind. It's an old mill, left useless because they've stripped it of trees and moved the river away from it with their flumes. It still has a little water from a creek. I could make rock drills there. It's in the hills not far from Frémont's rancho."

Chapter 19

ADALINE WROTE THE LETTER to Colonel Frémont, commending Gerard. Gerard wrote a letter of his own with details on the new machine. He took the letters to Sacramento and placed them in the hands of a man who drove for a freighting company, Russell, Majors, and Waddell. The letters were transported to Saint Joseph, Missouri, then put on a train to New York where Colonel Frémont awaited results from the presidential election. The speed of travel would not compete with what the Pony Express, established four years later by the same freighting company, would be able to claim nor for that matter not anything like the telegraph, which replaced the Pony Express in another year and a half, but the time for such exchanges was diminishing even then in 1856. Flocks of sheep, herds of cattle, light and heavy goods, exotic, commonplace, and manufactured goods came overland, a veritable flood in service to the non-indigenous California population, which in a few years had swelled from 8,000 to over 300,000. The response to Gerard's letters arrived within six weeks.

*

One afternoon early in November, alerted by Naja, Adaline stepped outside and caught sight of a wagon coming from the north. It was pulled by two mules, one of which she made out to be the flint colored one. She discerned the white horse, following on a lead. A few minutes later, the wagon pulled up in front of the casa and Gerard climbed down, knocking dust off his shirt and trousers with his hat. The wagon was loaded with supplies, as she would learn: iron, sheets of it to be drawn, and iron tubing, and what otherwise was required to outfit a forge. He reached into the wagon and took out a package. "For you," he said.

Her fingers parted the paper from around a blue dress decorated with white flowers. She ran her hands over it, then lifted it out and held it against her. "It's so smooth," she said.

"Silk," he said. "From China."

"But I didn't expect anything." Despite herself, she was pleased.

Gerard unharnessed his mules and turned them and his horse into the corral where the animals circumnavigated the confines while Adaline's stirred-up mounts trotted along the fence line in the adjacent pasture. The last of her heifers had calved several weeks ago and José had brought more cows down to sell to the army. Some could be seen grazing in the far pasture. Gerard collected his rifle from the wagon and walked with her to the house. He explained how he had journeyed first to Sacramento, then to Stockton, settling his affairs, back to Sacramento, where he received a letter from Mrs. Frémont in lieu of her husband. Finally, he went to San Francisco where he met with Mr. William Palmer as Mrs. Frémont's letter instructed him. He purchased the second mule, the wagon, and the supplies.

When they reached the kitchen, he leaned his rifle in a corner and took the letter from his vest, which he passed to her. It expressed in colonel's interest in the rock percussion machine and instructed Gerard to contact Palmer, Cooke, and Company in San Francisco, which had oversight of Las Mariposas. In the event that an advance was required, the letter said to seek a voucher from Mr. Palmer. Further negotiations would ensue at a future date. It said to give her best regards to Adaline Carson and to say that "I still hope to meet her. If we are unlucky with the elections perhaps it will be soon in California." The letter was signed, "Jessie Benton Frémont."

Gerard had brought an issue of the Sacramento Union with him, too, that published the story of the newly formed Republican party narrowly losing the October 14 state election in Pennsylvania. It was also defeated in Indiana, and therefore Frémont's defeat in the Electoral College was certain.

Adaline said, "They'll come then to California?"

"Frémont's man, Mr. Palmer, says he'll have to come. He has business here. Mrs. Frémont, I don't know." Gerard took the letter back. "The lady is enormously popular. I've contracted with Palmer to build two machines for Frémont. More would have to be negotiated."

"You held back?"

"It was mutual."

"Wise." To Adaline, the colonel and Mrs. Frémont occupied a panoply of privilege and powerful dominion, though she well remembered her visit to Frémont and still had the sense of something awry, some slight off-balance flickering, though she had no complaints about his arrangements for the slicks.

She filled a basin with water from a bucket.

Gerard washed his face and hands, then once again dug into his vest and handed her three ten dollar gold pieces. "That's Turner's." She clicked them down on the table. "Even that much is an act of generosity," he said, answering her question before she posed it. He moved to the back doorway and peered outside where in the sunlight the water specks glistened like mica in his hair.

As she stoked up the fire to heat tortillas and beans, he turned to her, adding that he'd purchased tracks, a hearth, an ingot of open hearth steel, and tools from a foundry in Sacramento. They were being carted up to Bear Valley via Mariposa by teamsters right now. He also had an order in for two boilers from the same foundry. He was filled with expectation, and he put it to her directly, "So, you are coming, no?"

"I'll come to see how it is, but keep my herd, and ask José to watch over it for a time. I have to hold back, too."

"Maybe they need beef in Bear Valley."

"Maybe."

Darkness came on while they ate. Afterwards, she went to the bedroom. She took off her shirt and canvas trousers and tried on the new dress. It proved smoother against her skin than she had imagined. It had cloth covered hasps running up one side. She crouched to light a fire in the fogón and heard Gerard's footfalls behind her. When he put his hand on her shoulder, she stood and turned to him, and he slid his hands down her ribs.

"Wait." She unhasped the dress and slipped it over her head. Carefully folding it up, she placed it on her dresser. In only her chemise she turned to him again. He lifted her off her feet and she tasted the sweetness in her throat. He lowered her to the pallet, unclasped his belt, came down to his knees, and pressed into her. Afterwards, they took their ease by lying on their backs and watching the play of light against the ceiling from the candle and fógon.

He touched the wooden crucifix that lay between her breasts. "You are Catholic?"

"I began with my mother whose spirit went to the land of the rising sun, and then I became Catholic with my father, then Presbyterian with my aunt, and then Catholic again with my father and Josefa. But my father was angered by a padre, Padre Antonio Martínez, and a woman forgave me for sins I never committed. I think I am nothing."

"I am Catholic. I suppose we are in sin."

Her thoughts turned to Pablo, who had given her the carved crucifix with the tiny, twisted figure of Christ, then shifted to Padre Antonio again, to Bishop Lamy, and back to Pablo, who had told her about the padre resisting the tithes Lamy tried to enforce, and how the padre's opinion was that the world was composed of more unruly elements than the bishop acknowledged. She thought of Frémont's alleged Catholic history, and of the newspapers' sympathetic bias to the Democrats' excoriation of Frémont, turning him into a papist bastard, and of California which was at least equal in its vitriol for the colonel. "Who judges?"

He smiled. "And the key?" He passed his hand along the bottom of one breast and fingered the iron key she kept suspended from the sinew next to the crucifix.

"For opening." She thought of Mr. Turner's gold, which she had not told Gerard about. She supposed she, too, contributed some unruliness to the world.

"I see."

Before he left the next morning, they agreed she would follow in a month. His first intention was to come back down to accompany her, but she, prideful of her independence, insisted she could travel alone. Because of the load he was hauling, he planned to go by the slower road up through Mariposa. He said, "You could come by the faster way directly from the west." He drew a map on paper. "It's steep but less traveled. It's near impossible for the wagons, so they don't go there. And there's not as much chance of encountering road agents on it. There'll be the Merced River and mining near the end of the trail, just before you reach Hornitos. From there, it's less than twenty miles to Bear Valley." He marked them out.

•

In the days that followed, Adaline turned over another bunch of cows to Alexis Godey's men, who paid her in scrip and took the cows off to Fort Tejon. She arranged with José to leave what remained of hers under his charge for the winter, together with Manchada and Hawk. She prepared her casa, separating the things she would take from what she would leave behind, and as night fell before the day of her departure lit a lamp in the kitchen and went outside to unearth her strongbox. The box thudded when she struck it with her shovel. She pried it out of the hole and lugged it into her kitchen, setting it next to her trunk.

She took the sinew from her neck and inserted the key. The dirt-encrusted lock resisted, but she bent over the hasp of the strongbox and twisted with both hands until it gave way. She lifted the lid, smelling the waft of dankness. Inside were the bundles wrapped in oil cloth, the gold and silver coins from sundry mints, bags that contained gold dust she'd taken in trade, and Mr. Turner's leather pouch. To this she added Frémont's scrip, notes, and next the coinage she had on hand, checking it against her ledger. She turned to Mr. Turner's pouch and ran her fingers over the nuggets, then weighed them on a scale. Seeing again how heavy the one large nugget registered—four ounces—she inhaled deeply. The sum of the scrip, notes, coinage, and of Mr. Turner's gold now came by her reckoning to over two thousand dollars.

Outside, the cool contracted the roof timbers, causing them to creak. Spooked, she went to the front door and looked warily outside. Naja found her, the ragtag of orange and white coming out of the darkness, and then the wet nose against her hand. Juana and José's house was unlit, but in the light of a half moon the silhouettes of cows stood beneath a stand of aspen. There was no one, no sound, nothing other than a gentle breeze passing through the trees. She retreated back inside and bolted both doors. Mixed with her disquietude she had a sense of something left undone. It came from unfathomable guilt deep within her nature, and she felt the chill again, as if something cold had passed through her to fashion a pocket of ice in her heart.

She wondered: What is it? A danger I don't see? Or what?

She moved the currency, drafts, scrip, and notes to her trunk, which she would take along, also Mr. Turner's pouch and the three ten dollar gold pieces. She would see to the scrip at the Wells Fargo office in Mariposa. Godey had sent word reassuring her that Colonel Frémont would redeem what he owed her, and she expected Mr. Turner's gold could be converted there, too. Up to now, she'd been unsure how to manage it. The remainder, including the coinage, the dust she'd taken in trade, which she judged totaled three hundred dollars, she returned to the strongbox. She reburied the strongbox as a vouchsafe, a cache she could return to if needed. When she was done she used a juniper bough to sweep the ground. She moved her trunk next to her pallet, laid out the Hawken and Damascus, and secured the pistol under her pillow.

Before dawn, she arose, packed her books into the trunk, also her astrolabe and other instruments, the scales, her mother's beaded bag, the turtle, and her clothing, including the blue dress, which she folded inside the wrapping paper. She broke out the travois with iron wheels. To this she secured the trunk, put the Damascus next to it, the buffalo robe over the top of everything, and lashed it down. She walked back into her casa. Most things she left just as they were, the dishes and bowls, furniture, the crockery she'd acquired. Naja was worrying her and she bent down and stroked the dog's ears. "You'll have to stay here with José and Juana."

She harnessed the travois to the white mule, Ghost, and saddled Slate. Her Hawken went into its scabbard and her Navy pistol she now wore on a cartridge belt that passed over her shoulder. She walked over to bid goodbye to José and Juana, who were working stretching out a heifer hide and staking it to the ground beneath the awning in preparation for cutting strips from the soft belly to braid into a reata. The three younger children romped next to the animal pens, and the twins were in the nearby hills with the cows. José and Juana stopped their work as Adaline drew near, José appearing slightly perplexed, as always, for though he was strong and expert with the animals and his children, he seemed otherwise subtly disengaged, as if he were cut adrift by the mysteries of the world that had proved more durable than he could ever hope to change.

Juana wondered if Adaline thought it was a good idea, her going off like this.

"I'll be back. I have things in there," she said, looking over her shoulder at her casa. She had determined not to tell them still about her strongbox, not wishing to compromise them.

Juana warned the trail might be hard. There could be snow.

"Not yet, I think. Not where I'm going." It was true there had been snow high in the mountains, but the winter weather had not begun in earnest.

Furrowing her brow, Juana fretted about the danger traveling alone, and so far.

"It's not so far. A week or eight days at very most."

But Juana warned she had heard there was more mining, now, more prospectors, the Chinese, Chileans, French, and the dangerous

Australians. Convicts, all of them. It was said there were thousands of miners, including bandits from Mexico. Some said that even Joaquín Murrieta lived on, that he killed wantonly.

Adaline said, "But I've heard Murrieta's head was displayed for all to see in a jar of whiskey."

Juana said it was not wise going off in the path of a man. The man should be here to escort her on the path. She said such respect from a man would be for the best, in order to protect her from Joaquín Murrieta to whom death meant nothing, not even the tale of his own death.

Adaline smiled. "Oh, Juana. I've told Gerard I want to come alone. I have my man's clothing on. I have a fast horse." José's eyes narrowed and he almost spoke but turned to scratch Naja's ears. The dog had taken position at his knee and Yeso lay just behind him. The exchange of looks between her and José revealed to her that though he knew her horse was fast, and Ghost too, yet he would be pulling the travois. She believed José had been about to question her, but she continued reassuring Juana: "Much of this journey I've made before."

Juana looked her up and down, surveying her moccasins and canvas trousers and the red underwear top and that peeped through the brown shirt. More than once Juana had expressed her admiration for the freedom Adaline seemed to have found. She herself could never be so, yet Adaline knew that Juana by circumstance and habit of loving and following her husband and children had accepted a way different from what she—Adaline—had chosen. Juana stood motionless. Her smile was mysterious and strong as if it came straight up from the earth through her legs to her face. She said she would pray for Adaline.

"Oh, Juana, if you pray for me, I will be pleased. Then I'll be safe."

"Momento." Juana stepped into her doorway and reappeared, holding a bundle wrapped in a cloth, which she put in Adaline's hands.

It was heavy and warm. By the scent of it, Adaline knew what it was: tortillas, boiled beef with peppers, and tamales with salt pork, salsa, and corn meal steamed inside corn husks. Of all things to eat, Adaline loved tamales most. "Gracias," she said.

Juana said that Adaline would travel better with food in her belly.

They all walked slowly around to where Adaline mounted Slate and took up the mule's lead. José lifted his hat while the three small children ran circles around their parents, filling the air with cries: "Adiós. Adiós, Adalina. Adalina, adiós." By the look on Juana's solemn face, Adaline believed she was already praying, and her experience with departures was reawakened. She told herself it was because of the sadness of leaving these people behind, José who had been like a father, instructing her how to keep cows, or Juana who'd always been kind to excess, or the children who were like little sisters and brothers to her, and even the adolescent twins.

Chapter 20

First there were four days of traveling along the great valley and Adaline caught sleep in her buffalo robe. By the morning of the fifth day, the mountains rose directly to the east. She went forward, her travois on wheels leaving two distinct trails in the dew. She came to a stream and crossed it, scaring up a flock of sandhill cranes from a nearby lake, then all manner of waterfowl exploded and the sky filled with birds of many colors. She headed northerly, happening upon the remains of a field, which was bewildering in its vastness. Ears of maize hung on bedraggled stalks and she stripped some off and stored them on her travois.

Turning northeasterly she marked the nether reaches of Bear Creek. Sunlight fell against the golden November grass and the path she followed merged with the road to the towns of Merced and Modesto and all the way to Stockton and over to the west to San Francisco. She would follow it for a piece before coming to the -Y-, one spur of which went on to the cities, and the other spur on the map Gerard had drawn for her made a direct ascent to Hornitos and Bear Valley, following the trace of the Merced River. Back the opposite way on the road lay the easier yet slower climb to Las Mariposas. She came near the -Y-, seeing how heavily traveled the main road was, packed hard by hooves and wheels.

In the afternoon, she set onto the rightward trail of the -Y- that cut into the hills. Her travois rattled and clattered in and out of the cuts. She leaned into Slate and urged him on. The trail narrowed and the climb grew steep as she circled on one switchback, Ghost and the travois following behind, then another long switchback, another, and another, and on one the mule's ears went back, which she took to mean the mule sensed something or someone. She dismounted between her animals. "Easy, Ghost. Easy," she whispered. Retrieving two cobs of maize, she stripped off the husks, offered them up to the mule and to Slate, hoping to keep them quiet.

She listened, then heard loose rock scared up. She thought she heard a solitary voice, followed by silence. Because of the complex of canyons, she couldn't tell where the sounds came from and she waited for what seemed a long time. Nuthatches materialized, working over the seed in thistle. A squirrel dropped onto a rock and scolded her. That was all. She mounted, rode a little further, and as it grew dark retreated off the trail into the bush. Disencumbering Ghost of the travois and her horse of its saddle and blanket, she put the animals on pickets and turned to the travois, lifted off her Damascus and positioned it alongside her pistol and Hawken, and spread out her buffalo robe. She ate two of Juana's tamales.

The night was uneasy. She fell asleep, then awakened with a jolt to several distant, reverberating gunshots, but as with the clattering rocks it was impossible to tell from what direction the shots issued. It fell silent again in the pitch black. Only the coyotes ruptured the air with their intermittent back and forth yipping. After an hour or two of listening, she dared to let herself sleep but an instant later, it seemed, she jerked awake. She'd been dreaming. Just now she'd dreamed of a huge book, the pages slowly turning and herself trying to stop them. A rock rolled. Horse hooves gathered. She sat up straight. Again there was a rustle like pages turning and she grew deeply confused as to where she was, even whether she was truly awake, dreaming or not dreaming, then she heard a rhythm in the sound.

Hush, hush, hush.

She peered through the bush. She made the sound out as the hiss of tule sandals treading lightly, and she discerned shapes, many of them passing in the faint light, naked legs, skirts, at least a score of apparitional figures. At the back of the procession came two more horses.

Indians.

Once they had moved some distance ahead, she led her mounts toward the opening and turned her eyes upward. Nothing. In the pale light of dawn, she detected faint hoofprints but mainly the mark of feet. She looked downwards, straining to see, and saw far below near the beginning of the -Y- another half-dozen men, their shapes on horseback flickering in and out of the light and then behind the trees. Not knowing who they were, she grew apprehensive. Maybe she should stay put and let them pass, but the possibility of waiting seemed intolerable. What then? She remembered Juana's anxiety and felt qualms over her pride in her independence. Finally, she moved out as quietly as the travois allowed, matching her pace to that of the Indians ahead.

Dawn passed into full morning and the ascending path wound around hills that arose from the shadowy formations to the east. She went along a ridge close to a waterway, smelling the spray in the air, and soon caught sight of a stream that passed around a bend. There was evidence here of mining, but no men, only mud discharged from banks into the creek and old placer fabrications. Off the trail she found a vantage point on the hills ahead. Yet higher on another flat, movement flickered across an opening and then changed into the file of Indians, slouched like a heavily laden snake. Looking downwards she saw nothing, only a fragment of the trail but not the bottom any longer, not the horsemen.

She pushed ahead. The occasional arrastra, sluice, or long tom appeared, and then a few men at work, shoveling and raking the gravel to free up the gold. She found it reassuring to have company in this fashion. Twice she was hailed and she touched her hand to the brim of her hat and rode on. Soon, the Merced River came into view. The force of its drop over rocks precipitated a stretch of whitewater and beneath a tongue of glossy water that appeared eerily still, fringed by more cascading whitewater. Fifty yards up the trail, water pooled again and a grassy bar crossed almost to a cutbank and overhanging escarpment. Deciding that the bar would be a good place to let her animals drink, she dismounted, led them onto it, and dropped Slate's reins and Ghost's lead. Then she spied something else in the water beneath the escarpment, and in an instant plunging fast upon her she hissed between her teeth, making her own snake sound.

It was a dead man, his head submerged in the water. She glanced back, down the waterway again, saw nothing there, but put her hand upon her pistol, turned round and edged farther up to where the river began to bend. Coming out to the water and to the view upstream afforded there, she pulled up short. Sluices had been broken, tools scattered, a chest had been axed open, and there lay the wracked bodies of three more men, two draped over the wreckage and one in the shallows. The one closest to her she recognized by his pinched eyes and his queue to be Chinese, his throat sliced so that the skin flapped in the current.

She edged down to where Slate and Ghost stood. She glanced to the sides and over her shoulder, her eyes searching in all directions, then warily led her animals out onto the flat of the bank. There was no one, no sound but the risible of the water. She advanced along the river until she had a full view of the wreckage. It had been an elaborate installation—sluice, long toms, a string of riffle boxes, a roundabout catwalk. There were the three bodies, and yet another fallen on the opposite bank. Hoof and boot prints circled everywhere. She looked around again, wondering how it happened that she had understood the general picture of momentous change in gold seeking, how she had known of mercenary conduct taking over the ends, the brutal jockeying for power and ascendancy, yet how this was the first she had seen of its murderous danger.

She mounted and returned to the trail, the qualms she'd felt in her belly now transformed into the chill that came out of her blood and closed upon her. Her travois chattered behind the mule, bouncing over the outcrops, and as soon as the trail offered a vantage of what lay ahead she paused to look. Her hands had begun to tremble. She took a deep breath. A skiff of mist hung over the craw of the long, northward bearing canyon, and there was a waterfall. The Indians moved steadily above it. She looked at the trail marked by footprints in the dust, mixed in with the sign of horses. She murmured to herself: "Maybe they didn't see it. Maybe they just passed by." The men who worked at the placer mining installations seemingly had not seen it either or hadn't placed the sounds. She told herself: "Move along. Be careful. Those others down below, you still don't know if they're there and, if so, who they are."

By then it was afternoon. She rode for several hours, bypassing mule-driven arrastras and the men working at them. When it grew dark she took a game path off the trail. She picketed Slate and Ghost and ate the last of Juana's tamales. She listened. Nothing. There was only the breeze blowing through the great oaks and further off the rush of the river. She lay down with her Hawken, Damascus, and pistol for company and slipped into a drowse, several times starting at what might have been a limb rubbing against another limb or the sound of a night visitor, raccoon or skunk. Only the forest sounds issued, but they grew menacing in the dark. Some distance away coyotes sang, the chorus of them shimmering like silver against the black void. When she fell into a fitful sleep, she dreamed again. Figures ghosted through: the spectral Chinese, the Indians who kept coming, countless numbers jostling each other as they passed into the book with its turning pages.

Hush, hush, hush.

She beheld Juana far away: ¡Adalina! ¡Vuelva! ¡Cuidado!

Then the head of Joaquín Murietta appeared. His swollen tongue admonished her from within a great jug, awash in a bath of whiskey, and a wind came up, turning round and around, sucking Joaquín and all the people into it. She came half-awake and snatched up her Damascus. She peered into the blackness and saw her trunk still lashed onto the travois just as it had been, and her animals standing there, and heard the river running. She saw a figure in a pale poncho walking away. It was Pablo, talking about the Santos coming from within the wood, about what loomed on the outside expressed what was inside them. There was a sharp cracking sound, the sound of a tree snapping, and Pablo vanished. She felt crazy. She dove deep into herself where her true, terrorized nature was hidden.

She took a deep breath and rose. Her hands shook as she saddled Slate and harnessed Ghost to the travois. In this way, she employed tasks to piece together the world. The sky paled with light. She picked her way toward the river and rode until she spotted the Indians above her. Skins were draped over their shoulders, and three white men rode on horseback, two bringing up the rear and one at the head. She looked down the trail again. The slopes were bathed in light and she saw movement stirring. The horsemen were there after all, ascending. She determined she had to pass by the Indians.

In the river were several more placer operations. The apparati, the double and triple long toms and the diversion flumes, grew more elaborate. She passed another large arrastra driven by two donkeys, grinding rock down for the gold. It was tended by four Mexicans, who sighted her. As she'd done before, she touched the brim of her hat. One man lifted his hat and held it in the air. She rode on, hoping that the three men ahead on horseback would take no interest in her. There was a time for caution, even retreat, she came to think, and a time to press forward.

Nearing the Indians on a flat, she noted a few women among them with cradleboards and several children on foot. Most were men. She took them to be from a lowland Miwok band not unlike the Emigdianos who had lived near José and Juana. Some of the men were lashed together with hemp rope. All walked with a slouch, barely lifting their feet. She pulled up beside the two horsemen at the rear. The one nearest, grizzled and grime covered, glowered at her, but the other paid her no heed whatsoever. He hunched forward and peered over the edge of the trail at the drop below. The grizzled man glared and loosed a whip and cracked it in the air above the Indians. "Clear the way! Make way!" Muttering as much to himself as to anyone, "Them savages will stop given any reason. Then we got to start them all up again."

The Indians pressed close, allowing an opening. Some looked back, their eyes following her as she approached, their expressions filled with fear. Adaline continued past them, taking care to keep Ghost close. The travois skittered along the edge. She despaired yet at the same time increased her distance from the Indians.

The man in front had yellow hair and a dead-grass beard. "You're headed where?"

"Bear Valley, thereabouts."

The man sniggered. "Thereabouts. There ain't hardly no thereabouts to it. Otherwise it's a lot of trouble you've gone to climbing this perpendicular."

"I'll be looking for Colonel Frémont."

The man looked sharply at her and she knew he had marked her as a woman. His lips hardly moved when he spoke, as if crafted out of stone, and the words were shaped somewhere down in his throat and spewed out in a slurry: "Where these savages is going. He's putting down a shaft, they say, and needs diggers. These verminous Diggers is what he'll get."

Adaline looked straight ahead, an angry flush rising at her neck. She mostly disbelieved the man and convinced herself that the Indians would be better off the sooner they got under Colonel Frémont's charge. She wondered about asking the man if he'd seen the slaughtered Chinese miners, or if he knew who the others were, coming behind them up the trail, but she let those things rest. "It's his rancho I'll be looking for."

"What business would a young woman have with him?"

She shot a quick glance at him, thinking—none of yours—then extended her half-lie further. "I'm carrying messages from Stockton."

"Stockton," the man said.

"And thence from San Francisco," she added.

"Thence!" the man said. "What's that?" Adaline thought she could almost hear his mind working, the heavy gear wheels grinding around their axles as he tried to calculate whether "thence" meant before or after. "Peavey," he said. "I'm Nick Peavey. And you?"

"Carson."

"Carson," he said, now looking at her yet again, running his eyes all the way down to her one moccasin in the stirrup and up her trousers to the Hawken in its scabbard. He looked at her mule and let his eyes rest on the rattling travois for a moment, then drew them along Slate's flank. "Looks like you'll be delivering more than messages." He paused. "Fair looking animals." He paused again and looked back at his charges, then added, "You related to one of them Carsons or just making use of their name?"

"If you mean Kit Carson, I'm his daughter."

This caused the man to stare at her. He began to laugh, what came out as a string of phlegmy barks flying from his chest. He bent nearly low enough to kiss his animal's neck. Coming up again, he ejaculated anew, "Haw! The outcome of his poking in a squaw's blanket!"

The sound of walking behind her became like a prayer of the book in her dream.

Hush, hush, hush.

"I'll be going on ahead," she said, pressing Slate forward. A moment later she could hear the man still laughing, and she peered back and saw him looking at her, his face rife with raucous delirium, and behind him the downcast heads of the Indians as the they toiled along. She glimpsed the full meaning of the unwritten. It was not just a geography, the white spaces on the maps marking out the unknown, but also people who resided in that white space, their lives unwritten and unknown, an agrapha of souls.

But why? Why is it this way? Why?

She nudged her horse to keep up the pace. She came upon a fork in the trail and a board with the crudely painted words: Hornitos. Bear Valley. It had an arrow pointing to the rightward way as Gerard's map said it should. She dismounted and scanned downwards, now seeing no one, not the Indians, nor the men coming behind them, only parts of the river glinting pewter colored in the distance. Above the mountains thunder clouds formed. She rode northeasterly and after another hour signs of mining came into view again. Up along the ledges she saw the outlines of the machines—the jaw crushers, arrastras, and chilean wheels. A stamp mill was built against a large ledge, and above what she thought must be a shaft stood a mule-drawn whim. She came into Hornitos. More arrastras and crushers were visible on the outskirts, and scattered adobes, stone buildings, the constructions with canvas roofs, and a cemetery up a hill with its stone markers shaped like the hornos from which the place took its name.

The road turned. Buildings amassed upon a main street, a livery stable, Reeb's Butcher Shop, a Wells Fargo office, a store called Gagliardos, and down a ways she saw the word "Pandería" on a facade, then "Taberna" on another one. She crossed a bridge over a creek and saw two new hotels and then another taberna in front of which were tied off three horses. She heard music coming from it, but except for two women lingering in the road in the shadows beyond the taberna no one was evident. Otherwise, the roadway was eerily empty. Adaline approached the women. One of them, who wore a dark shawl, seemed to be comforting the other. The other woman suddenly broke away and cried out in an animal wail that made Slate shy. The woman was cradling an infant, and in that instant of pulling on Slate's reins to hold him, Adaline sensed something terribly wrong. The second woman embraced the first, and Adaline's skin prickled as the first one emitted a low keening that formed the words: "¡No! ¡Por Dios, no!"

The woman in the shawl stepped back, still holding the other one by the elbows, whom Adaline marked as much the younger of the two. Adaline drew abreast of them. There was something between buildings that fell into her view. A solitary oak tree was there, which had a bare limb, and two forms wearing white trousers, the necks crazily askew, hanging by ropes. Instinctively her eyes shot back to tick off the elements—three horses tied in front of the taberna, music, the bereft woman, the strangely empty streets, the older woman holding the other, the younger one now moaning inconsolably, "¡Condena, multilación!"

The older woman looked up at Adaline and spoke in a hoarse whisper: "¡Salirse pronto!"

Adaline leaned into Slate and the horse jerked forward. Right behind came Ghost and the clattering travois. It was an instinctive response to the woman's tone and meaning: "Get away! Quickly!" She rode out of the town and along the well-traveled road, and then started up a long grade on which she slowed, at first for fear of jading her already weary animals and next because she perceived more horsemen riding ahead of her. Close by, the backs and hats of four riders configured in the furtive twilight. She slowed down the more until at last they veered off, going toward what must have been Bear Valley, though glimpsing it she barely recognized what the town had grown into. Several streets now were laid out with establishments and what looked to be a hotel. She rode on. Dark clouds churned above and a wind arose. She approached a great patch of silvery gray pitched at an angle to the earth and rode straight into the rain. While passing by a creek, she spied another closely knit encampment of canvas-topped shacks. Men were out working in spite of the downpour. They wore oilskins and kept digging at a wing dam where a creek was diverted. She made out more arrastras and rockers, and then the marker that Gerard had told her to watch for, a big, looming, and crashing stamp mill. It displayed a sign which she leaned toward to read: THE MERCED MINING COMPANY.

The rain turned to sleet and snow. She rode alongside a flume that fed into the mill, and spotted still more elevated wooden flumes, soaked to the color black and implanted one after another like huge accent marks upon the whitening hills. Several more men labored tenaciously, the snow on their shoulders. Voices rang out, together with the grating sounds of shovels, rakes and scrapers, and just to the side of her now, the racket of the stamp mill. The hooves of Slate and Ghost sucked in and out of the wet earth. There would be another creek past the stamp mill, Gerard had said. She found it and rode the trail alongside that passed behind a stand of junipers. Wagon wheels had gouged deep cuts here.

She pushed Slate over the brow of a hill to a flat through which the creek twined. Pausing, she saw what once must have been a conifer woods, reduced to stumpage. To her left was a stone dwelling. Down below a corral had been built beside the creek. Gerard's horse and his two mules stood in the snow. Above the corral and directly before her lay a long building with a shed roof and a wide entryway. White smoke curled from a makeshift chimney. There was a spot of flame within the dimness of the shed and she heard a hammer ringing upon an anvil. Gerard was there.

Safe. She was safe. It felt like a deliverance.

Gerard saw her and came out, held her by the arms, then embraced her. He carried her trunk into the stone house. They unhitched Ghost and unsaddled Slate and put the animals in the corral. Once inside the house, she told him about her journey, saying goodbye to Juana, José, and the children, going up the -Y-, the sounds at night, the fright of the murdered Chinese, the wreckage, gold mining operations everywhere, the Miwoks, their guards, and more white men below and before her, the two hanged men in Hornitos.

She was startled by how she grew distraught in the telling, almost as if she were experiencing it anew. She said the world seemed to have changed, but then she grew near to incoherent with fatigue. The last thing she remembered was Gerard putting her in bed and covering her with her bearskin robe, the softness of it, Gerard coming next to her, and herself falling into a deep sleep.

Chapter 21

THE NEXT MORNING they prepared coffee. Gerard repeated what he'd said the night before, that he hadn't realized the route had grown so dangerous. He now berated himself for his misjudgment. "I should have known." He said she was right, that the battles over access to gold had turned into all-out war, that the old mayhem had been replaced by a new and ruthless mayhem.

He pieced Adaline's journey together, surmising that the men who appeared behind her must have been the colonel's men, so, too, was the second posse of men on the high road, who must have besieged the town of Hornitos. Also, perhaps they had killed the Chinese miners before Adaline chanced on that scene. And there were the three horses she'd seen tied up in Hornitos. Maybe they were a part of the other group of men up ahead and had stopped at the taberna, or maybe they were operating on their own. Gerard guessed the two Mexicans had been hanged as an example. He said that for some life had little meaning here.

Adaline could still hear one woman telling her to get away and the other woman's moan.

¡Mutilación!

"The colonel has his vigilante enforcers. Vigilance Committees, they're called now," Gerard said. "He has the power to appoint deputies. The village of Hornitos is made up of Mexicans and Americans, with a few Chinese, Chileans, and Australians thrown in. It's known for its wildness. And for being one of Joaquín Murrieta's lairs from the old days."

"Murrieta," Adaline murmured.

It was as if Juana had sent an image of Murrieta's head with one of her prayers, flying up to warn Adaline. Indeed, within the confines of the place where she found herself—the stone house, the remains of a mill, the blacksmith's shed, down below the horses and mules in the corral, not far off a slash pile and flume to redirect the creek, everywhere the patches of melting snow—Adaline felt still shaken by the dreams she'd had.

She told Gerard about them.

"The Mexicans are defiant," Gerard said. "It's because of the royalty Frémont requires in return for mining on 'his land,' land they believe is theirs. They believe the Mariposa Grant was stolen as war booty, then enlarged by a mapping trick. And Frémont takes every opportunity to intimidate them." Gerard went on to say how it seemed nothing was as important to Frémont as gold, not determination of guilt or guiltlessness, not the terror and grief of the women, and not the Miwoks brought in to dig for him. "He's become like a man possessed."

Adaline thought of the damaged souls residing within the Indians she'd seen on the trail to here, and before that the Indians in the stockyard. Yet she remembered George, too, trusted by Frémont, and Johanna, trusted and taken in by him. She felt they, and she, too, were in circles of lamplight, nearing Frémont's circle. She said, "But Frémont will treat the Miwoks fairly, won't he?"

"Running for president nearly broke him. He's desperate for money. Gold and the power it brings is the measure of everything. Here, the law is Frémont's law. Peremptorily, men are shot, or hanged. Women raped." A distant look moved into Gerard's face. "I wish I had not given him a copy of the plans for the drill. And God knows I wish the machine were finished. Everything's turning into a corruption. As to your Miwoks, I can't say."

"I'll visit him," Adaline said. "Maybe I'll find some reassurance."

Gerard set his cup down, then said, "Come see what I've done." He moved outside to the shed, which to Adaline became a befuddling confusion of forge, benches, tongs, all manner of tools. Gerard showed how he had one machine to the point where its workings were clear. The hardened snout-like nose, he said, was capable of breaking up rock, even granite. The nose was mounted on the end of a rod which passed back and forth through a piston. Something of the old Gerard she knew surfaced when he touched it, his eyes glimmering. "It's something, isn't it."

"Yes, it is." It seemed Adaline as another phantom coming into being, formerly nothing more than an idea derived from the new Bessemer steel forging process.

Gerard said, "I've got two boilers on their way up from Sacramento. Screw jacks from Britain. Once those screw jacks get here it'll take maybe a week to finish and test it."

•

Two days later, Adaline rode past the stamp mill with its sign, THE MERCED MINING COMPANY. It had cams attached to iron boots, which turned on a shaft before crashing down and crumbling the rock. The mill was big, at least fifteen feet tall and twenty feet long. It had a hopper at its top into which the quartz was loaded. Below, the flow of water washed the bits of rock against a screen while two bedraggled men scraped the amalgamation onto a riffle mat, then watched for the separation of gold from crushed rock. She rode on, passing the shacks and coming to where the road from Hornitos met the one to Bear Valley and Mariposa. She put her knees to Slate and turned toward Frémont's rancho, built directly above the town of Bear Valley, which indeed now boasted a hotel, a livery stable, an outlet for Trabucco's Store. Its several streets were lined with makeshift houses.

Reaching the rancho, she saw that it, too, was in the process of transformation. She saw George Stilts helping to unload lumber from a wagon and she raised a hand to greet him. She also found a man, whom she learned was Henri, a chef, and a voluble French pastry cook, Mêmê, standing outside. She presumed the two were a couple.

She made acquaintance with Mêmê, who was overseeing preparations for Mrs. Frémont's arrival.

"Soon?" Adaline asked. "She'll be here soon?"

In response Mêmê gave Henri a sidelong look.

Just then the colonel emerged from the house. Learning that Adaline had traveled up by the Hornitos trail, he took her aside and insisted she tell him everything she'd seen. Startled by his sudden insistency, she said she'd heard gunshots one night.

"Nothing more?"

She hesitated out of a fear of being somehow implicated but went ahead and told him about the dead Chinese, the wrecked emplacement, the Miwoks she'd passed, the hanged men in Hornitos, and the two women.

"I see." He softened a little. "You must have had quite the journey. Those Chinese have been mining illegally. So, too, the Mexicans, who no doubt killed the Chinese. It seems to be taken for granted that I give permission gratis to whoever wants it."

"I see." She marked that the colonel had the story a little differently than did Gerard.

Frémont went on: "And the rock drill? Is it ready?"

"Soon. Gerard has one nearly ready. He has supplies coming."

"Good," he said. "Tell him I'm anticipating seeing it." He looked away with a distracted expression. "My wife is coming as soon as we add a room and a veranda," he said, gesturing at the wagons, one of which George and the men had completed unloading. They, together with the chef, Henri, now turned to unloading a wood burning cook stove.

Adaline said she hoped to meet Mrs. Frémont.

"And she you," the colonel replied, settling back on his heels and looking away again. She saw a twisting in his eyes, a glossy darkness as if from a jungle.

•

In February she ventured to the rancho again. She rode past the stamp mill and the workers, one of whom—Mick—liked to talk. Mick was one of the bedraggled pair. She'd been by here several times, going to the store in Bear Valley, and once the twenty-five miles to Mariposa where she visited the main Trabucco's and the Wells Fargo bank where she had converted Frémont's scrips and deposited most of her gold. On this day she rode up toward the Frémont's house, what Mick had told her some poked fun at by calling it the "White House." She saw that the new room and veranda were virtually complete. A barn was being built down the slope, together with separate men's and women's privies. In the yard stood covered cargo wagons and pulling teams. Men, including a Negro, were unloading multiple wagons. Stuffed chairs, a china cabinet, and an upright piano stood in a row on the veranda. Some rugs had been brought out of the house to hang on a line where despite the cold two Indian women beat the dust out of them, the eldest of whom, the one with the facial tattoos and dentalium necklace, was Johanna. She smiled at Adaline. Off to one side, Adaline caught sight of Mêmê again supervising the whole affair. She tied off Slate and went to inquire after the commotion.

"Of course, it's Madame," Mêmê said, smoothing her apron.

Adaline looked toward the house. "She's here?"

"Soon. Right now she's in San Francisco. We've turned the house upside down. What was in had to come out. Now, there's more going back in. There's wallpaper to hang!"

Adaline looked back at the windows. Figures weaved about and she could hear the colonel's stentorian voice.

Mêmê said, "But if things please the madame, maybe she'll hold back a little."

"Won't she like it here? After all that's been done for her?"

"She will say she does, but she will not. To make things worse, her father, the senator, has died."

"Oh," Adaline said. "I am sorry."

Mêmê placed her hands on her hips and appraised Adaline. Above her bodice, her chest blushed ruddy in the cold and strands of hair clung to her flushed cheeks. Taller than Adaline, she differed most markedly in ampleness—full hips, fulsome breast, and broad face.

"Perhaps I should stay to help you," Adaline said.

"Perhaps you should not. There's enough people underfoot here as it is."

Taken aback, Adaline next said something she would regret. Not that it was wrong, or untrue, but misplaced in the way that people caught off-balance sometimes blurt out what they most desire: "Mrs. Frémont has left word that I should visit."

"But it will be on Madame's time," Mêmê said summarily. Just then a sideboard was carried onto the veranda, past the line of furniture. While attempting to maneuver it through the doorway, it crashed against the jamb. Mêmê whirled around and shouted, "Tip it! Isaac! You have to tip it! Don't break the legs! Put it down!" She turned back. "The fools!" The Negro, whose name, Adaline gathered, was Isaac, set his end of the sideboard down as did the man on the other end. Isaac vanished, backing through the doorway into the house. Mêmê bent and picked a bottle out of a crate. "See here! Wine!" she said. "Cases of it!" She produced a pair of round tins. "Steak and kidney! Truffles from France! It's lucky the colonel has come into wealth." Back in the yard, several drovers continued unloading, all the while casting nervous glances at Mêmê. "A fortune's worth of English china! A piano, for goodness sake! And that clumsy darkie! Come up from San Francisco ahead of Madame! For what!" She gestured at Johanna and the other woman who kept beating at the rugs. "Them, too! Grub-eating slaves!"

Shocked, Adaline looked to Johanna and the young woman beside her and cast about for something to say. "I've no idea what truffles are."

"Nor caviar, I'd think," Mêmê said superciliously. "You'd best not raise your expectations but stay with your sour dough and wild hare." She made away, speaking over her shoulder. "There's no telling what people's fancies will turn to given a taste of something fine."

Moving to the veranda, Mêmê pushed in front of the man who remained and tested the weight of the sideboard by lifting it, then called out, "Henri!" Instead, George Stilts emerged. Putting his hands on one end of the sideboard, he caught Adaline's eye and gave her a wry expression of mock perseverance. Behind George she glimpsed the Colonel in the shadows, peering out. For an instant he looked at her, his eyes shining, but gave no sign of recognizing her. He disappeared. Then Henri appeared from within and came to Mêmê's rescue. George lifted and tipped his end and Henry followed suit with the other end. They went softly inside. Mêmê stood glowering after them. The women beside Adaline pounded at the rugs. Filled with an indescribable feeling of irrelevance, Adaline made her way back to Slate and rode quietly off.

•

By March they received word that the screw jacks had arrived. Adaline planned to retrieve them from Trabucca's main store in Las Mariposas. On the day she was to go she was awakened by a booming that shook the earth. She felt for Gerard next to her, but he had risen early and gone to work. She got up, picked her way to the doorway, and conjectured that the booming was another of the small earthquakes that were commonplace here or more likely the deep snow in the mountains slipping on itself and plummeting down the chutes. She moved along the side of the house, running a hand over its stones, and looking in the direction of the sound, past what was called Chinese Camp, high up and well off Frémont's Mariposa Grant, over in the direction of Yosemite and Mono Lake.

She had yet to see Yosemite or Mono Lake, but Gerard had described them. He spoke of Mono Lake as a place where they might settle once he finished the machines. Though he hadn't given up on his invention—far from it—his wariness of the colonel had only increased. She could keep her cows and raise them in Mono Lake, he'd said. He'd heard that meat was in demand there. There were mines and he could continue building machines. Mono Lake's vantage on the lowland was to the eastern desert lands, to Carson Valley, so named years ago by Frémont for her father. The lake was said to be filled with strange formations. She ruminated on all this and took pleasure in the chill air that coiled around her ankles, gazing above the juniper into the dawn.

She walked toward the house, stepping down to a landing where the corral below and the blacksmith's shed just across the way came into view. Two spots glowed in the shed, the coals in the forge, the coals in the hearth. Gerard had to correct a problem of overheating in the firing tube before he installed the screw jacks.

In the dim light inside the shed, which had grown familiar to her, she could make out the bins containing scraps of metal, the shovels, hand driven drills, a variety of tongs and hammers hanging from the walls, vises and anvils, the slack tub, and also the boilers that had come in from San Francisco. One of the boilers was installed and Gerard was half-visible, bent over his machine. The difficulty he was having was controlling the pressure from the boiler so that the piston would fire and then be caught by the built-in grippers, and fired again and again, but after running for a few minutes it either jammed or slipped by the grippers.

There came another boom, but farther away. Gerard looked up and cocked his head at her. She raised one hand and ducked back into the house, filled the percolator with water, took down the canister of ground coffee beans, and spooned some in the percolator, and put it on the wood burner. As it heated up, she dressed, replacing her nightshift with her canvas trousers, put on the old shirt with the fringes, tied a red bandana about her neck, and dragged a brush through the tangles in her hair. She put on her moccasins, her blue poncho, and carried the percolator and two cups to the shed. Gerard was crouched low, tending the fire under his boiler.

"Coffee," she said, filling the cups she set down on a bench. "Then I'll go."

Gerard stepped around his machine. He'd added two arched runners for the nose of the machine to slide up and down, mounted beneath the long piston. Just outside lay a stone channel by which the creek was routed in order to have water close by. "I want to try the grippers again. I'm going to score the tube, then burnish it. We'll have to test it on rock."

He tripped a lever and nudged the drill out through the piston, and flipped the lever and nudged the drill back in until it reseated with a click. "Like that. It'll have to do that on its own. I've cut a slit for a vent, which might help. The problem may be the recoil." Gerard ran his fingers over the drill. "But with a full head of steam, the screw jacks in place, and the hard surface of a rock wall for resistance, it might work." He lifted up his cup and sipped at it.

"Do you want me to stop by and see about bringing someone from the Frémont's?" she said. "Maybe George? He'd be pleased to come." She was all but certain that Mrs. Frémont was there by now, but after the discomfort of her previous visit she felt she'd come to need an additional reason for being there. It would be like ballast.

"Maybe in a couple of days. That way I'll be sure to have the screw jacks mounted." He sipped his coffee, then bent over the fire again. The boiler had its own firebox, and he'd set the whole of it on logs in the round. With the aid of a lever, he could slide it across the floor. He mused, "I still wish I'd figured how to compress air."

The shed grew illuminated and shadows began to form. As the pale of dawn increased, it began to rain lightly. Against the far wall gleamed the smooth side of a second boiler he'd ordered shipped up. Gerard's leather apron was blackened by the work at the fire and the skin drawn over his collarbones glistened with sweat. When he applied the bellows to the fire, smoke blew up in his face and he backed away, squinting. "Maybe rubber would do it," he'd said.

"Rubber?"

"Not impregnated linen," he'd said. "Something new like vulcanized rubber such as Hancock in England and Goodyear in this country are experimenting with. Then Hancock runs it through sulphur chloride to make it malleable. I could sew hoses out of that."

"Vulcanized," she murmured, remembering way back to Don Rámon's use of the same word and the anger it produced in Louis. Louis was shamed. But as to Gerard, she well knew he was considering how to contain and transfer compressed air. "Gerard," she said, smiling. "No."

"It would work. Hoses from the boiler to a turbine, then again to a compressor. Run compressed air off the boiler, replace the tracks with which the boiler was to be delivered to the rock with a lightweight hose, and simplify the pressure on the grippers. Maybe it would stop glazing. The hoses would be cooler. Then a compressor to operate the rock drill." He paused. "It's energy, that's all. How to deliver the energy to the drill efficiently. I'd still have to figure how the compressor would work. Another set of pistons, maybe. It would require a heavy gear wheel and an air-tight container."

She put a hand on her hip. "Gerard. Build it with the boiler first. Like you planned."

"Sometimes the answer lies by the side and can end up leading you into the center of a problem, like the hoses, for instance."

"Gerard."

He grinned at her. "I know."

Chapter 22

SHE RETURNED TO THE HOUSE, took up her Navy Colt, and put on her slouch hat and walked to the corral. She saddled Slate, then positioned herself next to the mule and, applying her knee to its ribs to make it blow, threw back her weight, pulling the cinch to its aparejo and bending to hook it before the mule sucked air back in. She swung up on Slate, rode by the house, and taking the turn at the crest of the hill, headed down past the stamp mill. She glanced at the men shoveling large lumps of quartzite, preparing to load them into the hopper. Mick did not meet her eye now. Along with the others he'd grown sullen. For the last several days, she and Gerard had heard talk about the terms of the Merced Company's lease and the quality of diggings allowed it. The gist seemed to be that the Colonel at all costs wished to keep the Merced away from the rich vein called the Black Drift that had been discovered in one of his mines.

The sun rose from behind the mountains, the ground fog and low clouds began to burn away, and with them the rain would pass. The ride to Las Mariposas would be twenty-five miles, first taking her past the road that led down through Hornitos, then past the lane that went up to the Frémont house, through Bear Valley, past the Osos Hotel and stores, and the shacks, hogans, and half-covered edifices that housed the miners. Slate splashed through a pond that had formed in the rutted roadway. Ghost sloshed close behind. The clouds began to break apart and scud across the sky, producing a sepia-like light. The pace of her animals quickened as she skirted Mount Bullion, what the Colonel had named for the riches it contained, and by his nickname, in honor of the late senator from Missouri, Mrs. Frémont's father. Her thoughts flowed freely as she rode, dwelling upon Mrs. Frémont, for whom she still held a fascination.

Adaline had been raised in Missouri, and Mrs. Frémont came from there. It seemed a pattern, the two different lives laid out parallel between two points there to here, halfway across the continent. Adaline had read that crowds clamored for Mrs. Frémont during her husband's candidacy, so spellbinding was she. Her portraits as they appeared in books and magazines showed a woman with an oval face, shining black hair brought close to her head, high brow, and large, dark eyes, and who, years ago, Adaline had come to believe, had sent her husband's book to a fourteen-year-old girl as a gift to travel with. Adaline wanted to thank her for that. She wanted to meet the woman, to know her.

She made good time, entering Las Mariposas early in the afternoon and threading her way amongst the mule teams and people strolling the boardwalks and street. She drew up in front of the store, what seemed an emporium compared to the outlet in Bear Valley. Indeed, Las Mariposas was built to support the several mines that drew from the Mother Lode, so the town was in all respects much more established than it had been not long before. She tied off her horse and mule at the rail, stepped in, and was greeted by Talley, a clerk hired by the proprietor. Talley bent behind the counter. There came a rattling and the thud of metal, what she supposed were the steel fittings, rivets, and valves come in from Bessemer in Britain, and the iron screw jacks. Talley heaved canvas sacks up one at a time on the counter until he had six bags in all. She opened one containing a screw jack, a heavy fitting that allowed for adjustment in two directions. Gerard had ordered four, two for the machine he had nearly ready, and two for the next one.

Talley had milk-blue eyes and an indentation on the left side of his brow where he'd been struck by a musket ball that penetrated his skull. A little cave of skin remained. Sometimes, if he wrinkled his brow, the skin would close over the indentation. When he looked across at her, the left eye twitched. "Will it do?"

He produced a voucher in the colonel's name, which she had to sign.

"I need more things," she said.

She toured the store, going past the prospecting tools to the foodstuffs and picking out flour, beans, coffee, pressed sugar, and tabasco to counter the pungency of their over-wintered meat. She carted her goods to the counter, and while Talley calculated the total she contemplated a rack of French wine that stood nearby, finally drawing two bottles from the rack.

"French," Talley said. "From France."

"I see." She had seen the language on the label. "Why French?"

"Ten dollars." Talley let out a sigh. "It's the effect of Mrs. Frémont over in Bear Valley."

"For certain she's here?"

"The Colonel picked her up in a coach, her and the children. She's a fine looking woman, all right, but now all the other women in town get high-falluting notions."

Adaline looked outside at the men and women bustling to and fro on the boardwalk. Her horse and mule stood at the rail, switching their tails. "For two?"

Talley's expression clouded, and then he understood. "Each."

"Five is too much."

"Eight," he said. "Came around the Cape. All the way from France. They're French, I say."

"Seven."

Talley closed his eyes. When he opened them, the left one twitched and the flap of skin over his hole almost closed. He didn't speak. She grasped the bottles by their necks, intending to return them to the rack, but Talley said, "All right." She placed the bottles back on the counter. Talley bent over, laboriously scrawling her purchases on an invoice. He revolved his sheet of numbers on the counter. She made it out, the hardware priced as previously agreed, and the wine, the flour, but the beans and sugar were high. "Put in one more bottle of wine." She pointed at the number in the column.

Talley raised his eyebrows, inducing the skin to pucker. "Seven dollars."

"No. Fifteen for the three."

"Sixteen."

She glanced through the window again. The sun's springtime light filled the street, and the numbers of people had increased. She'd heard one cargo wagon roll in, come up by the old highway, then yet another. They were no doubt hauling goods from the valley and distinguishable by the bells suspended from the drover's perch, used to warn off the bears and mountain cats. The pitch of the bells identified what the cargo was.

Talley saw her listening. "Mining machines."

"Mining machines?"

He lifted a hand, meaning to tell her to wait a minute. "Sixteen?"

"All right." She took the pouch from her pocket, poured a small pile of dust into a six-ounce measure, and pursed her lips as she watched Talley begin to add a pinch at a time.

He said, "The Merced has ordered monitors from Stockton."

She looked at his scale, which had the needle pointing straight up. She smiled at Talley. She knew he would try to distract her, then take an extra pinch of gold. "Oh?"

"They say the Australians down in Hornitos has mixed in with the Mexicans to make trouble," Talley said. "But the Merced pays a little more, which I can't calculate since the Merced is paying Frémont, too."

Inscrutable as it was, she knew that. These dealings had exacerbated her and Gerard's doubts over the Colonel.

"Frémont pays nobody nothing, 'cept a dying wage, which leaves him the cash to pay for what he wants. Like for them rock machines, if he pays. He ain't paid yet, right?" Talley paused. Adaline waited. He liked to gossip, too, and something told her not to let on how close

Gerard was to completing his work, or that they expected final payment for them soon. Talley said, "Rather let them Indians dig and die first, then the Greasers, or Welshmen, what have you. So, the company foments it."

Talley had succeeded in obfuscating. "Frémont's company does?"

"No. The Merced, I say." Having caught her interest, he dropped another pinch of dust onto his scale. "It'll be killing."

"And for you," she said. "If that last bit doesn't go back."

He chuckled and put the pinch back. "It's a kindness to you, remember that, keeping you alert," Talley said as he made a large pile of her goods. "You got to be alert."

She poured the remaining dust back into her pouch and began carrying her purchases outside. It took several trips and while she apportioned the weight on either side of Ghost's aparejo a whiff of perfume saluted her as two ladies in fancy skirts and velvet hats entered into the mercantile. She followed them to gather up the last of her things. They were examining bolts of yardage. When Talley came out from behind the counter, Adaline caught his sleeve. "Listen," she said. "What did you mean the Merced foments it?"

"It's the rights of proprietorship, that's all. Frémont owns everything underground. Trabucco's store, this one and the other he has. Frémont's got his hooks in them. Now the Merced's fighting back. That's what I mean." Talley bowed and displayed his hole all the way in to the skin the color of green phlegm at its bottom. "There's trouble brewing. I said them monitors being cargoed in ain't solely purchased by Frémont."

"I see," she said.

She made her exit and secured Ghost's aparejo. Not knowing whether or not Talley had merely unearthed a fragment and exaggerated it, as he was wont to do, made her uneasy. She swung up on Slate and started down the hill on the main street, which ran high up the bank above Mariposa Creek. In the brilliant sunlight the creek raged, near to overwhelming its banks. She rethreaded her way past the offices of the *Mariposa Gazette* and past the pack trains and cargo wagons, another three or four of which had meanwhile come up from the valley. Now, she marked the wagons with monitors resting in their beds, ready to be delivered, and pondered which of them were for Frémont, which were not. To her right and along the side of the street rustled five women in hoop skirts, as if they were heading for a tea. Behind them came a column of men with linen dusters worn over frock coats. Scattered everywhere roved the more coarsely dressed drovers, cargo handlers, prospectors, the Chileans and Mexicans. Two Chinese men with long queues abruptly retreated down a side street. She rode below the courthouse, two stories high with a clock tower that the colonel had ordered built.

Talley was right about that: Frémont owned it, as he owned all subsurface mineral rights beneath the houses, station, offices, saloon, mills, boarding house, Wells Fargo office, jail, cash store. Truly, the boo-jay metropolis had sprung up as if money had rained on the wilderness, producing changes that burst willy-nilly. New buildings and dwellings were made of brick. Some were under construction while others had been finished with leaded glass windows and fancy wrought iron balustrades. She had heard that some had wood trim within made from Nicaraguan mahogany and ponderous furniture brought from France by ship around Cape Horn just like Talley's wine.

She rode on, fashioning a one-person parade upon a horse the color of thunderclouds about its chest and head, running to pure black on the hindquarters, the big white mule trotting behind, the muffled clash of hardware in its aparejo. Adaline cut a figure, decked out in her bandolier and old Navy Colt, her knife, high moccasins, canvas trousers, her blue poncho, black slouch hat, her hair coming out to catch the light like obsidian, and the red bandanna fluttering. People glanced up, a few nodded, while those who didn't make her out must have wondered about the fiery young woman, gliding by on her fine horse. Certainly she was not one of the Indians out of California. Maybe she was Brazilian come for the gold, or a Mexican, or maybe one of the brazen Chileans. It depended upon how attuned were the onlookers to the appearance of feature and skin, the unending influx and the opportunism and hazard accompanying each group, seasoned miners from Wales or Ireland, the British Highlands, the Nordic countries, and France, Russia, Peru, Chile, China, convicts out of Australia, along with Mexicans who'd lived here longer than anyone except the Indians. And there came the deluge of Americans, a generation or two or three removed from their own amalgamation, spilling out from the South and East, loaded up with their raw sense of preeminence tantamount to religion. There were journeying Indians, such as Frémont's favored Delawares, or the Utes, Comanches, Cheyenne, even Arapaho.

Some might ask, "Who is that?" Then, "Who you say? His daughter?" They would fill in the spaces with their own conjectures as to how she came to cut such a figure. At the edge of town, she leaned forward and put her knees to Slate to quicken him up the hill northward, the mule in tow. Several hours passed before she went around Mount Bullion. Higher in the hills the stamp mills crashed. Upon entering Bear Valley at twilight, she could see the lamplight shining inside the Oso Hotel. Miners were arriving at the boarding hall, some lounging just outside of it, tipping their chairs against the facade. Men were on the roadway, too, Frémont's men, and a gang of Indians, Diggers moving toward the huts located behind the hotel. Their eyes glistened in the near darkness. Clouds moved in from the mountains, blocking out all but the faint, westward starlight as she rode on.

She began the climb uphill. Quieted now, the stamp mill loomed sepulchral. Judging from her animals' gait, they must have come upon an uneven surface, the effect of continued thaw, of a heavy freight of water from the higher hills upon the sodden ground. She allowed Slate to pick his way. Bushes and trees leading up to the stone house blocked out what light remained, and she determined there was no candle or lamp lit. Ahead, as best she could see, only a spark glowed in the work shed. Her eyes turned to the corral, searching out and catching sight of Gerard's white horse. She dismounted and tied off Slate and Ghost at the house, pushed the door open and eased inside the room, now blacker than the outside. Stumbling, she felt something awry, and fumbled for the lucifers in her shirt pocket, struck one, lit a candle, and turned around. The room was in disarray, pots and pans strewn over the floor, her trunk open, books and newsprint articles scattered. She picked her way to her trunk and found the lower compartment pried open, what it had held of her gold and coin missing.

A jolt shot through her—A thief? Here?

Hearing something, she whirled back toward the doorway. Things were more visible out there and she saw from the mule's position that the sound had come from its load, shifting while it lifted a hoof and set it down again. Otherwise the horse and mule were calm, biding their time. As if on cue, Gerard's white horse nickered. Slate turned his head toward the corral and nickered back softly.

She placed the candle on the table, took out her pistol, and stepped outside. She led her horse and mule, walking silently just in front of them. She stopped before the work shed, tied them off on a post, and now glimpsed faint embers of two fires, one back a ways in the forge and one closer, low in the center of the room. Slowly, her eyes adjusted to the darkness within, and then in a flash of an instant her scalp prickled. By the pale of his brow, she saw Gerard standing against the wall to the right, stock still. She whispered, "Gerard?" A piece of metal scraped against her foot, and in the faint light from the embers she could trace the outline of his hair and expression. She whispered again, "Gerard," and advancing carefully, reaching out to him, catching hold of his shirt, she touched something damp. She passed her hand sideways and sensed the incongruity of dampness and something cold and hard. Metal. Alarmed, she pulled on it. He pitched forward against her and she caught him, a terrible weight, heavy, something tipping against her that was much more than she could hold. She let go, struggling to step clear of him. Metal crashed to the ground and he fell sideways. Behind her, Slate and Ghost's hooves glanced across the ground.

Then there was nothing, no sound. She went for the lamp Gerard kept on the bench and backed up, pistol still in her right hand, feeling for it with her left hand. Finding it, she took out another lucifer but simply hung there for a long minute and took in a long, shuddering breath, then scraped the lucifer against the surface of the bench. It flamed, casting wild shadows. She lit the lamp, peered down, and to her horror saw exactly what she'd most feared, but not in this detail, not this detailed horror. Gerard had been impaled in the chest with the drill rod. The machine was angled sideways, and his body lay thrown a little further awry of it. Blood had flowed from his chest down to his stomach from where the drill rod had been affixed. The expression on his face was wild with terror. Some powerful force had driven the drill rod.

By the effect of the boiler upon the piston, perhaps.

Perhaps, just perhaps he'd impaled himself by accident.

But how? How could that be?

Asking herself that question and remembering the scattered contents of her trunk, she hastily set the lamp down and stumbled back outside the verge of its light, stopping.

Easy now.

She held her pistol steadily and in all-out alertness scanned her surroundings.

A thought flashed.

I'm alone here.

She heard water trickling.

She raised the gun and peered back into the crevices of the shop, skittered her eyes back at Gerard's prone form, and then down the mill site into the hopeless darkness, the obscurity that became increasingly palpable.

She moved. She saw to her mounts, first uncinching and next dumping Ghost's aparejo on the spot—tools, screw jacks, wine bottles, sack of beans, and all. Though she moved deliberately, her mind was racing, and thinking that she would have to find help, yet knowing it was absolutely dark and knowing further that the animals had to eat and that they'd do well to rest, too, she picked her way with them down the path to the corral. She unsaddled Slate, leaving the saddle at the ready, laid across a fence in the event she had to feel for it in the pitch black. Then she felt for loose hay in a stall and gave them some. She caught up Gerard's horse and lit another lucifer to find his bridle. She put it on him and paused for a moment, holding the lucifer aloft. She saw nothing untoward, just the shadowy shapes of horses and mules. She let the lucifer burn out and lifted her eyes toward the shed. She had left the lamp burning in the shed and could just make out Gerard's crumpled form and in the foreground Ghost's aparejo, the disarrayed heap. It seemed somehow as still as a phantasmal crèche, and the shock began to grow in her now, an unintelligible blackness penetrated her, and she tasted the gall as her stomach churned and her hands began to shake. She told herself to move.

She led Gerard's horse up to the stone house, tied him off to have him at the ready.

Ready for what?

She went in. The candle was half burned down and it slumped toward the table. She lit another, went to her knees before her trunk, and mindlessly sorted things out to put them away—newspaper, dime novels, her instruments and the Frémont exploration journal, some of Don Rámon's rocks, and her ledger book. Then it abruptly came to her. She stopped, registering how incapable she was of putting in order what was beyond her capacity to comprehend, what was completely and utterly disordered.

Not only what little gold I had here is gone.

But Josefa's little box of potions, too. Her jewelry.

What?

Gerard's gift, the blue silk dress and the fine paper it was wrapped in.

She backed against the wall, facing the doorway, and sank to the floor, pulled her buffalo robe over her knees, laid her pistol down, and stared into the night. A lump formed in her throat, and tears began to flow, which then gave way to stunned breathlessness. Finally, she wiped the tears from her face. Her hands were shaking again. Her whole body was shaking. She held her breath until it stopped. She heard water running in the creek and the more distant thudding in the flume in the hills above the house. Adaline jerked, then she saw the desert as if from far above. The man with no face traversed its endless expanse, leading a horse and followed by a great whirlwind, filling the sky with dust. Gerard's horse moved. He pulled at a clump of grass and put his nose through the doorway.

I left the door open.

His horse is there, standing, looking at me.

Gerard is dead.

The morning light began to filter in and across the way she watched it washing toward the blacksmith's shed, illuminating the heap from Ghost's aparejo and toward the inert percussion rock drill. If she stepped out to the landing, she would see Gerard's crumpled form. She heard distant booming, then the Merced Company men start up the stamp mill. The innards of the earth were piled. Pulverized rock spilled onto the screen. Soon, its remains would wash down and fill the valley with tailings and silt. The dredges would come out and the endless drudgery would go on. The men were unkempt, stringy-haired surgeons roving over the ruptured skin.

Chapter 23

AT THE BREAK OF DAWN, Adaline repacked what remained of her things in her trunk. She laid her guns down beside it. She walked down to the corral and saddled Slate and led him, Gerard's flint-colored mule, and Ghost and the travois back up to the house, tethering them next to Gerard's white horse. She loaded her trunk and guns onto the travois, and then led Ghost to the shed where she managed to move Gerard. She eased him out from under his percussion rock drill and stood him up and found how like Mr. Turner he was much heavier dead than she had imagined possible. She thrust her shoulder under his belly, dragged him several feet, and dumped him onto the travois. She lifted his legs, positioned him beside her trunk, and lashed him and the trunk down. In what seemed a crazed quest for order, she had a strange, blunted consciousness of what she was doing. Moving like a somnambulist, she put the screw jacks away in the shed, the food and wine bottles in the house.

She picked her way down the hill with her string of animals, including Gerard's white horse. Within a few minutes, she approached the deafening clamor of the Merced Company's stamp mill. Two men shoveled quartz into the mill, one the bedraggled Mick who hardly looked at her. In the thaw, water spewed everywhere, out of the leaky flume and over the banks of the creek. She turned on the road to Bear Valley, rode up the lane to the rancho where Mrs. Frémont stood on the veranda and glanced at her imperiously, distracted as she was by her toddler, little Frank. She did not know at first who Adaline was, then slowly came to a realization. She drew near, held Adaline by the shoulders, and saw the dead man in the travois, his chest crushed.

She said, "Adaline Carson? Is it you? My lands, what happened child?"

In discovering Gerard as she had, the jolt of it, and the sleepless night that followed, Adaline's face had taken on a pallor. She was unsteady on her feet. Mrs. Frémont called Mêmê and Henri to help. Adaline was led up the stairs and put to bed in the small room next to the parlor. It had a down-filled quilt and pillows. Adaline fell almost instantly into a deep sleep. Late that day, Mrs. Frémont had Mêmê rouse her from bed and take her to the parlor where she was given soup and bread. Through a window, Adaline saw George Stilts and Albert Lea, another Negro in Frémont's employ, down past the barn, digging a grave. It seemed unreal, parting with Gerard in almost the same way she'd met him, though then the hole was dug for another. Now, it belonged to Gerard.

•

According to Mrs. Frémont, Adaline suffered from a nervous disorder. For the first few days she slept and wandered about in a half-stunned state. Her legs were leaden. Several times, she sensed people watching her from behind, but when she turned to look no one was there, having metamorphosed into pillows stacked in a pile, or a chair with a wrap draped over it. Mrs. Frémont told her the cause of these visions was the assault and the loss she'd suffered. The effect of the growing insurrection, the drunken chouts, and the nightly near riots down at the Osos hotel couldn't have helped, either, she explained. Mrs. Frémont knew about threats to a loved one because during her husband's expedition into the Rockies she fell victim to fits of a prescient nervous disorder. "We women recognize when there's evil from the outside to be reckoned with," she said. "With the colonel, there were evil forces, but I knew when he was safe. He went to your father's house in Taos. It was before you came West."

Adaline knew about this. She remembered it as a topic of conversation between Josefa and her father, how Josefa had nursed Frémont back to health, serving him a chocolate drink every morning.

Mrs. Frémont insisted that Adaline stay. It was the least she could do, she said, and though it came in fits and starts Adaline's strength gradually returned. Adaline formed the practice of entering the parlor once she was dressed, and of visiting the women's privy, then going back to the parlor and pausing at the windows which overlooked the grounds outside, or walking straight into the kitchen, where she might find Mêmê or Mrs. Frémont. From the parlor one morning she heard a chorus of voices, all three children laughing and scurrying in the kitchen and Mêmê calling to them. A door that led outside clicked open and the chattering faded away. A man's voice now spoke up, as it often did. She knew it to be the colonel. Mrs. Frémont responded, and then opened the door between the parlor and kitchen. "Just as I thought. You're up." She was holding a teacup which she set down on a table. "I'll be back." She wore crinoline under her skirt, which crinkled as she returned to the kitchen.

Here, the table with a white damask cloth stood poised between two upholstered chairs. A rug with great red and yellow flowers woven into it lay on the floor. The shelf against the opposite wall was now entirely filled with books—not just *White Jacket, The Scarlet Letter,* and the colonel's own expedition journals. Adaline had asked about her copy of the journal, saying her father had thought maybe Mrs. Frémont had inserted it when she'd arranged to have the trunk shipped to Adaline way back when Adaline was just starting out for the West.

Mrs. Frémont displayed her impish side. "But, of course. Your father had told me that you liked to read. He said you were reading the journal."

"I was. And I did again," Adaline had said. "I know it practically by memory."

Also in the bookshelf were John Greenleaf Whittier's works, Longfellow's *Evangeline: A Tale of Acadie,* Maria Cummins' *The Lamplighter,*

Harriet Beecher Stowe's two volumes of *Uncle Tom's Cabin*, a book of essays by Ralph Waldo Emerson, and another by Henry David Thoreau. One book, Fanny Fern's *Ruth Hall*, Adaline had read a portion of and was startled by the breakneck pace of it. In a corner of the room stood a desk with a pile of papers, a quill, and pot of ink. A straight chair with a linen seat and a arching back was pulled up to it. Mrs. Frémont was keeping a record there, Adaline surmised.

Mrs. Frémont returned, holding a second teacup and a plate of pastries. "Mêmê made these." She stepped back and appraised Adaline. "Sit," she said. Adaline sat. Mrs. Frémont filled the tea cups and sat next to Adaline. Her dark hair was parted severely in the middle and combed back. She motioned to the plate. "Won't you try one?"

Adaline took a pastry. Just as Mrs. Frémont began explaining that Mêmê had gone off with the two boys, Charley and little Frank, on an outing, and that her daughter, Lily, despite her objections over being too old for the boys, had consented to join them. Colonel Frémont materialized in the doorway. Mrs. Frémont glanced up at him and then turned back to Adaline. "Business associates are expected on today's stage. But one never knows exactly when the stage will arrive, or even if it will come today."

"I see," Adaline said. The possibility of such guests explained the crinoline under Mrs. Frémont's skirts, her shining hair, and the cravat the colonel had tied around his neck.

The colonel announced that he would be taking several men to haul Gerard's rock percussion machines up Mount Bullion to the Pine Tree Mine. Another man was up at the mill site now, repairing and finishing the machines. "I have Gerard's plans," he said. "We need to see how well the drills work. We'll try them, then I'm going to show them to my attorney, also to an investor who's interested in them." Before Adaline could respond, snagged as she was on the thought that Gerard's invention was now passing away, the colonel continued, saying they had also uncovered signs pointing to Gerard's killers, but they were going to hold off apprehending anyone until they were certain. "It seems they worked for the Merced Company. Corrupt politics. And in the time since the court granted us another hearing, there have been rumors of the Merced jumping the Pine Tree. We're reinforcing all embattlements around the mine."

The growing tension between Frémont's miners and the Merced Company was precisely what Talley had forewarned against. From bits of household gossip, Adaline had become aware that Frémont's men were feverishly running tunnels along a vein left by an ancient riverbed, the Black Drift, at the Pine Tree Mine, and feeding the rock to his massive eight-stamp mills. The Merced Company, engaged in digging another adjacent tunnel, claimed it had a lease for it and hence for the Black Drift. The issue of ownership and of loopholes in the laws of possession, which the Merced men hoped to work to their advantage, had been held up in court and also were under consideration by the governor, hence the rumblings of insurrection. The colonel looked directly at her, adding, "Yet you need not bother yourself with this. I have men at the ready. For you, there's nothing now but the woods and sky and whatever may chance into your view and fancy. We need to take care, all of us." He kept gazing at her.

"I am careful," she said, a little affronted by the colonel's seeming condescension, yet catching herself at the presumptuous tone in her response. Mrs. Frémont, solicitous within the confines of her franchise, let her hand float to Adaline's wrist. Yet more unsettled, Adaline stared past the colonel at the wall opposite, a design on white paper exhibiting silver leaves and rose-colored buds. Through the window behind her, a cloud had moved away, permitting the sun to shine a rectangle of light and the precise silhouette of a tree branch upon the wall.

Abruptly, the colonel strode across the room and opened the door to the front veranda. The door swung shut and his boots thudded on the planks. Through those windows Adaline saw him stop to position his hat and look down to where Lea had brought his horse. She thought: There he is. The famous pathfinder, former governor, senator, presidential candidate, and now land magnate. Something defiant surfaced in the way he squared himself and stepped down to his

311

man and his mount, like one of the mystifying rocks, brecciate, what had once come out of the ground molten, flowing as liquid, adhered to other stones, and then cooling with these stones trapped inside itself. A gold nugget might be found in one but more often bits of garnet, amethyst, agate, jasper, and tourmaline. The colonel mounted his horse and rode off behind the trees that lined the lane.

Mrs. Frémont lifted her hand from Adaline's wrist, passed it through the air, and surprised Adaline by saying, "There is a part of my husband I cannot reach. It's what he saw, I believe, when your father was in his company. Everything was new, and fresh, and wild, an entirely new order of experience from anything anyone but the first adventurers had encountered. It turned out to be not what we wrote about in his reports. I'm sure it was something of a religious experience. It was often frightening to him, but it found an opening to his soul. It bears no resemblance to the world of banks and courts, the politics that plague him now. It was the fright, the terrible exhilaration in the journeying . . ."

Mrs. Frémont's voice had grown husky with emotion. She broke off for a moment and then collected herself, saying, ". . . the necessary fright and the other-worldliness as if it were an Eden that held God's love for all creatures. The hazard of His Being. Wind on their cheeks. Solid earth. The actual world. From it all came knowledge that cannot be shared. Not by optimism, nor with hope, nor in good spirit for improvement, but by a dark complicity, so hard was it, so filled with the blackness of killing. I have wondered if it was something of that order that drove Meriwether Lewis mad."

As she took this in, Adaline sensed dissonant chords clashing. There was the matter of "first adventurers," as Mrs. Frémont put it, among whom Adaline's father had been one, much earlier than the colonel. And there was her mother in the northern plains for whom what Mrs. Frémont called Eden had been simply the home into which she was born. How is it, she wondered, that Mrs. Frémont thinks what is new to her people, given to them, they believe, in all its shine, and not ancestral, not scarred up and twisted since time immemorial, and giving over its scars and twistings to the people born by countless generations into it? What Eden?

"Hopeful as everyone was for him," Mrs. Frémont said, "and as a price for the future of the nation, whereby he opened up the West for them, there must have been a kind of ruination in it, too. Revealed as a horror playing underneath the beauty of it all."

Adaline held her peace, thinking: Ruination? What of the ruin they brought with them?

Her brooding thoughts conjured dream images of the great book, filled with pages that kept secret what lay between the Colonel and his wife, page after page which Mrs. Frémont could not connect to what he had witnessed. He had kept it hidden from her, even though she wrote his journals down while he, as the rumors had it, paced and narrated by the fire late into the night, frenetic with reliving his adventures, exhausting himself that way. He could not bear to sit for the writing, and often could not complete his thoughts, terrifying as they sometimes were. In his impatience, he left it to her to ferret out and embellish. Wonderful as the journals were, for their science, particularly, it had to be said that what she knew only by conjecture she often named as fact, and sometimes what she suspected as fact about people, coming close to it, she expunged entirely. With such excisions she drove the whole of it toward an idealistic fancy, never mind what was harrowing, cold blooded, hidden within his sketchings, or kept concealed from her in his loins. This, Adaline had concluded, was how Mrs. Frémont contained the mercurial man within her equally mercurial and furtive romance.

It wasn't the power of desire, or of temptation that troubled her. Adaline understood that! Given the shortage of women in the wilderness, or for that matter, in the gold fields, she well comprehended how men were insatiable both in their desire and in their conspiracy to treat women as if they meant nothing, or if they were so privileged, as was the colonel, to have access to the lot, to rummage through their ranks and take the best.

313

The pages turned, shuffling one to the next as of Indians in tule sandals on a slow march to their work, the digging. That, too.

Hush, hush, hush . . .

"For me, this place is near enough to the wilderness," Mrs. Frémont added. For a long while, she gazed out the window toward where her husband had disappeared, and her voice shuddered: "For him, however, there are times when I know he would like to be done with this and to return to his expeditionary days." She fell silent for a moment, as if an owl had winged out looking for the words and not finding them returned to the night of her interior and settled there on a roost, adjusting its feathers. Mrs. Frémont reached for the teapot, refilled both cups, and clicked the pot down on the tray.

"Oh, child," she said. She leaned back in her chair and gazed at the wall. Adaline looked at it, too, the white upon which the sun, having swung a bit southward, now shone directly through the window behind the women, still imprinting a clear etching of the tree branch. Mrs. Frémont had seen to it that Albert Lea and Isaac planted gardens so that plots with flowers stretched alongside the house and all manner of vegetables and trees. This was a young persimmon tree already beginning to bear fruit. A bird landed, causing the branch to dip and gracefully recoil. "I don't envy you. Hard as this place is for me, it would be impossible for . . ." There was a hitch, a pause in which she trailed off.

Neither moved. Their gazes stayed fixed and Adaline wondered with what the sentence would be completed. A young woman bereft? Or the half-blood daughter of Kit Carson, or an Indian alone? The bird, by the outline of its crest a jay, reached down to peck at a green fruit. The image raised its head, screamed raucously, and bent to peck again. Adaline thrashed about in her mind for something to say. "I had thought to settle into one place for a time."

"Yes." Again Mrs. Frémont touched Adaline's arm and leaned toward her, her high brow smooth, her eyes filled with care, and her lips parted ever so slightly. "This new world calls for a different kind of forbearance. There was nothing like this ever before."

"I had thought to have a home and to live with the man I loved," Adaline said. The simplicity of the statement nearly brought tears to her eyes. She had had a man. She had had a home, after a fashion, but she was not married, and what she called a home was merely granted as a place to live. That man, whom she had learned to love, was dead. And then, in her mind, Adaline twisted as if in midair. She felt her body doing it, turning, and immediately a hopefulness washed over her as she remembered her cows, the care of them, and the vastness of her loneliness. The hopefulness ferried crosswise over the current of what she otherwise felt.

She had thought: No, no, no, I'm aggrieved that Gerard is dead, but I have to go on.

She thought: I'll go where we had talked about. I'll take my animals to watch over.

She said, "Do you think I could stable Ghost and Gerard's horse and the mules here while I go down after some of my cows? Perhaps I can ride down with one of the colonel's wagons."

"Of course, my dear," Mrs. Frémont replied matter-of-factly. "Sometimes I have felt like an osprey, rebuilding my nests in precarious places. But I know . . ." Her voice trailed off again and she gave Adaline's wrist a squeeze.

She's off in her own world.

Adaline considered this place with its servants, employees, and children, the shelves full of books, the sideboard in the next room. There were the stores in the barn, equipment, food supplies, more furniture, but she was impressed by how so much from the cart loads of goods she'd seen in the yard had found its way into the house, and by how systematic it all was. There were white curtains, now, in the parlor, tied open in sashes to admit the summer light, china and French figurines in ranks behind the glass doors of a cabinet, the chairs and matching chesterfield, and flowers from Mrs. Frémont's garden in two crystal vases set just so on top of the piano. The house was still to be enlarged under Mrs. Frémont's direction, yet another room added, a chimney built, and the veranda extended while the master of tens of thousands of acres, her husband, came and went. It hardly seemed precarious, yet Adaline had to grant that hazard could tell upon anyone. Mrs. Frémont had lost her first son. She had lost her house in San Francisco to fire. Her father's house had burned in the East, and then not long before Mrs. Frémont came West the Senator had died an agonizing death to rectal cancer.

As if reading her thoughts, Mrs. Frémont said, "I know I am fortunate. I've had my struggles but nothing compared to yours. Yet we have like natures. Willful and independent. Were we men, we would be powerful. Your education, what your father was so determined to secure for you, has served you well. It is a great mystery of the world, is it not, how the willing and the good can be born into either the best of conditions or the worst, and so, too, with the unwilling and evil. It's as if God dropped us all here like jackstraws, and our trial is to sort out in the short time we have on earth what He might have sorted out for us straightaway."

"Yes," Adaline said. As to her education, she was grateful for the reading and numbers she'd been taught in Fayette. Her eyes drifted down to the shelf before her, then to what hung above it, a framed poem, John Greenleaf Whittier's presidential endorsement, "The Pass of the Sierra." She even came to feel grateful for the nuns in Saint Louis, rapping her on the knuckles with sticks, flagellating her with switches in the dark corridors of the nunnery, and grabbing her by the collar as they passed the people dancing dervishes in the streets. They'd taught her what passed as manners to give her a sense of how to behave in other societies. She knew how to hold a teacup, how to sit in a chair, how to hold herself firm in this way against the world's cruelty. She said, "At times, though, I'm afraid that if I make one more mistake, I might be crushed."

"These mistakes . . ." Mrs. Frémont said. "Yes, if you make one, and in the press of panic make a second, and the third, then you're headed pell-mell for disaster. The world can be crushing. It's the bear in the bush. Don't provoke it." Mrs. Frémont's voice broke, causing Adaline to look sharply at her. She appeared suddenly pale. She picked up the teapot and said, "Won't you have more tea?"

Adaline held her cup directly under the spout to catch the tea.

Mrs. Frémont smiled. "Another pastry?"

"Thank you."

Mrs. Frémont looked at the wall again, sighing deeply.

There had, in fact, occurred an episode with a bear while Mrs. Frémont, her husband, and others rode on an outing part way up Mount Bullion. The colonel and Isaac had saved her from the encounter, indeed from even knowing there was a bear in the bush until she was safely home. There was the court martial from ten years ago, the times of the expeditions, the long separations from her husband, and the time she thought she'd lost him for good on the expedition into the Rocky Mountains. And then her own nervous disorder, which took the form of acute fatigue and "brain fever," according to Mêmê. So great was the pressure from within that the skin around her eyes and forehead had turned black, and then, as if by premonition, and though she was miles away, Mrs. Frémont claimed she knew when her husband was safe in Kit and Josefa's Taos home. Immediately, she recovered.

Adaline's eyes went to the neat stack of papers on the desk where lay documents pertaining to numerous suits against the colonel's holdings and now to the defense against the revolt of the Merced company. Through all this Mrs. Frémont maintained her ferocious ambition on behalf of her husband, and the insults he bore she took as cuts against herself. Adaline glanced at Mrs. Frémont and found something cleared away for her, the brush, leaving only the bear, and she had her own visionary premonition of Mrs. Frémont as an old woman, a widowed and infirm crone watched over by her fat, old maid daughter, Lily. She pictured her in a wicker wheelchair, nearly blind, bankrupt, and living in a California house provided by friends, yet crazed in her willfulness, and to the end ready to exercise all her powers to defend her dead husband.

Within the silhouette now, nearly a dozen jays flitted in and out of sight, battling over the green fruit, raising a cacophony. It was as though their shrieking brought a message from the world.

Finally, Mrs. Frémont spoke. "You are right. You should go back to your cows."

"Yes."

"Does the valley where you were supply you with enough resources?"

"I have thought of going to Mono Lake."

"Mono Lake? Above the Yosemite? Why, I've heard that's a gold camp!"

"Yes, they say there are strikes there, now."

"You would go back into the gold fields?"

"Yes, with cattle. They say there are shortages." She went on: "They also say there are rocks that float in water. White castles upon the water made of a soft rock." She was tempted to say that she had dreamed of such a place, a powerful dream of a presidio that overlooked the desert that had things Frémont had named for her father—Carson River, Carson Valley, and now Carson City.

"I see," Mrs. Frémont said. "You'll need to take someone to guide you. Perhaps George. He knows the way. Perhaps his sister, Johanna, would know it even better, since she comes from up there. I will ask the colonel if he can part with them for a time." Mrs. Frémont settled in her chair. "Pumice and tufa. Salts and calcium from the water. It's good that curiosity and the will to live have survived in you."

It was true. It was partly that, but partly also what she would never say to Mrs. Frémont—her wish to be away from her and the Colonel, too, and partly the practical in her envisioning, her need for a means of self-support, conjoined with the need for meat in the highland fields and by the army fort near Carson City, the opening of the mines in the hills, and then the vantage on the desert.

Chapter 24

THE COLONEL DID NOT WANT to part with George Stilts just yet. But when Adaline assured him that someone from the hacendia in the valley could return as far as Bear Valley with her—she thought José, or one or both of the twins—the colonel found an opening for her to travel in the company of a freight wagon. She rode to Las Mariposas, then went with the wagon toward the plain below, tracking the course of Mariposa and Owens Creeks. The colonel had given his word that the driver and two guards were to be trusted, yet Adaline stayed vigilant. When they stopped at night, she sought out a place removed from them. None of the three troubled her.

On the second day, she saw more incarcerated Indians marching ponderously, supervised by guards. The Indians moved to the side of the trail, making way for the wagon and horses. Throughout the landscape, the cacophony and bedlam had escalated. There were more canals and diversions, more sluices, more iron monitors were being hauled up to Las Mariposas. By the fourth day, as her group reached the bottom, she examined the booming stamp mills and the whistle and crash of steam driven dredges at work in the slackwaters, and still more Miwoks working in gangs with shovels, heavy hammers, picks, and buckets.

Once the wagon turned northward toward Stockton, she aimed south. Alone, she passed by fields planted with maize and now with winter wheat, too, and two afternoons later came upon her old casa.

A few cows were apparent and she deduced, given the season, that the remainder had been driven into the hills. Manchada and her ten-year-old horse, Hawk, grazed in the pasture. She tied Slate outside the casa and stepped inside, finding the pallet, chairs, shelf, and ceramic dishes all in place, but when she touched her hand to the table and removed it she left a diffuse claw-like mark in the dust. That stopped her. She sensed the ghost of Gerard at her back. She turned. Nothing. Nobody. The casa seemed untouched, only the filtering dust measured the five months that had passed. Stepping back outside, she made out a trace of Gerard's picture of the rock percussion machine scratched into the earth. It was still there.

She reentered and went through the back door, checking where she had buried her strongbox. By now the earth was packed hard there. She swung around as children's voices called out to her: "Adalina! Adalina!" Pedro and Maria darted toward her while Lucia trailed behind them. Adaline knelt and hugged each of the little ones. "Look at you. How you've grown," she exclaimed. She moved to Lucia and embraced her gently. Lucia's cheeks revealed a softness riding over the jaw, a sign of her passing into womanhood. Her eyes drooped, underscored by dark rings. "But look at you, now," Adaline said in Spanish. "What is wrong?"

Lucia turned away.

Adaline looked to their casa. She saw the shadow of a hunched-over woman in the breezeway. "And your mamá? She is in the casa?"

Lucia's eyes filled with tears while the two young ones grew solemn and looked to Lucia.

"¿Qué tienes? ¿Qué pasa chica?"

Lucia told her that her mother, Juana, had died three months ago. They had hoped to have another brother or sister. It turned out it was not one but two sisters. One sister lived. The younger came out stillborn and her mamá died.

"No. Oh, no," Adaline said, shocked. "Oh!" She took Lucia in her arms and held her tight, and felt the thin body quaking. Her own eyes filled with tears. Maria looked at the ground now and little Pedro stared straight out into the sky. Adaline released Lucia. "And your papá? He's out with the cows. Or he is here?"

"No, mí abuela," Lucia said.

Adaline glanced toward the house again. She slowly advanced while the children hung behind. Their grandmother, Juana's mother, acknowledged in Spanish that she knew who Adaline was. José and the two sons were away in the pastures and were expected home this evening, she said. Adaline should plan to eat with them. Her face was deeply wrinkled, but her hair was pulled back like Juana's had always worn hers, and also like Juana she scrutinized Adaline askance as if shades were half-drawn over her eyes.

In time, José and the twins, Ernesto and Eduardo, returned, and Naja came up to her. Adaline stroked the dog's chest and noted that her muzzle now looked lean with age. And the silver that had formerly grizzled José's beard and temples had so taken command that nearly all of his hair had turned silver. The world was constantly changing. The twin sons were growing beyond their adolescence and turning into cleanly built young men. More silent than Adaline remembered them, they, too, were carried by the sobering effects of loss. Everyone sat down at the table to beans and rice, strips of grilled beef, salsa, and corn tortillas. They dined enveloped within the ineffable memory of Juana.

After dinner came a murmur from an adjoining room. Abuela rose up and went and returned with a baby swaddled in a blanket, whom she handed over to Adaline. They called her Juanita. Little Juanita's wondrous, shining eyes were nestled in thick, dark lashes, and her tiny hand latched onto Adaline's small finger. Lucia carried the dishes away. There was mention of Juana's sister, who would come to fetch Juanita, but for now Abuela took care of the baby. A half hour later, she put her to bed, soon to be followed by the two young children. The twins departed to see to the animals, and Naja followed them. Lucia and Abuela stepped outside to draw water from the well.

Adaline and José sat at the table, drinking a tea Abuela had concocted from the prickly pear cactus. Adaline told José what had happened to Gerard, all of it, how he had struggled to build the rock percussion machine, and how he had it almost ready, and she had ridden into Las Mariposas to purchase the last parts, and she came back, found him dead, his machines wrecked, and now it was believed that the colonel's rivals had murdered him. Strange as it was, she felt an inner quiet telling José because he listened with such calm.

"It is very bad," he said. "Too much killing. I am sorry for you." He told her about the cows. All was well with the herd, he said. Not much disease. No thievery. From a hole in the wall he retrieved a box which contained coins and a promissory scrip. It was her share from what had been sold to the army at Fort Tejon. "Señor Godey was here. He said they wanted horses, too, but I don't have many of those. The army is preparing for something, I think," he said. "They are still fighting Indians, but there is something else. They are looking to the east."

Adaline examined the money and promissory scrip and asked if he was sure he wasn't giving up too much. José assured her that it was her share. They would see what to do with the remainder of the herd. "We had a good spring for calves," he added.

"I only want a few of them," she said. "Some cows with early spring calves. You keep the balance."

"Then I will still owe you," José said.

"If you let me pick what I take, the best for the journey, then we will be settled." Her mind flashed to the buried strongbox. She still had to dig it up. Suddenly, she was confused and overpowered by the lack of resolution everywhere, brought on by what José had mentioned about the East. She, too, had a premonition of something about to happen. Moreover, she had heard that the California lawmakers had formally enslaved some tribes, that the governor had recently called for the extermination of all Indians, and that it was not Frémont alone who considered Mexicans interlopers. She could not form her thoughts clearly enough to speak of this to José. "I am going to Mono Lake."

José's hands rested on the table, cupped around the güiro which held his tea. He looked steadily across at her. "I have heard of Lago Mono. It is very high in the mountains." He smiled. "Some say the ghosts go there to live in the white rocks that float upon the water."

"I have not heard of those ghosts." She smiled at him. "I have heard there are gold strikes and not much meat. The army is in the valley far below, on the other side of the mountains. To tell the truth, Bear Valley is an unlucky place for me." She took a sip of her tea.

"Juana did not think it was good for you to go. She did pray for you."

"Of course she did."

"She was not in pain at the end. The padre from the pueblo was here." As he regarded her, Adaline saw his eyes glistening. "My Juana always loved you."

"And I her."

"But it is so far away, Lago Mono. You could stay here. Cows will be sold here just as easily as there."

She looked over at Lucia, who had just entered carrying two buckets. She poured the water out of one to heat for the dishes. Abuela looked on. Adaline also loved Lucia and the younger children, and José's offer was tempting. She thought of it in a way that included dwelling in the company of José, for whom she held untold affection, but as Juana had been nearly old enough to be her mother, so, too, José was nearly old enough to be her grandfather, and he would need to be preeminent. Soon enough he would fall ill and die. Her high regard for him would become complicated and soon after compromised. She looked up at José and found him watching her. Sexual understanding flickered between them before he looked away.

"I must go," she said. "I don't like worrying about Colonel Frémont."

"You owe him nothing. Just cows."

"I want to see across the desert," she said. "I've been having dreams lately."

"Ah," José said. "I thought it would be something like that. El agüero."

"I don't know that word."

"A visitor in your dreams."

"Yes." She thought of the man with no face wandering in the desert, the whirlwind woman, and Gerard, too.

"Tomorrow, then, we will go up to divide the animals."

"Yes."

Lucia dumped the water outside the back door, returned, and said good night to them, kissing her Papá. Abuela went with her to the room where the baby slept.

Adaline said, "I will go to my casa, now."

José lifted a hand with which he bade her to stay. "When you first came, Juana thought you would help us to continue here on the Frémont land since you had the Colonel's blessing and Señor Godey's as well. At first that was our only interest in you, for we were afraid of losing our position. But then we came to like you, and we wished for you to continue here. My Juana had reason not to like you."

She cocked her head at the turn in subject. "Oh?"

"Do you remember that we told you our families each lived in this Alta California for a time? Our families were hacendados for the missions. We were old families here, long before the Americans came, though I was in service to a priest who took a liking to me. As a boy, I was taken from my family not far from here. Santa Lucia it is called. I knew my mother for only five years. They said my father was a soldier. I never knew him."

She sat still. Though she believed she knew what being in service to a priest meant for a boy, José's face betrayed nothing.

"Juana's people were first at San Luis Obispo, then San Francisco Solano, what is now called Sonoma." José sipped his tea and one of the buttons on his vest clinked against the table edge. "She was a Berreyesa. Does that mean anything to you?"

"I don't remember her family name. Perhaps I never knew it."

"We thought not. And we did not tell you this," José said. He smiled faintly. "There was another José, el tío de su padre. How do you say it?"

"Her father's uncle," Adaline said.

"Sí. José de los Berreyesa and his two nephews. They were twins." He smiled again and nodded toward the breezeway. His own twin sons had returned and outside the door they were talking softly. "Twins run in Juana's family. There are four that she knew of but never two sets with one mother. Perhaps that is what killed her. Agüero malo, the second one. But those twins I am talking about were Ramón and Francisco de Haro. They and their uncle were captured by your father at the water. They had come by boat. Each of them was made to kneel and shot in the head. They were two young men, or boys, truly, and one old man, surely not to be mistaken for Californio fighters." Jose's face had grown formidable, and his voice was husky in a way that she had never heard. "This was during the time of the American invasion, the very beginning of that war. It was near the Presidio Sonoma, thirteen years ago. We know they were carrying a dispatch of conciliation to Colonel Frémont."

He paused and sipped his tea. Adaline continued to sit still, but a creeping coldness filled her belly and passed up to her shoulders, for though she knew there was no mention of the incident in Frémont's journals, she had read a report of it in the form of an accusation by the Democrats during the presidential campaign. Frémont was said to countenance cold-blooded killing and her father portrayed as one who did his killing for him. She had felt the weight of complicity bearing down on her. But she thought that maybe someone else had done the shooting, or maybe her father just didn't want Frémont to be blamed for giving the order, as some claimed. She put the report out of her mind. But now she visualized the three on their knees, the hatless backs of their heads, the old man and two very young ones, the bullets tearing through the bone.

I am one of these Americans he speaks of.

Yet I am not one of those Americans.

I am the daughter of the man who was accused of having no mercy for three Mexicans, and there were more, many more to whom he showed no mercy.

And his commander, Frémont, who countenanced a killing for no reason except for the pleasure of power. For his convenience. The jungle in his face.

José lifted his hand again. "It is said that Frémont wanted to have the fame of conquest for himself. He took no interest in the message Don Berreyesa and his nephews brought to him from the generale, José Castro. Juana did not know them, the twins and Don Berreyesa. But in her family it is believed that their blood is on Colonel Frémont's hands, and your father is hated for his part in it.

The coldness grew in her listening. She beheld in a new light what always had been José's aloof deportment and the great trouble Juana must have had in treating her well at first. And now loomed the other side of her father, his fierce taciturnity, resolute obedience to orders, and unending respect for Colonel Frémont. She was deeply confused. "I did not know. I am sorry."

"It is not yours to be sorry for," José said. "Of course, you didn't know. Juana came to believe that you'd been sent as a mensajera, bringing the message that we should carry on."

Mensajera!

Next, still in the grip of her remorse, she thought: But I did know. I've always known, if not in the particulars then as a matter of general principle. And what does he mean, mensajera?

"You will need someone to ride back up with you. To keep the cows in order."

She could hardly look into his eyes. She'd meant to ask about that, of course. After a moment, she said, "As far as Bear Valley, perhaps. I think I have someone to ride to Mono Lake with me."

"It is decided then. The hermanos can watch over the casa and the rest of the vacas."

Chapter 25

THEY TRAVELED SLOWLY herding the cows, she with her coins and disinterred gold secured in Slate's saddlebags. In three weeks time they reached the outskirts of Las Mariposas where she left the cows in José's charge while she proceeded toward the Wells Fargo office. Las Mariposas was in a state of high disorder with armed men roaming the streets and lounging on the boardwalks. Mule teams were amassed two and three deep. In the Wells Fargo the clerk told her that the Merced Company had jumped the Pine Tree Mine. Colonel Frémont had petitioned the governor for aid in fighting them off, and the governor had dispatched five hundred California Volunteers. The clerk said that he guessed that Frémont had won this round with the Merced. She transferred her notes and consolidated her accounts, whereupon the clerk informed her that before the uprising the colonel had deposited five-hundred dollars in her name.

"I see," she said. "Thank you."

Coming from the Wells Fargo office, she spotted Talley out in front of his mercantile, posting an issue of the *Gazette*. He said not only had the Merced Company and the men of the Hornitos League jumped the Pine Tree Mine, but in response Frémont had threatened to blow up both the Pine Tree and Black Drift with the interlopers inside, including the Miwok diggers. He assured the men that they'd pay for their misdeeds in hell. Talley said it was true that the governor of California, upon receiving an express from Frémont, ordered the marshal of the state to gather up the force, and in addition the governor solicited aid from Nye of Stockton, the owner of a transport company, whose teamsters and guards came with convoys of wagons, loaded with arms. They had moved in three days ago, approaching the mines in the hills by way of Sonora, and past Hornitos and Bear Valley and up to Mount Bullion, but what they found when they arrived was a wonderful pall. The men of the Merced and Hornitos League had vanished.

"We had men enough for a war," Talley said. "It was over in a flash." He turned to the article in the *Gazette* and followed the lines with his finger until he came to the part that crowed over Frémont's victory: "'Frémont had been the subject of more bitter personal enmity and abuse than any man we have heard of. So far as we know there is no reason for it, and for the benefit of all concerned it should stop until it fully appears that he is the autocratical swindler, scoundrel, and rascal that it seems the heart's desire of some men to make out.' Ain't that fine?" Talley stepped back and chortled. "Autocratical he may be. But less of a swindler than them jumpers who's beleaguering him. Ain't we lucky . . . lucky as can be getting to choose which swindler we prefer to deal with?"

Adaline made her way to rejoin José and together they herded the cows to a meadow that lay beyond the road to Hornitos and northwest of Bear Valley. They had passed by the Osos Hotel, which was in even a greater state of tumult of mules and men than Las Mariposas had been. Wagons were lined up on both sides of the hotel and around a bend in the road. In the morning, she again left her herd under José's charge, and journeyed back in sight of the hotel where scores of mules were being harnessed. She rode up the lane toward the White House, along the fence to a screen of trees where she pulled up. Here, too, wagons were being prepared for departure. The Frémonts' stores of tinned and bottled goods, what Adaline had once heard Mêmê refer to as "le grocerie," had been raided and the remains dumped in the yard. Barrels and crates had been pilfered from the barn and scattered. New trails gouged and scarred the grass that emerged from the underbrush and crossed through the village of Indian huts below the house. The vegetable plot lay in ruins.

A wagon departed, passing Adaline, the drover ringing the bell and calling out to his team. Instantly, another team took its place and men materialized from the barn where they'd been camping out. Some set to harnessing the teams and loading the wagons while down below the sound of the departing wagon dwindled to its single tolling bell, falling in with other wagons setting out from the hotel. All the while, men's voices were calling out and the hooves of countless mules swelled to a din. There was a creaking of harnesses.

Frank and little Charley Frémont walked out from behind the house. Adaline caught sight of the colonel himself striding up the slope near the edge of the yard, immersed in conversation with a man carrying an umbrella and wearing a heavy overcoat. Considering that the sun would blaze before the day was far gone, the umbrella made some sense, but the overcoat was hard to fathom. Mêmê and Henri appeared behind the two boys and followed them into an open field beyond the barn and village of huts while a fatigued-looking Mrs. Frémont slipped out the front doorway of the house. Adaline approached on Slate, threading around the mules and wagons. She dismounted, tied off her horse, and stepped up to the veranda. Mrs. Frémont's smile was strained. "Now, more or less of disorder, and lingering threats, but it's back to our congenial quarters one hopes," she announced shakily. "Some of the men saw you coming yesterday, driving your herd. And you, I take it, have heard what's been happening while you were gone?"

"Yes," Adaline said. "What was stirring up when I left. The Merced men came out in the open and you and Mr. Frémont ended up with the state marshal's five hundred and Nye's men to defend the mines."

"Indeed. Defend them against men of Botany Bay and Sydney, criminals all, sent to the penal colony in Australia, and then come here to join up with the Mexicans of the Hornitos League, as they call themselves." Mrs. Frémont moved to a wicker settee positioned in a shadow on the veranda and dropped into it, making none of the noise of crinoline she'd made the last time Adaline had spoken with her. Her deeply pleated skirt fell close upon her legs. "They are an utterly unpredictable, murderous group, but the Colonel was a wonder. In the end, he hardly needed the governor's men." She patted the cushion next to her. "Won't you sit?"

Uneasily, Adaline sat down.

"You had a safe journey?"

"Yes, ma'am." She said she'd been by the Wells Fargo and found that the Colonel had paid her five hundred dollars. She guessed it was for Gerard's machines.

"Yes, it is," Mrs. Frémont said.

"Please tell him it's more than I expected."

"It's what you deserve," Mrs. Frémont said. "And now you've come for your mules and trunk. And Gerard's horse. George and Johanna have secured permission to travel with you."

"Have they now? Both of them? I'm grateful for that."

Mrs. Frémont reverted to her state of high nervousness as she went on. "The Colonel was a marvel, putting it down. 'The hour must have its man,' as Whittier said. They found your Gerard's killer, by the bye. He was caught during the night trying to steal mules, emboldened as he was, and then the colonel's men found him lurking in the hotel. They shot him on the spot."

Adaline said, "The killer was with the Merced?"

"Of course, just as we thought. The colonel deserves the thanks."

"There was only one?"

"I imagine so."

"The colonel was there?"

"Oh, I think not. His men, I say."

Adaline now looked toward the colonel where he had paused with the other man atop a hummock. He appeared straight and assured of himself, while the pale man with the overcoat and umbrella put her in mind of a barker. Her thoughts veered toward José and the twins, Juana, and the Haro brothers, and Gerard, and Gerard's killer's fate over which Mrs. Frémont passed so lightly. Adaline was all but certain there had to be at least two men involved in the killing of Gerard, possibly more. She felt a chill. She was haunted by the image of the buried hunk of metal in Gerard's chest. And she recalled what José had said when she told him the news of the mines while they escorted her little herd from Las Mariposas to the pasture beyond Bear Valley, how he had echoed Gerard's view of the colonel, how the colonel seemed charmed, charmed by his gold, charmed by the court's act of dragging its feet in hearing the suit brought by the Merced Company. Now he was charmed by the five hundred deputies the governor had sent. Nothing mattered, José would say, so long as there was room left for his gold. It all had been confirmed by the example of mayhem in retribution, for indeed Frémont's men could have found almost anyone and that would have sufficed as it had with the two hanged men in Hornitos. Killing was rendered not judicially with exactitude or purpose, but with careless and indifferent impatience and to instill dread.

Three men were busy hitching their mules to the wagon and loading their goods. More were prepared to travel alongside on horseback. They mounted up. The wagon moved ahead, the clash of its motion soon replaced by a tolling bell, and passed beyond the house, the screen of shrubs, and joined others setting out along the road down by the hotel. The horsemen followed. Several more mules were led from behind the barn, and across the yard the man with the umbrella and overcoat held Frémont's arm and spoke, gazing after the wagon.

"That's Horace Greeley. He loathes the sun." Mrs. Frémont's face looked pinched. "He came all this way from New York to persuade the colonel to run for president again, but the colonel will not. What a shame! But Mr. Greeley gives the best account of the mines in his *New York Tribune*. He's bitterly opposed to slavery. It's fine he saw the colonel in action. The eagle still flies here, putting his talons into the cowards."

Not knowing how to put together what she saw in Mrs. Frémont's words—the opposition to slavery, the East coast newspaperman, the politics, Negro servants here, Miwok slaves, the fortune the mines held, the colonel's action and his talons dripping with blood—Adaline said simply, "My herd awaits me."

"Yes, your cows." Mrs. Fremont sighed. She summoned Albert Lea and directed him to seek out George and inform him that Adaline was here and then to fetch her trunk. Albert disappeared into the barn, came back out, and entered the house. In a few minutes, George emerged from the barn with Ghost harnessed to the travois on wheels and tied him off next to Slate. He went back toward the barn, stopping at the corral at its side. Albert appeared on the veranda with her Damascus and her trunk, and Adaline stepped down and set to lashing her belongings onto the travois with a sisal rope while Albert held them in position.

George came astride his horse, leading one of Gerard's mules, and was shadowed by Johanna on Gerard's horse with Gerard's second mule. Mrs. Frémont rose from the settee and followed Albert into the house. When they returned, Albert carried a basket which Mrs. Frémont insisted that Adaline accept. It contained red cloth and capes, articles Mrs. Frémont believed the Indians favored, also knives and hatchets in case articles in trade were required. "Thank you," Adaline said, securing the basket on the travois. "For everything."

"You are your father's daughter, if possible even more single-minded than he," Mrs. Frémont said. A silence fell between them. Finally, Mrs. Frémont added, "What use would the Black Drift be to them when they cannot carry off the ore without resistance? Not in a wagon nor on roads without detection. And what use attempting to destroy Gerard's percussion drills, except to impede my husband? How could they be so emboldened?"

Albert disappeared into the barn and this time emerged with the other Negro, Isaac, carrying a load toward the waiting wagon with eight mules hitched to it. A file of three young Indian women materialized from the huts that dotted the southerly slope away from the house, bearing large bundles of clothing to be laundered.

"So, now," Mrs. Frémont said, "All the troubles usurped as in a nightmare and it developed for more good than evil. Up against the evil, good proved the greater, as is suitable."

"Yes," Adaline said, taking both of Mrs. Frémont's hands in her own. Disbelieving Mrs. Frémont's optimism, what seemed another romance, she was anxious to go. She bade Mrs. Frémont goodbye, and mounted up. She looked at the colonel and Horace Greeley, and nodded to the colonel as she fell in line with her retinue, and the Colonel touched the brim of his hat even as Greeley went on speaking to him. She remembered Henry, the Delaware, the Unalachtigo, and thought Horace Greeley must in his way be like him, though pale as a slug. His tools were different, yet he resembled one of the Delawares camped outside Frémont's expeditionary tent with strings of scalps. She guessed Greeley protected Frémont against attorneys, bankers, and rival companies with his newspaper and sought to make it possible for Frémont to act with impunity, to gouge out a hollow of law into which money flowed. José had been right. The colonel was charmed, but he required his mercenary collaborators around him, including the most devoted of them all, his wife.

•

José took his leave that evening, and in the morning Adaline, George, and Johanna set out to drive the cows eastward. They left the Mariposa Grant and went through a Chinese settlement where men labored over a placer mine with an elaborate series of sluices. A short road of dust ran between two rows of shanties, a joss house, an apothecary, and a mercantile. Some men wearing long queues turned out to watch the three, but they managed to hasten their cows through. Once away, George warned that they would have to watch their animals closely the next night. "You could see the hunger in their eyes as they looked at these beefs."

That night they took turns keeping watch, as they would each night, George taking his banjo from a bag and plucking it to calm the cows. The next day they penetrated deeper into the mountains and on that afternoon began a long descent into a canyon. She was glad for George and Johanna's presence. They were familiar with this country, as had been promised, and they were good at handling the cows. It was their calm, such as José had possessed. They coaxed the animals along until they reached the Merced River, which ran low due to the autumn season. George led them to a place where they could cross the river without difficulty. Next, they began the ascent, keeping to the north bank. The bottom was littered with huge granite boulders, which had tumbled from the towering formations above. Adaline contemplated the causes, rain and snow washing away, freeze and thaw, tremors in the earth. Avalanche chutes were cut into the mountains, some with stone still raw and others with bush cropping up around boulders. All around this place were signs of blowdowns, massive heaps of snapped-off trees.

They made camp in a spot where the cows could sniff out grass that sprouted in the shade of the boulders. Adaline settled in her buffalo robe on one side of the herd, and Johanna lay down close by. George positioned himself some forty yards away as were best for both decorum and vigilance. One red cow had become Adaline's favorite as she was given to ranging off in search of the best forage. The cow also knew her name, Rosarita, and would come up to Adaline when called or when she heard the rattling salt bucket. She would contemplate George when he plucked his banjo and did not bother to butt heads or to muscle her way amongst the other cows for dominion, yet the herd would tread in her path.

Adaline lay on her robe, looking at the stars and moon passing in and out behind clouds, listening to the breeze that soughed through the trees in this hollow of the earth, and her thoughts veered to the dead. She had finally begun to accept that Gerard was gone, having accustomed herself to spending mornings without him and to sleeping nights without rubbing her feet against his. Right now, she recognized, she most needed what had been granted her by his passing, to be left to herself, to be certain about going on.

At daybreak, Johanna had taken the lead as they picked their way along precipitous trails, the likes of which Adaline had never seen, not even the time she'd first journeyed over the Sierras on the sheep drive. Sometimes, they would be little more than a narrow cut in the granite. At other times, they ran over slate talus at the base of a cliff where the rock had slipped and now chattered under the animals' hooves. They lost a brindle bull calf, who slid down toward a stream and wedged himself between two trees. He pawed frantically at the air. One hind leg was broken and he bellowed wildly. George slipped off his horse and, dodging the hooves, slit the calf's throat, disemboweled and skinned it. The distraught mother cried out and began tramping in circles, backed up, and advanced on George as if to attack, but Adaline fended her off by positioning her horse before her. George wrapped the meat tightly in the section of oilcloth Johanna brought over to him from his pack mule, then lashed it alongside Adaline's trunk on the travois. "We don't want to waste it. Perhaps we will want to give it to those who are watching us."

"What?" Adaline said. "What do you mean watching?"

"Those who know we're here. The Shunta."

Adaline peered into the darkness amongst the trees. "Shunta?"

Johanna's smile worked through the pair of parallel tattoo marks, and once again Adaline believed she saw little animals twisting inside Johanna's cheeks. "Shunta. The Watching Eye." Johanna had confirmed by now that she was indeed a Kuzedika, or Flyeater, from a band that lived far above by the lake with the presidios, and that she did not intend to return to Frémont's rancho in Bear Valley.

Adaline had listened with great attention to stories George and Johanna told about their lives: Johanna's father had also been Kuzedika, but he was killed, and George's father was an American who took up with their mother. Now, the mother was dead too. George knelt beside the stream, washing his hands. Johanna joined him and George bade Adaline to do the same. "The bear will smell it. We don't want to spread the smell around." He washed his knife clean in the water. "The rest of the calf here will keep him busy. The bear likes to be first."

They assembled their gear and moved on. Often, the mother cow turned round and lowed for her dead calf, but George and Adaline forced her to go between them while Johanna moved the rest of the herd from the rear. Since leaving the Chinese, they hadn't seen a soul, but George counseled that the Watching Eye might make itself known at any moment. Adaline looked warily about. Though she didn't see anyone or anything but an owl, even now in the daylight. Her ears had further attenuated to the quiet. She heard the hooves of their animals, sometimes the groaning of limbs rubbing against each other in the breeze, and the exchanges of birds.

Trees of all descriptions appeared and disappeared in accordance with the ever-changing landforms, aspen and birch and willow near the water, oak in the open places, and fir, cedar, and intermittent pines emanating from crevices between the rocks. As the ground began to level, they came into a great valley and saw the big redwoods. Adaline had never seen trees this tall, stretching up as though into the ether, and when she dismounted and circled around one in the spongy earth she had to walk over twenty-five paces. She looked up at Johanna whose smile spread over her face and sparkled with pleasure. From the shade of the canopy overhead, the ground exhibited a patchwork of sunlight amidst low-lying currant bushes, grass, and ferns, now turning brown and yellow and red. She came upon a fallen redwood. New green was sprouting along its trunk, and upon further examination she beheld a phenomenon that occurred everywhere, young sprouts growing out of the dead.

"Look. The mother in them never dies," she said.

Judging from his expression, George was thinking about what she said. Finally he responded, "This is seen," he said. "That is the difference."

"Yet it is the same with all of them," Johanna said.

"You mean the mother of everything never dies?" Adaline said.

"No," Johanna said. "Each mother never dies."

"You see?" George said. "The mothers are different. They are all watching the world and they never die."

He kicked his horse and rode ahead, tracing a game trail that wound through the trees. His mule followed directly behind and the cows were set in motion by Adaline and Johanna. Above them rose sheer cliffs. Soil had slipped down to the bottom of this valley where things grew more densely, requiring that the riders and their herd slow down and proceed in a file. Toward midafternoon, they discovered a meandering creek, and the matted path had come to be beaten down and bore sign of elk and deer. Suddenly, a granite monolith reared into view. George pulled up short, let the cows pass, looked back at Johanna and exchanged words in their language with her, and to Adaline he said, "Tutokanula. It means a measuring worm because that is the only creature that could climb it. All the other animals tried. The mountain panther did the best, throwing himself up, but it was not enough."

From the trees near its bottom, two men appeared, wearing rabbit skin breech clouts and carrying bows. One of them also wore a white man's vest and a necklace of dentalium shells like the one Johanna wore. The cows stopped and Adaline rode slowly around them, spreading salt from her pouch to keep them calm while George rode out to speak to the men. They were glancing at Adaline and Johanna, and back to George. Finally the one with the vest spoke at length. When he finished, the two walked off slowly and disappeared among the trees. George returned and announced that soon they would come upon an encampment. The men said there'd been trouble, but he had promised there would come no such thing from them. "I told them to look," he said to Adaline. "We are not miners or settlers, though we come from down there and we are bringing these cows. I am a traveler, that is all, and I told them to look at Johanna, a Kuzedika from above. The one thinks he might even remember her. Then I asked him what he saw in you. He said you come from the plains far beyond the mountains."

This gave Adaline pause. "How does he know that?"

"Others have come from there in days past. He knows. Like myself, though you are white, you are Indian."

This was one of the few times she remembered being taken for exactly who she was, aside from Pablo long ago, the Comanche mezclado, and now George and Johanna. Not even Gerard had granted her that, seeming to want to look upon her as Kit Carson's daughter.

"And you are tall, too."

"Tall? I am not tall."

George smiled. "Not as tall as me, eh?" He explained how white men had come through not long before and killed several men. They took some women with them. Their people had moved their encampment. "I promised we would leave meat and that we would watch for their women. These men said they will meet us there."

The three rode past a waterfall which was higher even than the redwoods, as if pouring from the very sky. The air was filled with spray and a stream flowed out from the pool at its bottom. A little further east, they observed the ruins of the abandoned encampment, and after five hours of climbing came upon a remote place, the new settlement, where those who survived were preparing for winter, mainly old women, young children, and very few men. Some wore robes of rabbit skin and others wore almost nothing, even into the cool of the evening. Their dwellings had the same shape as the hogans of New Mexico Territory or the ones located around the Frémont White House. An old man who wore a woven headband and the two men whom George had spoken with previously were at work building another one, the two cutting long slabs of redwood bark and the old man tying them together with vines.

The man in the vest accepted the meat George offered. He parted the cloth to look at it, folded it back up carefully, and passed it on to an old woman. Adaline studied the women who had gathered acorns and were storing them in a cache fashioned from a large basket that stood above the ground, while others meticulously laid herbs in smaller baskets. From a tree hung several rabbits and squirrels. It was all the meat they had besides the beef, George told her. The man passed his necklace of dentalium shell to George, who in turn proffered it to Adaline and told her she was to keep it. George said these people had been advised to travel down below to one of the towns to buy food, but what were they to pay for it with? Besides, it tasted bad. Everyone had stopped now and was attending to the conversation. Adaline ran her fingers over the dentalium and looked at Johanna's necklace. Johanna smiled at her. Adaline thought about the gold in her saddle bags, about economies that did not match, what Frankie long ago had called uncodified trade.

Five of the men from the village worked at Frémont's Guadalupe Mine in the valley. Another twelve had formed a hunting party and journeyed further eastward where the Indians here believed the pillagers had gone, but the twelve did not know that since they had left before the other settlement was raided. The Indians held to the hope that the hunters would come upon the pillagers by surprise and rescue the women, but then again that seemed unlikely. The white men were in possession of powerful new guns. In recent years, the Indians made their summer home in the north near the headwaters of the Tuolumne, a place called Hechheche, but it had become too dangerous there. Therefore they had moved southward to their former encampment, only to learn they were in even greater danger than before. The men of the hunting party, the strongest men they had left, had gone for meat. George translated all this for Adaline. "They hoped to take deer and perhaps a bear." George said. "He says we should be careful if we head out that way. There are seven white men riding horses."

In other years these villagers would have moved lower yet into the foothills for the winter, but despite the cold and snow they decided to stay here in Lasamaiti. It was no longer safe by the mines with all the noise and drunken men. Once the snow fell, they hoped no one would dare come through here. Meanwhile they were trying to build up their stores. They knew they might starve. It was a prison of their own choosing.

A short distance away from the village, the grazing was good and the three herded the cows there where they built a small pen out of sisal. Once again, George took out his banjo and plucked at it, his long fingers searching out notes one at a time into the darkness. In the morning while Johanna watched the cows, Adaline and George returned to the village with Mrs. Frémont's basket and presented gifts of knives, hatchets, and swatches of red cloth. The man in the vest accepted a bit of the cloth and put it in a pocket, leaving out a corner of red for exhibition. Through George, Adaline told them they would leave a heifer as meat for the winter, then Adaline and George rode back to their camp, tied up the heifer, and with Johanna set out with the herd, while listening to the heifer's wailing echoes.

They entered another valley and passed through a stand of redwoods, at which point they picked up sign in the earth of men on horseback. The trail was not fresh, at least several days old, and it headed back to the northwest. The three continued eastward, beginning a long climb that would last four days. The path was difficult, particularly for Ghost who strained to pull the travois around the boulders. They moved in and out of changing climates as displayed by the differing plant life. Redwoods would not be seen again, and the cedars grew sparse. They entered into an open, wind-blown country where monolithic slabs of granite thrust straight up through the earth and spindly pine trees were bent and ravaged by weather.

Each night George found a small hollow and applied his fire drill to ignite a fire. Johanna and Adaline fetched kindling and firewood, heated their food, and tended the animals. Vigilance was required to insure the cows did not take fright and run off in the dark. Adaline's curiosity was piqued by this fierce country, and she was inspired to retrieve her measuring instruments from the trunk. She calculated their location: Latitude 37° 54' North. Longitude 119° 32' West. With the barometer she found that they were over 6,000 feet high. "The air is thinner here," she said. "There's less of it above the mercury." By the next night they had climbed to nearly 7,000 feet and the animals labored with their breathing. "They are used to more air. So are we. Everything is getting lighter up here," she said. She had her barometer out and George took a passing interest in it, but Johanna was fascinated by the tube and mercury, her face filling with pleasure as she examined the instrument.

"Lighter?" Johanna said.

"Less air," Adaline replied.

Johanna looked up, then down with the faint smile on her face.

The next night, they were over 7,000 feet, and deep howling began, softly at first. From its resonant timbre Adaline believed it was wolves.

"No. No wolves in these mountains," George said. "Not here."

The next night, a high-pitched barking persisted for over half an hour, answered by deeper, more sonorous wailing, like a lament. "There," she whispered. "Those are surely wolves. It must be. Don't you hear?"

George did not answer but only listened until it was quiet. He finally spoke with Johanna and Adaline awaited his verdict, but then he didn't speak, only pursing his lips.

On the third night, the singing continued in earnest, a full-throated barking against a back-up chorus of what Adaline surmised to be coyotes. This response came from a higher promontory, ricocheting against the rock cliffs from all directions at once. George, who had been plucking at his banjo, set it down and listened. Adaline watched how the calves were huddling up and the cows encircled them. The mothers stood still, ears twitching, eyes fixed to the dark.

"Look at them," she said. Her mind turned to the wolves on the Santa Fé Trail, the one that dug up the baby, and the feral dogs on the sheep drive, though she didn't believe these were dogs. She conjured up Ferine's hound, and then her thoughts reverted to that wistful time on the way home from Abiquiú when she and Pablo had talked about the minds of animals. How she missed Pablo! She came to believe that with Gerard gone, now, her being had turned back toward Pablo, that his person resided within her. Somehow the cows in the singularity of mind shared among themselves, discovered in their nature as if they were santeros carving themselves, represented a last vestige of her struggle for meaning against the vast loneliness she felt. "We have to watch out. Wolves can be bold."

Johanna spoke to George in their language, and then George, measured in his probity, said, "I understood there were few wolves in these mountains, but Johanna says they used to come sometimes."

On the fourth day, they arose over the crest of the ascent and dropped down into an high-elevation valley which promised good grass along a meandering creek. The first snow capped the peaks and the creek swelled with the melt. A storm overtook them. Black clouds wrapped the mountain tops immediately to the south, boiled over them, and whipped across the valley. Lightening bolts forced the three to take refuge under a stand of aspen in a depression next to more extensive granite outcroppings. They drew their horses and mules in close, holding them tightly, while the cows held fast and endured a pelting of rain and hail. In an hour, just when water had begun to pond in the depression, the storm was over.

They pressed on. Two hours passed and George suddenly stood up in his stirrups. Adaline turned back to check on Johanna and the cows, but Johanna motioned her to proceed. Pulling up beside George, Adaline spied far away the dark shapes, some moving about, some stationary. Here and there several hunkered together. They were yet too far away to make out in detail. Adaline and George rode forward onto a hummock above a bend in the stream which afforded them a better view. Adaline strained to see one shadowy shape, then another. They were timber wolves, and on the far perimeter coyotes feeding on something else, but on what she couldn't tell because of the tall grass in between meanderings of the stream. She noted large black-backed birds sidling through the grass. "Wolves," she said. "And coyotes, keeping their distance. Buzzards, too."

"Wolves," George said.

"Taking their fill."

Johanna had ridden up beside them. She looked and said, "Not good."

Adaline looked north of the myriad carrion eaters where, judging from the brows carved in the earth, there would be the stream to ford and just beyond that the hills to climb. She looked southward where granite boulders lay strewn about in their random way. "I believe we should go that way." She gestured with her head. A cold wind was now blowing westward over the top of the mountains, which seemed unusual, but at least they were downwind of the wolves and coyotes. "Maybe they won't trouble us, but we don't want to spook the herd." She herself felt tense, watching what she judged were fifteen or twenty wolves and nearly an equal number of coyotes.

She thought through what she had not said, what neither George nor Johanna had remarked upon: A wolf might take down an elk, or a deer, or even a sick bear, but there's a lot of them feeding out there, and if the vultures are there, it must be carrion several days old.

George said, "The coyotes will escape to safety when they see us coming."

"Maybe it will be the same with the wolves," Adaline said.

They rode back to the cows, whereupon she untied the restraining thong from her Hawken and pulled the gun from its sheath, checked her load, and slid it back into the sheath, leaving the thong loose. George did the same with his carbine. She checked her revolver, sliding its holster around from the small of her back. They picked their way forward. They were acting in concert and no words were necessary. First and foremost they had to find a place where it was safe for the cows, which early on had caught the scent of the wolves. The horses and mules caught the scents, too, and Adaline felt Slate twitching beneath her. The cows pulled in tight around Johanna, not wanting to move, but Adaline and George circled behind and helped Johanna force them to give ground and to keep them from bolting. They were on high alert, their hooves swishing through the grass.

They rode well southward, fashioning a long loop by first moving away and then swinging back from around a line of boulders that formed a natural barrier in which the cows could be secured. George turned them into it while Johanna and Adaline followed, pushing them toward the rocks. Adaline had spotted a keyhole between boulders and another brow of earth above the creek. She passed Ghost's lead to Johanna, also the poke with salt in it, and forged on until she reached the keyhole and looked at one wolf, then at a knot of them, noting that some were tearing at the meat on the ground while others started looking her direction, ears pricked. They knew she was there. The smell had grown more acrid. She checked behind her, seeing the cows still quiet in the makeshift corral and George now leaving his pack mule there and moving her way.

She turned her attention back to the wolves and to the coyotes still further off. When one wolf moved sideways, a crowd of magpies rose up from cover, shrieking to each other, and then ravens sifted upwards, so many of them that for a moment the sun darkened. They circled, making guttural staccato noises. Now, the wolves drifted farther off. She looked at the vultures parting the grass as they wove through it, then one took wing, followed by another, and a third, and from yet a further distance a condor turning along the flat until it ascended with great flaps of its wings. It was trailed by another condor. The two caught drafts and soared, piercing the air with their whistles.

The stream lay before her. Once more, she strained to see ahead and what now took form was what she had feared. There were people, people were being devoured, people cast about in all manner of positions, on their faces, on their backs, several poised to lift up their half-eaten bodies by one arm, some lifting an arm, or two arms to fend off the attackers, or else in supplication. She simply apprehended it now, the carnage spread everywhere across the valley, then again she looked behind her at the huddled cows beyond the keyhole between the boulders, held safe by Johanna. George was riding toward Adaline. She nudged Slate forward until she revealed herself fully out in the open. She counted corpses, twenty of them, twenty-five, maybe more. Numbness infused her limbs, an aghast disbelief, fear, and a roiling stirred in her gut.

The wolves drifted and taking that movement as a signal the coyotes slinked back toward the hills. Adaline moved to a chest-high boulder, dismounted, and tied Slate's reins to a bush. Now, without knowing exactly what she was doing—it was an inchoateness borne of the rage that formed itself—she leaned up against the rock, cradled her Hawken, and began shooting and reloading, taking out one wolf, wounding another, then George was beside her, and the reports of his carbine slammed into her ears. They took down six or seven of them.

The rest loped toward the hills in the path of the coyotes and within moments all had vanished. More ravens and magpies had flown up, skipping over to the human carrion that lay strewn farther away. Another four vultures rose, catching the drafts, and the remaining ravens, magpies, and blackbirds escalated their numbers, emanating from the dead.

She mounted Slate and rode across the creek. Footing was poor, but she made it to the opposite bank. George rode alongside her and they picked their way amongst the bodies, one after another. These were the women from the village, followed by their men endeavoring to head back with their winter stores, for there was the offal of two elk carcasses, a deer carcass, and one of a black bear. It seemed that the men had come upon the women. Or maybe the women cried for help. Maybe some were killed on the spot in order to entrap the men. They'd been shot down, the gunshots coming from Sharps by the look of the wounds. There were also saber wounds, including bloody gashes turned black on the top of each head where the scalp had been ripped away and the rest of them left, eaten away, their guts ripped apart, their eyes pecked out by birds, and here was the stench that is unlike any other. Adaline's teeth began to chatter.

She and George wove through, noting the marks of the hooves of horses evidently aiming downward. She rode awhile in that direction, vainly searching for survivors, but she detected only the tracks of the seven that the people of Lasamaiti had warned them about. She turned back. George had settled onto his horse and stared straight ahead, not looking, riding beside her. Her voice came out low. "The killers are headed down. They came in from the north and they've gone down by Sonora, three days ago at least. Maybe headed for Modesto. They've taken scalps for proof so they can collect bounty. It's too many here. Too many dead for us to bury." They crossed the stream again and rode around the granite boulders to Johanna and the herd. Adaline tried to stop her teeth from chattering. "Too many to understand or to bury or to burn. Too many."

George's face was set deep in darkness. His horse's hooves knocked against the granite which was like a slab underfoot. He took up his mule's lead. Johanna leaned forward on the white horse, her face set in even deeper darkness.

Adaline took Ghost's lead in her hand and started out, the travois rattling. She went behind the cows and cried out, "Hiyah!" A transfigurative violence swept through her. She dug her heels into Slate and set the cows in motion. "Hiyah!"

"Hiyah!" Johanna drew even with Adaline on the other flank.

George brought up the rear. "Hup! Hup! Hup!"

The birds dropped out of their gyre and the wild dogs slipped back out from the hills. The three drove the cows for a long time, neither stopping nor speaking, gazing straight ahead, riding back into the great book of the unwritten.

Before nightfall they came around a promontory and there beheld the strange presidios built upon the lake. They were unmistakably there, hundreds of them, large and small, sculpted in towers, columns, and tubes, topped with minarets, close to shore and also shooting outward toward the sky, seemingly afloat and looking like a magnificent white city, white upon water the color of cobalt.

Chapter 26

Mono Lake was in a dry country, receiving only fourteen inches a year of precipitation and that mainly from the snows of winter. Water evaporated from the lake during the warm season as fast as it was replenished, and because it had no outlets the lake was terminal. It was hypersaline, its water undrinkable, unfit for all creatures but brine shrimp, alkali flies, and the birds, the grebes, phalaropes, geese, plovers, swans, pelicans, and ducks that came along the Pacific flyway by the hundreds of thousands to feed upon the flies and shrimp. There were also the California gulls, vast flocks arriving seasonally and nesting on a black island called Negit.

Adaline kept a shack on the eastward slope of the mountains where she had arranged to pasture her cows, and a house near the lake in the town called Monoville. She stored her buffalo robe in the shack. Johanna lived between these abodes and Adaline would stop to visit when she passed by. They'd become close, as often happens with those who have experienced a ghastly occurrence together. What all three, George included, shared in the blackness of what they had witnessed had shaken them. George vowed never to return to Las Mariposas, or Bear Valley, or anywhere on the western slopes. Adaline took solace in growing her herd. George assisted her and spent hours searching out melodies on his banjo. Johanna immersed herself in the old ways of her people. They rarely spoke of the horror. Each understood that such killing had become commonplace, for five dollars per scalp was paid by several municipalities and twenty-five dollars per severed head by a few others. In addition, the courtship with mayhem birthed a bill passed by the California legislature that designated several tribes as slaves, this when a war was soon to be fought over the issue of slavery. The three absorbed this as a haunting of the evil.

The two women did speak of the summer heat, the cold in the winter, the tremors in the earth, and how in the early spring the snow was given to avalanche, a phenomenon of obliteration that continued to bewitch Adaline. Avalanches happened when warm south winds blew in, softening the snow on the slopes, and with the winds came more snow falling upon the slicks. Johanna was amazed that the white settlers dug their mines and built their dwellings within the hollows. She wondered if they believed they were in possession of such power that they could stop the snow as it settled on the slippage, then roared into the valleys, or, for that matter, if they believed they held sway over the earthquakes that also were a common occurrence here.

In March of 1859, near the end of Adaline's first complete winter at this place there was an avalanche in what was called Bloody Canyon. Two American men and a German woman had dwelled in a mill house there, and people dug desperately for their remains. They uncovered the dead men and Thea Grünig, who emerged alive after a day entombed. She'd managed in her frenzy to hollow out a cave, and when she finally emerged her face was as white as the snow, yet her only injury was a gash in her thigh. She was scarcely frostbitten. The men wrapped her in blankets and pulled her by sledge down the trail toward the nearest safe dwelling. As Thea was transported, she was given whiskey from a flask, whereupon she sat bolt upright and repeated over and over again in her own language, "Muss ich auch wandern in finsterer Schlucht." Her blue eyes seemed ready to blow out into the air. She cried out, "Mein Hirte! Mein Hirte!"

Later, one of the Germans told Adaline that Thea was questioning where her shepherd, the Lord, had gone, but then the Lord came back, choosing to return her to the living. Adaline relayed this to Johanna, trying to explain what it meant to be chosen according to

Thea's religion, and who the shepherd was, but her sense of it all crumbled because it exposed yet another, different kind of horror, one that veered ominously close to the killing they had seen together, yet then it was the perpetrators who regarded themselves as the chosen ones. Finally, she said, "She's not chosen, no matter what she thinks. No one is chosen in that way. It's just luck."

After considering for a moment, Johanna said, "Luck?"

Studying Johanna's face, with its tattoos and black eyes that snapped with the certainty of her question, and sensing that Johanna sought something in particular, Adaline was speechless.

•

As with settlements on the other side of the Sierras, hundreds of men came to Monoville. When Adaline first arrived, women were in a distinct minority and men began showing an interest in her. During that fall George was assisting with the cows, cutting out the heifers, moving the remaining herd down to the lower slopes for winter and with the help of two old men, castrating the bullocks. Adaline took the opportunity to fend off suitors by letting it be known she and George were married, an idea to which George did not object. Though he preferred the shack in the hills, he habituated himself to moving back and forth between it and town in order to vouchsafe Adaline's claim, yet rarely joined her in her buffalo robe in the shack or her pallet in town. He seemed almost devoid of sexual desire and in this way was like no other man she'd ever known.

The first to work the best sites for gold and silver had been Chileans and a few Mexicans. Australians, Germans, and Americans were soon lured by reports of strikes, and here, too, the Chinese managed to turn a profit on abandoned sites. Many of the men remained in Monoville just long enough for their fortunes to play out, arriving and departing like ghosts. A very few amassed their claims into mines, buying up the ditches, and there emerged a growing number of tradesmen, merchants, teamsters, and lumbermen. In accordance with patterns everywhere in the West, the moneyed mining companies began taking over the region.

Meanwhile, the Kuzedika, or Flyeaters, continued to dwindle as members of the tribe succumbed to disease and privation. In the fall, Adaline noted, small bands would travel into the Sierras to trade salt and obsidian gathered from the Glass Mountains and to harvest acorns and pine nuts. Some retreated into strongholds high on the western slopes in places like Lasamaiti for the winter. During the summer months, they would gather to harvest alkali fly pupae near the shores of the lake, a food source, rich in fat and protein, from which they took their name. But increasingly, many Kuzedika men vanished into the slave camps or were slaughtered. Johanna led a secluded life, holing up in her hogan outside of town.

For three years, Adaline found pleasure listening to George's banjo. She liked the twanging sounds of his fingers plucking out the tunes. In town, the notes seemed to resonate with the shapes of the white tufa, which she surveyed from her position next to him on the front porch. At other times, when they were out on the slopes, and when he played in order to soothe the cows, she thought that the banjo was George's way of going inward to search for himself. He appeared as though he were dreaming when he played, then one day when she went to the shack he was gone. His banjo stood propped against a wall, and she found her cows scattered. She rode around the hills seeking out the two old men to help her gather them up, then waited for George. Days passed and he didn't return.

She rode to town and asked Johanna about him. Johanna said that she'd been watching for him, too. Adaline said maybe he was called away or had gone on a hunt, but Johanna grew adamant. "No. He meant to stay nearby. He would have told us." She said she had begun to notice how he showed signs of looking from behind the shadows as if from a cage. Tears came to her eyes and she stared at her hands. At that moment, she was weaving willow branches into a basket and her fingers kept moving, twisting and pulling. She applied pitch from a piñon to make it watertight. "He's gone," she said. "Disappeared. It's just luck."

"But Johanna . . . No." Adaline said. Aghast, she let her voice trail off, pierced as she was by George's absence and also by what she now understood Johanna took luck to mean, that it was conjoined with doom.

Johanna said, "Our time is past. Too many dead. More dying. When we awake each morning, we are reminded of the pain of our loss. Yet not all people are bad. Surely the animals are not. George could not go on, seeking the little good that remains in the world."

Adaline could not bring herself to speak. To lie would be an insult. To speak the truth would only affirm what her friend had said about the dying. So, she was trapped. She recalled all her experiences with death and felt herself plummeting into a sadness akin to Johanna's but without Johanna's forbearance. She thought of her father's perpetrations long ago, and of what he called the susceptibility of his men to "go loco" in their killing of the Maidus and Yanas. She thought of Frémont and José de los Berreyesa and the de Haro twins. She thought of the ring on Louis's truncated finger, how the coldness of silver and turquoise dug into her throat as he grasped and hit her. Out of a hardening of her nature, her way of offsetting the pain, she entered into an entanglement with herself. She began to demand that the men she dealt with—the operator of the mercantile, the teamsters, the mine owners, the commander of the recently built fort down below in the valley, the lieutenant and his sergeant, and the cattle buyers—call her by the name Kit.

"Kit," she would say, her face twisted from her habit of sucking on the hole left by her missing molar and shining with the venom she felt for the white men, the bullies. "Call me Kit Carson."

•

The war came to the nation.

Before George disappeared, Adaline had been following the war from reports by migrants from the East, from the newspapers that found their way to her, and then from the telegraph. In 1861 she learned that the state of Missouri had been sundered against itself, that Colonel Frémont had been promoted to major general and placed in command of the Union Army at Saint Louis. He issued his own Emancipation Proclamation, independent of the president, only to be summarily removed from his command. She guessed Mrs. Frémont was in Missouri, too. She knew the man she had seen at the Frémont rancho with the overcoat, Horace Greeley, had entered a political fracas over the proclamation. Greeley accused Lincoln of holding back, of being compromised by his attempts to hold the Union together, and of inhumane behavior toward the slaves. She knew that there was killing and bloodletting on an enormous scale. She envisioned the fields strewn with bodies, blood soaking into the ground. She imagined the pervasive stink of it, the carrion eaters. All along the trails were echoes of killing while here at Monoville and in Carson City entrepreneurialism turned violent, the miners, loggers, mill owners, and Union officers using graft and brutality to wage their wars over control.

In 1862, Adaline had visited Carson City in order to secure more pastureland on the mountainsides. Military installations loomed, populated by "galvanized Yankees," or prisoners from the Confederacy who had been released in the East on the condition that they serve under Union officers in the West. Those installations were accompanied by an explosion in lumber milling. It was another "rush," a timber rush, the lumber used to build forts, dwellings, and serving the mines with new ways of supporting the deep tunnels. The need for beef became inexhaustible. Adaline could not increase her herd fast enough to satisfy demand, yet through breeding, and using her deposits in Monoville's Wells Fargo to purchase stock, and picking up the occasional slick, she had increased her herd from the original twelve to over eighty animals.

By 1862, the year George disappeared, the nation came to be completely transformed by war. Carson City became a supply city to the mines. It lay within the newly organized Territory of Nevada, a designation executed by Congress in order to conjoin the transcontinental routes to the Pacific and to give the Union access to gold and silver, which it was using to finance the war. The Comstock Lode had been discovered. With it came advances in technology, including much of what Gerard had foreseen—not only rock percussion machines but compressed air powering them, along with fans, hoisting engines, carts on tracks pulled by wire rope, newly processed rubber in the hydraulic hoses. The recently installed telegraph lines running from Fort Laramie, Omaha, and Saint Louis had their western terminus in Carson City. When she first heard of this, Adaline had thought it strange, the lines strung along much of the route she had traveled on the sheep drive. Now, poles were put up and words sent inside a wire.

•

To her surprise, she received not a telegram but a letter from her cousin, Susan. Mrs. Frémont had written to Adaline's father, who had the letter read to him, and who in turn reported Adaline's whereabouts to Jesse Nelson and Susan. Susan wrote they'd heard Louis Simmons had divorced Adaline, and since they hadn't heard from her for so long, nor anything about her, they feared the worst. She pleaded with her to write back and tell her that she was well.

Adaline responded immediately, noting that a town called Las Animas was Susan's home. She explained where she'd been, that she'd found a man named Gerard, but he had been killed. She said that although she'd come to harbor doubts about the Frémonts, she was grateful that Mrs. Frémont had written to her father. She told Susan about Alexis Godey, about José, Juana, and the children, about Johanna, and George, about the cows she'd brought over to Mono Lake, and about the scene of slaughter.

Susan's reply arrived several months later. "Your father is a colonel," she said. "He's training troops in Albuquerque. There was great excitement when he helped to fight off a Confederate invasion of the Territory from Texas." She added that he had sent Josefa and the children—there were five of them now—away from Taos. It was believed that Taos had become too dangerous. She said that there were wars everywhere, more wars in the shadow of the Civil War. Adaline wrote back, asking Susan to please explain what she meant. And she asked if she knew anything about Carrie Turner, since there was money waiting in the Wells Fargo for her.

Again months passed before Susan's reply arrived. She had no idea of Carrie Turner's whereabouts. The Territory simmered, she said. Differing Indian tribes had formed alliances with either the Confederates or the Union according to what they believed might further their cause, seizing on every opportunity for revenge and revolt. Bands within the tribes fought each other. In some places the French and the Spanish and especially the Mexicans sought opportunities for resurgence and like mercenaries passed through shifting alliances. There was an increase in the number of attacks on ranches. Indians and all manner of thieves rustled meat for sustenance or for the profit of selling it to this one or that of the armies, which were perpetually hungry. Ranchers hired private killers to protect their interests. Depredation was commonplace, as was slave trading. Indians, Mexicans, and runaway slaves were captured and sold by opportunists. Most prized of all were white women. Captives were traded from one tribe to another, or to the Mexicans, or marched to Texas and sold to the Confederates. Women were turned into prostitutes. Land claims were contested everywhere.

By the time she wrote her next letter, Adaline had begun to fall ill. Also, she had a softening of heart. She asked Susan about her children, remembering that Colonel Frémont had reported she and Jesse had them, and she inquired directly about Pablo. "The last I heard he was going to Durango to serve under Bishop Zubiria. I've come to believe he has been killed. Tell me if you heard anything about him."

A letter arrived in which Susan wrote that she had three children, one recently born, and two more siblings. Susan had asked her husband and Tom Boggs, who lived near them, about Pablo. "We think you are right about his service to Bishop Zubiria. Tom says Pablo was intractable, that he could be devilish," she wrote. "He says Pablo was returning to his pueblo to serve as a spokesman. Both Tom and Jesse think they heard that Pablo and the company he traveled with had been ambushed on the road from Durango. Yes, they believe he is dead."

As Adaline read the letter, she thought about the words "intractable" and "devilish." If he had been the Pablo she remembered, then intractable could mean that he was passionate and unswerving. Devilish could only mean that he would cause trouble if he believed it was called for. She thought Susan and Tom Boggs had it terribly wrong. Adaline remembered Pablo as the boy and later the young man who always saw two things at once. She sat out on the veranda of her house. She reread the letter, and stared at the word, "dead." It confirmed what she'd known in her heart of hearts for years. She heard a vivid sound like a tree cracking, and her hand, holding the letter, sank to her lap.

She saw La Muerte in her dreams that night, riding in a cart. The sickness was overtaking her. Her lungs were weakening. She was overpowered by an oppressive weight and still by the bloody Indian killing field where wolves fed on the dead, and the coyotes, ravens, vultures, and condors, the legs of people locked in their struggle to set the bodies aright, their outstretched hands. She thought of something she hadn't thought of for a long time, the infant she'd lost, what came to seem the progeny of a nightmare. She despaired of all she had left unfinished. Feeling desperate, she made a plan for her holdings, managed to put a blanket on Ghost, then struggled to get up on the mule. She rode to the Wells Fargo office, made arrangements for the sale of her herd, and for part of her money to be reserved for Johanna, another part to be transferred for José and the children, and a sum set aside for Carrie Turner, if ever she appeared to claim it. Back at her house, she took out her trunk and inspected her measuring instruments, the buntline books about her father, the old newspaper articles, Frémont's journal, the pages curled from being dampened by the river years ago, the old maps with huge white spaces, Don Ramón's rocks with fossils, her mother's worn beaded bag, and the beaded turtle.

She turned her thoughts to the children she had known, Lucia, Pedro, Maria, even little Juanita, and Teresina, Nicanor, and Juan. Her spirits rose a little as she thought of them, then her feelings about

Pablo resurged. She remembered what Frankie had said, that death was a foremost ordinary of the earth. "In between the beginning of your engendering and the end when you've engendered all you can, or want to, you still got your needs," Frankie had said. "At the end, the reaper takes his satisfaction . . . When and with who, he gives no answer . . . He just traipses along on his own time."

In the very early spring of 1863, although a mere twenty-six years old, her physical being was far from the hale and agile young woman luxuriating in her ability to careen about on her horse. These last weeks, she inhabited her house in Monoville. She would wrap herself in a blanket or her poncho and venture outside to seek solace in the lake that stretched to the horizon as if to the edge of the world. She took draughts from a bottle of laudanum, a tincture of opiates dissolved in brandy that she purchased for the relief it gave her from the ache in her belly and the fits of coughing. The lake came to be enshrouded in miraculous colors that transformed into shades of blue, gray, and black, in accordance with the condition of the sky, whether clouded, clear, or veiled by poconip fog. Small islands of differing hues speckled its length, black ones, brown, and almost white, and the two larger ones, the black one, Negit, and the lighter one, called Paoha, and then there sprung up the resplendent white formations of tufa that appeared larger the longer she looked. These were the shapes she'd first seen after crossing over from the site of the slaughter, what seemed so eerie at that initial sighting as if they were presidios.

She coughed up blood, the sputum crimson on her handkerchief. Her fascination with the lake grew near to overwhelming. She watched the thousands of birds flying above it, whirling down into it and up again. She took to believing it drained into the horizon and begged Johanna to escort her to that place. Johanna looked at her closely and said she would need to find a boat. She went off to make the arrangements. When she returned the next day she heard sounds as if of a struggle on the other side of the door. She went in and found Adaline fighting to pull her canvas trousers. Adaline's face was pallid and her cheeks were drawn. She sank to the edge of the bed, bending over and wrestling first one and then the other high moccasin up over her feet. When at last she straightened up she was beset with tremors, yet still she begged Johanna to take her. Johanna helped Adaline put on her red long john top, her shirt, and her poncho, then placed an additional blanket around shoulders. "Here," she said. "All right. We will go, but you must guard against the cold."

When Adaline suffered a paroxysm, Johanna undid the cap to her bottle of laudanum and Adaline took a drink. They went out, Johanna leading the way to the lake's shore, and in time they came upon a shallows. A crescent moon, so articulated that it seemed cut into the sky descended, while crimson light from the sun seeped over the tops of the Glass Mountains to the east. Ducks clucked to each other and swam into the reeds. The women passed along a draw, crossed over it, came upon a stand of Jeffrey pine, and turned back toward the lake. Johanna moved lightly amidst bush and stone while Adaline followed, clutching her blanket. They came out on an abutment from which Johanna began a descent. Adaline put her feet where Johanna had placed hers, marveling at how for Johanna walking was a rhythm, a right foot here, a left foot there. She imitated the rhythm of Johanna's feet and felt her body swaying to and fro as if fashioning a melody as it moved.

They approached a creek that flowed into the lake, forming a small estuary, and there a boat made from reeds rested. Johanna waded into the shallows, drew the boat near, and gestured to Adaline to give her the blanket and climb in. The boat was nearly round. It rode high in the water and when Adaline stepped in it tipped wildly to one side. She jerked herself to its center and with both hands grasped the tightly braided edge that ran all the way around. She looked sidelong at Johanna, who laughed softly, the little critters in her cheeks suddenly mobile. Adaline found herself smiling. A pair of swans were startled out from amongst the rushes. Johanna clambered in the boat, wrapped up Adaline securely, and used a long stick to pole the boat out of the shallows. As they moved amongst the reeds and around the tufa formations, more ducks flew in, pintails, redheads, mallards, and coots, all the while raising a muted clamor. Up on the shore Adaline saw geese. Johanna propelled the boat toward the two islands, Paoha and Negit, that lay in the center of a passageway that led to the horizon.

The moon grew pale as the sun rose in the east. Crimson transformed to rose, illuminating low wisps of clouds and flaring against the mountain slopes. The great volcanic hollow which wrapped around the lake remained in the darkness. Upon the lake's surface were reflected the pink clouds, sparks of the looping birds, and shadows of the white formations. Water bubbled up as they passed over a fissure in the bottom. Johanna went on, heading toward Paoha. She pointed out the birds floating before them, the phalaropes that spun and plunged their beaks into the water, seeking to make small rising whirlpools of brine shrimp. The phalaropes spiraled down, then spun up again.

The boat came close to the Negit, the dark island. Johanna stood and waved her pole in the air. Adaline heard the steady and raucous racket of a different kind of bird, some rising to wheel around. She saw a shelf and dark escarpment and in between picked out what at first she had imagined was the floor of the island, but then it moved. In fact, there were hundreds of gulls, or thousands, tens of thousands, in loosely formed nests on the ground, and up the slope to the escarpment they made a white carpet against the black island. The tumult of the gulls shifting about, winging up, and down, pilfering each other's nests, went on without end. Johanna poled the boat away and set out for what Adaline saw as the opening in the lake. The sun had risen far enough to burn off wisps of fog. Behind the boat, gulls winged circles in the air, and before it and on either side more birds rode up on the wind. Soon, all the birds Adaline had ever known, including the condors, vultures, the passenger pigeons, the ravens and crows, turned overhead in a great gyre. The boat glided silently in the channel to the edge of the lake. On the shoreline beyond, Adaline beheld the man with no face.

A whirlwind blew and spun and pirouetted into a water spout, turning the lake fierce. Darkness fell upon her. The moon was obliterated. La Muerte appeared to embrace her. The man with no face walked quickly away past the white palisades toward the horizon as she lifted into the wind.

Hush . . . hush . . . hush . . .

Postscript

May 1868, five years after Adaline's death

THE ARKANSAS RIVER was swollen with snow melt. Kit Carson had been ported across it to Fort Lyon, Colorado, and brought into the physician's quarters, which were rudely built of stone with mud chinking and pole rafters open to the roof. Spring floods the previous year had leveled the original Fort Lyon, and this, the second of several incarnations the fort would pass through over the years, had been thrown up in haste on higher ground and at some greater distance from the river by "fort Indians" and troops, detachments having derived from the Seventh Cavalry and Third and Fifth Infantries. These bluecoats are like the ants, always busy.

The floor, where Kit lay on a buffalo robe, as he had said was most comfortable to him, was made of raw oak, the color of winter weeds. A black Mexican blanket with red lightening bolts woven into its hems spread over him to the ribs. His head and shoulders were propped up on pillows in order to facilitate his breathing, which had become rasping, interrupted by occasional fits of coughing that terminated in a pause, a breathlessness that filled the room with the radiance of exhalation, then gave way to a succession of shallow gasps.

At the insistence of the physician, Doctor Tilton, he had been transported here from Boggsville, a place to which he had moved some two hundred miles from his home in Taos ten months previous, along with his wife, Josefa, and the children. Morning light washed over the Arkansas from the east and southerly and angled in obscure shafts through the windows made from sheep flesh in which the rust-colored veins traced an off-kilter geometry, their former alluviality upon the roundness of a sheep's body rendered into truncated planes and stood on edge. The doctor himself, who for diversion gave wide berth to his surgical applications, had scraped away the fat and stretched the skins onto frames.

•

Soon after moving his household to Boggsville, Kit had been called away in service to the government. He had traveled to the cities of the Northeast, but then, weakened and sick, he had come back to Josefa. It was a pattern of their lives, his departing and the longing for his return. He had stopped over with Jesse and Susan Nelson who themselves had moved to La Junta, Colorado, and Josefa had arrived with a carriage to meet him, although she was nearly nine months pregnant with their seventh child, who, like a gem taken from the earth, was to have arrived ensconced in the full shine of the father's reputation. There was also the prospect of the family's having land passed to them through the influence of friends, Tom Boggs and Lucien Maxwell, and also by virtue of a Spanish land grant to which Josefa, a Jamarillo and a Vigil, was claimant. Yet, seeing her husband's condition, his labored movement, his coat askew upon his frame, his fatigue, the gauntness of his jaw, and the bruise-colored swelling on his neck around which his shirt hung slack, she'd been struck cold. She took him straight away. He hunched under his coat in the carriage, which was driven by a man named Rivera. Josefa drew Kit close to her, frightened by how lacking in resilience he was.

"Ay, Chipita," he murmured. "Qué duro."

She searched his gray eyes, famous for their discernment. Illiterate though he was, his genius had been to read the script of the world, the humps, cuts, and defiles of landform, where opening allowed passage, and where not. He'd been alive to distant disturbances, as they might be carried by winging birds, or of puffs of dust filtering into the sky, or to the signals of pathways or of stones turned upon them. The dangerous or benign meaning such signs might contain had always been understood by him, except in the Canyon de Chelly in 1864 where following orders against his wishes he grew lost in himself. Now his eyes were fixed with fevered pinpoints of glitter in them like glass, what Josefa discerned as a signal of his breaking apart.

Rivera drove the team gently in the ruts along the twenty mile stretch of the Santa Fé Trail between La Junta and Boggsville. He was sobered by the magnitude of his errand, transporting the ailing hero, a brevet brigadier general, a man for whom people had names— Lobo, Fuete, Bi'éé Li Chíí'í, or Red Shirt, Rope Thrower, The Bleeder. From his perch, Rivera glanced to his left at the Arkansas where high water rushed up around the willow trunks and the fine evening light coursed through the branches that had swelled with their ochre color and a kind of pale purple, and which were budding and sprouting their new leaves, as were the tall cottonwoods. The banks shone bright with spring grass. The carriage's C-springs creaked and the mule team's hooves struck against the packed mud. Sometimes, Rivera could also hear the murmuring on the bench at his back as if of lovers in their bed, which caused him to consider the earth and its mysterious God, the kindness of this season when things arose, the resurrection of life, but how it was also the time of sacrifice, giving up, and death.

Josefa comforted her husband, lifting the old beaver hat he had removed to his knees and placing there the blanket with the lightening bolts that she had brought for him. She held his hat by the brim where she could feel the shiny place from his habit of constantly adjusting it to keep it square and looked at the gilt inscription on the inner band, barely legible through the years of wear:

> At 2 O'Clock
> Kit Carson
> from
> Major Carleton

That had been a gift in 1854, early in Kit's service to Major Carleton. Reading the signs, Kit predicted almost to the minute when they would come upon the Jicarilla Apaches they pursued, and then seeing them, the women and children among them, he'd a change of heart.

Josefa set the hat on the seat and placed her other hand so that her fingers rested on his wrist. She tried to give him hope by speaking of this child and the others, of the home they would build, yet she felt his struggle to hold his body straight and within herself the beginning of the sundering. Something had sheared in them. It was for the sake of Kit's appointment as Indian Agent for the Colorado Territory that they had left Taos, the place he had chosen as a young man to be his own. She had lived there all her life. She considered the customary early light flaring through the Sangre de Cristos upon the adobes, the call of women's voices and of the roosters, the bells of the cathedral tolling the hour. Better that than this, Josefa thought, as she slid her thumb into Kit's palm and clutched his hand to steady him against the rocking of the carriage, and tipped back her head so he wouldn't see her tears. Better that with its everyday uncertainties, even waiting for him to come from afar, than to have him arriving like this.

Two days after meeting Kit in La Junta, Josefa gave birth to Josefita, her seventh child. In another eight days, by April 23, Josefa was dead. Those who knew Kit believed that her death had caused him to bring an end to his own struggle, but truly she, perceiving the end of the long-loved coming and going of his person, the swing of his armature to the nation's drive wheel, had relinquished first. This was what he had most feared, and so he was reminded, despite the widespread killing that still went on everywhere in this time, that grief is first and foremost personal.

•

Kit had been brought to La Junta by carriage, driven by the Ute Agent, and prior to that by stage from Cheyenne to Denver, where he parted company with the four Ute chiefs with whom he'd been traveling. He and the chiefs had come from Boston to Chicago, then

Council Bluffs, and through the plains along the railroad line laid five months previous into Cheyenne. He had traveled to Boston from New York, and to New York by way of Philadelphia and Washington, D.C. where his old commander, John Frémont, searching out investors to rescue his failing fortunes in Las Mariposas, had seen him and urged him to seek medical attention. There, Kit had presented the Ute chiefs in delegation for the purpose of signing a treaty that would confine them to the western one-third of the Colorado Territory, an agreement made null and void from the moment of its ratification by post-Civil War adventurers coming West in floods.

He'd been asked, or required in the way that authority regularly tapped his willingness to obey, to continue with the chiefs through the cities of the Northeast so that they might be impressed by the overwhelming power and numbers of Americans, and that their savagery might be publicly observed in the antic mode of its acquiescence, their darkness juxtaposed to the odd apparel: frock coats and ornately beaded neck chokers, hairpipe breastplates, draperies of sinew, feather, dentalia, and bits of metal, leather aprons hung over their trousers, buskins decorated with buttons, blankets over buttoned-up flannel shirts, military epaulettes sewn into the shoulders of the blankets, feathers and flat brimmed hats. The meaning of these accoutrements was secret to them, even defiant. They posed for photographs with Kit, with politicians and dignitaries eager to have the record of their presence in the company of fame and inscrutability. When, because of his illness, Kit began declining such appointments, it was taken for arrogance.

One afternoon in New York's Metropolitan Hotel, Kit would awaken from a deep sleep and find his head cradled in one of the chief's hands and the other three gathered close around him. His gaze fixed upon the white curtains behind the men, billowing above the radiators. The windows had been thrown open to the noise below of passing dray, and to the reek of coal smoke and garbage, in order to allow his passage. He had called out to his Lord Jesus, the chief said, which Kit could not remember.

A day later, after receiving a wire about Kit's condition from her husband, Jessie Frémont sent Kit a message asking to see him. With her son, Frank, she would come down from her house near Tarrytown that overlooked the Hudson River. Kit was reluctant to be visited by so fine a lady in his room where bedrolls were scattered about the floor and the four-poster bed was used as a repository for articles of clothing, guns, knives, powder horns, hunks of lead and molds, quivers, arrows, bows, and spears. Elaborate arrangements of feather dangled from the hat rack. The room smelled of tobacco and a kind of dispirited sweat that floated with the scents of leather and the acrid desert medicines the chiefs kept in their pouches. Instead, Kit agreed to meet her in the hotel dining room.

Jessie was taken up with the rakish angulation the new Darwinism gave to her sense of the "fittest," and the Kit Carson she had come to know was preceded by what twenty-five years ago, before she'd even met him, had lodged as an alive thing in her imagination, libidinous and hot. But now, observing his pained movement as her son, Frank, led him through the French doors and across the carpet to where she waited at her table, and the effort it took for him to hang his hat on the hook, she was filled with pity. Kit's face was emaciated and he studied his chair before lowering himself into it. His hand shook, holding his cup. She grieved the quenching of the old smoldering in herself here on the other side of the "gulf like death," which was how she regarded the Civil War, the sadness of it, the loss, the political intrigue that had fed her husband's differences with Lincoln, and his removal from command. She had considered Lincoln guilty of appeasing pro-slavery factions and referred to him as "slimy."

She ordered cakes. From outside came the sound of hooves on the cobblestone and a cry. Kit looked to the window. A livery passed. Three men in suits and bowler hats ambled by. Behind them an old woman hawking fish was pushing her cart along the walk, and Kit listened to what became a dirge-like call into the vanishing, like the caw of a crow dropping behind a ridge. He looked between Jessie and Frank into the fireplace where a log shifted, hissing and throwing out onto the carpet a spray of sparks. He told Jessie about his experience in the hotel room. "I felt my head swoll," he said. "And the air stove out of me."

Watching him grow cognizant to the sounds, Jessie marveled at how, even now, he was like one of those wires attenuated to the telegraph key, sharp as a lynx, also how like was he to his daughter, who years ago had been so intent upon taking cows to Mono Lake and establishing a herd there, or how like she had been to him. Jessie said as much and with the memory a light came into her eyes. "Your daughter had a mind of her own," she said.

"Aye. Twister," Kit said. "We began to believe she was lost in them years. I'm glad she got to meet you. For my part, things was left unfinished with her, a rendevouz unkept."

They spoke of Kit's other children, about whose education he was concerned, and then Mrs. Frémont tried to persuade him to do what he would not, to come to her home, what she and her husband called Pocaho. She assured Kit that he could rest there and be under a doctor's care.

Kit was in awe of Mrs. Frémont, but in truth if given the choice he would have preferred to pass on in the room with the chiefs to being put on display in a fancy house. He felt excruciatingly lonely, despairing of the charade of his journey, and sorry for the trouble Jessie had already undertaken on his behalf. He cut a piece of the cake with his fork and put it in his mouth, sucking on the sweetness, and said softly, "I must take the chiefs to Boston. I gave my word to them. Then we go home, straight. Josefa must see me. If I was to die here without her, it would kill her. I must go to her."

It is bright to consider the line of his retreat, westerly and then southerly as if by a funneling of apparati retrograding through history—the train to Cheyenne, then stage coach, and two carriages, and after the grief from Josefa's death the carriage again, driven by Rivera, and finally the gurney upon a raft affixed by ropes through pulleys on posts from either side of the river which Rivera, a man with powerful arms and a torso thick as a horse, cranked onto an iron spool.

Doctor Tilton had advised Kit that his end was not far off. Knowing that Kit would want it stated clearly, Tilton had explained that death would come from suffocation or a hemorrhage if the aneurysm in his neck burst. Kit stated his preference for the latter, or better yet an overdose of the chloroform Tilton had been administering to ease the pain, but Tilton, following the watchful inaction his profession required, declined, saying, "I'm afraid that's God's business."

Kit reached up with one hand and touched his neck. "If it weren't for this, I could live to be a hundred."

"Yes," the doctor said. "I believe you could."

Another man, Aloys Scheurich, the husband of Kit and Josefa's niece, Teresina, and godfather to the Carson children, was in the room, standing next to the doctor. Scheurich was to oversee the disposition of the children and to witness any last wishes. He looked down at Kit, who lay propped against the wall, his face drawn and grainy looking, and his eyes half-closed to slits, his chest hardly moving. If it had been left to Scheurich, he would have granted Kit's request. He pictured it, bending over and pressing the chloroform-soaked muslin to Kit's face, and having to counter the body's instincts. Scheurich also wondered if he and the doctor were simply to leave, that left to his final reckonings, Kit might go quickly.

Scheurich glanced over at Tilton, a slender man, tall and bearded, who stood with a hand grasping one of the two iron stirrups that protruded from the foot of his examination table. Without speaking, Tilton raised his other hand in an indecipherable gesture. Scheurich felt uneasy, as if the doctor were claiming possession of a living relic.

Tilton had sought out Kit's memories of the old days before his life with Josefa, before his travels with Frémont, when he'd roved the West as a trapper and took on as his wife Waa-nibe and with her had two daughters. Kit himself seemed reconciled to finding pleasure in the memories and even in hearing Tilton read of the time from De Witt Peters' biography, *The Life and Adventures of Kit Carson, the Nestor of the Rocky Mountains*, though he'd said the author "laid it on a little thick." The book now rested alongside the porcelain chloroform canister between the examination table's two stirrups.

Kit's breath began to rasp again, making a sound like pebbles rolling in a sluice. Listening and knowing it would build into another paroxysm of coughing, Scheurich looked away toward the sheep flesh windows opposite him. Mounted on the wall above the windows was a buffalo head, and in a line on top of a roll top desk stood a stuffed beaver, a martin, and a bobcat that twisted and bared its incisors in pantomime of a snarl. Around the corner from the desk, near the doorway, and faintly illuminated by an oil lamp that hung from a rafter, two old flintlocks rested on pegs. The taxidermy was the doctor's own. He was a collector and antiquarian, one who had performed his first surgical service in the closing months of the war, whose medical applications, thus, were fiercely practical: amputations and cauterizings, setting broken limbs, digging out balls, slugs, and shrapnel, lancing pustules, administering opiates to quell the agony. His healing impulse had been darkened by the brutality of war. He sought refuge by passing into the latitudes his science offered him in this place still rife with the unknown.

A Ute woman in his service had been coming and going, bringing water or broth in a steel cup or taking the bowl in which Carson had spat his bloody sputum to rinse it clean at the well in the plaza. She came now, opening the door and then returning it to its slightly ajar position where the doctor had directed it to be for the sake of ventilation. She turned to Kit, her long blue skirt stirring up the dust motes, which as if charged, swirled in the pale light and settled around her as she knelt at his side. Gently, she tilted up his head and held the cup to his lips. Her black hair gleamed.

Kit took a swallow, coughed, and took another swallow. He looked at the woman with eyes that glittered with pain. She eased his head back to the pillow and pulled up the blanket to where Josefa's silver crucifix, which Kit wore on a chain around his neck, lay flat against his red underwear. The woman set the cup on the case beside him between his old beaver hat and a skull that had the phrenological regions marked out in black ink, from which she visibly shied, and then her eyes darted up in fright, jumping from the doctor to Scheurich. At first, Scheurich thought it was the skull, but he, too, felt something moving past him, churning and chill, a tight, wild, whirling gust as if a spinning mensajara had entered the room. The flame in the Franklin stove against the opposite wall bent back upon itself. The oil lamp's wick hissed while the lamp swung from its hook. For an instant, everything rocked like a ship at sea. When he looked at Kit, Scheurich observed that his friend's eyelids had opened a little more. The gray that had taken it all in turned to luminous silver. Behind the silver were spots of black.

Scheurich glanced over at Tilton who seemed not to have noticed anything untoward but had retrieved his book from between the stirrups and was seeking his place. The doctor leaned back and resumed reading aloud: "The two parties once more consolidated and started for the summer rendezvous which was appointed to be held on the Green River. Upon their arrival at this place, they found congregated all the principle trappers of the Rocky Mountains. They were divided into two camps and numbered about two hundred men. . . ."

The Ute woman left hastily. Her receding footfalls could be heard descending the steps and turning in the sand to her left where she would sit next to Rivera. They were hospitators, waiting, hunkering elbow to elbow, hips touching and their backs against the outer wall of the physician's quarters. They faced the river, which hummed and boomed. At a distance, the footsteps of soldiers following their errands scuffed against the earth. Cart wheels creaked. A peening hammer rang from the blacksmith's shop, the fort's flag snapped in the breeze, and soon would be snapping at half-mast.

Author's Note

ADALINE CARSON'S MOTHER was Waa-nibe, or Singing Grass, a Northern Arapaho woman. Adaline was born in 1837 or 1838, at either Fort Davy Crockett on the Colorado-Utah border, or more likely at Fort Hall in Idaho. Similarly there are two versions of the date of her death, one mounted on a plaque at Mono Lake puts it at 1859 and another, also at Mono Lake, but putting it later, for in 1862 the Mono County Court Records show her receiving one hundred dollars from a B.F. Snyder. The cause of her death is not known. In my portrayal I have chosen to have her die in 1863 of consumption, complicated by a stomach ailment and at the end by doses of laudanum. While in Mono Lake, it is reported that she took on the name Kit Carson.

That she had a younger sister who died by falling into a soap cauldron seems beyond question, yet it is not certain whether this happened in Taos or at Bent's Fort. Descendants of the Jaramillas and Vigils put it at Bent's Fort, but some historical accounts have it otherwise. It is known that her father gave Adaline over to the care of his sister, Mary Ann, in Fayette, Missouri in 1842, and that this provided the opportunity for him to meet Frémont and to be engaged as a scout for Frémont's upcoming expedition. It is unclear whether Adaline was enrolled in a Catholic school in Saint Louis or in a boarding school in Fayette, or, most likely, in each at different times. The school in Saint Louis probably came first. She did not receive a diploma from either, which may explain why records of her attendance prove elusive.

It is also known that her father visited her at least once in Missouri, following her aunt's concerns about her behavior, and that later on (in 1851) he brought her West along the Santa Fé Trail, along with her cousin, Susan, who had recently married Jesse Nelson. On this journey Kit and his men were delivering supplies to the Rayado and to Fort Union. Otherwise, the account of the wagon train is mainly fiction, although some episodes, such as the altercation Kit's group had with the Cheyenne, and earlier on John Chivington's appearance with the Wyandot, of whom he, in his guise as a Methodist missionary to the tribes, had charge, are based on historical fact. This is well before, as a colonel of the Colorado militia, Chivington led the 700 man force in the massacre of Cheyenne and Arapaho at Sand Creek, which occurred in November 1864. Kit did arrange for Adaline's marriage to his friend, Louis Simmons (or Symonds), and the two traveled with Kit to California on the sheep drive of 1853.

Subsequently, according to Jesse Nelson, Simmons said that Adaline was a wild girl and did not behave properly, and he left her. I have given her a voice, a speculative reason for the dissolution, and thus the cause of her leaving him. From that point on up to the time of her appearance at Mono Lake in the company of a man named George Stilts (or Stiles), nothing is known except that she disappeared into the gold fields. The picture of Pablo, the young man with whom she nearly escapes her marriage to Simmons is fiction, but the portrayal of Padre Martínez, his printing press, his prodigious memory, his concerns for his laity, his disagreements with the Vicar Lamy, and the Easter ceremony at Abiquiú are true in a representative way—not literally true, but consistent with the truth as it is reported. Similarly, the account of Josefa is a representative fiction, excepting the flashback to her part in witnessing the death of Charles Bent during the Taos Rebellion, which is true in fact.

The words uttered by John Charles Frémont and Jessie Benton Frémont are fictions. However, the circumstances surrounding the Frémonts, Don Rámon's tale of Bill Williams' cannibalism on Frémont's last exploration expedition in the Rockies, the manner in which Frémont acquired the Las Mariposas Grant, his role as the first Republican candidate for president, his "rancho" in Bear Valley, the "vigilance committees," the attempt to take over the Black Drift by the Merced Company, the governor's intervention following Frémont's appeal by sending the state marshal's five hundred men, and Nye's men, as well, and therefore Frémont's successful, if brief, victory over the Merced Company are all historically accurate. The same could be said for his portrayal as a failed businessman, his difficulties with Abraham Lincoln, his independently released "Emancipation Proclamation" during the Civil War, his subsequent removal from command, and Mrs. Frémont's view of Lincoln. Kit Carson's final journey to the East with the Ute chiefs, Mrs. Frémont's alarm at seeing his condition and her attempt to take him under her care are true, too. Gerard Perlot is an invention of the novel, but the sudden revolution in machinery put to use by the mining industry, including rock percussion machines, and the massive influx of corporate money in support of such machines and of the mining industry in general are accepted history. Similarly, the portrayal of the California settler population's nineteenth century murderous attitude toward the indigenous population is by and large accurate, as is the attitude of the Franciscans toward the indigenes and the Mexicans a hundred years earlier.

Nothing in the record comes from Adaline herself and very little from Kit, who, it was said, had favored her. We know nothing of her thoughts and feelings nor of how her experience informed her being. The treatment of Adaline is of the short life of a woman who has entered into my conjecture. True, it is challenging, to say the least, for a white man to write from the point of view of a young, half-Arapaho woman who lived in a willfully spirited, mercenary world, like the one we live in now.

I know what my old colleague and friend, Elizabeth Cook-Lynn, says in her remarkable book of essays, *A Separate Country: Essays on Post-Coloniality from Indian Country:* "American contemporary society emphasizes the attraction, indeed the seductiveness of taking on an imaginary persona of the American Indian, an indigenous anomaly, a deviation, like a planet divergent from its perihelion, helps the settler-American from another world take his false version of history and transform it into an 'experience' that is tolerable. It is another way to rewrite the invader's history of imperialism and arrogance, which is difficult to acknowledge in the midst of platitudes and piety that often pass for historiography. Finally, it is the quintessential method by which America, the essential nation in global affairs, sustains itself as a colonial power even in the face of a powerful and ubiquitous indigenous population [Texas Tech University Press, 2011, p 132]."

I have tried to avoid appropriating Adaline, to maintain a respectful distance from her. As I have portrayed her, she started out believing she had an appointment, or rendezvous, to keep with her father. As is often the case with children of the famous, this expectation was never fully realized. What such children may be left with is the bitter disappointment at not being able to take on the aura of the parent, which becomes compounded and even more galling when the parent—no matter how thoroughly he may change, and no matter how much he favored her—has earned a reputation of being a killer of like-blooded indigenous people. If nothing else, this novel is a fragile testimony to my efforts to understand the durability of American racism, particularly when it applies to women, and of our colonial practices, the language with which we attempt to explain such practices, our arrogance in the midst of platitudes, and the extraordinary contradiction of espousing the abolition of slaves while continuing to find new and sometimes more cruel ways to enslave them, and, more telling, our continuing enslavement and disenfranchisement of indigenous populations.

Acknowledgments

For the understanding they lent to me, I'm grateful to the aforementioned Elizabeth Cook-Lynn and her late husband, Clyde Lynn; to my friend, the late Rubén Trejo, to his daughters and son, Sonya, Tanya, and Eugenio, and their late mother Joanne Hammes; and to our son, Carson Keeble, and his wife, Melissa Peña, who doubled back to check out the Rayado for me, spent time in Taos with me, accompanied me to Poshuouinge and Abiquiú, and whose enthusiasm about most all things New Mexican was contagious. Thanks go to Napoleon Garcia, Sr. of Abiquiú; to Barbara Loste for help with the Spanish language passages; to Michelle Huneven and Jim Potter and their basecamp tent where my wife and I stayed while I researched in the Huntington; to Dan Sisson who supplied me with historical information; to my brother-in-law Jim Sheldon and his wife Nancy, who accompanied my wife and me on our last trip to Mariposa and Yosemite; and to Simon Ortiz who granted permission to quote his poem. Thanks for the patience of Denise Shannon, for the editorial skill of my friend, Christopher Howell, and, as always, I'm indebted in countless ways to my wife, Claire.

In addition, I wish to acknowledge with respect the authors of the some five hundred books I have gradually acquired on the subject, or subjects, of this novel; and the University of New Mexico Library in Albuquerque; the Kit Carson Research Center and the Kit Carson house, also the Martínez Hacienda in Taos, New Mexico; Eastern Washington University Library in Cheney, Washington; the Starsmore Center for Local History, the Colorado Springs Pioneers Museum in Colorado, and particularly to Laura Fuller for her efforts to track down Jesse Nelson's remarks and those of others through the Cragin Notebooks; and finally the Huntington Library Rare Books Collection in San Marino, California, from which I acquired detailed maps of mid-nineteenth century Mariposa, Bear Valley, and Hornitos.

About the Author

JOHN KEEBLE is the author of seven previous books, including the novels *Yellowfish* and *Broken Ground*, both recent University of Washington Press reprints, and University of Washington Press original, *The Shadows of Owls*. His short fiction collection, *Nocturnal America*, won the Prairie Schooner Prize for short fiction and was published by the University of Nebraska Press. He is also author of *Out of the Channel*, the definitive study of the Exxon Valdez disaster. Keeble taught at Eastern Washington University for more than thirty years, and has taught also at Grinnell College and the University of Alabama, and served as Distinguished Visiting Writer at Boise State University. With his wife Claire, he lives, in a house of his own construction, on a wooded hillside west of Spokane, Washington.